C0-ATP-567

BACH PERSPECTIVES

VOLUME FIVE

Bach in America

BACH PERSPECTIVES

VOLUME FIVE

Bach
Perspectives

VOLUME FIVE

Bach in America

Edited by Stephen A. Crist

UNIVERSITY OF ILLINOIS PRESS · URBANA AND CHICAGO

Manufactured in the
United States of America
C 5 4 3 2 1

∞ This book is printed
on acid-free paper.

ISSN 1072-1924
ISBN 0-252-02788-4

Bach Perspectives is
sponsored by the
American Bach Society
and produced under the
guidance of its Editorial
Board. For information
about the American Bach
Society, please see its
Web site at this URL:
www.americanbachsociety.org.

For
Robert L. Marshall
to mark his retirement from the
Editorial and Advisory Boards
of the
American Bach Society
and to celebrate his
distinguished contributions to
American Bach research

CONTENTS

PREFACE

This fifth volume of the series *Bach Perspectives* is simultaneously a continuation and a new beginning. It is a continuation of the series that was begun in 1995 and remains the primary publication of the American Bach Society. But it is also a new beginning in that it is being issued by a new publisher. The series was begun in partnership with the University of Nebraska Press. The American Bach Society remains especially grateful to this Press, not only for its willingness to enter into partnership with the Society, but also for the way in which the first four volumes were produced. For a variety of reasons a change of publisher became necessary. Our new partner is the University of Illinois Press, and we particularly appreciate the energy and enthusiasm of its staff, notably the director, Willis G. Regier, in establishing this new partnership.

The purpose of *Bach Perspectives*, however, remains the same: the publication of new research into the life and works of Johann Sebastian Bach within the musical, social, cultural, and religious contexts of his time, as well as of investigations into the reception of this music in later generations and of its impact on other composers.

When the first volume of *Bach Perspectives* appeared in 1995, Don O. Franklin suggested in the preface that the new publication venture represented a "coming of age" for American Bach research. It is therefore more than appropriate that the subject matter of this fifth volume, that marks a new beginning for the series, should deal with "Bach in America."

Robin A. Leaver, President
The American Bach Society

EDITOR'S PREFACE

Although this book had already been in preparation for several years, the final stages of editing took place around September 11, 2001, a date that is indelibly etched in the minds of Americans and that has assumed historic significance throughout the world. In the wake of the cataclysmic events of that day and their far-reaching consequences, it seems especially fitting that volume 5 of *Bach Perspectives* should be devoted to the topic "Bach in America."

During the period of mourning following the terrorist attacks in New York City and Washington, D.C., many people throughout North America derived great comfort and solace from hearing and performing the music of Johann Sebastian Bach. It may therefore seem surprising that Bach's music was virtually unknown in America before 1850. Indeed, his reputation has grown from the size of a mustard seed to a mountain in just 150 years, with much of the growth concentrated in the second half of the nineteenth century.

The essays in the present volume fall into three main divisions. The first group treats aspects of the nineteenth-century American reception of Bach. Barbara Owen's introductory article provides a broad-ranging overview of the terrain. Matthew Dirst then examines in detail the contributions of John Sullivan Dwight, especially through the publication of *Dwight's Journal of Music*, to the public acceptance of the composer. The next two essays offer case studies in the reception of Bach's music in a pair of major American cities. Michael Broyles describes how this repertory became known in Boston, and highlights in particular the influential work of John Knowles Paine and Eugene Thayer. Mary J. Greer's detailed account of Bach reception in New York City provides a counterpoint to Broyles's view of Boston, drawing special attention to the roles of Theodore Thomas and the Damrosch family in promoting Bach's music.

The next three articles concern genealogical origins and manuscript sources. First, Hans-Joachim Schulze weighs the evidence connecting the American descendants of August Reinhold Bach with Johann Sebastian Bach, concluding that the two branches of the Bach family apparently shared a common ancestor in the sixteenth century. Christoph Wolff then reports the results of his research on Friederica Sophia Bach, the wayward daughter of J. S. Bach's eldest son, Wilhelm Friedemann, whose grandson emigrated to the United States in the late nineteenth century. Peter Wollny's valuable contribution describes and evaluates several important manuscripts containing music by J. S. Bach and his circle, which were not included in Gerhard Herz's catalogue of *Bach Sources in America*.

The last two essays consider the influence of Johann Sebastian Bach on two major figures in American music. Carol K. Baron explores certain parallels between the music of Bach and Charles Ives, and discusses the role of Bach in Ives's education and compositional career. In the final chapter, I examine one facet of Bach's considerable impact on an important jazz musician, the pianist and composer Dave Brubeck.

I wish to thank George B. Stauffer, former president of the American Bach Society, for his collegial support and guidance throughout this project. I also am grateful to Robin A. Leaver, current president of the Society, for first suggesting the thematic focus of the volume, and to Gregory G. Butler for his editorial advice. M. Patrick Graham and Richard Wright, of Pitts Theology Library at Emory University, both offered invaluable technical assistance. In addition, I wish to acknowledge the contributions of three students at Emory University: Drew Boles, for preparing the musical examples; Julianne Yocum Erbrecht; and Peter Morin.

Stephen A. Crist
Atlanta, Georgia

ABBREVIATIONS

BDOK	Werner Neumann and Hans-Joachim Schulze, eds. *Bach-Dokumente.* 4 vols. Kassel: Bärenreiter; Leipzig: VEB Deutsche Verlag für Musik, 1963–78.
BG	[Bach-Gesamtausgabe.] *Johann Sebastian Bach's Werke.* Edited by the Bachgesellschaft. 47 vols. Leipzig: Breitkopf & Härtel, 1851–99.
BJ	*Bach-Jahrbuch.*
BMT	*Boston Musical Times.*
BWV	[Bach-Werke-Verzeichnis.] Wolfgang Schmieder, ed. *Thematisch-systematisches Verzeichnis der musikalischen Werke von Johann Sebastian Bach.* Rev. ed. Wiesbaden: Breitkopf & Härtel, 1990.
BWV ANH.	Appendix (*Anhang*) to the BWV.
DJM	*Dwight's Journal of Music.*
H.	E. Eugene Helm, ed. *Thematic Catalogue of the Works of Carl Philipp Emanuel Bach.* New Haven: Yale University Press, 1989.
HWV	[Händel-Werke-Verzeichnis.] Bernd Baselt, ed. *Thematisch-Systematisches Verzeichnis: Instrumentalmusik, Pasticci und Fragmente.* Händel-Handbuch, vol. 3. Kassel: Bärenreiter, 1986.
KB	Kritischer Bericht (critical report) of the NBA.
m./mm.	measure/measures.
mvt.	movement.
NBA	[Neue Bach-Ausgabe.] *Johann Sebastian Bach: Neue Ausgabe sämtlicher Werke.* Edited by the Johann-Sebastian-Bach-Institut, Göttingen, and the Bach-Archiv, Leipzig. Kassel: Bärenreiter; Leipzig: Deutscher Verlag für Musik, 1954–.
NBR	Hans T. David and Arthur Mendel, eds. *The New Bach Reader: A Life of Johann Sebastian Bach in Letters and Documents.* Revised and enlarged by Christoph Wolff. New York: W. W. Norton & Co., 1998.

NYP *New York Post.*

NYTI *New York Times.*

NYTR *New York Tribune.*

TVWV [Telemann-Vokalwerke-Verzeichnis.] Werner Menke, ed. *Thematisches Verzeichnis der Vokalwerke von Georg Philipp Telemann.* 2 vols. Frankfurt am Main: Klosterman, 1981–83.

W. Alfred Wotquenne, ed. *Catalogue thèmatique des oeuvres de Charles Philippe Emanuel Bach* (1714–1788). Leipzig: Breitkopf & Härtel, 1905. Reprint, Wiesbaden: Breitkopf & Härtel, 1972.

Bach Comes to America

Barbara Owen

The music of Johann Sebastian Bach became known in America much later than that of his contemporary, George Frideric Handel, or that of his sons and other relatives. Handel's music crossed the Atlantic Ocean during his own lifetime. Some of his large choral works, copied around 1738–49 and provided with German texts, are preserved in the archives of the Moravians of Bethlehem, Pennsylvania.[1] Portions of the oratorio *Messiah* were performed in New York in 1756, and thirty years later the "Hallelujah Chorus" was published in Worcester, Massachusetts.[2] The Handel and Haydn Society, still active today, was founded in Boston in 1815. Although commonly regarded as the first choral organization dedicated to Handel, the Handel and Haydn Society actually was preceded by a short-lived Handelian Society in Philadelphia, which gave its first concert in 1814.[3] From the mid-eighteenth century to the present, then, Handel's choral and instrumental music has resonated continuously on the North American continent.

Similarly, the works of other composers in the Bach family were heard in the American colonies long before those of Johann Sebastian, even though he subsequently has come to be regarded as the most prominent member of the clan. Most popular by far was the music of Johann Christian (the "English Bach"). His symphonies were performed in Boston as early as 1771, and on subsequent occasions in the latter decades of the eighteenth century. In 1786 an unidentified overture by J. C. Bach was included in a concert led by the expatriate Englishman William Selby.[4]

1. Howard Serwer, "Handel in Bethlehem," *Moravian Music Foundation Bulletin* 35, no. 1 (Spring–Summer 1980): 2–7.

2. Roger L. Hall, "Early Performances of Bach and Handel in America," *Journal of Church Music* 27, no. 5 (May 1985): 4.

3. Robert A. Gerson, *Music in Philadelphia* (Philadelphia: Theodore Presser, 1940), 88.

4. Cynthia Adams Hoover, "Epilogue to Secular Music in Early Massachusetts," in *Music in Homes and in Churches*, vol. 2 of *Music in Colonial Massachusetts, 1630–1820*, ed. Barbara Lambert (Boston: Colonial Society of Massachusetts, 1985), 814, 823.

While the English colonies favored Johann Christian, the Moravians of Pennsylvania and North Carolina performed concertos, symphonies, and trio sonatas by other members of the Bach family as well, including Carl Philipp Emanuel, Johann Ernst, and Johann Christoph Friedrich. Copies of compositions by J. C. F. Bach dating from as early as 1768 are found in the archives of the Moravian *collegia musica* of Bethlehem, Pennsylvania, and Salem, North Carolina, as are works by J. C. dating from 1780.[5] Some pieces by C. P. E. and J. C. F. Bach are transmitted only in manuscripts in the Moravian archives. Although the compositions by these various Bachs in Moravian sources are predominantly instrumental works, a number of C. P. E. Bach's vocal works (e.g., *Zwölf geistliche Oden und Lieder* [W. 195; H. 696] and *Die Israeliten in der Wüste* [W. 238; H. 775]) are preserved there as well.[6]

C. P. E. Bach's music probably was known in Philadelphia, too. In 1786 Alexander Reinagle (1756–1809), an English-born musician of Austrian ancestry and a friend and correspondent of C. P. E. Bach, arrived there and almost immediately became prominent in the city's musical life. During his first year in Philadelphia, Reinagle gave a series of twelve concerts. Among the works performed were an overture and a piano concerto ascribed to "Bach," which almost certainly were composed by C. P. E. Bach.[7]

In contrast with the popularity of the music of Handel and of J. S. Bach's sons in the latter half of the eighteenth century, Karl Kroeger has noted that "so far no evidence indicating the performance of Johann Sebastian Bach's music in eighteenth-century America has been found."[8] No one has yet disproved that statement, but J. Bunker Clark unearthed the earliest known American publication of a composition by J. S. Bach. A polonaise by "Sebastian Bach" appeared among a group of short pieces by Scarlatti, Haydn, and others in Johann Christian Gottlieb Graupner's *Rudiments of the Art of Playing on the Piano Forte* (Boston, 1806), a publication that was largely pla-

5. See Johann Christoph Friedrich Bach, *Four Early Sinfonias*, ed. Ewald V. Nolte, Recent Researches in the Music of the Classical Era 15 (Madison, Wisc.: A-R Editions, 1982), x–xii; also Karl Geiringer, "Unbeachtete Kompositionen des Bückeburger Bach," in *Festschrift Wilhelm Fischer zum 70. Geburtstag*, ed. Hans Zingerle (Innsbruck: Selbstverlag des Sprachwissenschaftlichen Seminars der Universität Innsbruck, 1956), 99–107.

6. Dr. Nola Reed Knouse, Director, Moravian Music Foundation, Winston-Salem, North Carolina, letter to volume editor, February 14, 2001. On the manuscript owned by Johann Friedrich Peter containing the "Spiritual Odes and Songs," see Pauline M. Fox, "Reflections on Moravian Music: A Study of Two Collections of Manuscript Books in Pennsylvania ca. 1800" (Ph.D. diss., New York University, 1997), 145–46.

7. Byron A. Wolverton, "Keyboard Music and Musicians in the Colonies and United States of America Before 1830" (Ph.D. diss., Indiana University, 1966), 328.

8. Karl Kroeger, "Johann Sebastian Bach in Nineteenth-Century America," *Bach: Journal of the Riemenschneider Bach Institute* 22, no. 1 (Spring–Summer 1991): 33.

giarized from a piano tutor with a similar title published in London in 1801 by Muzio Clementi.[9] It can hardly have been the most popular work in the volume, however, for it was omitted from the second, revised edition (1819), although two other anonymous polonaises, quite inferior to Bach's, were included.

If J. S. Bach made his first appearance in Boston, the second appearance may have been made in Bethlehem. In 1823 John Christian Till (1762–1844), a Moravian schoolmaster, musician, and piano builder, made a copy of the cantata *Ein feste Burg ist unser Gott* (BWV 80), which is the only manuscript of a J. S. Bach composition in the Moravian Archives. The source consists of three vocal parts, seven instrumental parts, and a keyboard score.[10] Since these materials are in such good condition, there is some question as to whether they ever were used in performance. If not, the American premiere of Cantata 80 may not have occurred until 1865, when part of it was sung by a sixty-voice chorus at Harvard University under the direction of John Knowles Paine.[11]

A decisive event in the early-nineteenth-century "Bach revival" in Europe was the 1829 performance of the St. Matthew Passion by the Berlin Singakademie, under the direction of Felix Mendelssohn. Mendelssohn's popularity in England helped to encourage the development of the Bach cult there, already established by Samuel Wesley and others. It was not long before the groundswell of enthusiasm for Bach's music began to make a few ripples in the New World. These can be attributed to three main factors: (1) American music periodicals routinely reprinted news from English and continental publications; (2) German and English musicians continued to emigrate to America; and (3) American musicians began traveling and studying abroad.

One of the first Americans to receive musical training overseas was A. N. Johnson (1817–92) of Boston, who studied in Germany in 1842–43. Shortly after his return, he published for the first time in this country sixteen of Bach's chorale settings (anonymously, as examples of "German chorals") in a "thorough-base" tutor described as "a New and Easy Method for Learning to Play Church Music upon the Piano Forte or Organ." From 1846 on Johnson also edited the *Boston Musical Gazette*, which included articles on Bach, excerpted from an English translation of Forkel's biography.[12]

Another musical traveler was the well-known teacher, editor, and choral director

9. J. Bunker Clark, "The Beginnings of Bach in America," in *American Musical Life in Context and Practice to 1865*, ed. James R. Heintze (New York: Garland, 1994), 339. Although Clark says that the piece is from the first French Suite, it actually is from the Sixth, the only one to include a polonaise.

10. See Ralph G. Schwarz, *Bach in Bethlehem* (Bethlehem, Pa.: Bach Choir of Bethlehem, 1998), 10–13.

11. John C. Schmidt, *The Life and Works of John Knowles Paine* (Ann Arbor, Mich.: UMI Research Press, 1980), 60.

12. Clark, "Beginnings of Bach in America," 340–41.

Lowell Mason (1792–1872). Mason seems to have held conflicting views about Bach. On the one hand, he rewarded his teenage son William with a grand piano for having learned and memorized a Fugue in F-sharp Major (presumably from the Well-Tempered Clavier).[13] At the same time, however, this advocate of congregational singing seems to have felt that Bach's chorales were unsuitable for such purposes, noting in 1854 that "congregations might as well undertake to sing Beethoven's Mass No. 2, as these [Bach] chorals, with all sorts of complicated and difficult harmony parts."[14]

Lutheran chorales had, of course, been sung in the American colonies by German settlers of the Lutheran, Reformed, and Moravian faiths from the eighteenth century onward, but not in Bach's settings. Mason himself made simplified arrangements of German chorales, as did others in the nineteenth century. However, none were attributed to Bach until 1845, when B. F. Baker and I. B. Woodbury, music directors of two Boston churches, published *The Choral: A Collection of Church Music Adapted to the Worship of All Denominations.* In this collection, a long-meter tune is described as "From the 'Choralgesange' of J. S. Bach," another melody is attributed simply to "John Seb. Bach," and a third, in common meter, is said to be "Arranged from the 'Gospel Passions Musick' of J. S. Bach" (see plate 1).

The latter heading suggests the interesting possibility that one of the compilers may have owned a version of the St. Matthew Passion by this date (and that the source was perhaps an English imprint). The first and last measures of this tune correspond to the melody (but not the rhythm) of the familiar Passion Chorale ("O Sacred Head,

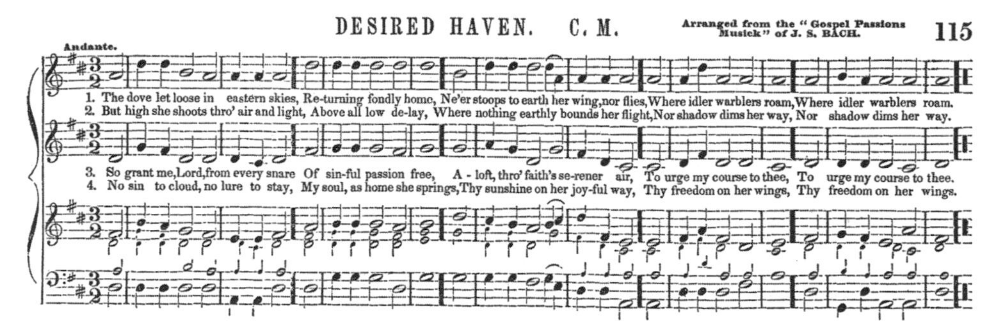

Plate 1. "Desired Haven," from B. F. Baker and I. B. Woodbury, *The Choral* (Boston: Otis, Broaders & Co., 1845). The melody is in the tenor line. Photo courtesy of Special Collections, Pitts Theology Library, Candler School of Theology, Emory University.

13. Ibid., 343–44.

14. Lowell Mason, *Musical Letters from Abroad* (New York: Mason Brothers, 1854), 301; quoted in Robert Stevenson, *Protestant Church Music in America* (New York: W. W. Norton, 1966), 82.

Now Wounded"). However, the intermediate measures appear to have been invented by Baker and Woodbury. (Lowell Mason probably would not have disapproved of such cavalier treatment, since the result was a hymn tune that was simple and easy to sing.)

As the nineteenth century progressed, other simplified adaptations from Bach's choral works began to appear with increasing frequency in compilations of choir music. A setting of Psalm 92 in *Hayter's Church Music: A Collection of Psalm and Hymn Tunes, Chants, Services, Anthems, &c.* (Boston, 1863), compiled by English-born A. U. Hayter, organist of Trinity Church in Boston, can be identified as a rhythmically altered version of Bach's harmonization of "Wachet auf" ("Sleepers, Wake") (see plate 2). Before long, excerpts from the cantatas began to appear. Albert J. Holden, compiler of *Holden's Sacred Music for Quartette Choirs* (New York, 1880), set the opening lines of

Plate 2. "Psalm XCII," from *Hayter's Church Music* (Boston: Oliver Ditson Co., 1863). Photo courtesy of Special Collections, Pitts Theology Library, Candler School of Theology, Emory University.

the aria "Mein gläubiges Herze" ("My Heart Ever Faithful") from Cantata 68, with Bach's accompaniment more or less intact, to the text of "Glory to Thee, My God, This Night" (again with the necessary rhythmic alterations).

If Lowell Mason was not an enthusiastic promoter of Bach's music, he nonetheless made an important (though probably inadvertent) contribution to the introduction of Bach to America. In 1852 Mason traveled to Germany, where he attended services at St. Thomas's in Leipzig and heard the choir perform unspecified "fine pieces" by Bach. In Frankfurt he also heard a vocal solo, which he described rather grudgingly as being "of a popular character, notwithstanding it is by Bach."[15] During the same year, Mason purchased the library of Johann Christian Heinrich Rinck (1770–1846) and had it shipped back to Boston. Rinck had acquired some of these materials from his teacher, Johann Christian Kittel (1732–1809), who was in turn a pupil of J. S. Bach. Although Rinck's name was well known among American organists who had studied from his popular organ tutor, and Mason may have assumed that the collection was worth acquiring on this basis alone, one wonders whether he had any idea of the treasures it contained.

Mason died in 1872 and his heirs gave his substantial library, including the Rinck Collection, to Yale University, where it attracted scant attention until recently. Yet it contains early copies of several preludes and fugues for organ, some preludes and fugues from book 1 of the Well-Tempered Clavier, and parts 3 and 4 of the *Clavierübung*, as well as the "Neumeister Collection" of chorale preludes, which includes a number of hitherto unknown works by Bach.[16]

Impetus to Bach performance everywhere came in the 1850s, with the beginning of the publication of his complete works in 1851 by the recently organized Bach-Gesellschaft in Germany, the crowning achievement of the "Bach revival." Eighteen American musicians and organizations are listed among the original subscribers, including Harvard College, the Harvard Musical Association, Yale College, and the Peabody Institute of Baltimore. A few music dealers also subscribed, presumably with resale in mind, and once the first volumes of the series were in print they became widely available.

It is possibly due to this increase in the availability of modern Bach scores that in 1853 three Boston pianists (Otto Dresel, Alfred Jaell, and William Scharfenberg, all from Germany), assisted by a string quartet (likewise composed of immigrants), performed Bach's Concerto in D Minor for Three Harpsichords and Strings (BWV 1063),

15. Mason, *Musical Letters from Abroad*, 52–53, 152.

16. Gerhard Herz, *Bach Sources in America* (Kassel: Bärenreiter, 1984), 205–11, 219–23, 246–47, 254–56, 268. See also Christoph Wolff, "Bach's Organ Music: Studies and Discoveries," *The Musical Times* 126 (1985): 149–52; and the introduction to Wolff's facsimile edition, *The Neumeister Collection of Chorale Preludes from the Bach Circle: Yale University Manuscript LM 4708* (New Haven: Yale University Press, 1986), reprinted in Christoph Wolff, *Bach: Essays on His Life and Music* (Cambridge, Mass.: Harvard University Press, 1991), 107–27.

the first recorded public performance of any major Bach work in America.[17] John S. Dwight called it "the great feature of the evening," praised "the perfect unity with which all moved together" (as well as the tone of Chickering's three pianos), and seized the opportunity to insert some historical information about the work. Dwight, an avowed votary of Bach who the previous year had published in his *Journal of Music* a translation of an article on Bach by Adolf Bernhard Marx, was clearly delighted with the performance. Indeed, he was quite carried away by "the neatness, the transparency, the easy continuous on-flow of the music" in the first movement, the "delicately piquant style of melody" in the second, and the "unity in variety" of the concluding fugue, which he likened to a mountain brook descending and spreading out upon a plain.[18] Dwight's discussion of the Bach concerto occupied nearly two whole columns; the other works on the program, by Beethoven, Chopin, Heller, and Hummel, rated but three brief paragraphs.

In 1858 Boston was also the scene of the first recorded performance of a Bach choral work longer than a hymn tune: the motet *Fürchte dich nicht* (BWV 228), which was sung by the Private Singing Club of Boston, and directed by Otto Dresel (1826–90), one of the pianists in the 1853 concerto performance.[19] Dresel, who emigrated to Boston in 1852, had been a student of Mendelssohn in Leipzig, which may explain his familiarity with and love of Bach's music.[20] His continuing devotion to Bach is confirmed by the fact that, in the course of thirteen piano concerts given in 1865, eleven different Bach works were performed.[21]

If any organist in America played Bach before the mid-century point, it would surely have been Dr. Edward Hodges (1796–1867), organist of New York's Trinity Church. However, the evidence for this is largely anecdotal. Hodges, who came to New York from England in 1839 after serving churches in his native Bristol, knew Samuel Wesley and seems to have been on the fringes of the English "Bach circle." He played a fugue by Bach—most likely from the Well-Tempered Clavier—at an organ dedication in Bristol in 1822, and an "Organ Pedal Fugue in G minor" as a duet at another dedication in 1836.[22] Hodges brought his well-worn copy of Wesley and Horn's edi-

17. This piece is identified incorrectly as the Concerto in C Major (BWV 1064) in H. Earle Johnson, *First Performances in America* (Detroit: Information Coordinators, 1979), 9.

18. John S. Dwight, "Otto Dresel's Fifth and Last Soiree," DJM 2, no. 22 (March 5, 1853): 174–75.

19. Johnson, *First Performances in America*, 15.

20. F. O. Jones, ed., *A Handbook of American Music and Musicians* (Canaseraga, N.Y.: F. O. Jones, 1886), 50.

21. Clark, "Beginnings of Bach in America," 343.

22. John Ogasapian, *English Cathedral Music in New York: Edward Hodges of Trinity Church* (Richmond, Va.: Organ Historical Society, 1994), 24–25, 86–87.

tion of the Well-Tempered Clavier with him to New York, and his daughter and biographer, Faustina Hasse Hodges, claimed that he played from it regularly.

Thus it is possible that Hodges played an occasional piece from the Well-Tempered Clavier as an organ voluntary after his arrival in New York. Moreover, he might even have played one of the "pedal fugues" at Trinity Church after 1846, when a large new organ by Henry Erben was completed to his specifications. This instrument had a twenty-five-note pedal keyboard beginning on C—one of the first in the country—which would allow the playing of many of Bach's preludes and fugues.[23] However, Hodges played his last service at Trinity Church in 1858, and there is no concrete evidence that any of Bach's music was performed there until a new chancel organ was dedicated in December of 1864, on which occasion Charles J. Hopkins played a "Toccata in F" by Bach (presumably BWV 540). More Bach probably was heard in Trinity Church after John P. Morgan became associate organist in 1868. Morgan had studied under Ernst Friedrich Richter and Moritz Hauptmann in Leipzig, and "played only the compositions of Bach, Merkel, and the contrapuntal school, disdaining to touch the works of modern French writers." It was not until 1875 that a Bach choral work was mentioned at this church, however: during Lent the choir sang the final chorus of the St. Matthew Passion.[24]

During the 1850s several gifted young American organists traveled to Europe to study, chiefly in Germany. Among them were John Knowles Paine (1839–1906) of Portland, Maine, later to become the first professor of music at Harvard University, and Dudley Buck (1839–1909) of Hartford, Connecticut, one of the most popular composers of church music in the late nineteenth century.

Paine studied in Berlin with Karl August Haupt (1810–91), a leading organ virtuoso who was an ardent promoter of Bach's organ music. Haupt introduced the young man from Maine to the wonders of Bach's preludes, fugues, and trio sonatas, which Paine soon performed in recitals to critical acclaim. Upon his return to America in 1861, Paine gave a recital at the First Parish Church in Portland, which included Bach works identified only as "fugues" and a "trio sonate." His program was attended by the editor of the *Boston Musical Times*, who described Paine as a "devoted worshiper" of Bach, who "revels in the wealth of the life-long labor of the illustrious master. . . . He is a missionary of Bach."[25] And so he indeed proved to be.

In 1863, after a wait of several years, a large organ built by the German firm of Walcker was installed in Boston's Music Hall. In front of it stood a bronze statue of Beetho-

23. Ibid., 159.

24. Arthur H. Messiter, *A History of the Choir and Music of Trinity Church, New York* (New York: Edwin S. Gorham, 1906), 106, 127, 158–59.

25. Schmidt, *Life and Works of John Knowles Paine*, 42.

ven, the reigning deity of Boston's musical Brahmins. But perched atop the pediment over the console was the stern-faced bust of an older master, prominently labeled in gilt letters, lest the uninitiated should not recognize him: "J. S. Bach." The recital given at the dedication of the organ on November 2, 1863, opened with Bach: first, Paine performed a "Grand Toccata in F" (probably BWV 540) and a "Trio Sonata in E flat" (BWV 525), and immediately thereafter one of Paine's students, Eugene Thayer, played a "Grand Fugue in G minor" (most probably BWV 542, or possibly 578 or 535).[26]

In a second recital three days later, Paine played Bach's Prelude and Fugue in A Minor (BWV 543 or 551) and a "Choral Varied; 'Christ the Lord to Jordan Came'" (presumably the two versions of *Christ, unser Herr, zum Jordan kam*, BWV 684 and 685, from Part 3 of the *Clavierübung*). On the same program George W. Morgan of New York, another Bach advocate, performed a "Fugue in D Major" (possibly BWV 580 or 532/2). In the space of a few days, then, Boston's music lovers were treated to a goodly selection of major Bach organ works—along with pieces by Mendelssohn, Antoine Édouard Batiste (1820–76), Louis James Alfred Lefébure-Wély (1817–69), Paine, Thayer, and the inevitable transcriptions.

In 1864 Paine was appointed to the faculty of Harvard University, where he would, over the years, direct many performances of Bach's choral and instrumental works and imbue his students with his own love of Bach's music. As early as 1866 one of them, George L. Osgood, presented a commencement speech on the appreciation of Bach's music.[27]

Dudley Buck studied with the noted recitalist and Bach advocate Johann Gottlob Schneider of Dresden and took courses at the conservatory in Leipzig, virtually in the shadow of Bach's *Thomaskirche.* Like Paine, Buck soon became adept at playing the master's preludes and fugues. Returning home a few years after Paine, in 1865, Buck immediately began a year-long series of organ concerts in Hartford, during which he performed at least six of Bach's preludes and fugues. In 1869 Buck moved to Chicago, where he became organist of St. James's Church, opened a teaching studio, and initiated another series of recitals. Like other recitalists of the period, his programs contained transcriptions and contemporary works (including his own). But a sampling of fifteen recital programs reveals that he also performed nine major works by Bach, including the Passacaglia in C Minor (BWV 582).[28] Following the tragic loss of his church and studio in the Great Chicago Fire (1871), Buck moved to Boston. During the 1870s he taught at the New England Conservatory and gave recitals in Boston's Music Hall,

26. *The Great Organ in the Boston Music Hall* (Boston: Ticknor & Fields, 1866), 74.

27. Clark, "Beginnings of Bach in America," 342.

28. William K. Gallo, "The Life and Church Music of Dudley Buck, 1839–1909" (Ph.D. diss., Catholic University of America, 1968), 18.

continuing the pattern of sandwiching Bach works between the transcriptions and contemporary compositions on his programs.

Like Paine, Buck was a kind of "missionary" for Bach—although Buck was more of a popularizer, whereas Paine worked primarily in academic circles. In an article for the *Musical Independent* in 1869, Buck averred that "Bach's day was the day of fugues upon the piano, as well as organ. They danced in fugue and reveled in canon. . . . It is hard for this generation to comprehend the truth of this, and yet there can be no question that the organ never so truly vindicates its claim as 'King of Instruments' as when heard in this style."[29]

After the new organ was installed in Boston's Music Hall in 1863, a series of weekly recitals was instituted. These continued for several years, and major Bach works were often featured. In the 1870s, students and faculty from the nearby New England Conservatory gave performances there, again frequently including the music of Bach. As large organs in concert halls and churches proliferated throughout America in the final decades of the nineteenth century, so too did organ recitals, an impressive number of which included at least one major composition by Bach.

The pupils and successors of Paine, Buck, Morgan, and Thayer continued to revel in the organ music of Bach, and several of their contemporaries (including S. P. Tuckerman of Boston, Samuel P. Warren of Montreal, and Clarence Eddy of New York) were subscribers to the Bach-Gesellschaft edition. As conservatories began to spring up in America in the 1860s and 1870s, Bach's works became an indispensible component in the curriculum for organ students—a tradition that continues to the present day. During the same period, Bach's music also became an integral part of the piano curriculum at these institutions. This is doubtless one of the reasons why American publishers began carrying the Well-Tempered Clavier in their catalogs, with Oliver Ditson leading the way as early as 1850.

It was mentioned earlier that Lowell Mason rewarded his son, William, with a piano for successfully learning a piece from the Well-Tempered Clavier. William Mason (1829–1908), who later achieved renown as a concert pianist, was another young American musician who studied in Germany around the same time as did Paine and Buck. In 1856, shortly after his return to Boston, Mason joined with William Scharfenberg and Henry C. Timm for a performance in New York of Bach's Concerto in D Minor for Three Harpsichords and Strings (BWV 1063).[30] Moreover, Mason is known to have performed in this work on at least three other occasions after moving to New York, all at Steinway Hall during the 1870s.[31] During his extensive recital career, Mason

29. Ibid.

30. Johnson, *First Performances in America*, 8–9.

31. Clark, "Beginnings of Bach in America," 344.

often included the music of Bach in his programs, and he also edited several volumes of Bach's keyboard works for the G. Schirmer publishing company.

One of the first advocates of Bach's orchestral and chamber works in America was Theodore Thomas (1835–1905), a German-born violinist and conductor who performed the Chaconne from Bach's Partita in D Minor for Solo Violin (BWV 1004) in New York as early as 1858. In the early 1860s Thomas founded his own orchestra, and he soon began programming music by Bach. Curiously, his initial offerings were transcriptions of organ pieces—perhaps inspired by the growing popularity of public organ recitals, which had familiarized audiences with works such as the Toccata in F Major (BWV 540) and the Passacaglia in C Minor (BWV 582), both of which were performed under Thomas's direction in 1865. But after 1867 Thomas also programmed the orchestral suites (No. 2 in B Minor [BWV 1067], first performed in 1874, was a favorite), the Brandenburg Concertos, and, in 1875, the Concerto in D Minor for Two Violins (BWV 1043).[32]

Thomas was not the only German-born conductor to begin performing Bach in America during this period. In 1870 Carl Zerrahn (1826–1909) slipped the air and gavotte from the Third Orchestral Suite in D Major (BWV 1068) into a program containing a Mozart symphony, an overture from an opera by Weber, and a Strauss waltz at the thirteenth annual music festival in Worcester, Massachusetts. Five years later, at the eighteenth festival, he devoted an entire program to vocal, organ, and chamber music by Bach and Handel.[33] In general, however, Zerrahn seems to have been less devoted to Bach than Thomas, Dresel, and his other German compatriots, and more a promoter of opera and contemporary music.

With regard to coverage in the press, Thomas, Paine, Dresel, William Mason, and others who performed Bach's music had an enthusiastic ally in John Sullivan Dwight (1813–93), the proper Bostonian editor of *Dwight's Journal of Music*. In 1869 Dwight wrote, "there is something in Bach that appeals to general sympathy, let him once be properly presented." Around the same time he also published a translation of Forkel's Bach biography, as well as an article on Bach's music. Not every reviewer shared Dwight's enthusiasm for Bach, however. In 1860 a writer for the *Boston Musical Times* dismissed violinist Julius Eichberg's performance of the Violin Concerto in A Minor (BWV 1041), noting that "Bach's concerto may be learned, but it is very heavy and uninspired."[34]

Compared with Bach's keyboard and ensemble music, serious performances of his choral works came relatively late to American concert life. Dresel's small choral group

32. Ibid., 346–47.

33. Raymond Morin, *The Worcester Music Festival, Its Background and History, 1858–1946* (Worcester, Mass.: Worcester County Musical Association, 1946), 29, 38.

34. Johnson, *First Performances in America*, 10.

had presented at least one motet in the 1850s, and Paine's students at Harvard had been performing cantatas since 1865, when portions of *Ein feste Burg ist unser Gott* (BWV 80) were sung during the commencement exercises. Yet it was not until the 1870s that Boston's prestigious Handel and Haydn Society set foot on Bach territory, with some performances of "selections" from the St. Matthew Passion under Zerrahn. A more complete performance had been announced for the 1870–71 season but was withdrawn as "unready." A fairly complete version with only minor cuts was offered in 1874, but it was not until 1879 that the entire work was performed.[35]

In view of the original proposed date of performance, it seems likely that the Handel and Haydn Society's interest in the St. Matthew Passion was spurred by the publication of the first American edition, late in 1869. It was edited, with both the German text and a new translation, by Dwight, who regarded the translation in the 1862 English edition as "too free, often ceasing to be a translation at all."[36] After having finally broken the ice in Bach performance, the Handel and Haydn Society followed this up in 1877 with parts 1 and 2 of the Christmas Oratorio (part 6 had to wait until 1883). However, not until 1887 did they attempt the B Minor Mass, and then only in a considerably abridged version.[37]

The choral conductors and singers were soon to catch up with the keyboard players and instrumentalists, though, and not all of them were based in the metropolitan areas of the East Coast. The first American musical group known to have appropriated Bach's name was formed around 1878 in Ohio, and by 1886 the Bach Society of Cleveland consisted of eighty voices, a twelve-piece string orchestra, and an organist. The director was Alfred Arthur, who, not surprisingly, had received his musical education in Boston and had studied under Julius Eichberg, the violinist who had performed Bach's A Minor Violin Concerto there in 1860.[38]

Also in Ohio, Theodore Thomas conducted the American premiere of several Bach choral works at the Cincinnati May Festival: the Magnificat in 1875, *Lobet Gott in seinen Reichen* (BWV 11) in 1882, and selections from the Mass in B Minor in 1886. The Magnificat was panned by an anonymous reviewer, who called it "the weakest thing the chorus has undertaken."[39] It may have been the chorus itself that was weak, how-

35. H. Earle Johnson, *Hallelujah, Amen! The Story of the Handel and Haydn Society of Boston* (Boston: Bruce Humphries, 1965), 109.

36. John S. Dwight, preface to *Passion Music, According to the Gospel of Matthew* (Boston: Oliver Ditson & Co., 1869).

37. Johnson, *Hallelujah, Amen!*, 250.

38. Jones, *Handbook of American Music and Musicians*, 9–10.

39. Kroeger, "Bach in Nineteenth-Century America," 38.

ever; amateur singers who have attempted to master the work's melismatic passages know that it is not for the faint-hearted. But Thomas was undeterred, and more and more of Bach's choral music continued to enter the mainstream concert repertoire as the century drew to a close.

Meanwhile, in Philadelphia, under the tutelage of the remarkable blind organist David Wood, a young man who would eventually put his indelible stamp upon American Bach performance was being nurtured in the music of the master. Wood's devotion to this composer was so strong that in 1894 at Philadelphia's Church of the New Jerusalem he performed an all-Bach organ recital, which included the Passacaglia in C Minor (BWV 582), the Prelude and Fugue in E-flat Major (BWV 552), the Toccata in D Minor (BWV 565), and the four-movement Pastorale in F Major (BWV 590), as well as two chorale preludes. However, his student, John Frederick Wolle (1863–1933), had played an all-Bach recital even earlier than this, at the Chicago World's Fair in 1893.[40]

J. Fred Wolle (as he was known) was born in Bethlehem, Pennsylvania, the son of a Moravian clergyman. Although David Wood had instilled in him a love of Bach's organ music, Wolle's lifelong commitment to Bach's choral works was kindled during his studies in Munich with Joseph Gabriel Rheinberger in 1884–85. Upon his return to Bethlehem in 1886, Wolle was appointed organist of the Moravian Church there. He also took charge of the Choral Union, which gave the first American performance of Bach's St. John Passion in 1888.

Despite having a good-sized chorus of 115 singers, Wolle worked under some handicaps in this performance. Movements were cut, a piano was needed (and possibly also the organ) to reinforce the rather weak string orchestra, and the Evangelist's part was spoken, not sung. But the soloists were praised, and the *Bethlehem Daily Times* pronounced the performance "a thorough success."[41] Thus encouraged, Wolle and the Choral Union successfully tackled the longer St. Matthew Passion in 1892, with additional singers from Lehigh University and the Moravian School. In 1894 Bach's Christmas Oratorio was performed by the Moravian Church choir, "assisted by others," under Wolle's direction.[42]

When Wolle initially attempted the Mass in B Minor, immediately following the St. Matthew Passion, it exceeded the capabilities of the Choral Union, which foundered on the shoals of the lengthy and formidable score and disbanded. But this merely deferred Wolle's dream. In December of 1898 his determination, fueled by the support of local

40. Gerson, *Music in Philadelphia*, 108.

41. Robin A. Leaver, "The Revival of the St. John Passion: History and Performance Practice," *Bach: Journal of the Riemenschneider Bach Institute* 20, no. 3 (1989): 49.

42. Robin A. Leaver, "New Light on the Pre-History of the Bach Choir of Bethlehem," *Bach: Journal of the Riemenschneider Bach Institute* 22, no. 2 (1991): 24–34, esp. 31 and 33.

music lovers, led to the founding of the celebrated Bethlehem Bach Choir. After fourteen months of preparation by the indomitable Wolle, the choir finally delivered a successful Mass in B Minor at the Moravian Church in March of 1900. Moreover, they performed the work in its uncut entirety, something no other American chorus had yet achieved. It was just the beginning of the Bethlehem Bach Choir's many Bach premieres.[43]

The year 1900 was, of course, the 150th anniversary of Bach's death. It also marked the completion of the publication of his complete works by the Bach-Gesellschaft, which had been initiated a half-century earlier. The success of the B Minor Mass performance in Bethlehem seems to have encouraged other choral groups: before the year was out, the Oratorio Society of New York had duplicated the feat, to be followed by Boston's Cecilia Society under B. J. Lang in 1901. By then, Wolle had already mounted what would become an ongoing series of annual Bach festivals, presenting on three successive days in May 1901 not only the Mass in B Minor, but the St. Matthew Passion and Christmas Oratorio as well.[44]

But the history of Bach in twentieth-century America must remain a topic for another day. Suffice it to say that by the end of the nineteenth century Bach's music was well on the way to becoming firmly entrenched in the repertoire of American choral groups, orchestras, chamber ensembles, singers, organists, pianists, and violinists. Some of his organ pieces, as well as the Well-Tempered Clavier and transcriptions of movements from choral and instrumental works, were among the very first selections (along with transcriptions of operatic overtures and all of Handel's *Messiah*) to be cut on paper rolls for mechanical playing after self-playing Aeolian residence organs were introduced in 1894—and one roll even provided a "music minus one" accompaniment for the so-called "Air on the G String."[45] This was but the beginning of a technological revolution that brought Bach's music into the homes of American music lovers via Edison's gramophone, Marconi's radio, and the digital media of today.

In the late-nineteenth and early-twentieth centuries, the music of Johann Sebastian Bach was abridged, transcribed, arranged, and reorchestrated at least as often as it was performed in its original form. Nonetheless, it was played, heard, and appreciated with increasing frequency. It took the entire second half of the nineteenth century to accomplish this introduction, thanks to the efforts of musicians such as Dresel, Paine, Eichberg, Buck, Mason, Thomas, Thayer, Morgan, Zerrahn, Wood, and Wolle, along with Dwight and other critics. By 1900, however, Bach most assuredly had arrived in America. And, fortunately for us a century later, he seems to be here to stay.

43. Raymond Walters, *The Bethlehem Bach Choir* (Boston: Houghton Mifflin, 1918), 45–48.

44. Ibid., 49–54.

45. Rollin Smith, *The Aeolian Pipe Organ and Its Music* (Richmond, Va.: Organ Historical Society, 1998), 155–56.

Doing Missionary Work
Dwight's Journal of Music *and the American Bach Awakening*

Matthew Dirst

During the nineteenth century—that great age of evangelism and revivals—musical salvation flowed across the Atlantic in one direction: due west. In fairly short order, American musical organizations and their patrons in New York, Boston, and other East Coast cities embraced the European classical canon of symphonies, operas, and chamber music in an effort to become more "civilized." By mid-century Beethoven, Mozart, Handel, and Haydn were household names.

American interest in the music of Johann Sebastian Bach, on the other hand, remained tepid until the 1870s. Why the long lag time in Bach's case? The biggest stumbling block was the music itself: his elaborate church pieces, intricate chamber music, and learned keyboard works severely taxed the talents, and likely the patience, of most musicians in antebellum America. Concert presenters and publishers could likewise hardly be counted on to promote music so far removed from the norm. The kind of private, connoisseur-driven Bach reception that obtained in Europe stood little chance on a continent that lacked composers of the first rank or large numbers of gifted amateurs or writers on music, from whose ranks European Bach enthusiasts tended to come. In short, in America the music of Bach was a tough sell.

Enter America's first music critic of real stature: John Sullivan Dwight (1813–93), whose eponymous *Journal* has been picked over by many music historians, but whose influential Bach advocacy has received scant attention. As editor of *Dwight's Journal of Music, A Paper of Art and Literature* (1852–81), Dwight played a prominent role in the musical thought and practice of a tumultuous era in our nation's history. A self-described "missionary of art," Dwight regarded the music of the European masters as not only a source of aesthetic pleasure but as an essential element in the proper development of American culture. The inaugural issue of his *Journal* states plainly that this was to be a "bulletin of progress" that would "represent the [musical] movement and at the same time help to guide it to [its] true end" (1:4).[1] Dwight found a receptive

1. This and all subsequent parenthetical references to volume and page numbers are to *Dwight's Journal*

audience among Bostonians in particular. This is clear from the *Journal*'s long association with Boston, where many music lovers came to share his essentially conservative tastes. But this was finally a periodical whose mission was national, not just local. To fill its pages Dwight borrowed liberally from English and continental writers (he often translated German and French materials himself). He also contributed the lion's share of new criticism and commentary. Elitist in tone but democratic in coverage, *Dwight's Journal* has long been recognized as the most detailed chronicle of musical life in late-nineteenth-century America—an impressive achievement for a venture that Dwight himself once characterized as his "last desperate (not very confident) grand *coup d'etat* to try to get a living."[2]

Compared with today's periodicals of culture, which tend toward either the popular or the academic, *Dwight's Journal* was really more of an evangelical tract. Its fundamental purpose, to win converts to the cause of fine music, was a mission for which its founder and sole editor was ideally suited. By all reports an awkward and unexceptional speaker, Dwight excelled as a writer on music; his enthusiasm for various utopian causes endows much of his criticism with an extraordinary degree of passion. From the Beethoven symphonies to the St. Matthew Passion, Dwight endeavored to make the European canon speak to American listeners by humanizing it in a peculiarly American way. More than anything else, Dwight wanted his compatriots to discover the same wholeness and profound satisfaction that he found in the classic masterworks.

What was it about Bach in particular that caused Dwight to champion his music so vigorously in the last dozen years of his *Journal?* Like European Bach enthusiasts, Dwight admired Bach's well-turned counterpoint and sublime melodies. He was fascinated with old genres and styles of composition, and with performing practices that differed significantly from modern approaches. He also was aware of Bach's influence on other composers. However, one other aspect of reception distinguished the awakening of American interest in Bach in the late nineteenth century from comparable (though earlier) developments in Europe. Dwight believed that Bach's greatest works had the power to transform the receptive listener with a uniquely personal kind of spiritual nourishment. He didn't want us merely to hear and appreciate this music, but somehow to be changed by it. Regardless of what one might think about such an argument, there is no denying that it resonated powerfully with Dwight's time and place: decades of evangelism had convinced many Americans that personal spirituality was

---

of Music: A Paper of Art and Literature (Boston: Edward Balch [1852–58], Oliver Ditson [1858–79], and Houghton, Osgood & Co. [1879–81], 1852–81; reprint, New York: Johnson Reprint Editions, 1968). All emphases are original, unless otherwise noted.

2. Irving Sablosky, *What They Heard: Music in America, 1852–1881, From the Pages of Dwight's Journal of Music* (Baton Rouge: Louisiana State University Press, 1986), 3.

not only desirable, but also necessary. Finding religion in Bach, Dwight was not so much worshipping a false god as he was arguing that in the experience of great works of art, one may encounter the divine.

A Reluctant Critic

Although enthusiastic about music from an early age, Dwight never intended it to become his life's work; he came to music criticism through the back door, only after rejecting a variety of other career paths.[3] A famously shy and even diffident man, Dwight was neither a member of a distinguished musical family nor a man with any noteworthy musical skills. The son of a prominent Boston physician, he received little formal training in music (among the Brahmin gentry, only young women took music lessons), though he learned to play both the clarinet and piano passably well. More important for his eventual career as a writer on music was the stimulating intellectual atmosphere of an upper-class Unitarian household, where he encountered a broad smattering of the latest European literature and thought.

While an undergraduate at Harvard, Dwight read German literature and the classics and participated in the first organizations on that venerable campus devoted to instrumental music. He remained active in one of these, the Pierian Sodality, after graduating in 1832 and he was one of the prime instigators of its 1837 transformation into the Harvard Musical Association, an organization that was for many years the most prominent chamber music society in Boston (it still exists and will concern us presently). Graduate study at the Harvard Divinity School followed, perhaps out of respect for his father, who had taken the same path. Although Dwight *fils* served barely a year as a Unitarian minister, he never abandoned an essentially Unitarian outlook. He viewed the world as an organic whole whose various parts, while under the control of a benevolent creator, could be manipulated for the benefit of humankind. His 1836 thesis on "The Proper Character of Poetry and Music for Public Worship" articulates just such a project for music. As his later work as a critic would affirm, music had to serve for more than just entertainment; it was the best means of deepening America's somewhat crude culture.

Dwight's dream of a better world through better music owes much to the idealist thought of Ralph Waldo Emerson and his followers, the transcendentalists, among whom Dwight found kindred spirits while a graduate student at Harvard. Though Emerson himself had little affinity for music, his associates were among the first American writers to take music seriously. Their journals are a treasure trove of infor-

3. There are two standard biographies of Dwight: George Willis Cooke, *John Sullivan Dwight: Brook-Farmer, Editor, and Critic of Music; A Biography* (Boston: Small, Maynard, 1898; reprint, New York: Da Capo Press, 1969), and Edward N. Waters, "John Sullivan Dwight: First American Critic of Music," *Musical Quarterly* 21 (1935): 69–88. The latter is reprinted in the Johnson edition of DJM 1:vii–xiii.

mation on the rise of a serious musical culture, especially in New England.[4] More important for the transcendentalists than music, however, were poetry and a life of introspection. This suited well the introverted John S. Dwight, whose first real love was poetry (his first publications were expert translations of German romantic verse). As his interest in music grew, he learned to divide his time between the two fields without ever losing sight of either one. Navigating with ease the leap from poems to symphonies, during the 1840s Dwight wrote about Beethoven with as much conviction as about Goethe and Schiller.[5]

Dwight's reputation as the "transcendentalist pope of music" reflects both a lifelong love of classical music and a persistent yearning for a transformed society in which music would play a prominent role. More than anything else, this latter preoccupation distinguishes Dwight's music criticism from that of his contemporaries, though his was but one of many voices agitating for the wholesale adoption of the classics in America. For decades Boston's leading musicians had been trying to improve the state of the art in the Massachusetts capital by introducing European music of a more serious nature. Instrumental music had never enjoyed much esteem in American cities. In theaters, instrumentalists were confined to the pit and only rarely featured by themselves. Furthermore, while New England Congregationalists extolled the virtues of psalmody, they shunned sonatas and symphonies. Gradually, however, an independent culture of instrumental music emerged, with figures like Dwight lending their support in a burgeoning musical press.

Dwight proved to be an especially effective advocate for Beethoven in Boston.[6] Two aspects of Dwight's long-standing espousal of Beethoven—one obvious, the other less so—set the stage for his later Bach advocacy. From his numerous essays and lectures on the Beethoven symphonies, Dwight learned how to influence public opinion, thereby redeeming his lackluster career as a preacher. He discovered, as Mark Grant aptly puts it, the "editorial pulpit function of music critics."[7] In addition, in his Beethoven

4. See Irving Lowens, "Writings about Music in the Periodicals of American Transcendentalism (1835–50)," *Journal of the American Musicological Society* 10 (1957): 71–85.

5. The best source of information on this formative stage in Dwight's career as a critic is Ora Frishberg Saloman, *Beethoven's Symphonies and J. S. Dwight: The Birth of American Music Criticism* (Boston: Northeastern University Press, 1995).

6. Before 1841 knowledge of the great symphonist rested on the occasional performance of excerpts on programs that favored the latest opera overtures, a smattering of songs and arias, perhaps a concerto, and the odd waltz or two, all served up in a festive stew without much thought as to the musical coherence of the program. See Michael Broyles, *"Music of the Highest Class": Elitism and Populism in Antebellum Boston* (New Haven: Yale University Press, 1991), esp. chap. 6, "Crisis in Secular Concert Activity: Disputes and Divergences."

7. Mark N. Grant, *Maestros of the Pen: A History of Classical Music Criticism in America* (Boston: Northeastern University Press, 1998), 46.

criticism Dwight propounded a distinctive argument: that the best music aided humanity by creating a healthy environment in its very sounding texture.

This interesting twist on the ancient concept of the harmony of the spheres—which fused together two of Dwight's central concerns, the power of music and humankind's need to get along—reflects yet another aspect of the reluctant critic's checkered career. Following his brief stint as a clergyman, Dwight embraced associationism, an offshoot of transcendentalism that preserved its idealism while rejecting the militant individualism of Emerson and his followers. Installing himself in the 1840s at Brook Farm (George Ripley's short-lived experiment in communal living in West Roxbury, Massachusetts), Dwight worked to refine his understanding of music in general and the symphony in particular. The essays he contributed to *The Harbinger* (the official organ of associationist thought and the most important of several journals for which Dwight wrote during this time) described a kind of music that few Americans knew. Accordingly, in introducing the Beethoven symphonies Dwight eschewed technical discussion and instead characterized these works in fairly abstract terms, stressing their universal appeal and moral force. Their worth, he maintained, derived in large part from their scoring: here was music that exemplified the associationist credo by placing the group above the individual in a world where everyone worked together toward a common goal. Making a clear distinction for his readers, Dwight held up this noble repertory while putting down the "mechanical finger-school" of the fashionable virtuoso, which served only to elevate star performers above both composer and orchestra. Thus Dwight lionized the best-known works of the European tradition as bearers of eternal values, the musical analogue of communal harmony.[8]

Like Beethoven, Bach too would eventually come to represent musical and societal well-being. Bach had the power to make "a wholesome, hearty strengthening beginning, putting all in cheerful, earnest humor for good true things to follow" (27:206). His music had a salutary effect on the performers as well: it put one "in the right state to play afterwards, it 'sounds so comfortable and makes one feel so comfortable'" (27:14). The effect was immediate; Dwight maintained that "we touch Bach and are strong" (29:182). Such pronouncements, which show the extent to which Dwight accepted unquestioningly the pious, *bürgerlich* Bach invented by earlier (mostly German) writers, are but the tip of the iceberg. Bach was such a frequent guest in the over 8,000 pages of *Dwight's Journal* that one may identify certain general themes in its many essays, reviews, and other notices. In what follows, we shall consider Dwight's Bach advocacy

8. My understanding of this aspect of Dwight's thinking about the Beethoven symphonies relies largely on Sterling F. Delano, "Music Criticism in *The Harbinger*," in Delano, *The Harbinger and New England Transcendentalism: A Portrait of Associationism in America* (Cranbury, N.J.: Associated University Presses, 1983); and Saloman, "Fourierist Aspects of Dwight's Major Essays, 1844–1845," in Saloman, *Beethoven's Symphonies and J. S. Dwight.*

within three broad phases of reception: (1) the dissemination of basic knowledge about Bach and his music, (2) instruction in the finer points of his art, and (3) the absorption of his major works into the repertory of America's premier performing organizations.

Getting Acquainted

Like its predecessors and virtually every other American periodical of its day that discussed music, *Dwight's Journal* regularly featured general articles on the lives and works of the major European composers. Information on Bach's life was readily available in English: a translation of Johann Nikolaus Forkel's Bach biography (1802) had been published in 1820, from which Dwight borrowed chapters 1–4, translating the rest afresh for his 1855–56 serialization of the work.[9] Excerpts from Carl Ludwig Hilgenfeldt's biography (1850) followed in 1867. The pages of the *Journal* also contained frequent comparisons of Bach and Handel, most of which merely reiterate familiar platitudes, such as the great irony that these "Saxon giants," born just a few miles from each other, never met.[10] The two were commonly said to have possessed similar talents but opposite personalities: Handel being the more worldly and outgoing, and Bach the more religious and inward.

Bach's allegedly devout nature brought forth a liberal amount of hyperbole and florid gravitas, including the familiar characterization of Bach as a staunch defender of the faith. By resisting the "theoretic pedantry" of Gottsched and his followers (according to Wilhelm Heinrich Riehl's *Musikalische Charakterköpfe*, 1853), and thereby preserving that which was "pure" and "chaste" in German art, Bach earned a comparison to the master masons and architects of the Gothic age: "In the believing mysticism of a child-like soul, and with the fantastic overflowing of wondrously intertwined forms, he built up cathedrals in tones, when people had long forgotten how to create them from

9. Forkel's biography appears in volume 8 of the *Journal*, from October 27, 1855 to January 19, 1856. The 1820 translation, long thought to have been the work of Augustus Frederic Christopher Kollmann, a leading figure in the English Bach movement, may have been made by another writer (see Michael Kassler, "The English Translations of Forkel's Life of Bach," in *Aspects of the English Bach Awakening*, ed. Michael Kassler [Aldershot: Ashgate, forthcoming]). Waters points out that the new translation of chapters 5–8 of Forkel constitutes one of the first examples of American Bach scholarship (Waters, "John Sullivan Dwight," DJM, 1:xi). Dwight's serialization of Forkel was not the first American publication of this seminal biography: excerpts had appeared earlier in Margaret Fuller's "Lives of the Great Composers," *The Dial* (October 1841): 174–85, and in an 1846 issue of *The [Boston] Musical Gazette*. On the latter excerpts, see J. Bunker Clark, "The Beginnings of Bach in America," in *American Musical Life in Context and Practice to 1865*, ed. James R. Heintze (New York: Garland, 1994), 341, 349 n. 16.

10. This was a common feature of contemporary English and German Bach criticism as well. The earliest such comparison known to me in an American journal is in an unsigned article entitled "The Pianoforte," *The Musical Magazine* 16 (August 3, 1839): 248–49.

stones." His life and works epitomized everything the romantics held dear: he was "an artist without a public, who sang in honor of God, and for his own pleasure" (8:258).

The belief that Bach was impervious to the mundane habits of his own culture as well as to pernicious foreign influence was common among German writers from the late eighteenth century onward. A Germanophile himself, Dwight published more than his fair share of this kind of rubbish, including the well-known exchange between Goethe and Carl Friedrich Zelter, in which the great poet demanded to know how the "French scum" could be lifted off the surface of Bach's music (as Zelter had rashly proposed) without damage to its essential structure (3:4). Dwight's subscribers, most of whom wouldn't have known a *coulé de tierce* from a *coulis de tomates,* surely paid greater heed to the more general observation that Bach's was an all but inscrutable art, for this was the point driven home repeatedly in the first few volumes of the *Journal.*

During these early years Dwight ventured only an occasional essay or excerpt on Bach; most were the work of other writers. From these infrequent notices the *Journal*'s subscribers learned that Handel's choral music was more striking and more immediately comprehensible, while Bach's was "the most difficult, and—its effect considered—the most thankless in existence" (6:123). As a correspondent from the *London Musical World* put it, Bach's is "magnificent music, but music without any relation whatever to the outside world, and therefore music which can never possibly have a chance of penetrating to the inmost heart of the crowd that constitutes nine-tenths of humanity" (13:122). Eventually Dwight affirmed this position but added an important caveat. Though Bach's music was too refined for most Americans, who had been taught to value only that which was "highly-colored, highly spiced, sensational," this should not prevent it from being heard, for "if we went solely by popularity, no great master work of poet, artist or musician ever would be brought out or known except in studies or by hearsay" (27:94). Dwight argued for a special place in the repertory for Bach by blending the antiquarian flavor of European reception with a dose of American sobriety. Bach became a kind of musical castor oil: his music was good for you even if you didn't like it. Dwight insisted further that Bach's works had to be preserved in all their purity, regardless of whether their import was apparent. Attempts to "popularize" them, especially those that stooped to vulgar arrangements (Dwight was particularly hard on poor Gounod), were routinely condemned as in "bad taste and almost sacrilege" (26:249).

Dwight occasionally reprinted more frankly propagandistic writings as well. One such piece, a translation of Friedrich Rochlitz's "On the taste for Sebastian Bach's compositions, especially those for keyboard," offers a compelling account of how an initial frustration with Bach could be overcome by diligent application.[11] Admitting that his first

11. The German original appeared in Rochlitz's *[Leipzig] Allgemeine musikalische Zeitung* 5, no. 31 (April 27, 1803): 509–22.

exposure to Bach's music as an impressionable chorister in the St. Thomas choir left him more confused than inspired, Rochlitz counseled perseverance, even though Bach's music "is *very* seldom what we commonly call agreeable, or flattering to the outward sense and to what passes over unconsciously from sense into feeling." It was worth the trouble, however, for Bach "offers indeed rich matter to the imagination, but seldom by direct appeals to it, always rather through the medium of thinking." Rochlitz's appeal to the intellectual pretensions of his readers was wholly in keeping with Dwight's own critical bent. The instructive ends of this "letter to a friend" were, moreover, not lost on the American critic, who knew comparatively little about Bach at this point in his career. Insisting that the novice had nothing to lose and everything to gain, Rochlitz cajoled with flattery, maintaining that "to one who cannot *think* during his artistic enjoyment, [Bach's] works are very little; such an one will never take home to himself their most essential excellence, nor will he even find it out." Tempering his rhetoric with more practical advice, Rochlitz recommended the four-part chorales and a number of preludes and fugues from the Well-Tempered Clavier as works that would engender a proper understanding of Bach's formidable art (12:209–10, 217–18).

Recognizing that professionals and amateurs alike in America knew little of Bach's output, Dwight dispensed advice on how best to listen to this kind of music. The biggest problem was overcoming fear of the unknown, and here personal experience served as a useful guide. A year-long European sojourn in 1861, when Dwight heard for the first time a good deal of Bach, had taught him that the best way to listen to Bach fugues was "with insatiable appetite, like love. Their suggestion is a story without end, and never tedious" (19:53). Dwight returned frequently to the latter point, protesting endlessly against the unjust association of Bach's name with only "heavy and uninteresting," "dull," and "dry" fugues. Challenging the "bugbear" that Bach belonged "to the stiff and mathematical school of the long past," Dwight asserted that Bach could be both "entertaining and delightful, as well as learned and profound" (24:358). Support for this view came from, among others, the Halle composer and Bach arranger Robert Franz, who challenged the *Journal*'s readers to look beyond the traditional ways of appreciating music (following the melody phrase by phrase, for example) and to focus instead on the entire contrapuntal fabric of a piece by Bach while forming a mental "image" of its many ideas. It was only this way, Franz maintained, that one could begin to appreciate and understand Bach's "seemingly confused, but really most richly artistic, organically developed complication of single parts" (27:102).

Gaining Expertise

Adjusting one's ears to Bach's uncommonly dense textures required hearing his music repeatedly, both at home and in the concert hall. Dwight lent his support to such activities with advance notices and reviews of Bach editions and performances in Boston and elsewhere. As the Europeans had done some fifty years earlier, Americans came to know Bach through his solo instrumental music; the works for larger ensembles (including the concerted church music) followed in due course. The keyboard works were a logical place to begin, as several were available in the United States by mid-century in inexpensive editions.[12]

In the reviews of Bach editions in *Dwight's Journal*, it was typical to play up the virtues of both music and edition while ignoring the latter's shortcomings. For example, in 1856 one of Dwight's correspondents announced the imminent publication of Chrysander's edition of all the Bach keyboard works. In Dwight's optimistic view, this edition would "enable hundreds, nay, thousands, who could not pay the high price of the former editions" to own and study this music. Commending it to American pianists, who were slowly warming to the charms of German keyboard music, Dwight reprinted in 1857 Chrysander's detailed preface, which describes the contents of each volume and provides concise definitions of the old dance types and keyboard genres found there (10:187, 194–95).[13] In the same year Dwight incorporated a review-essay that introduced a new edition of Bach's solo violin sonatas. The anonymous writer, after describing the "extraordinary manner" of these "little-known . . . musical treasure[s]," notes that Mendelssohn once composed a piano accompaniment for the famous Chaconne. The writer can't bring himself to recommend it, however, for the sonatas "ought to be played as Bach wrote them." Surprisingly, the same critic goes on to praise the latest edition of these works, a transcription for solo piano by Carl van Bruyck, for its pedagogical value. Van Bruyck completed the "building of the palace," so to speak, by filling out Bach's sometimes elliptical textures in the sonatas, much as Johann Philipp Kirnberger had done in the previous century for the Bach keyboard fugues (11:251).[14]

As this review shows, Dwight's age was broadly tolerant toward arrangements that tried to bring Bach's music into line with contemporary practices and tastes. The *Journal* spoke out against only the most egregious cases of editorial excess. One example is an 1866 translation of a review of Ignaz Moscheles' *Melodic-Contrapuntal Studies*, a publication comprising ten preludes from the Well-Tempered Clavier with obbligato cello melodies à la Gounod, which Dwight's uncredited writer disparaged as an "at-

12. Sixteen of Bach's four-part chorales appeared in A. N. Johnson's *Instructions in Thorough Base* (Boston: G. P. Reed, 1844), and the next decade witnessed the publication of American editions of the Well-Tempered Clavier (Boston: Oliver Ditson, 1850) and the organ works (New York: Peters, 1852), among others.

13. The mid-nineteenth-century change in American tastes in piano repertoire, from relatively lightweight French and Italianate pieces to the German classics, is described in Arthur Loesser, *Men, Women, and Pianos* (New York: Simon & Schuster, 1954), 469–70.

14. The review of the van Bruyck edition was originally published in the *Niederrheinische Musik-Zeitung*. For the 1773 Kirnberger harmonic analyses of Bach's fugues, see BDOK 3, no. 781.

tempt upon the life of that mighty genius, whose labor only now, after a whole century, has wrung from the world its long denied place in the history of Art." He rejected Moscheles' pastiche arrangements on account of the damage done to Bach's carefully calibrated preludes, and he deplored the fact that someone would add so indiscriminately to these works, "the foundation pillar and support of all composition." The edition is damned as "an offence not only against good taste [and] piety, but against all the fundamental perceptions on which our whole artistic culture rests" (26:249–50, 257–58). While such strong denunciations probably had little effect on sales of this or any other contemporary edition, the position of *Dwight's Journal* remained clear: Americans deserved reliable, affordable, and pedagogically sound editions of the classical repertory. In the case of Bach's music, original texts were preferable to arrangements, though the latter were occasionally of interest.

Among the *Journal*'s many reviews of Bach editions is a relatively early and rather hostile notice that warned about the potential dangers of even respectable editions. Robert Zimmer's "Thoughts upon the appearance of the third volume of the Bach Society in Leipzig" (translated by Alexander Wheelock Thayer) must have raised a few eyebrows among the handful of American subscribers to the Bach *Gesamtausgabe*. Originally published in Leipzig in pamphlet form, this aggressive diatribe dismisses the 1853 edition of the Inventions and Sinfonias, prepared by the Leipzig organist Carl Ferdinand Becker for the Bach-Gesellschaft, as little more than a knock-off of the existing Peters edition. By neglecting a crucial source (one that Peters had likewise ignored), Becker had squandered an opportunity to correct an edition that was "already in every musician's hands" (6:171–72, 179–80). While not many of Dwight's readers had cause for concern, Zimmer's agenda was one that resurfaced periodically in the pages of the *Journal:* to be worthwhile, a new edition must reflect the latest research and thinking about the repertory in question.

Concert reviews were likewise an obvious place to repeat the call for a wider audience for Bach's music in America. At a Harvard Musical Association concert in late 1861, Dwight so enjoyed a lone little piece of Bach, the Siciliano from the Sonata in E-flat Major for Flute and Keyboard (BWV 1031, delivered for the occasion on the violin), that he ventured to ask for more, opining that "there is no modern music fresher." Remembering fondly the effect of listening to the great virtuoso Joseph Joachim play this music in Dresden, Dwight felt "impatient that all our musical friends should know such enjoyment" (19:286). This came to pass in fairly short order: as the *éminence grise* behind the Harvard concerts, Dwight saw to it that they included periodic doses of Bach from the mid-1860s onward.[15] Dwight the editor likewise made sure

15. The Harvard Musical Association concerts began in 1844 at Dwight's instigation. Programming for the orchestral series was the responsibility of a committee that included Dwight, Otto Dresel,

that these concerts were advertised and reviewed regularly in the *Journal.* The same theme reappears in an 1862 review of one of John Knowles Paine's first organ recitals in Boston. Dwight noted approvingly that the program, which featured a substantial amount of Bach, attracted some "four or five hundred persons," and he was pleased "that even this number of people should manifest the desire to hear music for which the taste has been so little cultivated, and even the ear so little formed in our country." For Dwight this was "a sign of progress in a high direction" (20:367).

From the 1860s to the end of the century, performers and audiences alike in America favored works that have remained the cornerstone of the mainstream repertory. Concert pianists programmed the more contemplative preludes and fugues from the Well-Tempered Clavier (C Minor, C-sharp Minor, and F Minor from Book 1 were favorites) as well as familiar display pieces, such as the Italian Concerto (BWV 971) and the Chromatic Fantasia and Fugue (BWV 903). Organists found their way to the Passacaglia (BWV 582), the Pastorale (BWV 590), the Prelude and Fugue in A Minor (BWV 543), the Fantasia and Fugue in G Minor (BWV 542), the trio sonatas (BWV 525–30), and a handful of familiar chorale preludes. Among violinists, the Chaconne from the D Minor Partita (BWV 1004) was by far the most popular excerpt. Chamber groups and orchestras performed the celebrated "Air" from the Third Orchestral Suite (BWV 1068), occasionally in combination with one or two of the dances from the same work. They also essayed the multiple keyboard concertos, especially the two *a tre.*[16] At first the triple keyboard concertos were played by four pianists, one of whom realized the accompanying string parts. Dwight noted the Boston premiere of the D Minor (BWV 1063) in 1853 and of the C Major (BWV 1064) in 1864, both on Otto Dresel's chamber music programs in the Chickering piano factory's concert rooms. He characterized the latter composition as "no mere parade piece"; this was Bach at his finest, "full of joy in even-tempered life and solid work" (38:214). The D Minor Concerto first was heard in Boston in full orchestral dress in 1879. Both pieces eventually became staples of the orchestral repertory.

Beyond these familiar scores, the *Journal* records frequent performances of Heinrich Esser's orchestral transcription of the Toccata in F Major (BWV 540) on concerts of the Harvard Musical Association from the late 1860s onward. The Theodore Thomas Orchestra, launched in 1869 by its namesake and conductor as a touring ensemble, offered on the second program of its 1874–75 season Bach's Orchestral Suite in B Minor (BWV 1067), a work that Dwight found to be utterly charming, its dances "tan-

and others. See Arthur W. Hepner, *Pro bono artium musicarum: The Harvard Musical Association, 1837–1987* (Boston: The Association, 1987).

16. An edition of the Concerto in D Minor (BWV 1063) had been available since 1845.

talizingly short" (34:342). Thomas was also the first to program Bach's Magnificat in Boston, though the performance apparently left much to be desired (35:198–99).

On the subject of performance practice, *Dwight's Journal* was an outspoken advocate for a return to older ways of performing the music of Bach and his contemporaries. Though Dwight had no particular expertise in "historically informed performance," he was at least aware that the earlier repertory had its own proper means of performance, and that Bach's music in particular required something more than a kind of musical automatic pilot. Reviewing a performance of the D Minor Concerto for three keyboards in 1853, Dwight quoted the editor of the score, who maintained that "the hammering and lifeless mode of playing, now-a-days sometimes esteemed *Bach-ish*, must be utterly avoided; for the old pianists (harpsichordists) *sang* upon their instruments" (2:174). The so-called sewing-machine approach to baroque music was but one of many bad habits. An 1871 notice upbraids a pianist who intemperately added a few extra flourishes to the Chromatic Fantasia and Fugue (31:6), while an 1875 review faults Paine's monolithic approach to organ registration (34:390). Dwight returned to the latter issue with some frequency, wondering (as we still do) whether "old Bach . . . did actually allow himself no change of stops in his Fugue playing" (33:206). Bach's sonatas and suites for solo instruments, according to another critic, "demand great self-denial, presenting literally no opportunities for that dash and display so dear to all soloists." Joachim was singularly well suited to this kind of playing, even if his performance of Bach prompted the same critic to "occasionally fancy a want of what we would call romantic sentiment." Yet in the end Joachim's suppression of indulgence was thought to be entirely appropriate, even crucial, to proper performance of this music: "the absence . . . of this quality gives greater force to the rendering of these solos" (22:368). The lack of common ground with Bach meant that one had to rethink virtually every aspect of music-making, even those that had seemed self-evident. That a virtuoso of Joachim's caliber did so must have gratified Dwight and others who made frequent appeals for an approach to performing Bach that was fundamentally different from the prevailing mode.

Dwight occasionally had interesting things to say about not only the playing he witnessed but about the music itself. An 1869 review observes that Bach's E Minor Partita for solo keyboard (BWV 830) has some movements that "can hardly hold the attention awake, even when played so clearly and elegantly as they were." Dwight singles out the Courante in particular, which "in this as in nearly all Bach's Suites, is dry and lengthy" (29:151). More often, however, Dwight and his writers emphasized the grandeur and singularity of expression in Bach's instrumental works. Paradoxically, these pieces were attractive as novelties—they were so unlike everything else in the repertory that they could not fail to arouse comment—while simultaneously exemplifying the lasting values of a "strong, wholesome" culture. In this respect, the American Bach awakening was part of a larger renewal. As the United States emerged from the trauma of the Civil War, its musical institutions and consumers became ever more attuned to the European canon and less interested in the music of the nation's childhood. Like the other great composers venerated in the pages of *Dwight's Journal*, Bach injected timeless values and new vigor into a musical culture that was ready to expand its purview and flex its newfound muscles a little. That this was sometimes a messy process is undeniable. But even when a particular piece or movement didn't quite measure up, Dwight was firm in his belief that Americans needed to engage Bach's music and leave behind any preconceived notions about either the composer or his work. Even in Bach's legendarily difficult works, it was one's effort and application that counted the most. Some reviewers charitably excused unsatisfactory performances of Bach for precisely this reason. Dwight's own review of the Boston premiere of the Magnificat in 1876, for example, concedes the extraordinary demands this music placed even on professionals, most of whom were unaccustomed to such fare. On this occasion, Dwight could only shrug his shoulders at the inadequacy of both orchestra and chorus (35:198–99).

Although few (if any) of the first performances of Bach's music in this country were stellar, their very existence shows that America's fledgling musical institutions were responding to the call for a hearing of Bach's music, which was issued at regular intervals in *Dwight's Journal.* For years Dwight had been twisting arms in private as well. Making room for Bach's major works meant more than just backroom bartering with conductors and boards, however. It also meant convincing amateur singers, professional instrumentalists, and their public that this unfamiliar music was worth the considerable effort required. The critic's role as advocate thus became crucial as American choral societies finally took up Bach's sacred music in the closing decades of the nineteenth century.

Assimilating the Major Works

In support of this cause Dwight was at his most unabashedly proactive. As Adolf Bernhard Marx had done fifty years earlier for Mendelssohn and the Berlin Singakademie, Dwight paved the way for the first performances of Bach's major works in Boston and other American cities by agitating in his *Journal* for such presentations and by instructing readers in the finer points of these works, particularly the St. Matthew Passion. Among the first signs of American interest in this or any other of Bach's concerted vocal works were Dwight's carefully aimed salvos to the members of the Handel and Haydn Society's board of directors, who had to be convinced of the merits of such music before any rehearsals or performances of it could be scheduled. That this project took many years owes partly to the nature of the organization. Founded in 1815 as an amateur chorus with the aim of improving standards of sacred music, the Handel and Haydn Society grew exponentially during Dwight's lifetime, from an original sixteen singers in 1816 to several hundred in the 1820s and more than 600 during the 1870s. Consisting largely of middle-class amateurs, the chorus was run by a board of directors who considered the performance of oratorios to be merely one of the organization's activities, not its primary purpose. Until the late 1860s, when Dwight's persistent needling began to have some effect, they were quite content to recycle at the Society's triennial festival the same handful of well-known oratorios—*Messiah*, *The Creation*, and *Elijah* were the favorites—with occasional holiday performances of *Messiah* as well. Despite Dwight's long-standing affiliation with the Society (he completed a volume on its history), his status as both a prominent critic and a Unitarian intellectual decreed that his influence on its programming would be hard-won and a long time in coming.[17]

The conservative outlook of the Handel and Haydn Society and their audience, although surely a factor in the organization's longevity, meant that Bach made slow progress in Boston. The technical demands of a work like the St. Matthew Passion put an extraordinary burden on the soloists especially. Moreover, this composition required several instruments that were obsolete by this time. Until they were sure that the public would respond favorably, the Handel and Haydn Society board members were simply not willing to make the necessary commitments of time and money. Unfazed, Dwight began his campaign in 1854 with a notice about the work's first performance in London. He then sustained it for some twenty-five years, through partial performances and the infrequent airing of excerpts, until at last Bach's entire passion setting was heard in the Boston Music Hall on Good Friday in 1879—exactly fifty years after the Berlin Singakademie's first performances.

Comparisons with other nineteenth-century premieres of the work are instructive. The Berlin Singakademie (in 1829) and the London Bach Society (in 1854) likewise began their public presentations of Bach not with a modest work but with the opera-length St. Matthew Passion. The Berlin chorus had been rehearsing various bits and pieces of Bach for years, but Zelter was not willing to program any of it until Mendelssohn convinced him otherwise. In the end, the Singakademie presented Bach's passion shorn of most of its arias, with recomposed recitatives, and with a modicum of additional rearrangement; the result was practically a new work.[18] The Handel and

17. Charles C. Perkins and John S. Dwight, *History of the Handel and Haydn Society*, vol. 1 (Boston: Mudge, 1883; reprint, New York: Da Capo Press, 1977).

18. Martin Geck, *Die Wiederentdeckung der Matthäus-Passion im 19. Jahrhundert: Die zeitgenössischen Dokumente und ihre ideengeschichtliche Deutung* (Regensburg: Gustav Bosse, 1967), 34–60, provides a wealth of source-critical information on and contemporary reactions to the 1829 Berlin performance. For a concise description of the cuts Mendelssohn made and his reasons for doing so, see also Michael Marissen, "Religious Aims in Mendelssohn's 1829 Berlin-Singakademie Performances of Bach's St. Matthew Passion," *Musical Quarterly* 77 (1993): 718–26.

Haydn Society began instead with excerpts: the 1871 premiere included barely a quarter of the whole, while subsequent performances in 1874 and 1876 each added steadily more. Although piecemeal performances of major works were in fact going out of style, this strategy proved to be shrewd for the St. Matthew Passion. Those who found the excerpts objectionable were mollified by the remainder of the program.

Other Boston concert organizations had already presented various excerpts from the work; mostly prominently, "Erbarme dich" appeared on several orchestral programs of the Harvard Musical Association. Reviewing an 1871 performance of this beloved aria, Dwight acknowledged that such outings were only partially successful; the soloists often were overwhelmed by music for which they had not been adequately trained. The occasional piece by Bach was nevertheless important:

> For so long as he remains a stranger to us, we have not yet penetrated into the holy of holies of the temple of harmony, nor is our life intrinsically musical. Like an old masterpiece of painting, an Aria like this must be brought out from time to time—the same piece—and seen in a better and better light, with better skill of exhibition (or performance) and better preparation on the hearer's part: and while we listen or muse afterwards, the fire will surely burn within us. (30:398)

Evidently it did. Subsequent performances of this and other excerpts eventually raised the necessary enthusiasm—and courage—for a complete St. Matthew Passion.

In a remarkable display of impartiality, the *Journal* carried reviews of the work's Boston premiere that ranged from the hostile to the hagiographic. Bach's passion drew strong reactions from some critics, one of whom found it abstruse and "generally too severe for the average modern taste" (31:30). Writers for the major newspapers were generally more positive; some even sounded the very themes Dwight had already articulated in his extensive advance promotion of the work. The critic for the *Daily Advertiser*, for example, was surprised to find that the St. Matthew Passion required a whole new way of listening: Bach's melodies "transcen[d] the form of ordinary melody" (31:29). For some (including Dwight) the strange beauty of Bach's art was in fact its primary virtue. Weighing in a few weeks after reprinting the reviews of his colleagues, Dwight detected in the Handel and Haydn Society's performance "a new revelation of sublimity and beauty." The work, he rhapsodized, "led us farther into the inmost sanctuary of tones than any revelation thereof that had been vouchsafed to us before" (31:46).

With such comments Dwight adopted a rhetorical mode he had not used since his Beethoven essays of the 1840s. But in contrast to his earlier, all-encompassing characterization of Beethoven, Dwight saw Bach as the humble evangelist. The responsibility of the listener was clear: American audiences were the fortunate recipients of a musical message akin to Logos (the manifestation of God in the world), which they were obliged to share with all who would listen. The Handel and Haydn Society was simply a first step; Dwight then entreated other musical organizations and Americans in general to take up the cause.

One finds in *Dwight's Journal* countless similar exhortations to do right by Bach, to keep his music alive and thus perpetuate his legacy. In an 1867 issue, for example, at the end of an extended discussion of the Magnificat, Robert Franz admonished the *Journal*'s subscribers that "a work of Art first gains its true significance when it can actually exercise before all the world the power which the artist has lent to it: *he* has done his duty, now let those, who call themselves his followers, do theirs!" (27:126). Americans eventually signed on, no doubt emboldened by the increasing frequency of Bach's music on programs in Boston, New York, and even midwestern cities, where sizable numbers of German immigrants retained a taste for such fare. (Cincinnati heard performances of Cantata 80, *Ein feste Burg ist unser Gott*, in 1880 and excerpts from the B Minor Mass in 1886, a full year before the latter work was performed in its entirety by the Handel and Haydn Society.)[19] Dwight took great satisfaction in every stage of this development, crowing in 1869 that while the St. Matthew Passion "may never be popular . . . it will be, it is already, in such demand, that it cannot be kept out of the market or the concert-room much longer" (29:94). This was no mere wishful thinking: the Handel and Haydn Society began rehearsing the work the very next year. By the time Boston's premier chorus took up the call, there was a good deal of enthusiasm in the city for Bach. Not all of it was exactly helpful, however, as Dwight dutifully noted in the pages of his *Journal*.

Reviews of the Boston performances of the St. Matthew Passion in the 1870s describe a lively concert environment. The Music Hall was evidently a fairly noisy place; not even a Bach passion could quell the Handel and Haydn Society's boisterous public. Audiences routinely disregarded requests for no applause, often interrupting between sections and occasionally even demanding the repetition of favorite choruses ("Sind Blitze, sind Donner" regularly created a sensation). Nor did the musicians display much finesse or good taste; they were doing their level best just to learn the notes and paid little attention to either dynamics or phrasing. One writer faulted the 1874 performance for its "dead level of uniform loudness," a problem no doubt exacerbated by the large number of performers (eighty-five in the orchestra and six hundred in the chorus). Balance problems went uncorrected in the solos as well. The same reviewer

19. H. Earle Johnson, *Hallelujah, Amen! The Story of the Handel and Haydn Society of Boston* (Boston: Bruce Humphries, 1965), 250; and Johnson, *First Performances in America* (Detroit: Information Coordinators, 1979), 13. The *Journal* records a much earlier performance of the "Crucifixus" from the B Minor Mass in Boston in 1858, an event that "much increased the desire we have long felt to hear the [work] complete" (13:37).

complained that in one aria, the soloist's "voice, though her mouth was open and sound was certainly issuing from it, was drowned completely for several bars" (34:229). Dwight, too, criticized the Handel and Haydn Society chorus for its indiscriminately loud singing, and he occasionally took swipes at the conductor, Carl Zerrahn, for his choice of tempi. Despite these and other such quibbles, however, critics on the whole regarded these performances as successful and as an excellent foundation for further excursions into Bach's little-known oeuvre. In January 1878 Dwight professed great satisfaction that the members of the chorus "have by this time learned that [Bach] is worth studying." "Their rapid progress," he continues (not without irony?), "gives the fairest hopes for the future" (37:159).

During these years the *Journal* devoted considerable space to one particularly problematic aspect of performing Bach's concerted music in the late nineteenth century: realization of the continuo. With the steady expansion of orchestral and choral forces and the disappearance of the continuo group from ensemble playing, it became necessary to reinforce the often sparse textures of baroque music by either orchestrating the continuo or assigning it to a keyboard player, who oftentimes had no idea how to realize figures. Both solutions required considerable extra work (new parts to be created and/or realized) and neither was entirely successful, as attested by reviews in the *Journal* of Bach performances in Europe and the United States. Reporting on the 1865 Berlin premiere of the Magnificat, for example, Dwight's correspondent regrets that a "rather thin" harmonium was used instead of an organ (25:12). The lack of a suitable organ apparently was a common problem. In a letter to Eduard Hanslick published in the *Journal* in 1871, Robert Franz complained that concert hall and even church organs were often either too large or not at the correct pitch or temperament for playing with an orchestra (31:118). The problem was so acute that sometimes keyboard instruments were dispensed with entirely. Two years later George Alexander MacFarren reported that the current fashion in England was to accompany recitatives on both cello and double bass, "assigning the articulation of the harmony more particularly to the former" (33:114).

For his part, Dwight gave enthusiastic support to Franz's radical but immensely popular solutions to the problem of continuo realization in editions of Bach's sacred vocal works. Unlike the willful arrangements of Gounod or Moscheles, the Franz editions were "a veritable reproduction of Bach's works according to clear principles and on an extensive scale" (19:198). As the excerpt from the Magnificat shows (see plate 1), Franz supplied not only a fully realized organ part; he provided an orchestral realization as well, using strings and winds in dialogue with each other to flesh out Bach's bass line. The result is clever indeed.

Despite the artfully shaped dynamics and articulation of the added lines in the upper strings and winds, these parts draw little attention to themselves. They serve instead

Plate 1. "Quia fecit mihi magna" from Bach's Magnificat, as edited and arranged by Robert Franz and published by Leuckart (Leipzig) in 1864. Photo courtesy of Eda Kuhn Loeb Music Library, Harvard University.

to amplify a gently ambling bass (whose keyboard realization, already explicit in Franz's organ part, may or may not have been feasible in every circumstance) and to reinforce important structural points in the aria. In performances that featured hundreds of singers and big orchestras, Franz's orchestrations solved the most obvious problems of dynamic balance; in a solo such as this, the additional volume of the accompaniment was undoubtedly a useful foil for the opera singer hired for the occasion. Franz's arrangements quickly became the industry standard, so much so that one admiring reviewer described his edition of the St. Matthew Passion, heard at the 1874 Handel and Haydn Society concert, as "in every way so perfect, so completely in accordance with Bach's style, that one can easily imagine Bach's having done it himself" (34:236).

An Ongoing Project

By the late 1870s, then, Dwight had achieved his goal with the Handel and Haydn Society, and he had managed in the process to articulate for Bach a central role as "high priest" in America's rapidly expanding musical culture. As befits the creation of such an exalted figure, his music needed to be handled with care. Reviewing a Boston performance of the motet *Singet dem Herrn* (BWV 225) in 1879, Dwight worried that "the popular sort of admiration which clings to *Trovatores*, *Carmens*, and the like, might, if it only could get hold of one of these great works of Bach, prove fatal to its freshness, dim its celestial purity, and drag it down into the category of things commonplace and hackneyed." Instead of subjecting Bach to "the *furore* and clapping of hands [at] each new nine-days' wonder," Dwight wanted Americans to wrestle quietly with this music, much as one does with one's own conscience. In order to appreciate its incomparable riches one had to be willing to subordinate the merely entertaining to the truly profound: "To enter truly into the spirit, into the divine rest and beauty, of Bach's music," Dwight observed, "one must have known some deep experience" (39:45–46).

A capacity for *Innerlichkeit*, something Dwight inherited from German idealist philosophy as filtered through American transcendentalism, was essential for a full understanding of what Bach had to offer. As Dwight observed in one of his last comparisons of Bach and Handel, *Messiah* is "*universal*, speaking for mankind at large," while the St. Matthew Passion "goes down into the individual, private soul, pleads for and with the contrite and believing heart, and lends sympathetic voice to every Christian's *personal* and private feeling to and for the Saviour." Bach's infinite capacity for human empathy led to an epiphany of sorts—a metaphysical transfer quite unlike anything offered by the music of other composers—in those willing and able to hear what Bach had to tell them. Although the story of the Passion is hardly easygoing, Bach's genius is such that "the hearer's soul is not depressed, but raised to an atmosphere of all serenity and sweetness." "The music . . . brings out the *heart* of the tragedy, causes the spirit to shine through it." Bach's music, finally, overwhelms the "narrow and traditional" text in favor of a message that is both eternal and deeply personal (34:225).

While we tend nowadays to favor a kind of musical exegesis that is more in keeping with orthodox Lutheran thinking, Dwight's thoughtful reading of the St. Matthew Passion is a useful reminder that Bach's music can resonate equally with those of a more personal (not to say pious) religious persuasion. The ease with which Dwight shuttled between the public and private domains establishes some common ground with the more famous revival of the St. Matthew Passion in Berlin in 1829. In the most detailed review of this performance, Marx noted that it was akin to "a religious ceremony which one should repeat quietly to oneself, not report."[20] Dwight simply went one step further. By claiming Bach's music for all humanity while simultaneously encouraging the individual listener to come to grips with it in his or her own way, he effectively severed the St. Matthew Passion not only from its liturgical context but from its very connection with traditional Christian thinking. The work became an object of public veneration for listeners whose personal experience of it was ultimately more important than the story it conveyed. Though Dwight did not want his contemporaries to ignore the text or meaning of the gospel story, his primary purpose was to arouse enthusiasm among people who had no frame of reference for Bach's music and thus needed to be encouraged to take it to heart. In contrast to his earlier thinking on the communal nature of orchestral music, meaning in Bach's Passion was thus fundamentally personal, not corporate.

In this kind of writing one can see, finally, how influential Emerson's model of the poet-priest remained for Dwight. Decades after his flirtation with associationist utopias, Dwight's thinking about the role of music in society and his conception of Bach in particular retained a kind of naïve idealism. Bach was a figure unlike any other in the pantheon, a composer for Americans to revere as an oracle of the divine. An excerpt from an article Dwight skimmed in early 1871 from the *London Orchestra* makes this vision explicit:

> For splendor of language, perspicuity of subject, novelty of idea, grasp of the technical, and mastery over all the science of music, Bach has no equal; and yet all these high possessions are as nothing in comparison with the sweetness, love, and affection—the angelic tenderness of his spirit. . . . Bach held a pure sympathy with the Evangelist—he shared his emotion and his thought; his spirit was present at the Brook, the Garden, the Palace, the Judgment Hall, and Mount Calvary. (30:419)

Not to be outdone, in an 1881 review of a Harvard Musical Association orchestral concert that included the "Pastorale" from Bach's Christmas Oratorio, Dwight praised

20. Geck, *Die Wiederentdeckung der Matthäus-Passion*, 56.

this little gem as "something out of the sincere heart and soul of music, something to transport one from all thought of audience and outward surroundings, into the pure realm of the ideal, giving a foretaste of heaven and the life immortal" (41:14). Here was the least earthbound of composers, a figure whose music could finally achieve the dream, which Dwight had harbored since his youth, of a better world through deep human experience.

Though his musical values were patently old-fashioned, Dwight's highly charged conception of Bach found a sympathetic ear in a nation that had lived through the age of evangelical revivalism and was searching, by the century's last decades, for tangible cultural manifestations of the divine. Having absorbed a few Handel oratorios, the Mozart and Beethoven symphonies, and a good deal else of the classical canon besides, American musical institutions and their audiences were ready to expand the repertory back in time and to incorporate works that were characterized as challenging but ultimately rewarding. The process of assimilation was slow, but no less profound for the time it took. Dwight's own description of Bach's gradual progress in America sums it up best. Noting in an 1869 review of a performance at Harvard that Cantata 21, *Ich hatte viel Bekümmernis,* was a new experience for virtually everyone present, Dwight admitted:

> There will be all shades of conflicting testimony, from those who found it mournful, slow and tedious, to those whose deepest sensibilities, both musical and spiritual, were strongly drawn to it and charmed with it. We safely say that it was enjoyed precisely in the degree (1) of each individual listener's acquaintance with the music and with Bach in general, and (2) in proportion to each one's depth of nature and of moral experience. There were many in whose hearts those serious, yet serene, sustaining harmonies found warmest welcome; and there are many among cultivated music-lovers, and even some uncultivated, who, the more they become acquainted with Bach, the more do they enjoy it, love it, and find peace and health and comfort in it beyond any other music. It is the music that will *wear* best of all. All true musicians come to this acknowledgment. (35:207)

With the St. Matthew Passion finally complete in Boston a few years later, Dwight could congratulate himself on a mission well done. Bach had been accorded an enthusiastic reception in America's cradle, and his music would soon be making its way across the continent. Though the *Journal*'s own star soon faded (it ceased publication in 1881), Bach has indeed continued to wear well, both in America and around the world.

Haupt's Boys

Lobbying for Bach in Nineteenth-Century Boston

Michael Broyles

Before 1850 J. S. Bach was little known in America. Standard works of Handel and Haydn, such as *Messiah* and *The Creation*, formed the core of the repertoire of the oratorio societies in New England and the mid-Atlantic states. These groups, which sponsored the most elaborate concert vocal programs of the Federal period, seldom performed Bach's music; thus there were many Handel and Haydn Societies but no Bach Societies. Orchestras and chamber ensembles, which came into their own only in the 1840s, avoided Bach almost entirely. His name does not even appear in the opening volume of Vera Brodsky Lawrence's study of nineteenth-century musical life in New York, the most complete compilation of musical activity and performances in any American city.[1] The situation in Boston was similar. Unlike Beethoven, Mozart, or even Clementi, Bach's music simply was not programmed there.

This state of affairs is not entirely surprising, as Bach also was not frequently performed in Europe in the early nineteenth century. Although his instrumental music was better known, certainly few of Bach's vocal works were heard before 1829 (the year of Mendelssohn's famous performance of the St. Matthew Passion in Berlin). Interest in Bach developed more slowly in the United States. But it did increase, beginning in the 1850s. I will concentrate on a single city, Boston, and consider how and why this happened.[2]

1. Vera Brodsky Lawrence, *Resonances, 1836–1850*, vol. 1 of *Strong on Music: The New York Music Scene in the Days of George Templeton Strong, 1836–1875* (New York: Oxford University Press, 1988).

2. Boston in this instance is more paradigmatic than exceptional; consequently, events there had some resonance for the country as a whole. This is partly because by the second half of the century musical life began to assume a relatively uniform quality throughout America, thanks to the railroad.

* * *

More than any other musician, John Knowles Paine was the acknowledged spearhead behind the "Bach revival" in Boston. Music critic John S. Dwight wrote that in 1861 Paine was "our chief exponent, practically, of the great organ music of Bach."[3] Paine's colleagues at Harvard recognized this, too. *The Harvard Graduates Magazine* noted in 1906: "When Paine returned to America after his three years of study, he was active mainly as a concert-organist stirring a new interest in this branch of music and especially in the works of Bach. The building of the great organ for the Boston Music Hall is ascribed largely to his influence."[4]

But Paine was hardly alone in his efforts to promote Bach's music. Dwight himself was also an advocate, as was Theodore Thomas, a prominent musician in New York City who regularly appeared in Boston from 1869 on. Next to Paine, however, a lesser-known figure, Eugene Thayer, was central to raising the public consciousness about Bach. Like Paine, Thayer was an organist, and it was through that medium more than any other that Bach advocacy unfolded. Although they were nearly the same age, Thayer was a protégé of Paine. Their devotion to Bach can be traced to a common source: Karl August Haupt, with whom they both studied in Berlin, Paine in the 1850s and Thayer in the 1860s.

Haupt was considered one of the outstanding German organists of his time, and the principal exponent of Bach's music in Germany. He had studied with August Wilhelm Bach (no relation to Johann Sebastian), who was celebrated in the early nineteenth century for his ability to improvise in the style of his illustrious namesake. Haupt's teaching was legendary, and he attracted over thirty American students in the second half of the nineteenth century. Paine was probably the most famous.[5]

As a boy Paine had studied piano and organ with Hermann Kotzschmar in Portland, Maine. His teacher had emigrated to the United States in 1848 as part of the Saxonia Orchestra. Unfortunately, it soon disbanded, but Kotzschmar was able to secure a position in Portland as director of a theater orchestra. Shortly thereafter he was also appointed organist at the First Parish Church, and like most musicians at this time, he earned his living by a variety of means.

3. John S. Dwight, "The History of Music in Boston," in *The Memorial History of Boston*, 4 vols., ed. Justin Winson (Boston: Ticknor & Co., 1881), 4:443.

4. Philip H. Goepp, "John Knowles Paine," *The Harvard Graduates' Magazine* 15 (September 1906): 22. We will later see that only the first half of this statement is true.

5. In the same year that Paine went to Berlin, Carl Freiherrn von Ledebur described Haupt as "gegenwärtig jedenfalls einer der ausgezeichnesten Orgel-Virtuosen" ("at present, in any case, one of the most excellent organ virtuosi"). *Tonkünstler-Lexicon Berlins* (Berlin: Ludwig Rauh, 1861), 227.

Since his father ran a music store, Paine probably received more encouragement for his piano studies than most American boys at the time. Paine's own professional career began at the age of eighteen, when his father died unexpectedly. Three days later, Paine began advertising for piano pupils. He stayed in Portland for two more years, teaching and appearing in local concerts, until he decided to go to Europe for further study, probably at Kotzschmar's recommendation.

Paine's choice of Berlin is odd under the circumstances, since Kotzschmar was from Dresden and would have had connections mostly in Saxony. But on arriving in Boston Paine met Alexander Wheelock Thayer, librarian, journalist, and diplomat, who was preparing to return to Berlin to gather material for his biography of Beethoven. Thayer's invitation to accompany him meant that Paine would have a guide and an easier entrée into the musical world of Berlin. Whether Paine knew of Haupt before meeting Thayer is not known.

Paine quickly impressed Haupt with his talent and industry. Haupt soon predicted that Paine would become a "great" organist and some twenty years later still spoke highly of him. After three years of study Paine gave several concerts in Berlin and then London which won him high praise from the critics, especially for his Bach interpretations. He also attracted the notice of Clara Schumann, widow of Robert Schumann and celebrated pianist in her own right. *The Diarist* in 1860 reported: "Paine is the topic of talk in all the musical circles. Clara Schumann has heard of him, and I took him down to her a day or two since. He is to go again and play some of his music—a sonata, and fugues."[6]

Paine's future was uncertain when he returned to the States. The Civil War had begun, curtailing many musical activities, and Paine had no job; how he avoided the draft is unclear. After a brief time in Portland he was invited to give an organ recital at the Tremont Temple in Boston. Dwight's *Journal* and the *Boston Musical Times* were both enthusiastic; his playing of Bach in particular was praised. They were pleased because the music he played was not that of the virtuoso school, although Paine clearly was a virtuoso. According to the *Times*, "The music performed was of the severest and purest character. . . . He chose the best music, and trusted to his capabilities to render it in artistic style." Similarly, Dwight noted that the *Concert Variations on the Austrian Hymn* "were exceedingly ingenious and interesting, with no clap-trap about them, showing the labor of a composer and not of a show organist."[7]

Paine was playing a cat-and-mouse game with Boston. He let it be known that he

6. John C. Schmidt, *The Life and Works of John Knowles Paine* (Ann Arbor, Mich.: UMI Research Press, 1980), 37, 40.

7. *Boston Musical Times* 2, no. 15 (Nov. 30, 1861): 229 (hereafter abbreviated as BMT); *Dwight's Journal of Music* 20, no. 6 (Nov. 9, 1861): 254 (hereafter DJM).

would settle there "if sufficient encouragement is held out to him."[8] A second concert, which featured Bach's Fantasia and Fugue in G Minor (BWV 542), solidified his position. According to the *Times*, this recital "strengthened the opinions which were formed after his first performances. His management of the instrument; his thorough mastery of all its mechanical difficulties; his conscientious rendering of the recondite harmonies of Bach, and his own able arrangements for the instrument, has raised him at once to the front rank of organists."[9]

By now Paine had been offered the position of organist at the West Church. He also planned to teach piano, organ, and theory; according to the *Times*, "he will give particular attention to the construction of military bands, a department of music in which he is particularly well versed."[10] The church job was sufficient to keep Paine in Boston; what he did with military bands is not known. As an organist, however, he distinguished himself sufficiently that three years later he was appointed as professor of music at Harvard College. Thus began the phase of his career for which he is best known.

Paine lobbied for Johann Sebastian Bach from his first appearance in Boston. Prior to this concert he met with the editor of the *Musical Times*, who reported:

> [Paine] is a devoted worshiper of . . . Johann Sebastian Bach. He revels in the wealth of the life-long labor of the illustrious master. He would have the world love Bach as he loves him, and he sincerely believes that the world has only to know him as he knows him to love him equally as well. He is a missionary of Bach, and Bach has no more enthusiastic a worshiper, nor so admirable an interpreter in the United or Disunited States of America.[11]

How much help did Bach need at this time? On the one hand, Bach was no longer the unknown that he had been earlier in the century; his music (mostly instrumental works) was beginning to appear on programs in the 1850s. For instance, the Concerto in D Minor for Three Harpsichords (BWV 1063) was played on pianos in Boston in 1853 by Otto Dresel, Alfred Jaell, and William Scharfenberg, and in New York in 1856 by Scharfenberg, William Mason, and Henry C. Timm. On the other hand, critical opinion had coalesced. While the critics found much to like about Bach, they also faulted him for being cold, dry, and antiquated. Bach's music was for the head, not the heart, and would appeal only to the few. The following remarks were typical: "Composed at the time when such music was just emerging from the fugue, it has neither passion nor

8. BMT 2, no. 15 (Nov. 30, 1861): 229.

9. BMT 3, no. 1 (March 1, 1862): 5.

10. BMT 2, no. 15 (Nov. 30, 1861): 229.

11. BMT 2, no. 11 (Aug. 10, 1861): 166.

rhetoric to recommend it, nor yet transcendental harmonies. But still, it was proper to play it, as a relic of the past." It is "suggesting of antiquarianism but of a flavor that to the modern musical palate smacks unpleasantly of the *mummy.* But, no lapse of time can conceal the clearness and breadth of the design or the purity and consistency of the musical form." And it "possesses nothing of human sentiment or passion."[12]

As late as 1860 Bach was still considered a scientific and archaic composer, of interest mainly to connoisseurs. In March of that year Julius Eichberg played Bach's Violin Concerto in A Minor (BWV 1041) in Boston. Eichberg had recently come to Boston from Europe. An acclaimed prodigy, he studied composition with François-Joseph Fétis, and violin with Charles de Bériot and Lambert Meerts in Brussels. After a successful career in Germany and Switzerland he went to New York in 1857, motivated by a desire to see the New World and an attempt to alleviate his bad health. He enjoyed favor in New York as well, and then became musical director of the Boston Museum in 1858. The *Boston Musical Times* commented on Eichberg's Bach performance:

> The selection of instrumental music was not calculated to interest many. Bach's concerto may be learned, but it is very heavy and uninspired. We regretted that so admirable a performer as Mr. Eichberg certainly is, should pass by the fine solos of the great writers for the violin, to select some antiquated compositions which have little beside antiquity to commend them. We should have been glad to hear him in music worthy of his powers.[13]

One prominent Boston critic who took exception to these views was John S. Dwight, who was ready to offer a passionate defense of Bach. In 1859, when Eichberg played the Chaconne from Bach's Partita in D Minor (BWV 1004), with Mendelssohn's accompaniment, Dwight waxed eloquent:

> The piece is the richest and grandest of all violin solo pieces that we chance to know. What a stately progress from beginning to end! how full of wayside beauties! how boldly it anticipates the modern virtuoso brilliancies! And then what a whole it is in itself in respect to harmony, Mendelssohn's judicious accompaniments but carrying out its suggestions a little here and there![14]

Some years later, in 1871, when the C Major Triple-Keyboard Concerto was performed again, Dwight still felt compelled to defend Bach's music against the current tides: "If you think it enough to call it homely, conventional, old fashioned, you have yet to

12. Comments by Theodore Hagen and William Henry Fry, quoted in Vera Brodsky Lawrence, *Reverberations, 1850–1856*, vol. 2 of *Strong on Music: The New York Music Scene in the Days of George Templeton Strong* (Chicago: University of Chicago Press, 1995), 2:734.

13. BMT 1, no. 4 (April 1, 1860): 57.

14. DJM 26, no. 9 (Nov. 26, 1859): 279.

become well acquainted with it. When you are *blasé* and sick of the more highly seasoned modern *made dishes*, you will find wholesome and refreshing food in this old Bach."[15]

Ironically, Dwight himself had helped to perpetuate the notion that Bach was more a musician of thought than feeling. In 1846 he gave a series of lectures in New York, the content of which was reported in the *New York Daily Tribune*. The second one divided the history of music into three eras:

1. The Scientific Era, exemplified by Bach.
2. The Expressive Era, represented by Mozart and Beethoven.
3. The Age of Effect, illustrated by Paganini and the Modern Piano.[16]

Dwight's decision to represent the earlier period with Bach, rather than Handel, is telling, for Handel was far better known in the United States in the 1840s. Dwight clearly was an advocate of Bach, as is evident from the content of his journal in its early years. For instance, he frequently included European articles on Bach, especially on the emerging Bach-Gesellschaft edition, and in a thirteen-part series he reprinted much of Forkel's biography of Bach.[17] At the same time, however, Dwight still held to the standard mid-nineteenth-century interpretation, articulated in his lectures: Bach, as representative of the "scientific," is opposed to Mozart and Beethoven, who embody the "expressive." They all stand poles apart from the "virtuoso," who was criticized throughout the nineteenth century as nothing more than empty show.

* * *

Eugene Thayer came to serious music study relatively late in life, a situation not uncommon in antebellum America. He was born in Mendon, Massachusetts, on December 11, 1838, and his family moved to a farm on the edge of Worcester in 1845. Except for his grandfather Arnold Taft accompanying the choir and congregation on the bass viol at the Chestnut Hill Meeting House, there is no record of musical talent in the Thayer family.[18] Thayer's earliest musical experiences consisted of playing the

15. DJM 30, no. 11 (March 11, 1871): 415.

16. *New York Daily Tribune*, March 25, 1846, 1. These lectures were probably based on an earlier set that had been presented in Boston in 1842.

17. "Musical Correspondence: From Berlin," DJM 6, no. 22 (March 3, 1855): 171–72, and 6, no. 23 (March 10, 1855): 179–80; "Life of John Sebastian Bach; With a Critical View of His Compositions, by J. N. Forkel," DJM 8, no. 4 (Oct. 27, 1855): 25–26; 8, no. 5 (Nov. 3, 1855): 33–34; 8, no. 6 (Nov. 10, 1855): 41–42; 8, no. 7 (Nov. 17, 1855): 49–50; 8, no. 8 (Nov. 24, 1855): 58–59; 8, no. 9 (Dec. 1, 1855): 66–67; 8, no. 10 (Dec. 8, 1855): 74–75; 8, no. 11 (Dec. 15, 1855): 82–83; 8, no. 12 (Dec. 22, 1855): 90–91; 8, no. 13 (Dec. 29, 1855): 98; 8, no. 14 (January 5, 1856): 106; 8, no. 15 (January 12, 1856): 114; 8, no. 16 (January 19, 1856): 122–23.

18. Most of the information about Thayer's early life comes from a biographical sketch written by

guitar, mostly to accompany popular songs, and absorbing the music of gypsies who frequently camped in South Worcester. He seems to have had a fascination for gypsies, frequently suffering parental discipline for stealing away to their camp.

At some undetermined point, probably in his teens, Thayer began organ lessons (Sumner Salter observed that "his serious study of music did not begin until he was somewhat mature in years").[19] He first studied with Edward Cummings in Worcester, then with Paine. In 1865 he went to Berlin to work with Haupt, probably at Paine's suggestion.

Despite his late start, Thayer succeeded with Haupt. In large measure this was because of his work habits and discipline, which Haupt, who had been trained in the old German school, respected.[20] Thayer gives us a precise picture of his habits. In an open letter to young organists, he discusses how to organize a day:

> First hour, thirty minutes studies, new; thirty minutes music, old—eight to nine A.M.
> Second hour, thirty minutes out-doors; thirty minutes music, new—nine to ten A.M.
> Third hour, thirty minutes studies, new; thirty minutes music, new—ten to eleven A.M.
> Fourth hour, thirty minutes out-doors; thirty minutes music, old—eleven to twelve.
> Fifth hour, lunch or dinner—twelve to one.
> Sixth hour, sleep, rest, read, or out-doors—one to two P.M.
> Seventh hour, ditto, or any amusement—two to three P.M.
> Eighth hour, thirty minutes studies, new; thirty minutes music, new—three to four P.M.
> Ninth hour, thirty minutes studies, old; thirty minutes out-doors—four to five P.M.
> Tenth hour, thirty minutes music, old; thirty minutes reading music—five to six P.M.
> Eleventh hour, supper and recreation—six to seven P.M.
> Twelfth hour, start for a good concert, if possible—seven to eight P.M.[21]

Thayer argues that taking eleven hours is the most efficient way to get in five or six hours of practice. He also encourages the student to rest, and not to skip the midday meal, realizing that practicing when exhausted or hungry is not productive.

---

his daughter Louise Friedel Thayer, which appeared in *The American Organist* 16, no. 8 (Aug. 1933): 403–7. A second, less detailed source is Sumner Salter's "Eugene Thayer," in *The Musician* (December 1912); reprinted in *The Tracker* 14, no. 1 (Fall 1969): 7–8. Salter was a friend of Thayer.

19. Salter, "Eugene Thayer," 7.

20. Paine and Thayer were similar in this regard. Paine's reputation for industry was legendary, as witnessed both by contemporary accounts from his youthful colleagues, and by Haupt's own remembrance of them some twenty years later.

21. *The Tracker* 19, no. 1 (Fall 1974): 17. According to *The Tracker*, the letter originally appeared in *Folio* (December 1882).

Shortly after returning to Worcester, Thayer was invited to succeed B. J. Lang as organist at the South Congregational Church in Boston.[22] He subsequently held several other organ positions in Boston over the next fifteen years: at the Arlington Street Church, the Hollis Street Church, the Old First Unitarian Church, the New England Church, and the Harvard Street Church. Thayer moved to the Fifth Avenue Presbyterian Church in New York in 1881, and in the same year he received an honorary doctorate in music from Wooster University (Wooster, Ohio). In 1889, after several years of failing health, he took his own life.

Even before Thayer went to Berlin he had become an advocate of Bach, probably through Paine's influence. Although he was recognized as one of the better organists in New England, before he went abroad he enjoyed only moderate success, according to reviews.[23] Only after returning from his studies with Haupt did Thayer begin to have a significant impact on the American musical scene, and only then did his authority as performer and teacher begin to be felt.

While Paine was the more prominent musician in the 1860s and 1870s, and his overall influence was greater, Thayer was the more important advocate of Bach on the organ. Paine, of course, wore many hats: pianist, organist, composer, professor. After the early 1860s his work at Harvard and his compositional activities eclipsed his fame as an organist. Thayer, however, remained throughout his life primarily an organist.[24] Except for producing a few compositions, mostly for the organ, and considerable accompanying on the piano (he toured briefly with Ole Bull, whom he had met in Europe), Thayer focused almost exclusively on organ performance.

Thayer's most important contribution to musical life in Boston was the series of free organ recitals that he inaugurated in 1869.[25] These were held weekly during the season, and according to contemporary sources at least half of each program consisted of the music of Bach. Thayer's pupils often performed, rather than Thayer himself, but according to Dwight the recitals drew good crowds.[26] Dwight notes that Thayer gave sixteen recitals in 1869–70, and the *Boston Musical Times* indicates that by June of 1871 they totaled twenty-nine. These performances drew enough interest that Dwight could report, "The Organ Concerts largely show that Bach is in the wind."[27] Accord-

22. BMT 6, no. 6 (June 2, 1866): 83.

23. BMT 5, no. 5 (May 7, 1864): 68.

24. Only in the last five years of his life did Thayer's compositional work exceed his performance activity, and that was because he curtailed his performing due to increasing illness.

25. Louise Friedel Thayer gives the date as 1869, and Dwight implies the same, while Salter gives 1868.

26. DJM 30, no. 17 (Nov. 5, 1870): 373.

27. DJM 29, no. 15 (Oct. 9, 1869): 116.

ing to Salter, Thayer gave his 105th and last organ recital in 1878.[28] The following program, from October 14, 1870, is typical:

Toccata et Fuga in D minor	Bach
Vorspiel: Wir glauben all'n einen Gott	Bach
For two manuals and double Pedals	
Fugue in A minor	Bach
Master Shelton	
Orgel Studien, No. 3	Schumann
Vorspiele: Ich ruf zu Dir; Gottes Sohn	
ist Kommen	Bach
Master Shelton	
Fifth Organ Concerto	Handel[29]

Presumably the Handel concerto was played by Thayer.

Thayer was also very influential as a teacher. His pupils included Edward Fischer and George W. Chadwick, composer of the Second New England School and later director of the New England Conservatory, and he especially encouraged women in their studies. As the programs of his weekly recitals indicate, Bach's music was essential to his pedagogy. Thayer published several pedagogical volumes, most of which were collections of organ music.

* * *

For Thayer and for Paine (at least at first), Bach advocacy was clearly tied to the organ. This was possible because of two recent developments in Boston: (1) the growth of interest in the organ in the middle of the nineteenth century as new and larger instruments were built, and (2) the organ's emancipation from its subservient role as an accompanying instrument in church. Organs had been in New England since the early eighteenth century, and toward the beginning of the nineteenth century they replaced the bass viol and even the violin in most churches as the principal instrument for accompanying congregational singing. Their role beyond that was circumscribed, however. Remnants of Puritanism made Congregational churches wary of too much instrumental display. This carried over even to the Unitarian churches, where the liturgy was more open. Unitarians catered to the upper strata of Boston society, who were overwhelmingly indifferent and occasionally even hostile to elaborate music, whether sacred or secular. With little support from the wealthy class in Boston, secular music did not flourish. Episcopal or Anglican churches embraced a more music-friendly liturgy, but they represented a relatively small percentage of the population.

28. Salter, "Eugene Thayer," 7.

29. DJM 30, no. 17 (Nov. 5, 1870): 343.

There was another limiting factor: the level of organ playing was not high, even though a few organists in Boston did have impressive credentials. George K. Jackson emigrated from England in 1796 and gradually made his way up the East Coast, living in New York for almost ten years before settling in Boston. An imposing man of over three hundred pounds, he let no one forget his title, "Mus. Doc.," a trait that worked against him in Federal Boston. It is difficult to know to what extent his pomp masked a real talent. George J. Webb, also from England, entered deeply into the musical culture of Boston. Like Paine, however, his activities encompassed many areas, and he did not concentrate on the organ. Probably the finest organist in Boston in the early nineteenth century was Charles Zeuner, who came from Germany in 1830, about the same time as Webb. Zeuner's talents were such that Lowell Mason, president of the Boston Handel and Haydn Society, peremptorily fired Sophie Ostinelli, who had been organist for eleven years, a move that almost provoked a split in the organization. Though Ostinelli was considered to be a competent organist, Zeuner had one particular ability beyond her: he could play orchestral scores on the organ. Outside of church, this seemed the principal role for the organ, as an accompaniment when an orchestra was not available. Zeuner stayed in Boston less than ten years, and in 1857 took his own life.

W. S. B. Mathews, writing in 1889, stated that "scientific organ playing in this country goes back hardly more than a generation." He described four national schools of organ playing: German, French, English, and American. The American "in the olden time [i.e., the early nineteenth century] consisted in playing a few pleasing melodies upon fancy stops of impossible orchestra coloring, with pedal parts put in according to the French school" (by "the French school" he meant "consisting mainly of detached fundamentals"). This was not a style conducive to realizing the complex polyphony of J. S. Bach. Webb even admitted to Mathews that in his time (the 1830s through the 1850s) not a single organist in Boston was capable of playing a Bach fugue.[30]

When Lowell Mason made his first trip to Europe in 1837 he indirectly acknowledged the relatively low level of organ playing in Boston. He was mostly unimpressed with the quality of vocal and choral performance in Europe, often comparing European ensembles unfavorably with those in Boston. Yet he was astounded by the organ performances that he heard; nothing in Boston could compare with it. Mason was dazzled by the playing of August Wilhelm Bach, Haupt's teacher, and Johann Schneider of Dresden. He commented, "I hardly know which played with the greatest skill, he [Schneider] or Mr. Bach of Berlin—both were excellent, and by far surpassed any organ playing I ever heard in this style [contrapuntal as opposed to orchestral]." Mason attempted to compare Bach and Schneider with Thomas Adams of London, and later with Jacques Vogt of Switzerland, both noted for their ability to imitate the ef-

30. W. S. B. Mathews, *A Hundred Years of Music in America* (Chicago: G. L. Howe, 1889), 236–37.

fects of the orchestra on the organ, but then admitted that "the styles are so different there is no comparison between them."[31]

Part of Paine's early success after returning from Europe was related to the distinction between what Mason had termed the "contrapuntal" and "orchestral" styles of organ performance. Paine is credited with introducing the contrapuntal style into Boston. At the end of the nineteenth century, Frederick Field Bullard summarized Paine's contribution as follows:

> In 1861, he returned to this country, and gave a series of organ concerts, in which he introduced to the American public the principal compositions of Bach and Thiele [Louis Thiele, with whom Paine also studied]. During these first years Paine's reputation as an organist was exceedingly brilliant, his taste and style placing him almost alone as an exponent of the classical school.[32]

Here Bullard uses "classical" to mean the old style. Before going abroad Paine had appeared in public mostly on the piano. When he did perform on the organ, it was in a more traditional nineteenth-century manner, such as accompanying for performances of *Messiah* in Portland.

Paine's impact was great, because of his ability and frequent performances. But he was not the first organist to play Bach in Boston. That honor probably goes to George W. Morgan, a British organist who held positions at Westminster Abbey and St. Paul's Cathedral in London before immigrating to the United States in 1853. He settled in New York but appeared occasionally in Boston. Bach's organ fugues were first heard in Boston at his concert at the Tremont Temple in 1859.[33]

Paine and Thayer's activity coincided with a boom in organ construction in Boston. This was fortunate because, as Mathews observes, even if an organist had been capable of playing Bach fugues in the early nineteenth century, no organ existed that could do them justice.[34] Neither Paine nor Thayer was responsible for the organ boom, but both benefited from its synergy. Paine's first recital (in 1861 at the Tremont Temple) was given on an organ that had been constructed by the Hook Brothers in 1853–54. The new instrument, the Hooks' first with four manuals, replaced a two-manual organ that they had installed there in 1845 (the reason they had this opportunity was that the Temple burned to the ground in 1852).

31. *A Yankee Musician in Europe: The 1837 Journals of Lowell Mason*, edited and with an introduction by Michael Broyles (Ann Arbor, Mich.: UMI Research Press, 1990), 66.

32. Frederick Field Bullard, "Music in Boston. Zerrahn, Paine, Land and Chadwick," *Musical Courier* 37, no. 3 (July 4, 1898).

33. Mathews, *Hundred Years of Music in America*, 238.

34. Ibid., 237.

In 1863, soon after Paine's first appearances, one of the largest organs in the world was installed in the Boston Music Hall. Jabez B. Upham, president of the Boston Music Hall Association, was the motivator behind it. After conceiving the idea in 1852, he worked for four years to secure financial backing, examined organs in Europe, and discussed specifications with European organ builders. By 1856 he had secured sufficient monetary support, and selected Eberhard Frederick Walcker of Ludwigsburg, Germany. Walcker completed the organ by 1861, but its shipment was delayed over concern about the safety of an Atlantic crossing in the early days of the Civil War. The instrument finally arrived in Boston in February of 1863.

The Boston Music Hall organ had four manuals, a split pedalboard, eighty-nine stops, and 5,479 pipes.[35] It was by far the largest organ in America and was considered one of the "three or four largest in the world."[36] The imposing appearance of its elaborately carved walnut case, built in the United States, did much to contribute to interest in the instrument.

At the inaugural concert the entire house of 2,654 was sold out, at the unprecedented price of $3.00 (most classical tickets sold for $1.00), and curiosity about the organ was such that Dwight believed the house would have filled at $5.00.[37] The instrument itself was clearly the focus of the evening. It was covered by a green veil, which was lifted after an introductory ode read by the well-known actress Charlotte Cushman. To enhance the visual effect, a special electric (actually carbon arc) light was installed; the Music Hall, like most theaters and concert halls, normally was lit by much dimmer gas light.[38] The effect of the carbon arc light was, in a word, electrifying. *Harper's* described the organ's case as "so floridly ornate that the impression is bewildering." Likewise, Dwight characterized the effect of the light as "startling, brilliant," and noted that "the dazzling, unquiet, tremulous light was a new and irresistible distraction." He was concerned, however, that the visual spectacle deflected attention away from the music.[39]

Six organists were chosen to perform at the concert: Paine, Thayer, George W. Morgan, B. J. Lang, S. P. Tuckerman, and John H. Willcox. The first half consisted

35. Dwight, "History of Music in Boston," 4:436. Ochse, who provides a detailed list of stops, states that the organ contained eighty-four ranks and ninety-six draw-stops. See Orpha Ochse, *The History of the Organ in the United States* (Bloomington: Indiana University Press, 1975), 201–3.

36. DJM 23, no. 17 (Nov. 14, 1863): 133.

37. Ibid.

38. Though Schmidt calls it an "electric" light, this could be misleading, since Edison's invention (what we think of as electrical lighting) still lay almost twenty years in the future. See Schmidt, *Life and Works of John Knowles Paine*, 54.

39. DJM 23, no. 17 (Nov. 14, 1863): 133; *Harper's New Monthly Magazine* 27 (January 1864): 275. The *Harper's* quotation is cited in Schmidt, *Life and Works of John Knowles Paine*, 54.

of all Bach. Paine played the Toccata in F Major (presumably BWV 540, a work he performed so frequently that it became a kind of signature piece for him) and the Trio Sonata in E-flat Major "for two Manuals and Pedal" (BWV 525), while Thayer played the "Grand Fugue in G minor" (probably BWV 542, or possibly 535 or 578). The second half of the program, selected specifically to illustrate the major schools of organ music, included works by Handel, Mendelssohn, Palestrina (a transcription from a Mass), Purcell (a movement from an anthem), and Lefébure-Wély. The concert closed with Handel's "Hallelujah Chorus."

The reactions to Bach's music were mixed. Dwight's review was laudatory, and he carried elsewhere in the same issue a biographical account (from the *New American Cyclopoedia*) that characterized Bach as "in some respects, the greatest musician that has lived." Dwight chastised the audience while praising Bach's composition: "Those who knew how good it was, and therefore listened, were pleased and edified. *They* did not find the *Toccata* all a great roaring and fatiguing noise, but felt its mighty inspiration, its refreshing grandeur, its inexhaustible suggestions as of the ocean rolling in upon the beach."[40] Other critics, however, were less positive. The *Boston Musical Magazine* found fault with Paine's manner of interpretation: "The fugues of Bach, difficult though they be—with winding roulades and chromatic passages—with questions and answers—are not relished when played with a full, unvarying organ from beginning to end."[41] Paine learned this style from Haupt, who believed that Bach's fugues should be played with full organ, and with little variation in color or dynamics. The famous poet Julia Ward Howe was entirely unsympathetic to the organ, which she considered to be an architectural monstrosity. At the same time, she found much to admire in Bach and Paine, noting that "the chief feature of the evening was Mr. Paine's masterly presentation of the compositions of Sebastian Bach." She concluded her peroration with a reference to the organ as the equivalent of one hundred instruments in an orchestra: "Give me the hundred lights, say I, but of the single lights, give me Paine."[42]

Nearly twenty years later, Dwight attempted to put into perspective both this concert and a subsequent one that Paine gave on the organ:

> Fortunately the return, shortly before this time, of Mr. Paine from his studies in Germany, full of the music and traditions of Sebastian Bach, brought that greatest of all organ music into frequent hearing through the medium of this new gigantic instrument, and his efforts found emulous and able seconding in several of the organ-

40. DJM 23, no. 17 (Nov. 14, 1863): 133.

41. BMT 4, no. 9 (Nov. 3, 1863): 2.

42. *Commonwealth* (Nov. 13, 1863). Quoted in Barbara Owen, *The Organ in New England: An Account of the Use and Manufacture to the End of the Nineteenth Century* (Raleigh, N.C.: Sunbury Press, 1979), 241–42.

ists just named. It must be confessed, with some shame now, that those organ concerts for a year or two gave far more of the highest class of organ compositions than we have had a chance to hear more recently.[43]

One of the reasons that organ concerts were less common in 1881 than in 1863 was that the Music Hall organ had fallen into disrepair and disuse. The instrument remained in the Music Hall for only about twenty years. The new Boston Symphony Orchestra, founded in 1881, needed more space on stage, and succeeded in having the organ removed in 1884. The largest organ in America, built at a cost of $60,000, was then sold at auction for a mere $5,000. It was to have been set up at the New England Conservatory, but instead remained in storage for twelve years, until the warehouse was torn down to make way for a tennis court. This time it was sold for $1,500 to Edward F. Searles of Methuen, Massachusetts, who built a special hall for it.[44]

Despite its eventual slide into obscurity, however, the instrument in Boston's Music Hall did serve as a focus of Bach's organ music for several years. Dwight saw it as the opportunity Bach needed in Boston; he hoped that the Music Hall organ would lead to a triumph similar to what had occurred when the Boston Academy Orchestra began playing Beethoven symphonies in 1842. And he justified its massive size, as well as Paine's style of playing it at full throttle, as "the proper organ tone [for the] large utterance of godlike thoughts."[45] In 1867 Dwight reported that the organ was still played at noon on Wednesdays and Saturdays, and sometimes on Sunday evenings. A variety of artists participated, including Paine, whose performances Dwight singled out, and a Mr. Pearce from Philadelphia.[46] While the exact format of the concerts is not known, they may have been predecessors of the free organ recitals that Thayer inaugurated in 1869.

The installation of the Music Hall organ seems to have generated a period of major organ construction in New England. Several large instruments appeared in the 1860s and 1870s. Though some were in concert halls, most were in churches. Some of the church organs, however, were as large as those in concert halls—for instance, the instruments in the Holy Cross Cathedral (1875), Old South Church (1875), and Trinity Church (1877). But the largest and most important was "The Great Worcester Organ," built in Mechanics Hall, Worcester, in 1864. Not quite as large as the Music Hall organ, it nevertheless had four manuals, fifty-two stops, and 3,504 pipes.[47] For

43. Dwight, "History of Music in Boston," 4:436.

44. Ochse, *History of the Organ in the United States*, 204–5.

45. DJM 23, no. 17 (Nov. 14, 1863): 134.

46. DJM 27, no. 14 (Sept. 28, 1867): 162.

47. BMT 5, no. 12 (Dec. 3, 1864): 180.

the inaugural concert Thayer, a native of Worcester, was one of the invited organists. He played Bach's Toccata in F Major (BWV 540), a work that was becoming well known in New England through Paine's frequent performances of it.

* * *

By 1865 Paine was spending most of his time in Cambridge. In addition to his continuing organ performances, he was beginning to explore Bach's vocal music, a repertory that had hitherto been relatively neglected in the Boston area. One of the duties that Paine inherited was directing Harvard's Chapel Choir. For Commemoration Day, a ceremony marking the end of the Civil War in 1865, he performed parts of Bach's cantata *Ein feste Burg ist unser Gott* (BWV 80). The next year Paine announced a series of three subscription concerts in June, designed to raise funds for repairs to the organ.[48] The first two programs featured Bach organ works (including the Toccata in F Major), but the third included two arias and the final chorus from the St. Matthew Passion (BWV 244).

Over the next few years, the Passion gradually infiltrated into the Boston musical world. In 1868, at a concert of the Harvard Musical Association (which was in Boston, not Cambridge, and which had long since broken its affiliation with Harvard), Mrs. C. A. Barry and Bernhard Listemann performed the alto aria "Erbarme dich, mein Gott."[49] In 1869 Thayer presented two organ transcriptions from the St. Matthew Passion: "Ich will bei meinem Jesu wachen, So schlafen unsre Sünden ein," and "Wir setzen uns mit Tränen nieder." That same year the Handel and Haydn Society announced that it would undertake the Passion.[50]

Dwight was ecstatic. The Society had considered it the previous season, and had procured the Robert Franz edition of the performance parts, but had deemed it too difficult in the time remaining in the season. There had been some uncertainty over the plans of the Handel and Haydn Society in 1869, but in August Dwight felt confident enough to announce, "This time, it appears to be really a settled thing that Bach's great *Passion Music* (after the Gospel of St. Matthew), will be taken up and studied with the design of producing it in Passion Week." Ditson and Company were to jointly publish a piano-vocal arrangement.[51] Dwight lauded Ditson's move as a "bold venture and an honorable one." Regarding the Handel and Haydn's Society's efforts, he wrote: "For our old Oratorio Society, too, it is a rare, bold undertaking; perhaps the boldest step they could take." He was convinced that "Bach's *Matthew Passion* is bound to take

48. Schmidt, *Life and Works of John Knowles Paine*, 61–63.

49. DJM 28, no. 20 (Dec. 19, 1868): 366.

50. DJM 29, no. 12 (Aug. 28, 1869): 95.

51. In fact, they did not actually do so until 1895.

its place in the repertoire of the great Choral Societies in this country, as it has long since done all over Germany. . . . With us it is a question of time only."[52]

The time was slightly longer than Dwight had predicted, for the performance did not take place until May 13, 1871. And even then the Society did not perform the entire work (that did not occur until 1879). A Mr. Bowman, who described the event in Dwight's *Journal*, stated that they presented "a portion of Sebastian Bach's passion music from St. Matthew's Gospel."[53] A decade later, in the *Memorial History of Boston*, Dwight noted that they originally performed less than half of the work; that they presented "more generous portions" of it in 1874; and that on Good Friday in 1879, when the society originally planned its first performance, they performed it "with a completeness such as we do not read of even in England or Germany."[54]

The 1871 concert was nevertheless considered an important milestone. Bowman claimed explicitly that this was the first performance of Bach's passion music in the United States, and he considered it "one of the pivotal points" of the week-long Handel and Haydn Society Festival. Dwight called it "the most courageous venture in the history of this or any choral body in America." Both Dwight and Bowman also found it necessary to reiterate a by-then-familiar theme. Dwight referred to the Society's "resolute grappling with the difficulties and the doubtful popularity of the *St. Matthew Passion*."[55] Similarly, Bowman stated:

> Whatever may be the inclinations of individual taste, or however this person may find the music antiquated, or that other may find it dull, the fact remains, and is beyond all question or dispute, that the music itself is beautiful, not only in spiritually but materially. Those who fail to find it so may rest assured that the fault is in them, and not in it.[56]

By this time the spiritual as well as the intellectual qualities of Bach were being asserted. The ground had shifted towards an idealistic, transcendent vision of music. The people themselves were responsible for its success or failure; rather than bringing the level of music down to where the people were, the people must elevate themselves up to the music.

52. DJM 29, no. 12 (Aug. 28, 1869): 94.

53. DJM 31, no. 9 (July 29, 1871): 69.

54. Dwight, "History of Music in Boston," 4:451.

55. Ibid.

56. DJM 31, no. 9 (July 29, 1871): 69.

* * *

In addition to his performances on the organ and his direction of the choir at Harvard, Paine advocated for Bach in a third and very direct way: through his teaching and public lectures. In 1874 Paine introduced a course in music history at Harvard that was designed not for the trained musician but for the general student. This was in some respects a precursor of the "music appreciation" courses that later populated American higher education, and it gained considerable popularity. From an initial enrollment of six, it grew to eighty-one students in 1884–85. This figure remained the peak until Paine's last two years (1903–5), when 121 and 98 students enrolled respectively.[57]

Paine's widest audience came in 1870–71 when he gave a series of public lectures on the history of music. These were undoubtedly what became his course materials, which he later published as *The History of Music to the Death of Schubert.*[58] They reveal more precisely than any other source what Paine thought about Bach.

Claiming to follow Friedrich Rochlitz, Paine first parallels Bach and Handel, a shrewd move since Handel was already revered in the United States. He notes their similar backgrounds and common character: "as men, they were upright, straightforward, and firm, heart and soul, in the Christian faith." (To think otherwise of the composer of *Messiah* would have been inconceivable in nineteenth-century America.) He then contrasts Handel, the worldly figure, with Bach, who "sought no higher post, and only when a new one was offered him did he accept it thankfully as the gift of Providence." Bach's "only aspiration [was] to do his duty faithfully," and "fully satisfied, returned to his simple home."[59]

Not surprisingly, Paine interprets Bach within the sacred tradition. He compares him to Palestrina, about whom he had previously lectured. To Paine, "Bach is the highest representative of Protestant church music," and he considers Bach's passions to be on a level unmatched by any other oratorio, except *Messiah*. He also defends Bach, using language that had become a standard litany in postbellum Boston: "Those who find his music cold and passionless are simply ignorant of his style, which must first become familiar, or else they are incapacitated by nature from being moved and elevated by his music."[60]

57. A complete list of Paine's annual class enrollments is found in appendix 2 of Schmidt, *Life and Works of John Knowles Paine*, 713–17. Arthur Foote's scrapbook, in the Harvard University Archives, provides further details about Paine's classes, including lists of students, their grades, and copies of several examinations.

58. John Knowles Paine, *The History of Music to the Death of Schubert* (Boston: Ginn & Co., 1907; reprint, New York: Da Capo, [n.d.]).

59. Ibid., 219.

60. Ibid., 227–28.

Paine's emphasis on Bach's passions came when they were just gaining currency in Boston. But Paine does not ignore Bach the instrumental composer. He considers Bach to be the "founder of modern instrumental music" and places him on a level with Beethoven, just as he had equated Bach with Handel in the vocal realm. Paine's choice of pieces to discuss is characteristic of his time. He considers the Well-Tempered Clavier at some length, then mentions the Orchestral Suite in D Major (BWV 1068), which had received several performances in Boston, and briefly lauds the organ music, which contains "the very soul of his genius." He mentions specific pieces that had been heard in Boston: the Toccata in F Major, the Passacaglia in C Minor (BWV 582), several fugues, and the six trio sonatas (BWV 525–30).[61] There is no mention of any concertos (even the Concerto in D Minor for Three Harpsichords, or the Italian Concerto), or of the music for solo violin and solo cello.[62]

A contemporary report of Paine's lectures suggests that they differ little from the treatment in his book, but with some interesting embellishments. In the lectures Paine clearly elevates Bach above Handel, calling Bach "the greatest sacred composer and the most intellectual musician who ever lived." He finds Handel's works to be old-fashioned but claims that "Bach's music cannot grow antiquated."[63] He speaks of Bach as the true founder of instrumental music and calls attention to the individuality of his compositions. Citing Carl Maria von Weber, he refers to Bach as a Romantic master, putting to rest the notion of Bach the cold, passionless intellectual. Paine organizes Bach's instrumental music by function, in the manner of eighteenth-century classifications, dividing it into four categories:

1. Church music for the organ.
2. Sacred music for the home (most of his pieces for keyboard and violin, as well as the Well-Tempered Clavier).
3. Lighter secular pieces (Paine provides no examples).
4. Concert music (concertos and sonatas).[64]

61. Ibid., 230, 232–33.

62. The absence of the Italian Concerto (BWV 971) is puzzling, since Paine played this piece when he delivered his public lectures in 1871. Paine's choice of the Italian Concerto may be hard to explain with regard to the content of his lecture, but psychologically it was a wise decision. According to the report, the audience was much delighted with it. See DJM 30, no. 27 (March 25, 1871): 420.

63. Ibid.

64. Paine's use of the terms *sacred* and *secular* is in keeping with Dwight and nineteenth-century views of sacralization, which considered all serious, abstract, instrumental music as sacred. The more abstract, the more sacred a piece was, in Dwight's view. This is most clearly articulated in his "Address, Delivered before the Harvard Musical Association, Aug. 25, 1841," printed in *Musical Magazine* 3 (Aug. 28, 1841): 257–72.

* * *

Bach never became the box-office icon that Beethoven was in the late 1800s, or that Wagner would become around the turn of the century. With the demise of Dwight's *Journal* in 1881 and the founding of the Boston Symphony Orchestra in the same year, the musical center of gravity in Boston shifted to the orchestra, a direction that had been apparent for some time. The generation after Paine—George W. Chadwick, Arthur Foote, and Amy Cheney Beach—was much less interested in the organ and sacred music. Even Paine himself wrote no organ works after 1865. And while he did continue to produce large choral pieces, these are eclectic works that blend both Renaissance and Bach-style polyphony with Romantic harmony, color, and thematic treatment, manifesting the considerable influence of Felix Mendelssohn. Except for the *Fuga Giocosa* (1884), a playful piece for piano based on the popular ditty, "Over the Fence or Out, Boys," Bach seems not to have been a major factor in Paine's later life. Yet Paine had paved the way for Bach: first his instrumental music (primarily for the organ), and then his vocal works, particularly the St. Matthew Passion. Although Bach would never become a popular composer, as Dwight and others predicted, nevertheless he was established and respected. He was part of the canon, and the music-going public would at least recognize and acknowledge his profundity. Paine and Thayer, drawing inspiration from Haupt, had made sure of that.

"The Public . . . Would Probably Prefer Something that Appeals Less to the Brain and More to the Senses"

The Reception of Bach's Music in New York City, 1855–1900

Mary J. Greer

A significant chapter in the history of American performances of Bach's music begins in New York City. Of the forty chamber, orchestral, and choral compositions by Johann Sebastian Bach that were presented in the United States before 1901, twenty-five received their American premiere in New York.[1] This article provides an overview of the Bach works that were performed in New York between 1855 and 1900 (see the appendix for a chronological list), describes the form in which they were presented, profiles the individuals who played a leading role in promoting his music, and traces the ways in which the attitudes of musicians, critics, and the public toward the composer evolved over the course of these five decades.

The neglect of Bach's music prior to 1855 is attributable to a combination of factors, some global, some local. Only a small proportion of the repertory was available before 1851, when the publication of the first edition of his complete works commenced. Few American musicians were equal to the technical demands posed by his compositions. There was no call for performances of his music on the part of critics or the public for, to the extent that Bach's name was familiar at all, it was almost uni-

1. This figure includes chamber, orchestral, and choral pieces by Bach that were presented in complete or near-complete form. While performances of Bach's works for organ and other keyboard instruments also took place in the nineteenth century, they do not fall within the scope of this study.

versally associated with music that was old-fashioned and cerebral. Above all, no one had stepped forward to champion his music.

Circumstances became more auspicious for the performance of Bach's music in New York beginning in the mid-1850s, when several of the city's leading musicians founded a chamber music series devoted to serious classical repertory. Among the players was the German-born violinist Theodore Thomas (1835–1905) who, initially in his capacity as a soloist and chamber musician, and later as a conductor and arranger, did more than any other individual to promote Bach's music in New York.[2] Another German immigrant, Leopold Damrosch (1832–85), also played a leading role in introducing Bach works to New York audiences. In 1873 he founded the Oratorio Society which, over the course of the next three decades, presented the New York premieres of both the St. Matthew Passion (in 1880) and the B Minor Mass (in 1900).[3]

The appearance of successive volumes of Bach's complete works between 1851 and 1899 made many compositions available for study and performance for the first time.[4] Another significant development was the publication in the 1870s and 1880s of Philipp Spitta's monumental study of Bach, which provided a wealth of new information about the composer's life and works and the performing conditions of his time.[5]

Overview of Bach Repertory Performed in New York between 1855 and 1900

The overall picture of performances of Bach's music during the latter half of the nineteenth century is decidedly mixed (see table 1 for Bach works performed in New York, ordered according to genre). On the one hand, nearly all types of pieces—organ works,[6] pieces for other solo keyboard instruments, chamber works, concertos, orchestral

2. Thomas was born in Germany in 1835 and began playing the violin as a young child. He moved to New York with his family in 1845 and in his teens earned a reputation as a gifted soloist and chamber player.

3. Later on, Leopold Damrosch's two sons, Frank (1859–1937) and Walter (1862–1950), also played significant roles in fostering an appreciation for the music of Bach.

4. BG. The music critic Henry T. Finck highlighted the importance of this edition in a review written in February 1900: "Half a century ago the Bach Society was founded in Leipzig and since that time a volume of Bach's works has appeared nearly every year. Of the forty-four volumes printed as many as thirty are vocal music—nine volumes of passions, oratorios and masses, four of chamber music with voice, and seventeen of church cantatas." *New York Post*, Feb. 14, 1900, 7, col. 4 (hereafter abbreviated as NYP).

5. The German edition of Spitta's book appeared in 1873–80 and the English translation followed in 1884–85.

6. Nineteenth-century performances of Bach's organ works in New York are not discussed in this article unless they were heard in the form of an orchestral transcription.

Table 1. Works by J. S. Bach Performed on Chamber, Symphonic, and Choral Programs in New York City, 1855–1900, in Order of BWV

No.[a]	*Genre*	*BWV No.*	*Work*	*Date of First Performance*[b]	*Subsequent Performances*
120	Sacred Cantatas	6/1	Opening chorus of "Abide with Us" (*Bleib bei uns*)	Feb. 13, 1900	
128		12/1	First movement of *Weinen, Klagen, Sorgen, Zagen*	Apr. 26, 1900 (AmPr)	
80		21	"My Spirit was in Heaviness" (*Ich hatte viel Bekümmernis*)	Mar. 17, 1883	
77		26	"Vain and Fleeting" (*Ach wie flüchtig*)	Apr. 20–21, 1882 (AmPr)	
12		37	"Who Believed, and is Baptized" (*Wer da gläubet und getauft wird*)	1865 (AmPr)	
117		41	Excerpts from *Jesu, nun sei gepreiset*	Feb. 13, 1900 (AmPr)	
126		60	Excerpts from *O Ewigkeit, du Donnerwort*	Apr. 26, 1900 (AmPr)	
130		67/6	Aria with chorus from *Halt im Gedächtnis Jesum Christ*	Apr. 26, 1900 (AmPr)	
70		80	"A Stronghold Sure" (*Ein feste Burg*, arr. by Theodore Thomas)	Feb. 12, 1881	Feb. 19, 1881; May 2, 1882
50		106	"God's Time is the Best" (*Gottes Zeit ist die allerbeste Zeit*, arr. by Robert Franz)	Mar. 15, 1877 (AmPr)	
124		198	"Ode of Mourning" (*Trauerode*)	Mar. 15, 1900 (AmPr)	

No.[a]	*Genre*	BWV *No.*	*Work*	*Date of First Performance*[b]	*Subsequent Performances*
122	Secular Cantatas	204/8	Soprano aria from *Ich bin in mir vergnügt* (*Von der Vergnügsamkeit*)	Feb. 13, 1900 (AmPr)	
129		211	Coffee Cantata (*Schweigt stille, plaudert nicht*)	Apr. 26, 1900	
118		213/5	Echo aria from "Hercules in Indecision" (*Hercules auf dem Scheidewege*)	Feb. 13, 1900 (AmPr)	
123		214	*Tönet, ihr Pauken*	Feb. 13, 1900 (AmPr)	
14	Motets	ANH. 159	8-part motet, "I Wrestle and Pray" (*Ich lasse dich nicht, du segnest mich denn*)	Mar. 13, 1869 (AmPr)	
109		225	Motet No. 4, "Sing Ye to the Lord" (*Singet dem Herrn*)	Mar. 3, 1894	
125	Masses	232	Mass in B Minor (substantial excerpts)	Apr. 5, 1900	Nov. 24, 1900
121	Latin Choral Works	238	Sanctus in D Major	Feb. 13, 1900 (AmPr)	Apr. 26, 1900
21	Passions	244/42	Aria, "Give Me Back My Dearest Master" ("Gebt mir meinen Jesum wieder") from the St. Matthew Passion	Nov. 22, 1873	
27		244/39	"Have Mercy upon Me" ("Erbarme dich, mein Gott") from the St. Matthew Passion	Feb. 26, 1874	Apr. 25, 1874; Feb. 18, 1882

No.[a]	*Genre*	BWV No.	*Work*	*Date of First Performance*[b]	*Subsequent Performances*
67		244	St. Matthew Passion (about half the work was given)	Mar. 17–18, 1880	Mar. 12–13, 1884; Mar. 7–8, 1888; Mar. 1 and 3, 1892; Feb. 23–24, 1894; Apr. 12–13, 1895
15	Oratorios	248/II/10	Sinfonia from the Christmas Oratorio	Aug. 10, 1871	Aug. 15, 1872; June 11, 1874; Nov. 13, 1875; Feb. 15, 1890; Apr. 12, 1890
43		248/II/19	"Cradle Song" ("Schlafe, mein Liebster") from the Christmas Oratorio	Nov. 13, 1875	Jan. 18, 1879
85		248/I–II	Christmas Oratorio, Parts I and II (arr. by Robert Franz)	Dec. 20, 1884	Dec. 8, 1898 (Part II only)
22	4-Part Chorales	188/6	"In God in Whom I Trust" (*Auf meinen lieben Gott trau ich in Angst und Not*)	Dec. 3, 1873	Apr. 12, 1898
24		386	"Now to the Eternal God" (prob. *Nun danket alle Gott*)	Feb. 26, 1874	
119	Organ Works	525	Organ Sonata in E-flat Major (orch. transcr. by Herman Hans Wetzler)	Feb. 13, 1900	
		536	Prelude and Fugue in A Major for Organ	May 5, 1881	

No.[a]	Genre	BWV No.	Work	Date of First Performance[b]	Subsequent Performances
10		540	Toccata in F Major (orch. transcr. by Heinrich Esser)	Jan. 7, 1865 (AmPr)	May 7, 1881; Nov. 10, 1883; Mar. 29, 1884; Feb. 9, 1889
90		prob. 551 (poss. 543 or 561)	[Organ] Fugue in A Minor (arr. for strings by Josef Hellmesberger)	Dec. 6, 1887 (AmPr)	Jan. 21, 1888; Feb. 9, 1889
11		582	Passacaglia in C Minor for Organ (orch. transcr. by Heinrich Esser)	Apr. 8, 1865 (AmPr)	Aug. 28, 1873; July 22, 1875; Apr. 17, 1886
29		unknown	Prelude and Fugue [orch. transcr.]	June 18, 1874	Aug. 16, 1891
37		unknown	Prelude [orch. transcr.]	May 27, 1875	
39		unknown	Prelude, Chorale, and Fugue [orch. transcr.]	July 8, 1875	
56		unknown	"Chorale and Fugue" [orch. transcr.]	June 2, 1878	June 10, 1878; Sept. 12, 1878
69		903	Chromatic Fantasy and Fugue (orch. transcr. by George F. Bristow)	Apr. 20, 1880 (AmPr)	
44		971	Italian Concerto	Dec. 27, 1875	
1		846	*Méditation sur le Premier Prélude de Piano de S. Bach* (arr. for violin, cello, and piano by Charles Gounod)	Dec. 18, 1855	

No.[a]	*Genre*	BWV *No.*	*Work*	*Date of First Performance*[b]	*Subsequent Performances*
4	Works for Violin Solo	1004/5	Chaconne in D Minor (with piano accomp. by Mendelssohn)	Apr. 17, 1858	Nov. 23, 1858 (piano acc. by Schumann); Apr. 14, 1860
31		1004/5	Chaconne in D Minor (orch. transcr. by Joachim Raff)	Dec. 12, 1874 (AmPr)	Dec. 19, 1874; Jan. 18, 1875; Mar. 13, 1875; July 1, 1875
65		1006/1, 1003/3, 1006/3	Prelude, Adagio, Gavotte, and Rondo (arr. for strings by Sigismund Bachrich)	Jan. 20, 1880 (AmPr)	Jan. 24, 1880
107		prob. 1006	"Adagio and Gavotte from Suite in E" [prob. Partita No. 3 for Violin] (arr. for string orchestra)	Apr. 15, 1893 (AmPr)	
7		1016	Sonata No. 3 in E Major for Violin and Piano	Mar. 24, 1863	
113		1016	Sonata No. 3 in E Major for Violin and Cembalo (orch. transcr. by Theodore Thomas)	Mar. 5, 1897 (AmPr)	
9		1018	Sonata No. 5 in F Minor for Violin and Piano	Mar. 8, 1864	
96		1018	"Largo and Allegro" [Sonata No. 5 in F Minor for Violin and Cembalo] (orch. transcr. by Theodore Thomas)	Jan. 19, 1889	
102		1018	Sonata No. 5 in F Minor for Violin and Cembalo (orch. transcr. by Theodore Thomas)	Apr. 12, 1890 (AmPr)	Apr. 19, 1890; Mar. 23, 1896

No.[a]	Genre	BWV No.	Work	Date of First Performance[b]	Subsequent Performances
35	Concertos	1043	Concerto in D Minor for Two Violins	Feb. 6, 1875	Dec. 10, 1881
87		1044	Concerto for Piano, Flute, Violin, and String Orchestra	Mar. 21, 1885 (AmPr)	
95		1046	Brandenburg Concerto No. 1	Nov. 2, 1888 (AmPr)	
26		1048	Brandenburg Concerto No. 3	Feb. 28, 1874 (AmPr)	Mar. 11, 1881; Jan. 19, 1884; Feb. 11, 1888
112		1051	Brandenburg Concerto No. 6	Dec. 17, 1896 (AmPr)	
54		1052	Concerto No. 1 in D Minor for Clavier	Jan. 12, 1878	
8		1061	Concerto in C Major for Two Pianos	Apr. 21, 1863 (AmPr)	Dec. 27, 1875
2		1063	Concerto in D Minor for Three Pianos	Feb. 26, 1856 (AmPr)	Apr. 10, 1858; Apr. 25, 1873; Dec. 27, 1875; May 19, 1877; Jan. 5, 1878
47		1065	Concerto in A Minor for Four Pianos	Dec. 27, 1875 (AmPr)	

No.[a]	Genre	BWV No.	Work	Date of First Performance[b]	Subsequent Performances
48	Orchestral Works	1066	Suite No. 1 in C Major 1. Overture 2. Forlano 3. Bourrée 4. Passepied	Mar. 25, 1876 (AmPr)	
30		1067	Suite No. 2 in B Minor 1. Grave-Fugue 2. Sarabande 3. Polonaise et Double 4. Badinerie	Nov. 28, 1874	Jan. 16, 1875; Mar. 13, 1886
104		prob 1067	"Sarabande, andante, and bourrée" [prob. Suite No. 2 in B Minor]	Jan. 17, 1891	
13		1068	Suite No. 3 in D Major	Oct. 26, 1867 (AmPr)	Apr. 26, 1873; Feb. 1, 1877; Sept. 16, 1875; Apr. 14, 1877; June 17, 1878; Feb. 3, 1883; Mar. 21, 1885; Jan. 14, 1888; Apr. 6, 1889; Mar. 14, 1898 [and numerous others]

No.[a]	*Genre*	*BWV No.*	*Work*	*Date of First Performance*[b]	*Subsequent Performances*
19		1068	Air and Gavotte [from Suite No. 3 in D Major]	June 5, 1873	
23		1068	Air on the G String from Suite No. 3 in D Major	Dec. 3, 1873	May 25, 1878; July 18, 1878; Aug. 29, 1878; Sept. 16, 1878; Sept. 28, 1878 [and numerous others]
68		1068	Air [transcr. for cello] from Suite No. 3 in D Major	Mar. 19, 1880	

[a]Numbers in this column refer to the numbers in the appendix (pp. 106–14).
[b]AmPr = American premiere.

compositions, sacred and secular cantatas, motets, Masses, passions, oratorios, and four-part chorales—had been performed at least once in New York by the end of 1900. However, many of these genres were represented by only one or two works, and received only a single performance. Organ works and chamber pieces were frequently presented in the form of orchestral transcriptions rather than as Bach originally conceived them.

Furthermore, only about forty-two pieces or extended sections of works by Bach—a small fraction of the surviving repertory—were performed in the city during the nineteenth century.[7] There are also surprising gaps: there are no records of any performances of the St. John Passion, the Easter or Ascension Oratorios, the Magnificat, or any of the Lutheran Masses. Only eight of the 200 surviving sacred cantatas were presented in complete or near-complete form. Nonetheless, in comparison to other major American cities, New York was the leader in performances of Bach's music.

Bach performances in New York evolved in three phases that correlate closely with the founding of various instrumental and vocal ensembles. Between 1856 and 1864 only solo and chamber works, or solo pieces arranged for a chamber ensemble, were presented under the auspices of the Mason-Thomas Chamber Series. During the next eight years (1865–73), nearly all the Bach works that were performed appeared on Theodore Thomas's symphony programs and consisted of orchestral pieces or transcriptions of organ or chamber compositions. The founding of the Oratorio Society in 1873 led to more regular performances of Bach's sacred choral repertory.[8] Symphonic performances of Bach works continued through the end of the century.

The Mason-Thomas Chamber Music Series and the Music of Bach, 1856–64

Between 1856 and 1864 two concertos by Bach and three works for violin, or violin and piano, were presented on programs of the Mason-Thomas Chamber Music Series (see table 2).[9] Accounts of these early performances reveal that Bach's compositions held little appeal for contemporary listeners and were chiefly of historic inter-

7. This figure does not include solo keyboard works and organ compositions that were performed in solo recitals and do not fall within the parameters of this study.

8. Only two of Bach's choral works appear to have been presented in New York prior to 1873. The cantata "Who Believed, and is Baptized" (BWV 37) was performed in 1865, and the motet "I Wrestle and Pray" (BWV ANH. 159) was presented in March 1869.

9. Thomas's three performances between 1858 and 1860 of the Chaconne from Violin Partita No. 2 in D Minor (BWV 1004/5) were with piano accompaniment by Mendelssohn or Schumann. The monthly chamber music series that was founded in 1855 by violinist Theodore Thomas and pianist William Mason existed under a variety of names, including "Mason & Bergmann's Musical Matinées" and "Mason & Thomas' Classical Matinées" (later "Soirées").

Table 2. Works by Bach Performed at the Mason-Thomas Chamber Concerts, 1856–64

Date	BWV *No.*	*Work*	*Performers*
Feb. 26, 1856	1063	Concerto in D Minor for Three Pianos	William Scharfenberg, Henry C. Timm, and William Mason, pianos; Bergmann, Thomas, Mosenthal, Matzka, and Preusser, strings
Apr. 10, 1858			Same performers
Apr. 17, 1858	1004/5	Chaconne (with piano accomp. by Mendelssohn)	Theodore Thomas and William Mason
Nov. 23, 1858		(piano accomp. by Schumann)	Theodore Thomas and prob. William Mason
Apr. 14, 1860		[with piano accomp.]	Theodore Thomas
Mar. 24, 1863	1016	Sonata No. 3 in E Major for Violin and Piano	Theodore Thomas and William Mason
Apr. 21, 1863	1061	Concerto in C Major for Two Claviers	Henry C. Timm and William Mason, soloists
Mar. 8, 1864	1018	Sonata No. 5 in F Minor for Violin and Piano	Theodore Thomas and William Mason

est. After attending the American premiere of the Triple Concerto in D Minor in February 1856, the music commentator for the *Times* observed:

> The final novelty—Bach's Concerto, . . . a hale [and] hearty old patriarch, who is not ashamed of his age and his old fashioned ways . . . [is] more of a curiosity than an enjoyment. It is very old and very respectable. . . . [A]lthough we think that the collusion of three pianos with five stringed instruments is an abominable and malicious conspiracy, . . . it was admirably performed by Messrs. Scharfenberg, Timm, Mason, Bergmann, Thomas, Mosenthal, Matzka and Preusser. Our only regret was that they did not appear in perukes and kneebreeches.[10]

Another reviewer commented that, in his experience, Bach's "music . . . is so liable to be unfortunate in its interpretation, that his name in a programme is usually more a drawback than an attraction." On this occasion, however, he was pleasantly surprised

10. *New York Times*, Feb. 27, 1856, 4, col. 4 (hereafter abbreviated as NYTI).

when the "accomplished performance" resulted in "an entire removal from the monotonous and checkered effect of the ordinary flat Bach task."[11]

Critics praised Thomas's performances of the Chaconne in April and November of 1858, but found themselves at a loss for words when it came to assessing the unfamiliar work itself. One commentator characterized it as "a strange composition, which must be heard often to be thoroughly appreciated." But he did acknowledge that, even on a first hearing, "you discover enough to wish to know it better."[12]

Theodore Thomas as Conductor and Orchestrator of Bach's Music

Notable as the chamber music concerts and Thomas's role in them were, his most enduring contributions to the musical life of New York and as an advocate of Bach's music were in his capacity as a conductor. Between 1862 and 1891 he directed three different New York orchestras: Thomas' Orchestra (1867–78), the Brooklyn Philharmonic (1862–91), and the New York Philharmonic (1877–91). Over the course of these three decades he did more than any other single individual to raise the level of playing and promote an appreciation for Bach's music in New York (see plate 1).[13]

During the thirteen seasons Thomas led the Philharmonic Society of New York, he built it into one of the finest symphonies in America, on a par with some of the best European ensembles.[14] In a review that appeared in December 1881, the *Times* music critic Frederick A. Schwab reported, "[As usual] the audience . . . filled the house. . . . The tone was as firm and imposing as ever, and justified the claim that New-Yorkers may make that there is no such orchestra to be heard in this country, and no superior in Europe." Describing the Philharmonic's performance of the Third Brandenburg Concerto on February 11, 1888, the *Times* commentator William J. Henderson wrote, "The excellence of the Philharmonic orchestra this season has hereto-

11. This review appeared in an unidentified New York newspaper and was quoted in *Dwight's Journal of Music* (hereafter DJM) 8, no. 23 (March 8, 1856): 180–81.

12. DJM 13, no. 5 (May 1, 1858): 40, describing Thomas's performance on April 17, 1858, of the Chaconne with a piano accompaniment by Mendelssohn.

13. Thomas' Orchestra had sixty players, but the number occasionally increased to eighty. Thomas's tenure as conductor of the Brooklyn and New York Philharmonic Orchestras was interrupted when he moved to Cincinnati from 1878 to 1880, but he regained his positions upon his return to New York in the fall of 1880. In 1891 he accepted a call to become conductor of the Chicago Symphony. The orchestra visited New York in March 1896 and 1898, and performed works of Bach. Thomas died in Chicago in January 1905.

14. The Philharmonic Society numbered about 100 players at the time. Thomas introduced low pitch into the orchestra during the 1882–83 season. See George P. Upton, ed., *Theodore Thomas: A Musical Autobiography*, 2 vols. (Chicago: A. C. McClurg & Co., 1905), 1:92.

Plate 1. Theodore Thomas and his Orchestra in Steinway Hall, New York.
Courtesy of the Library of Congress.

fore been mentioned . . . and it only remains to add that its work yesterday was conspicuous for sonority, dignity, precision, and effective gradations."[15]

Thomas, an early subscriber to the complete edition of Bach's works, was a staunch proponent of his music. His three most notable contributions vis-à-vis the music of Bach lay in his sustained efforts to introduce the composer's works to the public, assembling and training performers who were equal to the exacting technical challenges of the music, and making his own orchestral arrangements and transcriptions of pieces by Bach.

Thomas's pioneering role in fostering an appreciation for Bach's music was recognized during his own lifetime. Writing in 1889, William S. B. Mathews characterized Thomas's distinctive contributions to the New York Philharmonic Society as follows: "He revived Bach's works and introduced the compositions of the modern school, headed by Berlioz, Liszt, Brahms, Rubinstein, Saint-Saëns, etc." He added, Thomas

15. Frederick A. Schwab, NYTI, Dec. 11, 1881, 9, col. 1; William J. Henderson, NYTI, Feb. 11, 1888, 4, col. 7. William James Henderson (1855–1937) served as music critic for the *New York Times* from 1887 to 1902, and for the *New York Sun* from 1902 to 1937 (see plate 3 [p. 93]).

"has given programmes ranging from the preludes, fugues and antique fancies of Bach to the latest cogitations of the French ballet writers, and including everything between."[16] Following a performance of Bach's First Orchestral Suite in March 1876, John R. G. Hassard, the music critic for the *Tribune*, observed that three orchestral suites by Bach had been published and that they were indebted to Thomas for their knowledge of them all.[17] In February 1889, after hearing presentations of orchestral transcriptions of Bach's Toccata in F Major and Fugue in A Minor, the *Times* critic Henderson wrote,

> The musical world owes Theodore Thomas thanks for many things, and one of them is his persistent playing of Bach. . . . The public . . . would probably prefer something that appeals less to the brain and more to the senses; but the public has got to be taught that music is an art, not a pastime, and every dose of Bach carries conviction with it.[18]

Following Thomas's death in 1905, many newspapers printed commemorative articles praising him for fostering an appreciation of classical music and for raising the level of playing in American orchestras. In a commentary that appeared in the *Northwestern Christian Advocate*, the writer singled out Thomas's sustained advocacy of Bach as one of his most significant accomplishments:

> Thomas . . . decided to educate the musical taste of the people of this country. . . . He had a . . . conviction that any people might be brought to appreciate what was best in music if they had it properly presented and presented often enough. . . . The task before him was tremendous. First, he had to create an orchestra and mould musicians to his ideals; . . . then he had to woo a public which could not be compelled. He played Bach; the people cried for Strauss waltzes; he gave them Strauss and more Bach. . . . For forty years Mr. Thomas went on with this work.[19]

Between 1865 and 1898 Thomas led performances of twenty different works, or sections of works, by Bach in New York (see table 3).[20] These included three orchestral suites, four concertos, three orchestral transcriptions of chamber works, transcriptions of four organ works and the Chromatic Fantasy and Fugue, the first two parts

16. W. S. B. Mathews, *A Hundred Years of Music in America* (Chicago: G. L. Howe, 1889), 413, 425.

17. John R. G. Hassard, *New York Tribune*, March 27, 1876, 4, col. 6 (hereafter abbreviated as NYTR). John Rose Greene Hassard (1836–88) served as music critic for the *New York Tribune* between 1866 and 1884. Thomas' Orchestra performed the Suite No. 3 in D Major (BWV 1068), or sometimes just the Air, on numerous occasions, and it became a particular favorite of audiences.

18. NYTI, Feb. 9, 1889, 4, col. 7. The transcription of the Toccata in F Major was by Heinrich Esser.

19. *Northwestern Christian Advocate* (Chicago). Quoted in Upton, ed., *Theodore Thomas*, 1:306–7.

20. Thomas conducted performances of two works by Bach when the Chicago Symphony visited New York in March of 1896 and 1898.

Table 3. Works by Bach Conducted by Theodore Thomas, 1865–98, with Date of First Performance

Work	*Date of First Performance*
Orchestral Suites	
Suite No. 1 in C Major, BWV 1066	1876
Suite No. 2 in B Minor, BWV 1067	1874
Suite No. 3 in D Major, BWV 1068	1867
Concertos	
Concerto in D Minor for Three Pianos, BWV 1063	1873
Brandenburg Concerto No. 3, BWV 1048	1874
Concerto in D Minor for Two Violins and Orchestra, BWV 1043	1875
Concerto for Piano, Flute, and Violin, BWV 1044	1885
Orchestral Transcriptions of Chamber Works	
Chaconne in D Minor, BWV 1004/5, orch. transcr. by Joachim Raff	1874
Prelude, Adagio, Gavotte, and Rondo, movements from BWV 1006 and 1003, arr. for strings by Sigismund Bachrich	1880
Sonata No. 5 in F Minor for Violin and Cembalo, BWV 1018, transcr. by Theodore Thomas	1890
Orchestral Transcriptions of Organ Works	
Toccata in F Major, BWV 540 (orch. transcr. by Heinrich Esser)	1865
Fugue for Organ in A Minor, prob. BWV 551 (orch. transcr. by Josef Hellmesberger)	1887
Passacaglia for Organ in C Minor, BWV 582 (orch. transcr. by Heinrich Esser)	1865
Prelude and Fugue	1874
Prelude	1875
Prelude, Chorale, and Fugue	1875
Chorale and Fugue	1878
Orchestral Transcriptions of the Chromatic Fantasy and Fugue, BWV 903 (orch. transcr. by George F. Bristow)	1880
Christmas Oratorio, Parts I and II, BWV 248	1884
Excerpts:	
Sinfonia, BWV 248/II/10	1871
Sinfonia and "Cradle Song" ("Schlafe, mein Liebster"), BWV 248/II/10 and 19	1875

Table 3. Works by Bach Conducted by Theodore Thomas (*continued*)

Work	*Date of First Performance*
Sacred Cantatas	
"My spirit was in heaviness" (*Ich hatte viel Bekümmernis*), BWV 21	1883
"A Stronghold Sure" (*Ein feste Burg*), BWV 80, arr. by Theodore Thomas	1881
Motet	
The eight-part motet "I Wrestle and Pray" (*Ich lasse dich nicht, du segnest mich denn*), BWV ANH. 159	1869
Arias from the St. Matthew Passion:	
"Give me Back my Dearest Master" ("Gebt mir meinen Jesum wieder"), BWV 244/42	1873
"O, pardon me, my God" ("Erbarme dich, mein Gott"), BWV 244/39	1874

of the Christmas Oratorio, two sacred cantatas, a motet, and two arias from the St. Matthew Passion. Of the twenty pieces, only eleven were presented in complete, or near-complete, form and with the instruments (or modern replacements) Bach called for: the orchestral suites, concertos, the first two parts of the Christmas Oratorio, the sacred cantatas, and the motet. Fully 40 percent of the Bach works that Thomas conducted in New York consisted of orchestral transcriptions of pieces that were initially conceived for a chamber ensemble or solo keyboard instrument. As arrangements and transcriptions constitute such a significant proportion of the Bach repertory that was performed in New York, and as the performing medium has a direct bearing on the reception of Bach's music, this subject will be considered at some length.

The Debate over Arrangements and Transcriptions

Throughout the second half of the nineteenth century, purists and pragmatists argued over the value of making orchestral transcriptions of solo or chamber works.[21] Most critics were receptive to orchestral transcriptions—if well executed—of works by Bach that would otherwise not have been performed. However, at times even the pragma-

21. The term "transcription" is employed to refer to a work that was orchestrated for a different combination of instruments than the composer had originally called for. The term "arrangement" designates a piece that was modified for performance on modern instruments. In the latter case, obsolete instruments were replaced by their nearest modern equivalents, and new parts were usually added to create a fuller sound suited to large concert halls.

tists faulted an orchestrator for choosing a piece that did not lend itself to orchestration in the first place, or for ineptitude in carrying out the task.

The debate over the merits of transcriptions surfaced as early as January 1865, when Thomas led a performance of Heinrich Esser's transcription of the Toccata in F Major. The *Times* critic felt that little had been gained by the orchestrator's efforts: "The Toccata in F, by Bach . . . has been newly instrumented by Esser, and without . . . adding to its effectiveness. The organ is grand enough for such productions. For that instrument, the Toccata is striking, quaint and pleasing."[22] Henry C. Watson, the commentator for the *Tribune*, on the other hand, welcomed the production of "this favorite organ piece of the old composer" in an orchestral form.[23] However, he was less taken with Esser's arrangement of Bach's Passacaglia, which he heard three months later:

> [The] "Passacaglia" is not as well calculated for orchestral development as his "Toc[c]ata" in F. . . . It is deficient in contrast and strong points and consequently admits of but little coloring. It is finely instrumented, the subject being well distributed through the orchestra, but the effect is very monotonous.[24]

The *Times* critic was even more withering in his appraisal of the transcription:

> [T]he . . . "passacaglia" of Bach . . . is a fair representation of the treadmill . . . [and] to the native weight of the composition Herr Esser has added the superior dullness of his instrumentation. . . . His idea of instrumentation appears to be a wheezy mingling of all the instruments with an occasional hiccough on the double basses. The "passacaglia" with its jaw-breaking return to one idea, certainly gains nothing from Herr Esser's colorless and insipid treatment.[25]

Joachim Raff's orchestration of Bach's Chaconne, which was performed a decade later, elicited contrasting responses from commentators. Hassard, the *Tribune* critic, was favorably disposed toward transcriptions and wrote that Raff had admirably preserved Bach's "pure, simple, majestic style . . . and given us such a score as we can imagine Bach might have made had he undertaken to adapt this charming dance measure to a well equipped modern orchestra." The critic for the *Times*, on the other hand, observed drily that "the utility of achievements of this sort does not impress us strongly." However, after hearing the same work a month later, he admitted that Raff's arrangement of the "Ciacona" contained "a few passages which grow upon one."[26]

22. NYTI, Jan. 9, 1865, 4, col. 6.

23. NYTR, Jan. 9, 1865, 5, col. 5. Henry Cood Watson (1818–75) was music critic for the *Tribune* from 1863 to 1867.

24. NYTR, April 10, 1865, 4, col. 6.

25. NYTI, April 10, 1865, 5, col. 2.

26. NYTR, Dec. 14, 1874, 4, col. 5; NYTI, Dec. 13, 1874, 6, col. 6; NYTI, Jan. 19, 1875, 4, col. 7.

In an article that appeared in January 1880 Hassard praised Sigismund Bachrich's composite arrangement for strings of three movements taken from two different violin sonatas by Bach, which was "most beautifully and effectively done" and "quite in Bach's spirit."[27] He also defended transcriptions per se, noting that Bach and other leading composers had made numerous arrangements that involved the substitution of one or more instruments for others. In addition, he observed that no violinists of their own day played the unaccompanied sonatas and partitas in their original form and that, consequently, if the works were not heard in arrangements, it was unlikely that they would be heard at all.

Three months later, in a lengthy rejoinder to the vigorous criticism occasioned by the performance of George Bristow's orchestral transcription of the Chromatic Fantasia and Fugue, Hassard wrote:

> Mr. Bristow's excellent arrangement for the orchestra of Bach's Chromatic Fantasia and Fugue has called out a vigorous protest; not that it is ill done, but because transcriptions are assumed to be improper. Critic after critic has taken up the chorus of condemnation. . . . Whenever a master of the orchestra undertakes to score a composition originally designed for something else, the rigorists cry out: "You shall not, you shall not!" but . . . they do not tell us *why* he shall not. Meanwhile the ablest musicians continue the practice, to the great pleasure and advantage of the public.[28]

He pointed out that Bach himself arranged Vivaldi's violin sonatas for the harpsichord, and argued that transcriptions in no way take the place of or alter the original piece but exist independent of it.

Theodore Thomas was notable not only as a conductor of Bach's music, but also as an arranger and orchestrator. His arrangements of "A Stronghold Sure" and the Second Orchestral Suite and two transcriptions of Sonatas for Violin and Cembalo (No. 5 in F Minor and No. 3 in E Major) were performed in New York between 1881 and 1897.[29]

27. NYTR, Jan. 25, 1880, 7, col. 1. Sigismund Bachrich lived from 1841 until 1913. The arrangement of movements from Violin Sonatas No. 6 in E Major and No. 3 in A Minor (BWV 1006/1, 1003/3, and 1006/3) was performed by both the Brooklyn Philharmonic and the Philharmonic Society on separate occasions in January 1880.

28. NYTR, May 2, 1880, 7, col. 1.

29. The violin part in No. 5 in F Minor is assigned to the violins and violas, and the piano part to the woodwinds and basses. Thomas also led a performance by the Brooklyn Philharmonic of a work identified only as "Largo and Allegro" (presumably BWV 1018), on Jan. 19, 1889. Thomas's orchestral transcription of Sonata No. 3 in E Major for Violin and Cembalo was presented by the New York Philharmonic Society with Anton Seidl conducting in March 1897. According to George Upton, Thomas also arranged the "Andante and Allegro" from Bach's Sonata No. 2 in A Major (BWV 1015) for the violin section of the orchestra. However, there is no record that this was ever performed in New York. See Upton, ed., *Theodore Thomas*, 1:211.

Contemporary reviews of Thomas's arrangements and transcriptions nearly always commended him for his technical knowledge of the resources of the orchestra and for remaining true to the spirit of the original composition.[30] In February 1881 Hassard praised his "splendid accompaniments" to *Ein feste Burg ist unser Gott* (BWV 80). He described for his readers the challenge that Thomas faced in arranging the work: he had to adapt the score to "the greatly increased resources of the modern orchestra, while . . . religiously preserving the spirit of the original." He praised Thomas for accomplishing this difficult and delicate task with notable success.[31]

After hearing Thomas's arrangement of the cantata just over a year later at the May Musical Festival, Hassard was even more complimentary of Thomas's skill, writing that he was virtually in a class by himself:

> It is remarkable that, while [Thomas] surpasses even Robert Franz in fidelity to the original, he has allowed himself a freedom in the use of new agencies of expression upon which, so far as we can discover, no other adapter of the archaic classics has ever ventured. . . . In the union of reverence and boldness his method is unique, and the splendid result is vindication.

Hassard continued,

> [Thomas] has not only adhered closely to the style of the master but he has literally used the master's own materials, and supplied lost accompaniments without the employment of a figure not found in the work itself. In providing substitutes for obsolete instruments he shows his intimate knowledge of the characteristics of the orchestra.[32]

However, when Thomas's orchestral transcription of Bach's Sonata No. 3 in E Major (BWV 1016) was performed a decade and a half later, in March 1897, critical reaction was mixed. Henderson wrote a scathing review of both the transcription and the performance:

> It is not quite possible to tell why Mr. Thomas made his orchestration of the Bach sonata, and it is altogether impossible to tell why the Philharmonic Society played it in such a dead style. . . . There was no delicacy, and little shading, and the solo passages—except that of Mr. Sam Franko on the viola—were inexcusably maltreated.[33]

30. For example, after hearing Thomas's transcription of the "Largo and Allegro" (presumably from the Sonata No. 5 in F Minor), William James Henderson remarked that the music was "excellently arranged by Mr. Thomas, whose ability in orchestration is once more finely displayed." NYTI, Jan. 19, 1889, 4, col. 7.

31. NYTR, Feb. 13, 1881, 7, col. 1. In his review, Henry T. Finck noted that "in the first chorus [of Thomas's transcription] the heavy imposing subject of the chorale is laid in the orchestra, chiefly for the trumpets and tubas." NYP, Feb. 14, 1881, 4, col. 7.

32. NYTR, May 3, 1882, 5, col. 1.

33. NYTI, March 6, 1897, 6, col. 7. Anton Seidl conducted the Philharmonic Society's performance on this occasion.

Henry Edward Krehbiel, the *Tribune* critic, on the other hand, though conceding that purists might object to orchestral transcriptions of chamber works, commended Thomas for making arrangements of rarely performed works which enabled "hundreds" to hear beautiful music they never would have come to know otherwise. He praised Thomas's discreet orchestration of the sonata, writing that he has "rescued it from archaism; the music pulsated with life." In short, "the sonata, in its new dress, is a distinct acquisition to the too small repertory of practicable Bach pieces."[34]

Symphonic and Choral Performances of Works by Bach in New York, 1865–1900

The remainder of this article is devoted to a chronological survey of representative symphonic and choral performances of Bach's music that took place in New York between 1865 and 1900. Contemporary reviews are cited frequently, as they provide the most immediate information we have about the nature of the forces involved, the quality of the performances, and the ways in which nineteenth-century audiences responded. The men who played key roles in introducing Bach's music to New York audiences and the groups they led—the Oratorio Society, the New York Symphony Society, the Musical Art Society, and the Bach Singers—are also profiled as they appeared on the scene.

A performance of Bach's Third Orchestral Suite by Thomas' Orchestra in the fall of 1867 elicited warm praise both for the level of playing as well as for the work itself. "This exquisite composition," the *Times* critic wrote, was "given by the orchestra with positive faultlessness, and the lovely *cavatina* . . . drew forth a spontaneous and emphatic endorsement."[35]

In the fall of 1866 Thomas founded the Choral Society to facilitate the performance of choral-orchestral repertory, and two and one-half years later he led this group, along with the Mendelssohn Union and Thomas' Orchestra, in a performance of the eight-part motet, "I Wrestle and Pray" (*Ich lasse dich nicht, du segnest mich denn*, BWV ANH. 159).[36] Hassard described the piece as "a grand work, partly in the fugue style, but containing also a severely beautiful choral[e]."[37]

A performance of Bach's Triple Concerto in D Minor (BWV 1063) in April 1873 with Anton Rubinstein, Sebastian Bach Mills, and William Mason as soloists elicited mixed

34. NYTR, March 8, 1897, 6, col. 6. Henry Edward Krehbiel (1854–1923) was music critic for the *New York Tribune* from 1880 to 1923. He also wrote program notes for important New York concerts.

35. NYTI, Oct. 28, 1867, 4, col. 6.

36. Daniel R. Melamed has shown that this work, formerly attributed to Johann Christoph Bach, is by J. S. Bach. See Daniel R. Melamed, "The Authorship of the Motet *Ich lasse dich nicht* (BWV ANH. 159)," *Journal of the American Musicological Society* 41 (1988): 491–526.

37. NYTR, March 15, 1869, 5, col. 3.

reactions from commentators and the audience. While the *Times* critic found the work to be overly complex, he reported that the audience responded enthusiastically:

> The three artists appeared, somewhat after the fashion of an enlarged edition of the Siamese twins, and delivered [the concerto] with unimpeachable precision. . . . We are, however, by no means willing to accept the applause of the audience as the result of the concerto's impression; the work is elaborate and exacting, but its effectiveness is in indirect proportion to its elaborateness and its exigencies.[38]

Hassard, on the other hand, described the concerto as "a most delightful work, short, bright, and hearty." While he conceded that the piece might well conjure up images of "bagwigs and hair powder" to contemporary listeners, it was nonetheless "full of the beauty which never becomes antiquated and the majesty that is never dull."[39]

* * *

The Oratorio Society, which Leopold Damrosch founded in 1873, soon earned a solid reputation for the high quality of its repertory as well as its performances.[40] In his account of the group's first concert in December 1873, which included the Bach chorale "In God in Whom I Trust" and the "Air on the G String," Hassard observed that choral pieces by Bach were rarely performed in New York, and that the group showed promise that augured well for the future.[41] He noted that the repertory was not particularly challenging, but reported that the singing was marked by "correct intonation, firm attack, and a great deal of expression," qualities, he added, "which are painfully missed in the concerts of older organizations." He observed that "Damrosch [took] the *tempi* of most of the choruses with more freedom than has been customary in New York, varying the accent and expression by that means with rather striking effect."[42]

38. NYTI, April 26, 1873, 6, col. 7.

39. NYTR, April 26, 1873, 7, col. 2.

40. Leopold Damrosch was born in Posen, Germany (now part of Poland) in 1832 and, after earning a medical degree in Berlin, decided on a musical career. He held several conducting positions in Breslau from 1858 to 1871, when he was named conductor of the Männergesangverein Arion in New York City. In 1873 Damrosch founded the Oratorio Society. He served as conductor of the Philharmonic Society during the 1876–77 season and in 1878 established the New York Symphony Society, conducting it and the Oratorio Society until his death in February 1885.

41. The Society comprised not more than fifty or sixty members, he guessed, and were "largely recruited . . . from German families of the highest class—a section of the community which manifests a better taste and warmer enthusiasm for music, and much more perseverance in the drudgery that vocal societies must undergo, than any other nationality." J. R. G. Hassard, NYTR, Dec. 4, 1873, 5, col. 3.

42. Ibid.

Theodore Thomas regarded Leopold Damrosch's arrival in New York as a threat, and relations between the two conductors were antagonistic, despite—or perhaps because of—the fact that both men were gifted German-born musicians, dedicated to the highest standards of repertory and performance and staunch advocates of Bach's music. Their conducting styles, however, were very different. In 1889 William Mathews described Theodore Thomas's approach as follows: "Mr. Thomas' ideal of musical effect is typically that of instruments. His notion of rhythm is instrumental, when the main bond of unity in long movements is the rhythmic pulsation and the rhythmic motivation."[43] This accords with the recollections of Leopold Damrosch's son Walter who, writing many years later, contrasted Thomas's conducting style with that of his father:

> Thomas . . . had always striven for great cleanliness of execution, a metronomical accuracy and rigidity of tempo, and a strict and literal . . . observance of the signs put down by the composers. . . . My father['s] . . . readings were emotionally more intense. He was the first conductor in this country to make those fine and delicate gradations in tempo according to the inner demands of the music.[44]

Under Leopold Damrosch's direction, the Oratorio Society developed into one of the most enduring choral groups in the city. The group performed at least two cantatas by Bach, the *Actus tragicus* (BWV 106) and "Vain and Fleeting" (*Ach wie flüchtig, ach wie nichtig*, BWV 26), in its first decade of existence. It also presented the first New York performances of both the St. Matthew Passion and the B Minor Mass. Works of Bach performed between 1873 and 1900 by the Oratorio and Symphony Societies under the direction of Leopold, Walter, or Frank Damrosch are listed in table 4.

* * *

By the mid-1870s critics were generally favorably disposed to Bach's music, although the frequent appearance of the word "quaint" in reviews reveals the extent to which it was still regarded as something of a novelty. For instance, in a review of a performance by Thomas' Orchestra in February 1874 of the Third Brandenburg Concerto, Hassard wrote that in its "quaint and beautiful measures . . . formal elegance and spontaneous grace are . . . inimitably combined." One is reminded of the "stately gayety of a light footed giant."[45]

The New York premiere in November 1874 of Bach's Orchestral Suite in B Minor

43. Mathews, *Hundred Years of Music in America*, 424.

44. Walter Damrosch, *My Musical Life* (New York: Charles Scribner's Sons, 1926), 24.

45. Hassard praised the playing of the strings in particular. The concerto was performed by seventeen violins and violas, six cellos, and one bass. NYTR, March 2, 1874, 7, col. 2.

Table 4. Works by Bach Performed by the Oratorio Society and Symphony Society, under the Direction of Leopold, Walter, or Frank Damrosch, 1873–1900

Date	*Work*	*Conductor/Collaborators*
Dec. 3, 1873	Chorale, "In God in Whom I trust"	Leopold Damrosch
	Air on the G String (BWV 1068)	Leopold Damrosch
Mar. 15, 1877	*Gottes Zeit ist die allerbeste Zeit* (*Actus tragicus*, BWV 106)[a]	Leopold Damrosch
Jan. 12, 1878	Concerto No. 1 in D Minor for Clavier (BWV 1052)	Damrosch Orchestra, Leopold Damrosch, B. Boekelman, piano
Mar. 18, 1880	St. Matthew Passion	Leopold Damrosch, boy choir from Trinity Parish; Symphony Society
Mar. 13, 1884		Walter Damrosch, Symphony Society
Mar. 8, 1888		Walter Damrosch
Mar. 3, 1892		Walter Damrosch, Symphony Orchestra, Boy Choir
Feb. 24, 1894		Walter Damrosch, "Chorus of 500," Symphony Orchestra, Boys' Choir
Apr. 12–13, 1895		Walter Damrosch, Boy Choir of St. James's Church
Apr. 21, 1882	"Vain and Fleeting" (*Ach wie flüchtig*, BWV 26)	Leopold Damrosch, Symphony Society
Nov. 2, 1888	Brandenburg Concerto No. 1	Walter Damrosch; Dannreuther, violin; Symphony Society
Apr. 5, 1900	Mass in B Minor	Frank Damrosch
Nov. 24, 1900		Frank Damrosch

[a]BWV 106 was performed in an arrangement by Robert Franz, with two clarinets and two bassoons added.

also received favorable notices. The *Times* critic described the work as "a series of dance-tunes, quaint and rather dignified, instrumented with matchless ingenuity and contrapuntal skill [that is] decidedly interesting from an historical standpoint." It was performed on this occasion "with unimpeachable clearness and delicacy."[46] Hassard was even more impressed by the work, writing that it utterly belied the academic stereotype of Bach that persisted in the mind of the general public:

> The Suite . . . is one of those fresh, charming, simple, melodious pieces in which this most fascinating of the grand old masters . . . stands far above rivalry or imitation. With just enough formalism to give it a quaint air of old-fashioned elegance, it is entirely free from the scholastic dryness which the popular mind ignorantly associates with the name of Bach.

46. NYTI, Nov. 29, 1874, 6, col. 6.

He conjectured that the fine performance "must have roused a general desire to see the name of Bach oftener on our concert bills."[47]

A performance in February 1875 of Bach's Concerto in D Minor for Two Violins and Orchestra (BWV 1043) elicited mixed responses. Hassard reported that the performance was a "remarkable triumph" and that the audience had received it with genuine enthusiasm. He described the entire composition in glowing terms:

> The first movement is a marvelous piece of counterpoint; the second, a most delicious melody; . . . the third reverts to the spirit of the first. It is the Largo which most quickly captivates the unlearned listener; but the whole work is a glorious one, whose greatness becomes more and more impressive at every repeated hearing.[48]

The *Times* reviewer, on the other hand, praised only the second movement: "[The] *largo* was listened to with manifest pleasure, a delicious motive being developed with faultless taste as well as with consummate art, the ultrascientific tendencies of the writer not being yielded to sufficiently to rob the harmonies of their fluency and clearness." However, in his view, the first and third movements had "more affinity with elaborate bowing exercises for the violin than with anything intended to charm the ear."[49]

In late December 1875 Hans von Bülow organized a concert that took place at Chickering Hall and featured four keyboard concertos by Bach: the Italian Concerto, the Concerto in C Major for Two Pianos (BWV 1061), the Concerto in D Minor for Three Pianos (BWV 1063), and the Concerto in A Minor for Four Pianos (BWV 1065). Hassard described the event as "one of the most remarkable piano-forte concerts ever heard in New-York." Von Bülow, Richard Hoffman, Marion Brown (a pupil of von Bülow's), and Mrs. Charles B. Foote (a pupil of Mr. Hoffman's) were the piano soloists; the accompanying string ensemble included four violins, two violas, two violoncellos, and two basses.[50]

The *Times* music critic, Frederick A. Schwab, described the Italian Concerto as "full of tune and quaintness" and praised von Bülow's performance, which was "striking as an exhibition of technique and almost as inspiriting." While the playing in the remainder of the concert was "precise and animated," he wondered "if the presentation of

47. NYTR, Nov. 30, 1874, 4, col. 5.

48. NYTR, Feb. 8, 1875, 4, col. 6.

49. NYTI, Feb. 7, 1875, 6, col. 6.

50. NYTR, Dec. 28, 1875, 5, col. 1. Hassard noted that "the strengthening of the simple quartet for which Bach wrote was not only justifiable, but necessary, since the modern piano is vastly more powerful than the harpsichord of his time."

one of the three [concertos] would not have [sufficed] for the glorification of Bach and the edification of a miscellaneous public."[51]

When the Triple Concerto was performed again two years later, Schwab remained unimpressed by the work. He also noted that it "did not move the assemblage to anything approaching enthusiasm," despite the precision and tastefulness of the performance. He concluded drily that, "as a rule, nothing can be less interesting in a large concert hall than Bach's piano music, and three pianists are just thrice as tedious as one, in handling most of the old musician's legacies to students of harmony and counterpoint."[52]

It would be difficult to imagine a more favorable account of a performance of the First Orchestral Suite which occurred in March 1876 than the one written by Hassard:

> The performance of this fascinating work was a quarter-hour of unalloyed delight. Rarely can Bach have had a more sympathetic and highly finished interpretation. The ensemble of the strings was perfect; the expression was beautiful, every man playing as if he loved his work, and the difficult reed trios were executed with a technical precision and purity of tone which we have never heard equaled by any other hautboy or bassoon players.[53]

Schwab was also favorably impressed by the work, writing that it is "full of melody and piquancy [and] has just enough flavor of the antique to make it representative of the Bach period without appearing at all dry or formal."[54]

The American premiere of "God's Time Is the Best" (the *Actus tragicus*) by the Oratorio Society in March 1877 also earned glowing reviews. Hassard wrote that "the cantata . . . is one of the noblest and most beautiful of [Bach's] shorter choral works, and is distinguished . . . for its dramatic truth and . . . [suffused with] rare poetic feeling." He observed that the work's original scoring was "for a small and very peculiar orchestra" with strings consisting of two viole da gamba, cello, and contrabass, and no violins, and winds represented only by two flutes. In Robert Franz's arrangement (which was performed on this occasion), the viola takes the place of the obsolete viola da gamba, and two clarinets and two bassoons have been added. The singers, he wrote, gave "firm and spirited" readings of the choruses under Leopold Damrosch's direction. Schwab characterized the cantata as "fresh and tuneful," and was particularly impressed by Bach's ingeniousness in interpreting and suitably coloring the plaintive

51. NYTI, Dec. 28, 1875, 4, col. 5. Frederick A. Schwab (1844–1927) served as music critic for the *Times* from about 1875 until about 1890.

52. NYTI, Jan. 6, 1878, 7, col. 4.

53. NYTR, March 27, 1876, 4, col. 6.

54. NYTI, March 27, 1876, 5, col. 2.

words, and by the "almost theatric skill"—which would compel even the admiration of Wagner—with which he handled the voices and instruments. In a third review that appeared in *Dwight's Journal,* the commentator praised the excellent performance of the "poetical and stirring composition." He particularly admired the cantata's "fidelity to the sentiments expressed in the texts," the simple, plaintive accompaniment, and its "deep feeling and . . . great variety of expression."[55]

Leopold Damrosch founded the Symphony Society of New York in the fall of 1877. In his review of the group's performance of Bach's Concerto No. 1 in D Minor, which took place the following January, Schwab observed that the piece did not have broad audience appeal: "The concerto . . . addresses itself to students of the piano rather than to the public. Its ideas are interesting chiefly through their development, and the listener who expects to find in them loftiness or sweetness, or, indeed, anything beyond fluency and a graceful ornateness, is doomed to disappointment."[56]

* * *

A significant milestone was attained in March 1880 when Leopold Damrosch led the Oratorio and Symphony Societies in the first New York performance of the St. Matthew Passion.[57] Schwab praised the Oratorio Society for its superb performance of the monumental work and commended the musical public for seizing the rare opportunity to hear the piece by attending in force both the public dress rehearsal as well as the concert.[58]

Hassard, Schwab, and the reviewer for the *Post* acknowledged that, on a first hearing, the Passion might prove difficult for an unschooled listener. Nonetheless, Schwab was confident that anyone with the slightest musical taste could hardly fail to be impressed by the work's grandeur and beauty. Hassard also commended the Society for distributing John Dwight's excellent program notes, for "Bach's Passion is singularly unlike all the music with which we are familiar; not in its deep religious sentiment and its ineffable tenderness and sorrow . . . but in the form of its melodies and the manner of treating the musical idea."[59]

55. Hassard, NYTR, March 16, 1877, 5, col. 2; Schwab, NYTI, March 16, 1877, 5, col. 2; DJM 37, no. 1 (April 14, 1877): 4.

56. NYTI, Jan. 13, 1878, 7, col. 4.

57. The St. Matthew Passion was revived by Felix Mendelssohn in Berlin on March 11, 1829, and was performed in London on May 6, 1854. The Handel and Haydn Society presented the American premiere of the Passion on Good Friday in 1879, at Music Hall in Boston. The work was performed in English in New York.

58. Schwab, NYTI, March 19, 1880, 5, col. 2.

59. NYTR, March 19, 1880, 5, col. 1.

While New York critics commended Damrosch for taking "judicious" cuts, which allowed the work to be performed in three hours rather than five, the reviewer for the Boston-based *Dwight's Journal* observed somewhat condescendingly that in New York "little more than half of the work was given. Here the whole required two concerts on one day (Good Friday)."[60]

The critics for both the *Times* and the *Post* praised the contributions of the chorus. Schwab wrote, "every number of the work which the chorus was called upon for was exceedingly well done, and none in the latter part more beautifully than the choral[e], 'O head, all bruised and wounded.'" The review in the *Post* was even more complimentary: "[T]he chorus was excellent last night throughout and produced magnificent effects."[61]

While the reviewers were unanimous in applauding Damrosch for his energy and enterprise in producing the Passion, they all faulted him both for his exceedingly slow tempos, particularly in the solo numbers, and for his poor choice of soloists. The *Post* reviewer wrote: "The tempi of all solos, particularly of the recitation, were taken very slowly, more so than is warranted by the spirit of the works, and we are sorry to add that Dr. Damrosch was unfortunate in the choice of his soloists, not one of whom was satisfactory."[62]

While Schwab conceded that Bach's music placed great demands on them and doubtless lay outside their previous musical experience, in his view "the two ladies were particularly unsatisfactory and wearisome. Neither of them seemed to have any grasp of the music or the ability to infuse any pathos or character into it. They both sang in a mere perfunctory manner, and both of them were so faulty in their enunciation that even with the printed copy of the words it was well nigh impossible to follow them."[63]

The critics also concurred that the choice of venue, St. George's Church, Stuyvesant Square, was unfortunate. The commentator in *Dwight's Journal* went so far as to write:

> What promised to be a most important event of the season, the performance under Dr. Damrosch, of Bach's *St. Matthew Passion Music*, seems to have fallen rather short of expectation. It needs our Boston Music Hall to display the forces for so great a work to good advantage. . . . The separation of the orchestra into two distinct divisions, being necessary by the conveniences of St. George's Church . . . seriously marred its success.[64]

60. About half the Passion was performed on this occasion. DJM 40, no. 1016 (March 27, 1880): 56.

61. NYTI, March 19, 1880, 5, col. 2; NYP, March 19, 1880, 4, col. 7.

62. NYP, March 19, 1880, 4, col. 7.

63. NYTI, March 19, 1880, 5, col. 2.

64. DJM 40, no. 1016 (March 27, 1880): 56.

Hassard also observed that the ensemble suffered as a result of the unfavorable disposition of the singers and players in the church:

> The chorus was placed on temporary benches covering the chancel; the orchestra was necessarily divided into two wings, pushed back under the galleries and wholly separated from each other by the body of singers. As a natural consequence, the voices and the band were not always together. The arrangement was the more to be regretted because the chorus, having had little experience in this kind of music, needed all the help it could get, and creditable as its efforts generally were, it was not quite at its ease.[65]

Schwab also found it regrettable that the lengthy work had been presented in the church rather than Steinway Hall, but for an entirely different reason: "to be requested to sit quietly for three hours and a half continuously in a [crowded and uncomfortable] pew is too much for endurance, even on Sundays."[66]

* * *

Shortly after his return to New York in the fall of 1880, after a two-year sojourn in Cincinnati, Theodore Thomas established both the New York Chorus Society and the Brooklyn Philharmonic Chorus to collaborate with the New York and Brooklyn Philharmonic Orchestras. Between 1881 and 1884 he led performances of two Bach cantatas as well as the first two parts of the Christmas Oratorio (see table 5).

Thomas's performance of "A Stronghold Sure" on February 12, 1881, received a glowing review in the *Tribune*. "Ein feste Burg," Hassard wrote, is one of Bach's finest choral works, "from the purity and nobility of its character, the beauty and richness of its counterpoint, and from the manner in which it preserves and expresses the manliness, the firm religious zeal and the spirit of earnest faith of the Reformation." He went on to praise, in the highest possible terms, the work of the 480 singers of the New York and Brooklyn Philharmonic Choruses and the New York Philharmonic

Table 5. Choral Works by Bach Performed under the Direction of Theodore Thomas, 1881–84

Work	*Date*
"A Stronghold Sure" (BWV 80)	Feb. 12, 1881, Feb. 19, 1881, and May 2, 1882
"My Spirit was in Heaviness" (BWV 21)	Mar. 17, 1883
Christmas Oratorio, Parts I and II (BWV 248)	Dec. 20, 1884

65. NYTR, March 19, 1880, 5, col. 1.

66. NYTI, March 19, 1880, 5, col. 2.

Society. The performance "was one of those . . . of which one hears but two or three in a lifetime."[67]

Schwab also gave a favorable account of the performance of the same work that took place in Brooklyn a week later. The playing of the orchestra deserved "nothing but praise" and "was marked by . . . unity and perfection." While the recently formed chorus had not yet achieved a level of distinction, it had improved considerably. The hall, he reported, was filled to capacity.[68]

Henry T. Finck described the Third Brandenburg Concerto, which the Philharmonic Society performed in March 1881, as "a bright, healthy and powerful work" that "when rendered by a string orchestra of such strength and efficiency as that of the Philharmonic Society, and inspired by Mr. Thomas's manly spirit, became one of the most interesting numbers on the program."[69] Schwab also praised the precision and power of the ensemble, and enumerated the forces that took part in the performance: seventy-eight strings, including thirty-six violins, fourteen violas, fourteen cellos, fourteen double basses, and twenty-two reeds, brass, and percussion instruments.[70]

When the Concerto in D Minor for Two Violins was performed in December of that year, Finck reported that the fine performance delivered by Hermann Brandt and Richard Arnold, both members of the first violin section of the Philharmonic Society, attested to the rapid progress that America was making in music. They played "with a thorough comprehension of the author's intention and a perfection of technique that many a travelling virtuoso might have envied." Finck continued:

> Bach has shown in many of his compositions [such] as . . . the last chorus of his Passion music, that he can stir the soul as deeply as any master. Such works as this concerto, however, appeal less to the emotions than to the intellect, which delights in tracing the outlines of the beautiful pattern by pursuing the thread of melody as it appears.[71]

While Schwab agreed that the concerto was admirably performed by the two soloists, in his view the work itself possessed "no interest to any one but a violinist."[72]

The Oratorio Society's performance of "Vain and Fleeting" (BWV 26) in April 1882 earned mixed reviews. While Schwab found the cantata "most interesting, and [certain]

67. NYTR, Feb. 13, 1881, 7, col. 1.

68. NYTI, Feb. 19, 1881, 4, col. 7.

69. NYP, March 12, 1881, 5, col. 8. Henry Theophilus Finck (1854–1926), a Harvard graduate, served as music critic for the *Nation* and the *New York Evening Post* from 1881 to 1924.

70. NYTI, March 13, 1881, 6, col. 7. Schwab reported that an identical number of players performed in the Philharmonic's concert on Dec. 10, 1881. NYTI, Dec. 11, 1881, 9, col. 1.

71. NYP, Dec. 12, 1881, 3, col. 8.

72. NYTI, Dec. 11, 1881, 9, col. 1.

to make an impression," Hassard wrote that, although the chorus and soloists had delivered a fine performance, the work itself was decidedly inferior to "A Stronghold Sure" "in learning, in beauty and in effectiveness," and had not "a tithe of [its] power."[73]

* * *

One of the most notable events in Thomas's thirty-year conducting career in New York was the May Festival of Music, which took place May 2–6, 1882, at the Seventh Regiment Armory. Schwab described the setting: "The stage is a vast amphitheatre, composed of tier upon tier of seats, rising from Mr. Thomas's stand almost to the roof of the armory. . . . [T]here are accommodations on the platform for 2,100 people, 1,800 chorus singers and 300 instrumental musicians."[74] The singers included members of the New York Chorus Society, the Brooklyn Philharmonic Chorus and five additional groups from Boston, Philadelphia, Worcester, Massachusetts, Baltimore, and Reading, Pennsylvania. Over 5,000 people attended the opening night concert.

The program opened with Thomas's arrangement of "A Stronghold Sure" (BWV 80), which was performed by 1,750 singers.[75] Finck gave a glowing account of the concert:

> The . . . choruses formed a body of sound so compact, harmonious, and reliable, that it seems almost fabulous to state that on this occasion they sang together for the first time. With the exception of a few passages, where [they] dragged a little, everything was sung with precision, correct shading, animation and brilliant effect. . . . The grand old chorale of Luther's which closes the . . . Cantata was so superbly sung that the audience broke out in prolonged and enthusiastic applause.

He observed that the performance must have made everyone eager to hear some more of Bach's cantatas, "in which inexhaustible treasures of thought and emotion are deposited."[76]

Finck pointed out that Bach himself employed vastly different performing forces: boys in place of female sopranos, and only twelve singers and eighteen instrumentalists in place of 1,800 singers and 300 instrumentalists. Nor did Bach have all the instruments which Mr. Thomas, "with much skill and taste," had added to the score. "But," he concluded confidently, "there can be no doubt as to which of these versions Bach himself would have preferred could he have heard them both."[77]

73. NYTI, April 21, 1882, 5, col. 3; NYTR, April 22, 1882, 5, col. 1.

74. NYTI, May 3, 1882, 4, col. 7.

75. The performance of Cantata 80 included only movements 1, 3, 5, 6, and 8 (both duets, nos. 2 and 7, and the soprano aria, no. 4, were omitted). NYTR, May 3, 1882, 5, col. 1.

76. NYP, May 4, 1882, 4, col. 6.

77. Ibid.

Hassard also reported that "the chorus and orchestra showed literally every good quality." The singing, like the music itself, was characterized by strength, assurance, precision, and majesty. While some people listened "with a little perplexity" to the work's opening chorus (which, Schwab noted, "suffered somewhat . . . from indecision on the part of the singers"), they "gradually yielded to [its] spell."[78]

The New York premiere of "My Spirit Was in Heaviness" (*Ich hatte viel Bekümmernis*, BWV 21), which took place ten months later (in March 1883), earned mixed critiques.[79] In Schwab's view the cantata itself was "a great addition to the répertoire." However, at least in the dress rehearsal, the recently formed Chorus Society showed occasional "timidity and uncertainty . . . which resulted in some ragged singing," and the sound of the orchestra often overwhelmed the chorus. Finck reported that the audience that attended the actual concert, though not large, was exceedingly enthusiastic: "Almost every number was warmly applauded, and several would have been encored if Mr. Thomas had shown any disposition to favor such demands." He praised the amateur New York Chorus Society for its "unity of sentiment, precision of movement, and delicate effects of shading." "The soloists," he wrote, "were quite satisfactory, and the orchestra was the Philharmonic—*i.e.*, it was as good as an orchestra can be."[80]

* * *

Henry T. Finck's glowing review of Reginald L. Poole's biography of Bach, which appeared in the July 5, 1883, issue of the *Nation*, closed with the following remarks:

> Poole's little biography of Bach . . . cannot be sufficiently recommended to all musical persons. Nothing could be better for the cause of musical culture in this country than an effort to give greater vogue to Bach's compositions. Hitherto they have been unduly neglected, although some of our musical societies have repeatedly endeavored to dispel the popular illusion that Bach is only an erudite, pedantic scribe, without any warm red blood in his veins. So far is this from being the case that repeated hearing and careful study of his works always end in making enthusiasts of the performers as well as of the audience. . . . There are Bach societies in Berlin, Hamburg, Leipzig, Königsberg, London, and other cities. . . . When shall we have the privilege of adding New York to this list?[81]

78. NYTI, May 3, 1882, 4, col. 7; NYTR, May 3, 1882, 5, col. 1.

79. Robert Franz's arrangement of the cantata was performed on this occasion. The tenor aria, "Rejoice, oh, my spirit" ("Erfreue dich, Seele," no. 10), was omitted.

80. NYTI, March 17, 1883, 4, col. 7; NYP, March 19, 1883, 4, col. 2.

81. *The Nation* 37, no. 940 (July 5, 1883): 16–18. The biography was Reginald Lane Poole, *Sebastian Bach*, Francis Hueffer's "Great Musicians" Series 7 (London: S. Low, Marston & Co.; New York: Chas. Scribner's Sons, 1882).

In an article dated the same day, Schwab cites this review and echoes many of Finck's sentiments. While professional musicians and critics had the most profound admiration for Bach's music, he observed, the public at large had not yet come to share their appreciation of the composer. He continued: "[I]t is a common error to regard Bach simply as a learned musician . . . whose works were written . . . to illustrate the metaphysical principles underlying his art [rather] than to arouse the emotions of the human soul."[82] He heartily endorsed Finck's idea of establishing a Bach society in New York and hoped that the suggestion would not be neglected.

After its initial performance of the St. Matthew Passion in March 1880, the Oratorio Society presented the work on five more occasions between 1882 and 1895. Schwab gave a glowing account of the concert that took place in March 1884 under the direction of Walter Damrosch.[83] The *Tribune* critic remarked upon both the high quality of the performance and the audience's attentiveness, which reflected the strides that had been made in recent years in "choral culture" as well as in elevating the general level of musical taste in New York. "Simple curiosity might have attracted such an audience," he wrote, "but it was something better which held it almost spell-bound for three hours, and which stirred up an enthusiasm that repeatedly broke out in applause."[84] He noted that the Oratorio Society was the first chorus in New York capable of doing justice to the great oratorios and, while the work of the chorus was uneven, it appeared to the best advantage in the chorales and the closing number.

Although progress had been made in cultivating an appreciation for Bach's music in New York by the mid-1880s, it nonetheless remained an ongoing challenge, as several reviews of a performance of the first two parts of the Christmas Oratorio in December 1884 attest.[85] Both Finck and Krehbiel commended Thomas and the Brooklyn Philharmonic for presenting the oratorio, which, Finck observed, "was a welcome substitute for the annual 'Messiah.'" "A large portion of the public," Krehbiel noted, "persists in regarding Bach as the personification of dry formations' pedantry and pure

82. NYTI, July 5, 1883, 4, col. 6.

83. NYTI, March 13, 1884, 4, col. 6. Walter Damrosch was born in Breslau in 1862 and studied composition and piano in Germany and New York. When his father began his season of German opera at the Metropolitan Opera in 1884, Walter became assistant conductor. After his father's death a year later, he continued in that position under Anton Seidl. He succeeded his father as conductor of the Oratorio and New York Symphony Societies and was active in the Oratorio Society until he resigned in 1898. He died in 1950.

84. NYTR, March 17, 1884, 5, col. 1. Both John R. G. Hassard and Henry E. Krehbiel served as music critics for the *Tribune* in 1884. As critics did not sign their reviews in the nineteenth century, the author of this article cannot be established with certainty.

85. These sections of the Christmas Oratorio were performed in an arrangement by Robert Franz.

Plate 2. Henry E. Krehbiel, on the right, with two unidentified gentlemen. Krehbiel (1854–1923) was music critic for the *New York Tribune* from 1880 to 1923. Reproduced by permission of the Music Division, New York Public Library for the Performing Arts, Astor, Lenox, and Tilden Foundations.

mathematics in music instead of what he is, the most many-sided and poetical composer that the art has yet developed."[86]

Finck adopted a more optimistic stance:

> It is a significant sign of the times that the New York Chorus Society has the names of Bach and Schumann in the motto of its programmes. . . . Hitherto Handel has been the composer of the people . . . while Bach has been the composer for musicians. But popular taste gradually, if slowly, approaches that of the leading musicians; and there is reason to hope that before another decade has passed Bach's music of the future will have become the music of the present, after waiting two centuries.

"Bach," he continued, is "full of melodious charm and a harmonic wealth that is inexhaustible." The performance of the oratorio itself was "as impressive as could have been desired," although he wished that Thomas had taken somewhat slower tempos in the chorales.[87]

Schwab gave a generally favorable account of the chorus, orchestra, and soloists. "The chorus," he wrote, "was sonorous and well balanced. Though occasionally ragged, it was generally strong and precise, . . . and the choral[e]s . . . were well sung." The "large and brilliant audience," he commented drily, "distributed its applause with some judgment and much generosity."[88]

March 21, 1885, was the bicentenary of Bach's birth, and the Brooklyn Philharmonic observed the anniversary by performing the Orchestral Suite No. 3 and the Concerto for Piano, Flute, and Violin (BWV 1044). Krehbiel took other New York performing groups to task for failing to observe the occasion, and for not doing enough to foster an appreciation for Bach's music during their regular concert seasons. While the concert was not a celebration worthy of "the greatest musician that ever lived," he wrote, it was nonetheless welcome as the only commemoration held in New York.[89]

Critics were in agreement that, of the two Bach works on the program, the Orchestral Suite had greater audience appeal than the Concerto. Finck wrote that "the gay rhythms of the [Suite's] gavotte caused a universal smile of pleasure to spread over the audience. The reception of [the piece] was so warm as to suggest the notion that we

86. NYP, Dec. 22, 1884, 2, col. 4. Krehbiel also wrote that "the singing [of the chorus] was generally prompt and hearty, on the whole vigorous rather than refined. . . . [T]here was a deal of delicacy of tone and lovely expression . . . in the chorales, . . . the congregational effect of which, however, was lost in the rapid tempo indicated by Mr. Thomas." NYTR, Dec. 21, 1884, 9, col. 1.

87. NYP, Dec. 22, 1884, 2, col. 4.

88. NYTI, Dec. 21, 1884, 8, col. 7.

89. Only the Overture, Air, and Gavottes I and II from the Suite were performed on this occasion. NYTR, March 23, 1885, 4, col. 6.

have arrived at a period in our musical culture when it will be safe to play Bach's instrumental works frequently."[90]

The concerto elicited mixed responses. In Finck's view, "like everything that Bach wrote it is fascinating and marvellously constructed, and not merely a 'show-piece,' like so many modern concertos." Krehbiel reported that "the quaint old work was delivered . . . with all the reverence that a relic of a great genius ought to inspire." Schwab opined that, while the concerto inspired "respectful attention," it was "a trifle tedious" and strictly of historic interest.[91]

In their accounts of the Oratorio Society's performances of the St. Matthew Passion in March 1888, both Henderson and Krehbiel drew attention to the considerable gap that remained between the public's appreciation for Bach and the high esteem in which the composer was held by musicians. Krehbiel noted that the Passion contained much that was still "foreign to the popular taste," but added that "Walter Damrosch could not do wiser than to perpetuate the tradition of a periodical revival of the grand old work."[92] Henderson wrote:

> To-day musicians know the power of this wonderful genius; . . . students and professors of the divine art bow their heads when Bach's name is spoken, and play him religiously year in and year out, whether the light and fickle public likes him or not. . . . No doubt many who can hear with pleasure the symphonies of Beethoven and the music dramas of Wagner wonder why musicians insist upon giving them constitutional doses of Sebastian Bach, accompanied with persistent reiteration of the assertion that this is good for them.

However, rather than asking why his music appears on programs so often, he continued, they should "wonder why so little is done in this great musical centre of the West to systematically publish the beauties of this man's works." He urged "musicians [to] continue . . . [administering] Bach as a tonic for the system of the musical public."[93]

The commentators recognized that the public did not bear sole responsibility for its reluctance to embrace Bach's music. Henderson delivered a blistering critique of the public dress rehearsal of the Passion, which took place "in the presence of a large and somnolescent audience" and was "without spirit and pitifully cold." While several of the chorales were sung "with attention to dynamic gradation and agreeable results," he reported, the dramatic choruses that called for force and color were "weak and misty," and the playing of the orchestra was intolerably slovenly.[94]

90. NYP, March 23, 1885, 2, col. 5.

91. Ibid.; NYTR, March 23, 1885, 4, col. 6; NYTI, March 21, 1885, 4, col. 5.

92. NYTR, March 9, 1888, 4, col. 6.

93. NYTI, March 8, 1888, 4, col. 7.

94. Ibid.

Plate 3. William James Henderson (1855–1937) served as music critic for the *New York Times* from 1887 to 1902, and for the *New York Sun* from 1902 to 1937. Reproduced by permission of the Music Division, New York Public Library for the Performing Arts, Astor, Lenox, and Tilden Foundations.

The critics agreed that, though far from perfect, the soloists were more satisfactory than the chorus or the orchestra. However Henderson noted that the baritone and bass, both German, had difficulty pronouncing the English words. The tenor "sang with a pleasant quality of voice and with accurate intonation," he reported, "but with no more expression than a hand organ." The work of the soprano was extremely irregular: sometimes "more than tolerable," and at other times "too bad for description." "Such presentations," he observed bluntly, "will not spread the gospel of Bach."[95]

After hearing the performance that took place the next day, Finck wrote:

> If the taste for good music were as well developed in this country as the liking for the theatre or for literature, it would be possible to give this work once a week throughout the season. It would have to be better interpreted, however, than it was last

95. Ibid.

> evening. . . . Several numbers were entirely spoiled by a confusion among the performers, and the whole work was sadly deficient in shading. It was not customary in Bach's day to indicate dynamic marks of expression in the score . . . but they exist in the spirit of the music all the same. . . . Mr. Damrosch, however, allowed his forces to sing and play in a mezzoforte almost all the time, ignoring even those fortes, pianos, and sforzandos which are marked, and on which the life of the music depends. . . . In the chorales, on the other hand, shading was introduced, and the result was that the chorales received almost the only spontaneous applause of the evening.[96]

Krehbiel gave the performance a mixed review. He echoed many of his colleagues' views and also pointed out that the soloists were not well versed in baroque performance style. While the soprano and alto soloists sang with "painstaking fidelity to the printed page, and there was much beauty in their tones," he commented, "they disclosed unfamiliarity with the style demanded by the music."[97]

* * *

Krehbiel's account of the Symphony Society's performance of the First Brandenburg Concerto in November 1888 reflects a nascent awareness of historical performance practice. He pointed out the inherent difficulties of performing with a modern orchestra works that had been composed for a much smaller ensemble, and urged conductors not to ignore the evidence of their own ears when performing the works of Bach and Handel. On this occasion, he wrote: "[A] better effect would have been attained . . . if the gross disproportion in sound between the band and the violin obbligato . . . had been lessened by the reduction of the orchestra. . . . We ought to hear the same balance of tone that the old composer imagined." Finck agreed that "the parts [were] overladen, and the playing deficient in relief and clear definition, so as to be even confused, and certainly misleading to any who do not know the effect of this music rightly given."[98]

Finck later reported that the large audience that attended the Oratorio Society's performance of the St. Matthew Passion in March 1892 "bore witness to the fact that Bach [was] at last meeting with some of the recognition he [deserved]." Nearly always more generous in his assessments of concerts than his colleagues, he added,

> [T]he performance . . . was on the whole the best that has ever been given under Mr. Damrosch's baton. The chorales were superbly sung with delicious tone and excellent shading. The more elaborate choruses offered difficulties which were not always so smoothly overcome, although the execution as a rule was good, and a fine sonority was attained, especially in the first chorus, where a beautiful tone-color was added

96. NYP, March 9, 1888, 7, col. 1.

97. NYTR, March 9, 1888, 4, col. 6.

98. NYTR, Nov. 4, 1888, 7, col. 2; NYP, Nov. 5, 1888, 7, col. 2.

> by a boy choir of one hundred. Some fine effects were missed by Mr. Damrosch's neglect of the art of broadening out at a climax—combining a ritardando with a crescendo. The soloists were well chosen and most of them did justice to their parts.[99]

In Krehbiel's opinion, by contrast, the Society had sunk into a "rut of mediocrity." While it sang the chorales well—though sometimes "with a languishing sentimentality"—the choruses "were sung languidly and without . . . expressiveness." The quality of the soloists, on the other hand, was exceptionally high.[100]

* * *

In 1893 Frank Damrosch founded the Musical Art Society, a professional chorus with about fifty-five members, to present the finest choral music with a special emphasis on *a cappella* repertory and contemporary choral works.[101] In its first seven seasons the Society presented at least four works by Bach (see table 6).

The group's inaugural concert, which took place in March 1894 and included a performance of Bach's motet, "Sing Ye to the Lord," earned favorable reviews. Krehbiel wrote that the group filled a conspicuous gap in the New York musical scene. He acknowledged that the concert had a few weak points—in particular he wished that "Damrosch had been a little more temperate in his tempo" in the performance of the motet. The work also seemed to call for a fuller sound but, he added, "that is always the case with [Bach]."[102]

Table 6. Works by Bach Performed by the Musical Art Society, 1894–1900

Date	*Work*
Mar. 3, 1894	Motet No. 4 "Sing Ye to the Lord" (*Singet dem Herrn*, BWV 225)
Dec. 17, 1896	Brandenburg Concerto No. 6 in B-flat Major (BWV 1051)
Dec. 8, 1898	Christmas Oratorio, Part II (BWV 248/II)
Mar. 15, 1900	"Ode of Mourning" (*Trauerode*, BWV 198)

99. NYP, March 4, 1892, 6, col. 1.

100. NYTR, March 4, 1892, 6, col. 6.

101. Frank Damrosch was born in Breslau, Germany, in 1859 and moved to New York with his family in 1871. He served as chorus master at the Metropolitan Opera from 1885 to 1892. In 1893 he founded the Musical Art Society of New York. A year later he established the People's Choral Union, with a primarily working-class membership of 500. In 1898 he succeeded his brother Walter as conductor of the Oratorio Society which their father had founded. He died in 1937.

102. NYTR, March 4, 1894, 4, col. 3; NYTR, March 5, 1894, 7, col. 1. William Henderson, the *Times* critic, reported that the chorus consisted of some of the finest solo talent in New York and comprised sixteen sopranos, fifteen altos, twelve tenors, and twelve basses. NYTI, March 4, 1894, 3, col. 3.

The remarks that follow reveal volumes about what constituted an ideal "Bach sound" at the end of the nineteenth century: "His is the voice of universal humanity, and no matter how great the amplitude of sound there always seems to be room for a more sonorous proclamation. In his instrumental no less than in his vocal works the voice of Bach is as the voice of a great multitude . . . saying, 'Alleluia, for the Lord God Omnipotent reigneth!'"[103]

Both Henderson and Krehbiel panned the Oratorio Society's performances of the St. Matthew Passion in April 1895. Krehbiel went so far as to write that, unless the piece was performed "with a more enthusiastic and reverent spirit and a more serious determination to sound the full depths of Bach's music," it would be better not to perform it at all. The quality of the group fell short of the high standard it had attained in former years, and their singing failed to convey the "majesty, the pathos and the thrilling power of the work."[104] Henderson also reported that the performance evidenced "a plentiful lack of rehearsal," and that none of the soloists was equal to the considerable challenges posed by the work:

> Mrs. Bishop [the soprano soloist] sang all of her music with an abundance of open, pallid tones, without accuracy of intonation, and with a style which for inflexibility and general rawness could hardly be surpassed. Mrs. Alves [the contralto soloist] . . . has fallen to forcing her lower tones unmercifully and indulging in a most exaggerated vibrato. . . . [The] tone production [of Mr. Thies, the Evangelist] was not a model of method, and his treatment of some of his consonants . . . was original and not charming. His phrasing in the air "With Jesus I Will Watch" was governed not by musical taste, but by the capacity of his lungs, which was generally exhausted in the most unexpected places. Mr. Beresford sang . . . in a cumbersome style.[105]

The Musical Art Society's performance of the Sixth Brandenburg Concerto in December 1896 represented a pioneering effort to perform a work by Bach on the instruments for which it was originally written in a "historically informed" way.[106] Commentators drew particular attention to the novelty of employing viole da gamba, which Finck described as "a sort of mongrel of half-viola half-'cello parentage, a miniature 'cello, or an overgrown viola held between the knees." In an article that appeared several days before the concert took place, Krehbiel pointed out that the instrument's characteristically "soft and nasal tone" was essential to the performance because "the

103. NYTR, March 5, 1894, 7, col. 1.

104. NYTR, April 13, 1895, 7, col. 2.

105. NYTI, April 14, 1895, 4, col. 7.

106. The performance of Bach's Brandenburg Concerto No. 6 marked a departure from the group's usual (choral) repertory.

concerto can not be heard as Bach and his contemporaries heard it unless the instruments are used."[107] His choice of words reflects the distance that had been traveled in the preceding decades with regard to performance practice. Rather than arranging baroque works for modern instruments and ensembles—the approach taken earlier in the century—musicians at the end of the nineteenth century attempted to recreate the sounds that Bach and the listeners of his time might have heard.

Morris Steinert of New Haven, Connecticut, helped the Society "make the concerto sound as it sounded in the music room of the Margrave of Brandenburg 175 years ago," by loaning the group five viole da gamba from his collection.[108] In addition to these instruments, the orchestra comprised twelve violas, three cellos, and two double basses. Given the imbalance of instruments, it is hardly surprising to read in Finck's account of the performance that "the viole da gamba were overbalanced by the violas, 'cellos, and basses, so that one could get an idea of their tone color only in a very vague way. . . . [T]he viola color was so much louder than the viola da gamba that the archaic effect was lost."[109]

In his review of the concert, Krehbiel highlighted another problematic aspect of performance practice, namely whether the continuo part should be played on an organ or harpsichord: "In the slow movement . . . the harmonies were filled out on the organ. . . . Historical correctness would have been subserved better, perhaps, had this been done on a harpsichord. . . . [However] the organ would have served nicely had not Mr. Carl made it altogether too prominent."[110]

Henderson gave a favorable account of a performance of the second part of the Christmas Oratorio in December 1898, in which the Musical Art Society was joined by the People's Choral Union. Members of the Musical Society who were on the stage of Carnegie Hall performed the solos, and the contralto aria was sung by all the contraltos in unison. The 900 members of the People's Choral Union who were seated in the hall's uppermost gallery were commended for their singing of the chorales.[111]

A performance of Bach's "Ode of Mourning" (BWV 198) in March 1900, in which the same two groups again joined forces, earned mostly favorable reviews. However, in Henderson's opinion,

107. NYP, Dec. 18, 1896, 7, col. 1; NYTR, Dec. 13, 1896, 3, col. 1.

108. Three of the gambas had four strings, Krehbiel reported, and two had six. One was of Italian make and attributed to Maggini, one of Spanish, one of English (Barak Norman, 1688–1740), and two of German (from Munich and Ulm); there was also a violoncello piccolo. NYTR, Dec. 13, 1896, 3, col. 1.

109. NYP, Dec. 18, 1896, 7, col. 1.

110. NYTR, Dec. 18, 1896, 6, col. 6.

111. NYTI, Dec. 9, 1898, 6, col. 7.

> the "Trauer Ode" would have made a deeper impression on the hearers if Mr. Damrosch had seen fit to vary his tempi a little. But it is the general fault of Bach performances here that the works are read through with a rigidity of style which is supposed to be in accordance with the genius of Bach. Dynamic shading, indeed, there was in Mr. Damrosch's reading, but something more might have been done with the movement.

He praised the continuo playing of the organist and commended Damrosch for using "the piano to accentuate the strokes of the bell, thus taking advantage of modern means to produce in its fullness an effect plainly in the mind of Bach when he wrote the continuo."[112]

* * *

An indication of the increased interest in performing Bach's choral works was the founding in the fall of 1899 of the Bach Singers of New York, the first choral group in the city devoted exclusively to Bach's music. The group was formed by Theodore Björksten and was composed of approximately twenty professional solo singers; instrumentalists were engaged on an ad hoc basis. Its formation was particularly opportune, Henderson observed, given the "daily multiplying" signs that a Bach revival was currently under way in New York. In his review of the Bach Singers' first concert Henderson noted that, while the Musical Art Society had done much toward familiarizing the public with the music of the older masters, until now New York had not had a society devoted wholly to performing the works of Bach.[113]

The group's first concert took place in February 1900 and featured the following selections:

1. Excerpts from *Jesu, nun sei gepreiset* (BWV 41),
2. The echo aria (movement 5) from "Hercules in Indecision" (*Hercules auf dem Scheidewege*, BWV 213),
3. An orchestral transcription, by Herman Hans Wetzler, of the Organ Sonata in E-flat Major (BWV 525),
4. *Bleib bei uns* (BWV 6),
5. The Sanctus in D Major (BWV 238),
6. The soprano aria (movement 8) from *Von der Vergnügsamkeit* (also known as *Ich bin in mir vergnügt*, BWV 204), and
7. *Tönet, ihr Pauken!* (BWV 214).[114]

Critics were generally supportive of the group's first effort. Finck commented that

112. NYTI, March 16, 1900, 6, col. 7.

113. NYTI, Sept. 24, 1899, 20, col. 3, and Feb. 14, 1900, 7, col. 3.

114. NYTR, Feb. 4, 1900, 8, col. 1.

> for a lover of what is best in music, [Bach's church cantatas] constitute a veritable Klondike [a rich site of gold deposits in northwestern Canada]. It takes enthusiasm, daring, and hard work to get at these treasures . . . and every pioneer deserves the most cordial encouragement. . . . Mr. Björksten's choir of twenty singers . . . acquitted itself creditably of its task on the whole—a task often of incredible difficulty.

He also noted that the concert had attracted "a good-sized audience" and that there was "abundant applause."[115]

Henderson observed that, while the chorus was small and not yet well trained, its efforts were at least earnest and deserving of encouragement. Although the performance was by no means flawless, the choruses in *Jesu, nun sei gepreiset* and the soprano aria from *Von der Vergnügsamkeit* were enjoyable. "The Sanctus pleased the audience so much that it had to be repeated, a compliment not often paid to music of this character," he noted. The orchestra, on the other hand, "was not brilliant in any respect."[116]

Both Finck and Henderson voiced the concern that devoting an entire concert to the music of Bach might be too much of one thing. Finck wrote, "The chief drawback was the length of the concert. Two hours of novelties—even though those novelties be a century and a half old—prove too much of a strain on the average listener."[117]

Wetzler's orchestral transcription of the Organ Sonata in E-flat Major earned mixed reviews. Finck observed that while "one may question the propriety of such an arrangement at a special Bach concert, . . . it must be conceded that Mr. Wetzler did his work well, and entirely in the spirit of Bach, who would have doubtless joined the audience in its extremely cordial applause. The last movement was played with such animation that Mr. Wetzler had to repeat it."[118] Henderson, on the other hand, criticized the transcription and wondered why Wetzler had bothered to orchestrate it. "Perhaps," he conjectured sarcastically, "he thought that Bach did not know enough to do so."[119]

Henderson provided information about the specific instruments that were employed in the concert as well as the capabilities of the players. After noting that the trumpets played out of tune in the first cantata, he pointed out that "they were not trumpets, but cornets. We have no trumpeters who can play these trumpet parts. The soprano aria, with its lovely accompaniment of oboes and oboe d'amore—the latter represented

115. NYP, Feb. 14, 1900, 7, col. 4.

116. NYTI, Feb. 14, 1900, 7, col. 3.

117. NYP, Feb. 14, 1900, 7, col. 4.

118. Ibid.

119. NYTI, Feb. 14, 1900, 7, col. 3. "This work," Henderson wrote disparagingly in a review published four days later, "was quite the opposite of the domestic cat, in that it was both harmful and unnecessary." NYTI, Feb. 18, 1900, 18, col. 2.

by an English horn—was heard with pleasure." In a follow-up article that appeared four days later, he wrote at greater length about the issue of historical performance practice, observing that, although the Bach Singers apparently intended to present Bach's compositions "in a manner as near to that of the time of the composer as possible," there did not seem to be a consensus regarding just what that was. However he did concede that the authorities were undecided on this subject. He noted that "even the great work of Dr. Spitta does not altogether clear up the matter."[120]

The proportion of instrumentalists to singers was in keeping with performing conditions in Bach's day, Henderson reported.[121] However, on this occasion, the playing left much to be desired: the horns were "obstreperous" and the trumpets were "wretchedly played." Furthermore, Wetzler's inept treatment of the organ continuo part revealed volumes about his lack of familiarity with the traditions of Bach; it was hardly surprising that he had made an orchestral transcription of an organ sonata.

Although Henderson remained supportive of the existence of a society devoted to performing Bach's music, he observed drily that "the singing of the Bach Singers will stand a good deal of improvement." In addition,

> every one concerned in this laudable enterprise will find it necessary to devote much time to the study of the authoritative writers on the subject of Bach and the music of his day. There are many problems to be settled, and while it is not likely that the new society will settle them, it must decide for itself what line it will pursue when it approaches the debatable ground.[122]

At their second concert, which took place ten weeks later, the Bach Singers presented

1. Excerpts from *O Ewigkeit, du Donnerwort* (BWV 60),
2. The Sanctus in D Major (BWV 238),
3. The first movement of *Weinen, Klagen, Sorgen, Zagen* (BWV 12),
4. The "Coffee Cantata" (*Schweigt stille, plaudert nicht*, BWV 211), and
5. The aria with chorus (movement 6) from *Halt im Gedächtnis Jesum Christ* (BWV 67).

120. NYTI, Feb. 14, 1900, 7, col. 3, and Feb. 18, 1900, 18, col. 2.

121. "The choir of the Thomas Church, in which the cantatas for New Year's were performed, was a small one, while instrumental players were plenty. . . . In Bach's time the orchestra usually outnumbered the singers by at least a third. We are told that in the Neue Kirche under Gerlach there were only four singers and ten instrumentalists. And Spitta records that Bach, in his memorial of Aug. 23, 1730, fixed the number of singers at twelve and that of the orchestra and organist at eighteen." This lengthy description of performing conditions in Bach's day attests to the increase in knowledge since the publication of Spitta's book, as well as the continued growth in interest in historical performance practice. NYTI, Feb. 18, 1900, 18, col. 2.

122. Ibid.

According to the reviews, the audience thoroughly enjoyed the performance of the humorous "Coffee Cantata" but found the other cantatas to be less accessible. The concert earned mixed critiques. Finck wrote that Björksten had opened up a new source of enjoyment to music lovers and pointed out that, until recently, the hundreds of Bach cantatas had been sealed books to concert-goers, partly because of their difficulty. These cantatas, he continued, though written in the eighteenth century, were largely novelties, many having only recently been printed for the first time in the edition of Bach's complete works. The performance generated "an amount of applause which would astonish those who fancy that Bach is for dry intellectual contemplation only." The Sanctus, which had been performed at the first concert, was repeated by request and was again sung "with remarkable choral virtuosity." The chorus was heard to particular advantage in the chorales. The bass soloist, Mr. Bispham, "simply covered himself with glory"; he was in splendid voice, and sang with intelligent enthusiasm. It was altogether an enjoyable concert, Finck wrote, and boded well for the society's future. In Henderson's estimation, the group's second concert was much better than the first, and he commended the ensemble for the progress it had made.[123]

Krehbiel, on the other hand, found the quality of the concert to be so mediocre that he doubted whether their programs would advance the cause of Bach's music. In his view, "the singing of the choir was decidedly rude, and as far as tempi are concerned we confess that Mr. Björksten is incomprehensible. Hornpipes and double shuffles in the midst of such solemn music as that of the church cantatas and masses by the old Leipsic cantor are inconceivable things, yet these are what Mr. Björksten seems to be trying to exploit."[124]

* * *

The Oratorio Society gave the first New York performance of Bach's Mass in B Minor on April 5, 1900, nine days after the work received its American premiere in Bethlehem, Pennsylvania.[125] The significance of these first two American performances of the Mass was not lost on contemporary commentators.[126] Several days beforehand,

123. NYP, April 27, 1900, 7, col. 2; NYTI, April 27, 1900, 9, col. 2.

124. NYTR, April 27, 1900, 6, col. 5.

125. The "Gratias agimus tibi" in the Gloria and everything after the Sanctus ("Osanna," "Benedictus," "Agnus Dei," and "Dona nobis pacem") were not performed on this occasion in the New York performance. Six choruses and five solo numbers from the B Minor Mass were performed on May 19, 1886, at the May Festival in Cincinnati, with Theodore Thomas conducting. Six choruses and six solos were performed by the Handel and Haydn Society in Boston on Feb. 27, 1887. The entire work received its first American performance on March 27, 1900, in Bethlehem, Pennsylvania. See H. Earle Johnson, *First Performances in America* (Detroit: Information Coordinators, 1979), 18–19.

126. Articles about the forthcoming performances appeared in the *Tribune* on March 18, 1900, pt. 3, 8, col. 2, and in the *Times* on March 25, 1900, 18, col. 5.

Henderson eloquently explained why the upcoming performance would be such a notable event:

> Ever since the revival of interest in Bach's music under the lead of Schumann and Mendelssohn, about seventy years ago, this mass has held an almost unique place in the estimation of musical authorities as one of the greatest and most profound—also as one of the most difficult—choral works ever written. It marks the summit of Bach's achievement in this field. . . . [I]f all the other music of the master should be lost, this mass alone would reveal all the characteristic qualities of his art and give a true idea of his matchless strength and the depth of his musical inspiration.[127]

Henderson noted that the musicians were approaching the music with a new awareness of historical performance practice:

> To heighten the effectiveness of the performance and to obtain the characteristic effects aimed at by Bach in his orchestral accompaniments, Mr. Damrosch has made up his orchestra in accordance with the tonal balance usual in Bach's day, differing from that of modern times chiefly in the greater prominence given to the wood wind, and in the use of the oboe d'amore.

Damrosch had procured two oboes d'amore from Germany for the occasion and assigned two oboists to learn how to play them. Henderson enumerated the instruments that were employed in the performance: twelve first violins, ten second violins, eight violas, four cellos, five double basses, four flutes, four oboes, two oboes d'amore, two bassoons, three trumpets in D, one solo horn, tympani, and organ. "Special care has been taken with the trumpet parts," he noted, for they "are so high as to be extremely difficult for modern players." He also informed his readers which movements would be omitted at the forthcoming performance.[128]

The concert took place in Carnegie Hall, which was filled to capacity. Henderson observed that both the size and attentiveness of the audience attested to the progress that had been made in raising the musical taste of the public.[129] Many members of the audience brought along scores, which they followed as they listened to the piece. Some of the more rousing sections of the Mass, such as "Cum Sancto Spiritu," were met with enthusiastic applause.

While the performance had "many striking merits," Henderson wrote, the overall quality was uneven. On the whole, the chorus deserved the warm reception the audience gave it, but the contributions of the soloists and orchestra were less satisfactory. Three of the four soloists were found wanting in terms of tone quality, phrasing, and

127. NYTI, April 1, 1900, 20, col. 3.

128. Ibid.; NYTI, March 25, 1900, 18, col. 5, and April 1, 1900, 20, col. 3.

129. NYTI, April 6, 1900, 2, col. 5.

intonation. The orchestra was "ragged . . . and also left much to be desired in the matter of intonation. . . . The horn obbligato was well played, but the trumpets were only fairly successful in their formidable task. The solo violin was poor in tone and not at all distinguished in style." Nonetheless, he concluded, the Oratorio Society deserved "praise for going so far toward impressive achievement."[130]

Krehbiel rendered a more generous appraisal of the concert, observing that the last choral concert in New York of comparable importance was the Society's first performance, twenty years earlier, of the St. Matthew Passion under the direction of Frank Damrosch's father, Leopold. The chorus, he reported, had not only mastered the difficult music, but sang with confidence, spirit, and expressivity. He, too, was unimpressed by three of the soloists, but pointed out that the music placed demands on them that lay outside the scope of current vocal training. He concluded that, if performances of Bach's music were to continue, soloists would have to receive training in the appropriate style of singing.[131]

Finck wrote that, while the performance was not great or inspiring, it had many merits. The choruses were sung with precision and a good body of tone, but the men were outnumbered by the women. In the orchestra Damrosch endeavored with success to restore the tonal conditions of Bach's time, but unfortunately he had insufficient control of his players, and "they did some very queer things." Overall, the weakness of the performance lay in the monotony of conception and the lack of expression. In Finck's opinion,

> the choral works [of Bach] still await a master mind to reveal their full eloquence. The difficulty [of interpreting them] is increased by the fact that even such inadequate expression marks as we have today were not in use in Bach's day. One of the accepted traditions is that every Bach chorus must end with a combined crescendo and ritardando. Bülow has protested against this notion, yet as a rule it holds good, and by the use of this simple method Mr. Damrosch secured some pompous effects last night which aroused the enthusiastic applause of a large audience.[132]

In a letter to the editor of the *Times* published in November 1900, "an unprofessional music critic" conveyed his impressions of the Oratorio Society's performance of the Mass that had taken place several days earlier. In general, he wrote, "the performance was exhilarating, impressive, and whole souled," but there were some short-

130. NYTI, April 6, 1900, 2, col. 5. Krehbiel also reported that the tone quality, phrasing, and intonation of the bass was superior to that of the other three vocal soloists. NYTR, April 6, 1900, 7, col. 1.

131. NYTR, April 6, 1900, 7, col. 1. Krehbiel also wrote: "If we are to have a Bach cult we should study the Bach style in solo singing, which is much further from the modern manner rooted in the drama than our singers suspect."

132. NYP, April 6, 1900, 7, col. 5.

comings. First, as the women in the chorus outnumbered the men by about two to one, the women's voices overpowered those of the men. The tone quality of the tenors was sometimes thin and reedy. He faulted Frank Damrosch for taking brisk tempos and complained, "Why must we always hear quick choral movements of the eighteenth century taken at such a pace that their abounding coloratura passages are blurred or mutilated?" In his view, the organ droned too much, and the vocal soloists failed to grasp the solemnity of their numbers. Their "hateful and amateurish vibrato" caricatured "the venerable words of the mass and the wonderful music of Bach." Though the solos "would make admirable love songs, . . . that is no reason why they should be sung like drawing room ballads."[133]

Conclusion

By the end of the nineteenth century, under the leadership of Theodore Thomas, Leopold Damrosch, and Damrosch's sons, Frank and Walter, Bach's music had attained an enduring place in the concert life of New York. Despite resistance on the part of audiences, these musicians persevered in including Bach's works on their programs and gradually succeeded in winning a devoted—if not sizable—following for his music.

Credit is also due to nineteenth-century music critics for this development. While mid-century commentators were often no more able to grasp Bach's archaic style than the public at large, their successors—John R. G. Hassard, Frederick A. Schwab, Henry E. Krehbiel, Henry T. Finck, and William J. Henderson—were more sophisticated and better informed about Bach's music. They were passionate and eloquent advocates of his compositions and generally lent their support to the various individuals and groups who performed them.

Over the course of the latter half of the nineteenth century, a widening gap between critics' appreciation for Bach and the general public's reluctance to embrace his music is apparent. Commentators repeatedly urged their readers to adopt a more receptive attitude to Bach's music and played an important role in educating the public about details of his compositions and aspects of historical performance practice.

Between 1855 and 1900, as this article has chronicled, not only did the repertory of Bach's works that were performed expand from a small number of chamber pieces to include orchestral and choral works, but attitudes toward Bach's music also underwent a considerable change. A significant trend was a growing awareness of historical performance practice on the part of musicians and critics. Armed with Spitta's pioneering study of Bach, by 1880 conductors were in a position to make historically informed choices as they approached the performance of Bach's music. By the close of the nine-

133. Letter to the Editor, NYTI, Nov. 27, 1900, 8, col. 6.

teenth century many performers attempted to present Bach's works with the size of ensemble and on the instruments for which they were intended.

Despite the progress that was made in broadening the scope of the repertory that was performed, and in the approach to performance practice and matters of style, Bach's music was still not widely appreciated at the end of the nineteenth century. This is attributable to three principal factors: the public's inability to shed its preconceptions of Bach's music as more likely to engage the intellect than appeal to the emotions; heavy orchestral renditions of complex works that obscured Bach's original intentions (half of all the instrumental pieces by Bach that were presented in New York during the nineteenth century were performed as orchestral transcriptions); and technical and stylistic shortcomings on the part of players and singers.

Spitta's biography of Bach provided a wealth of new information about the performing conditions of his day. However, even when conductors were committed to employing the instruments that Bach intended, violas da gamba, oboes d'amore, and the like were not readily available, and they had to go to great lengths to procure them. An even greater challenge lay in training performers on these instruments; commentators reported that nineteenth-century trumpet players were simply not able to play Bach's exceedingly high trumpet parts. In addition to mastering the technical difficulties of the music, musicians had to be instructed in performing traditions that had lapsed since the middle of the eighteenth century.

While only a small percentage of Bach's works were heard in New York in the second half of the nineteenth century, these performances laid the groundwork for the more comprehensive Bach revival that occurred in the twentieth century. Many issues that late nineteenth-century performers of Bach's music wrestled with—such as the balance between singers and players, or the difficulty of recreating eighteenth-century performing styles and traditions—are still being debated by performers and critics over a century later.

APPENDIX

Works by J. S. Bach Performed on Chamber, Symphonic, and Choral Programs in New York City, 1855–1900

No.	*Date*	*BWV No.*	*Work*[a]	*Performers*
1	Dec. 18, 1855	846	*Méditation sur le Premier Prélude de Piano de S. Bach* (arr. for violin, cello, and piano by Charles Gounod)	Mason & Bergmann's Musical Matinées; Theodore Thomas, Carl Bergmann, William Mason
2	Feb. 26, 1856	1063	Concerto in D Minor for Three Pianos (AmPr)	Mason & Bergmann's Musical Matinées; William Scharfenberg, Henry C. Timm, and William Mason, Bergmann, Thomas, Mosenthal, Matzka, and Preusser
3	Apr. 10, 1858	1063	Concerto in D Minor for Three Pianos	Mason & Thomas' Classical Matinées; Scharfenberg, Timm, and Mason, Thomas, Mosenthal, Matzka, Bergmann, and Preusser
4	Apr. 17, 1858	1004/5	Chaconne in D Minor (with piano accomp. by Mendelssohn)	Mason & Thomas' Classical Matinées; Theodore Thomas, violin, and William Mason, piano
5	Nov. 23, 1858	1004/5	Chaconne in D Minor (with piano accomp. by Schumann)	Mason & Thomas' Classical Matinées; Theodore Thomas, violin; pianist unknown
6	Apr. 14, 1860	1004/5	Chaconne in D Minor (with piano accomp.)	Mason & Thomas' Classical Soirées; Theodore Thomas, violin; pianist unknown
7	Mar. 24, 1863	1016	Sonata No. 3 in E Major for Violin and Piano	William Mason and Theodore Thomas' Soirées of Chamber Music
8	Apr. 21, 1863	1061	Concerto in C Major for Two Pianos (AmPr)	William Mason and Theodore Thomas' Soirées of Chamber Music; Henry C. Timm and William Mason
9	Mar. 8, 1864	1018	Sonata No. 5 in F Minor for Violin and Piano	Mason & Thomas' Soirées of Chamber Music; Theodore Thomas and William Mason
10	Jan. 7, 1865	540	Toccata in F Major (orch. transcr. by Heinrich Esser) (AmPr)	Thomas' Symphony Soirées; "a grand orchestra of sixty"

Appendix (*continued*)

No.	*Date*	*BWV No.*	*Work*[a]	*Performers*
11	Apr. 8, 1865	582	Passacaglia in C Minor for Organ (orch. transcr. by Heinrich Esser) (AmPr)	Thomas' Symphonic Soirées
12	1865	37	"Who Believed, and is Baptized" (*Wer da gläubet und getauft wird*) (AmPr)	New-York Harmonic Society
13	Oct. 26, 1867	1068	Suite No. 3 in D Major (AmPr)	Thomas' Symphony Soirées
14	Mar. 13, 1869	ANH.159	8-part motet, "I Wrestle and Pray" (*Ich lasse dich nicht, du segnest mich denn*) (AmPr)	Thomas' Orchestra, Choral Society, Mendelssohn Union
15	Aug. 10, 1871	248/II/10	Sinfonia from the Christmas Oratorio	Thomas' Orchestra
16	Aug. 15, 1872	248/II/10	Sinfonia from the Christmas Oratorio	Thomas' Orchestra
17	Apr. 25, 1873	1063	Concerto in D Minor for Three Pianos	Anton Rubinstein, Sebastian Bach Mills, William Mason, pianos; strings of Thomas' Orchestra
18	Apr. 26, 1873	1068	Suite No. 3 in D Major	Thomas' Orchestra ("increased to 100 Performers for this occasion")
19	June 5, 1873	1068	Air and Gavotte [from Suite No. 3 in D Major]	Thomas' Orchestra
20	Aug. 28, 1873	582	Passacaglia in C Minor for Organ (orch. transcr. by Heinrich Esser)	Thomas' Orchestra
21	Nov. 22, 1873	244/42	"Give Me Back My Dearest Master" ("Gebt mir meinen Jesum wieder") from the St. Matthew Passion	Thomas' Orchestra; Myron W. Whitney, bass
22	Dec. 3, 1873	188/6	Chorale: "In God in Whom I trust" (*Auf meinen lieben Gott trau ich in Angst und Not*)	Oratorio Society, Leopold Damrosch, cond.
23	Dec. 3, 1873	1068	Air on the G String from Suite No. 3 in D Major	Oratorio Society concert, Leopold Damrosch, cond.
24	Feb. 26, 1874	386	Chorale: "Now to the Eternal God" (prob. *Nun danket alle Gott*)	Oratorio Society, Leopold Damrosch, cond.
25	Feb. 26, 1874	244/39	"Have Mercy upon Me" ("Erbarme dich, mein Gott") from the St. Matthew Passion	Oratorio Society, Leopold Damrosch, cond.; Ida Karfunkel, contralto
26	Feb. 28, 1874	1048	Brandenburg Concerto No. 3 (AmPr)	Thomas' Orchestra

Appendix (*continued*)

No.	*Date*	*BWV No.*	*Work*[a]	*Performers*
27	Apr. 25, 1874	244/39	"O, pardon me, my God" ("Erbarme dich, mein Gott") from the St. Matthew Passion	Thomas' Orchestra; Adelaide Phillipps, contralto
28	June 11, 1874	248/II/10	Sinfonia from the Christmas Oratorio	Thomas' Orchestra
29	June 18, 1874	unknown organ work	Prelude and Fugue [orch. transcr.]	Thomas' Orchestra
30	Nov. 28, 1874	1067	Suite No. 2 in B Minor 1. Grave–Fugue 2. Sarabande 3. Polonaise et Double 4. Badinerie (NYPr)	Thomas' Orchestra
31	Dec. 12, 1874	1004/5	Chaconne in D Minor (orch. transcr. by Joachim Raff) (AmPr)	Philharmonic Society ("100 Performers"), Carl Bergmann, cond.
32	Dec. 19, 1874	1004/5	Chaconne in D Minor (orch. transcr. by Joachim Raff)	Thomas' Orchestra
33	Jan. 16, 1875	1067	Suite No. 2 in B Minor	Brooklyn Philharmonic, Theodore Thomas, cond.
34	Jan. 18, 1875	1004/5	Chaconne (orch. transcr. by Joachim Raff)	Thomas' Orchestra
35	Feb. 6, 1875	1043	Concerto in D Minor for Two Violins (NYPr)	Thomas' Orchestra; S. E. Jacobsohn and Richard Arnold, soloists
36	Mar. 13, 1875	1004/5	Chaconne (orch. transcr. by Joachim Raff)	Brooklyn Philharmonic, Theodore Thomas, cond.
37	May 27, 1875	unknown organ work	Prelude [orch. transcr.]	Thomas' Orchestra
38	July 1, 1875	1004/5	Chaconne [orch. transcr.]	Thomas' Orchestra
39	July 8, 1875	unknown organ work	Prelude, Chorale, and Fugue [orch. transcr.]	Thomas' Orchestra
40	July 22, 1875	582	Passacaglia in C Minor for Organ (orch. transcr. by Heinrich Esser)	Thomas' Orchestra
41	Sept. 16, 1875	1068	Suite No. 3 in D Major	Thomas' Orchestra
42	Nov. 13, 1875	248/II/10	Sinfonia from the Christmas Oratorio	Thomas' Orchestra
43	Nov. 13, 1875	248/II/19	"Cradle Song" ("Schlafe, mein Liebster") from the Christmas Oratorio	Thomas' Orchestra; Antoinette Sterling, contralto
44	Dec. 27, 1875	971	Italian Concerto	Concert organized by Hans von Bülow; von Bülow, soloist

Appendix (*continued*)

No.	*Date*	BWV *No.*	*Work*[a]	*Performers*
45	Dec. 27, 1875	1061	Concerto in C Major for Two Pianos	Concert organized by Hans von Bülow; von Bülow and Richard Hoffman, soloists
46	Dec. 27, 1875	1063	Concerto in D Minor for Three Pianos	Concert organized by Hans von Bülow; von Bülow, Richard Hoffman, and Marion Brown, soloists
47	Dec. 27, 1875	1065	Concerto in A Minor for Four Pianos (AmPr)	Concert organized by Hans von Bülow; von Bülow, Richard Hoffman, Marion Brown, Mrs. Charles B. Foote, soloists
48	Mar. 25, 1876	1066	Suite No. 1 in C Major 1. Overture 2. Forlano 3. Bourrée 4. Passepied (AmPr)	Thomas' Orchestra
49	Feb. 1, 1877	1068	Suite No. 3 in D Major	Thomas' Orchestra
50	Mar. 15, 1877	106	"God's Time is the Best" (*Gottes Zeit ist die allerbeste Zeit*) (arr. by Robert Franz) (AmPr)	Oratorio Society, Philharmonic Orchestra, Leopold Damrosch, cond.
51	Apr. 14, 1877	1068	Suite No. 3 in D Major	Brooklyn Philharmonic, Theodore Thomas, cond.
52	May 19, 1877	1063	Concerto in D Minor for Three Pianos	William Mason, Anna Essipoff, and Frederick Boscovitz, soloists
53	Jan. 5, 1878	1063	Concerto in D Minor for Three Pianos	Thomas' Orchestra; Richard Hofmann, William Mason, and Ferdinand Dulcken, soloists; ("Eighty-five Performers")
54	Jan. 12, 1878	1052	Concerto No. 1 in D Minor for Clavier (NYPr)	Damrosch Orchestra, Leopold Damrosch, cond.; B. Boekelman, soloist
55	May 25, 1878	1068	Air from Suite No. 3 in D Major	Thomas' Orchestra
56	June 2, 1878	unknown organ work	"Chorale and Fugue" [orch. transcr.]	Thomas' Orchestra
57	June 10, 1878	unknown organ work	"Chorale and Fugue" [orch. transcr.]	Thomas' Orchestra
58	June 17, 1878	1068	Suite No. 3 in D Major	Thomas' Orchestra
59	July 18, 1878	1068	Air from Suite No. 3 in D Major	Thomas' Orchestra
60	Aug. 29, 1878	1068	Air from Suite No. 3 in D Major	Thomas' Orchestra

Appendix (*continued*)

No.	*Date*	*BWV No.*	*Work*[a]	*Performers*
61	Sept. 12, 1878	unknown organ work	"Chorale and Fugue" [orch. transcr.]	Thomas' Orchestra
62	Sept. 16, 1878	1068	Air from Suite No. 3 in D Major	Thomas' Orchestra
63	Sept. 28, 1878	1068	Air from Suite No. 3 in D Major	Thomas' Orchestra
64	Jan. 18, 1879	248/II/19	"Slumber Song" ("Schlafe, mein Liebster") from the Christmas Oratorio	Brooklyn Philharmonic, Theodore Thomas, cond.; Annie Louise Cary, soloist
65	Jan. 20, 1880	1006/1, 1003/3, 1006/3	Prelude, Adagio, Gavotte, and Rondo (arr. for strings by Sigismund Bachrich) (AmPr)	Brooklyn Philharmonic, Theodore Thomas, cond.
66	Jan. 24, 1880	1006/1, 1003/3, 1006/3	Prelude, Adagio, Gavotte, and Rondo (arr. for strings by Sigismund Bachrich)	Philharmonic Society, Theodore Thomas, cond.
67	Mar. 17–18, 1880	244	St. Matthew Passion (about half the work was performed) (NYPr)	Oratorio Society, Choir of Boys from Trinity Parish, Symphony Society, Leopold Damrosch, cond.
68	Mar. 19, 1880	1068	Air [transcr. for cello] from Suite No. 3 in D Major	Mr. Herman chamber music concert; Mr. Werner, cellist
69	Apr. 20, 1880	903	Chromatic Fantasy and Fugue (orch. transcr. by George F. Bristow) (AmPr)	Brooklyn Philharmonic, Theodore Thomas, cond.
70	Feb. 12, 1881	80	"A Stronghold Sure" (*Ein feste Burg*) (arr. by Theodore Thomas) (NYPr)	New-York Chorus, Brooklyn Philharmonic Chorus, Philharmonic Society, Theodore Thomas, cond.
71	Feb. 19, 1881	80	"A Stronghold Sure" (*Ein feste Burg*) (arr. by Theodore Thomas)	New-York Chorus, Brooklyn Philharmonic Chorus, Brooklyn Philharmonic, Theodore Thomas, cond.
72	Mar. 11, 1881	1048	Brandenburg Concerto No. 3	Philharmonic Society, Theodore Thomas, cond.
73	May 5, 1881	536	Prelude and Fugue in A Major for Organ	prob. Walter Damrosch [Part of May Festival, Oratorio Society, Leopold Damrosch, cond.]
74	May 7, 1881	540	Toccata in F Major [orch. transcr.]	Festival Orchestra, Leopold Damrosch, cond.
75	Dec. 10, 1881	1043	Concerto in D Minor for Two Violins	Philharmonic Society, Theodore Thomas, cond.; Hermann Brandt and Richard Arnold, soloists

Appendix (*continued*)

No.	*Date*	BWV *No.*	*Work*[a]	*Performers*
76	Feb. 18, 1882	244/39	"O, pardon me" ("Erbarme dich, mein Gott") from the St. Matthew Passion	Brooklyn Philharmonic, Theodore Thomas, cond.; Annie Louise Cary, contralto
77	Apr. 20–21, 1882	26	"Vain and Fleeting" (*Ach wie flüchtig*) (AmPr)	Oratorio Society, Symphony Society, Leopold Damrosch, cond.
78	May 2, 1882	80	"A Stronghold Sure" (*Ein feste Burg*)	Festival Chorus and Orchestra
79	Feb. 3, 1883	1068	Suite No. 3 in D Major	Brooklyn Philharmonic, Theodore Thomas, cond.
80	Mar. 17, 1883	21	"My Spirit was in Heaviness" (*Ich hatte viel Bekümmernis*) (NYPr)	New-York Chorus Society, Theodore Thomas, cond.
81	Nov. 10, 1883	540	Toccata in F Major (orch. transcr. by Heinrich Esser)	Philharmonic Society, Theodore Thomas, cond.
82	Jan. 19, 1884	1048	Brandenburg Concerto No. 3	Philharmonic Society, Theodore Thomas, cond.
83	Mar. 12–13, 1884	244	St. Matthew Passion	Oratorio Society, Symphony Society, Walter Damrosch, cond.
84	Mar. 29, 1884	540	Toccata in F Major (orch. transcr. by Heinrich Esser)	Brooklyn Philharmonic, Theodore Thomas, cond.
85	Dec. 20, 1884	248/I–II	Christmas Oratorio, Parts I and II (arr. by Robert Franz) (NYPr)	Brooklyn Philharmonic, Brooklyn Philharmonic Chorus, Theodore Thomas, cond.
86	Mar. 21, 1885	1068	Suite No. 3 in D Major (Overture, Air and Gavottes I and II) (Pr)	Brooklyn Philharmonic, Theodore Thomas, cond.
87	Mar. 21, 1885	1044	Concerto for Piano, Flute, Violin, and String Orchestra (AmPr)	Brooklyn Philharmonic, Theodore Thomas, cond., Richard Hoffman, Mr. Oesterle, and Hermann Brandt, soloists
88	Mar. 13, 1886	1067	Suite No. 2 in B Minor	Philharmonic Society, Theodore Thomas, cond.
89	Apr. 17, 1886	582	Passacaglia in C Minor for Organ (orch. transcr. by Heinrich Esser)	Brooklyn Philharmonic, Theodore Thomas, cond.
90	Dec. 6, 1887	prob. 551 (poss. 543 or 561)	[Organ] Fugue in A Minor (arr. for strings by Josef Hellmesberger) (AmPr)	Theodore Thomas' Concerts
91	Jan. 14, 1888	1068	Suite No. 3 in D Major	Philharmonic Society, Theodore Thomas, cond.

Appendix (*continued*)

No.	*Date*	*BWV No.*	*Work*[a]	*Performers*
92	Jan. 21, 1888	prob. 551 (poss. 543 or 561)	[Organ] Fugue in A Minor (arr. for strings by Josef Hellmesberger)	Brooklyn Philharmonic, Theodore Thomas, cond.
93	Feb. 11, 1888	1048	Brandenburg Concerto No. 3	Philharmonic Society, Theodore Thomas, cond.
94	Mar. 7–8, 1888	244	St. Matthew Passion	Oratorio Society, Walter Damrosch, cond.
95	Nov. 2, 1888	1046	Brandenburg Concerto No. 1 (AmPr)	Symphony Society, Walter Damrosch, cond.
96	Jan. 19, 1889	1018	"Largo and Allegro" [Sonata No. 5 in F Minor for Violin and Cembalo] (orch. transcr. by Theodore Thomas)	Brooklyn Philharmonic, Theodore Thomas, cond.
97	Feb. 9, 1889	540	Toccata in F Major (orch. transcr. by Heinrich Esser)	Philharmonic Society, Theodore Thomas, cond.
98	Feb. 9, 1889	prob. 551 (poss. 543 or 561)	[Organ] Fugue in A Minor [orch. transcr.]	Philharmonic Society, Theodore Thomas, cond.
99	Apr. 6, 1889	1068	Suite No. 3 in D Major	Brooklyn Philharmonic, Theodore Thomas, cond.
100	Feb. 15, 1890	248/II/10	Sinfonia from the Christmas Oratorio	Brooklyn Philharmonic, Theodore Thomas, cond.
101	Apr. 12, 1890	248/II/10	Sinfonia from the Christmas Oratorio	Philharmonic Society, Theodore Thomas, cond.
102	Apr. 12, 1890	1018	Sonata in F Minor for Violin and Cembalo (orch. transcr. by Theodore Thomas) (AmPr)	Philharmonic Society, Theodore Thomas, cond.
103	Apr. 19, 1890	1018	Sonata in F Minor for Violin and Cembalo (orch. transcr. by Theodore Thomas)	Brooklyn Philharmonic, Theodore Thomas, cond.
104	Jan. 17, 1891	prob. 1067	"Sarabande, andante, and bourrée" [prob. Suite No. 2 in B Minor]	Brooklyn Philharmonic, Theodore Thomas, cond.
105	Aug. 16, 1891	unknown organ work	Prelude and Fugue [orch. transcr.]	Farewell Concert in New York of Theodore Thomas
106	Mar. 1 and 3, 1892	244	St. Matthew Passion	Oratorio Society, Symphony Orchestra, Boy Choir, Walter Damrosch, cond.
107	Apr. 15, 1893	prob. 1006	"Adagio and Gavotte from Suite in E" [prob. Partita No. 3 for Violin] (arr. for string orchestra) (AmPr)	Symphony Society, Walter Damrosch, cond.

Appendix (*continued*)

No.	*Date*	*BWV No.*	*Work*[a]	*Performers*
108	Feb. 23–24, 1894	244	St. Matthew Passion	Oratorio Society ("Chorus of 500"), Symphony Orchestra, Boy Choir, Walter Damrosch, cond.
109	Mar. 3, 1894	225	Motet No. 4, "Sing Ye to the Lord" (*Singet dem Herrn*) (NYPr)	Musical Art Society ("Chorus of Fifty Soloists"), Frank Damrosch, cond.
110	Apr. 12–13, 1895	244	St. Matthew Passion	Oratorio Society, Boy Choir of St. James's Church, Walter Damrosch, cond.
111	Mar. 23, 1896	1018	Sonata in F Minor for Violin and Cembalo (orch. transcr. by Theodore Thomas)	Chicago Orchestra, Theodore Thomas, cond.
112	Dec. 17, 1896	1051	Brandenburg Concerto No. 6 (AmPr)	Musical Art Society, Frank Damrosch, cond.
113	Mar. 5, 1897	1016	Sonata No. 3 in E Major for Violin and Cembalo (orch. transcr. by Theodore Thomas) (AmPr)	Philharmonic Society, Anton Seidl, cond.
114	Mar. 14, 1898	1068	Suite No. 3 in D Major	Chicago Orchestra, Theodore Thomas, cond.
115	Apr. 12, 1898	188/6	Chorale: "In God in Whom I Trust" (*Auf meinen lieben Gott trau ich in Angst und Not*)	Oratorio Society, Walter Damrosch, cond.
116	Dec. 8, 1898	248/II	Christmas Oratorio, Part II	Musical Art Society ("chorus of 60 artists"), People's Choral Union, ("with an orchestra and chorus of 900"), Frank Damrosch, cond.
117	Feb. 13, 1900	41	Excerpts from *Jesu, nun sei gepreiset* (AmPr)	Bach Singers, Theodore Björksten, cond.
118	Feb. 13, 1900	213/5	Echo aria from "Hercules in Indecision" (*Hercules auf dem Scheidewege*) (AmPr)	Bach Singers, Theodore Björksten, cond.
119	Feb. 13, 1900	525	Organ Sonata in E-flat Major (orch. transcr. by Herman Hans Wetzler)	Bach Singers; Theodore Björksten, cond.
120	Feb. 13, 1900	6/1	Opening chorus of "Abide with Us" (*Bleib bei uns*)	Bach Singers, Theodore Björksten, cond.
121	Feb. 13, 1900	238	Sanctus in D Major (AmPr)	Bach Singers, Theodore Björksten, cond.

Appendix (*continued*)

No.	*Date*	*BWV No.*	*Work*[a]	*Performers*
122	Feb. 13, 1900	204/8	Soprano aria from *Von der Vergnügsamkeit* (*Ich bin in mir vergnügt*) (AmPr)	Bach Singers, Theodore Björksten, cond.
123	Feb. 13, 1900	214	*Tönet, ihr Pauken* (AmPr)	Bach Singers, Theodore Björksten, cond.
124	Mar. 15, 1900	198	"Ode of Mourning" (*Trauerode*) (AmPr)	Musical Art Society, People's Choral Union, Frank Damrosch, cond.
125	Apr. 5, 1900	232	Mass in B Minor (substantial excerpts) (NYPr)	Oratorio Society, Frank Damrosch, cond.
126	Apr. 26, 1900	60	Excerpts from *O Ewigkeit, du Donnerwort* (AmPr)	Bach Singers, Theodore Björksten, cond.
127	Apr. 26, 1900	238	Sanctus in D Major	Bach Singers, Theodore Björksten, cond.
128	Apr. 26, 1900	12/1	First movement of *Weinen, Klagen, Sorgen, Zagen* (AmPr)	Bach Singers, Theodore Björksten, cond.
129	Apr. 26, 1900	211	Coffee Cantata (*Schweigt stille, plaudert nicht*) (NYPr)	Bach Singers, Theodore Björksten, cond.
130	Apr. 26, 1900	67/6	Aria with chorus from *Halt im Gedächtnis Jesum Christ* (AmPr)	Bach Singers, Theodore Björksten, cond.
131	Nov. 24, 1900	232	Mass in B Minor (substantial excerpts)	Oratorio Society, Frank Damrosch, cond.

[a]*Additional abbreviations:* AmPr = American premiere; NYPr = New York premiere; Pr = premiere.

"A Lineal Descendant of the Great Musician, John Sebastian Bach"?

Bach Descendants in the United States and the Problem of Family Oral Tradition

Hans-Joachim Schulze

Oral tradition in the exploration of family histories is often subject to the reproach of inaccuracy and to the danger of confusion. On the other hand, it is the source that can lend a little color to the mere framework of authentic data that usually appears rather spartan. When—for whatever reasons—oral tradition remains the *only* source, the explorer will soon find himself on very thin ice.

Such experience was also to be Johann Sebastian Bach's when in the autumn of 1735 he designed his family genealogy with explanatory commentary, titled "Origin of the Musical Bach Family."[1] The information he was able to gather (especially about his earliest ancestors) reached back to the sixteenth century, but it was lacking in precise and unquestionable dates. While we must be grateful to the Cantor of St. Thomas's in Leipzig for recording the family tradition, we nonetheless remain unable to close gaps of information about the two earliest generations or to resolve these unmistakable contradictions.

This pertains first of all to the oldest ancestor Veit ("Vitus") Bach, "white-bread baker" in Hungary, who had to leave his home territory because he was Lutheran and who settled in Wechmar near Gotha, Thuringia—though not leaving in headlong flight, for apparently he was able to sell his real estate. It has not been possible to substantiate any details about Veit Bach's former home (probably in present-day Slovakia), his dates, or the precise time of his persecution.

1. NBR, 283.

In addition, it pertains to his son Johannes Bach, who is supposed to have been a town piper's apprentice in Gotha and to have been in his master's service for some time. He was said to have returned to Wechmar after his father's death, when the castle of Grimmenstein—later replaced by the baroque castle of Friedenstein in Gotha—was destroyed, and to have taken over the parental estate and gotten married. At his death in 1626, he was survived by his widow and three sons, Johannes, Christoph, and Heinrich (born in 1604, 1613, and 1615, respectively). Since the castle of Grimmenstein was destroyed as early as 1567, though, it seems doubtful whether these biographical data refer only to one person. We shall return to this point.

* * *

Two hundred and fifty years later, Walter Wadepuhl of Palm Beach Gardens, Florida, then a senior among Goethe scholars, faced a comparable predicament in his exploration of family history.[2] Quite accidentally, he had found a township named Goethe on an antiquated map of the state of South Carolina. Growing curious, he visited the region and encountered a number of people bearing this name (spelled variously in its Anglicized forms), who even held a Goethe-family reunion every year, though they did not realize a possible connection with the family of the great poet. Wadepuhl's numerous attempts at tracing his lead led to a dead end because family documents were destroyed by flames during the twentieth century or official archives had become victims of the Civil War. In spite of these obstacles, it was possible to identify the brothers Georg and Heinrich Goethe as the oldest bearers of the name. The younger one (Heinrich) served in the Revolutionary War in 1779 and had remained single (he died in 1791); the older one (Georg, who died in 1786) was married in about 1772 and was the progenitor of a large family lineage. Only one of the descendants, the farmer Thomas Goethe in Tillman, South Carolina, remembered from accounts by older members of the family that his great-great-great-grandfather was related to the poet and that he had to leave Germany because of theft.

The only matter that can be connected with this hint of scandal is the so-called Gretchen episode from the year 1764, which Goethe mentioned in *Dichtung und Wahrheit*, albeit in rather disguised form. In the description of his circle of friends and their nightly adventures, Goethe intimates details, such as "daring mystifications," "foolish police affairs," "mischievous money-nipping," and other insidious things, as well as forgeries and further actions liable to punishment. He himself (at that time fourteen years of age), his "good cousins" whose names he withholds, and particularly Gretchen whom he adores, he declares as totally innocent and in no way part of these

2. Walter Wadepuhl, "Die amerikanischen Goethes und ihre Beziehungen zum Dichter Johann Wolfgang von Goethe," *Goethe-Jahrbuch* 99 (1982): 284–98, esp. 295–98.

illegalities. In reality, the damage done was apparently more serious. But since the Goethes were highly reputable Frankfurt citizens, the case was hushed up as much as possible. Gretchen had to leave town, Johann Wolfgang Goethe was kept under house arrest, and the "good cousins" were banned to America as "black sheep"—as Wadepuhl was able to verify. Coming from England, they must have arrived in Charleston, South Carolina, on the *Dragon* in the fall of 1764 and moved farther west a few years later. In Europe, nothing was heard of them again.

* * *

In the same year Walter Wadepuhl published his extended and complicated investigations—here merely summarized—John F. Erdle of Boise, Idaho, referred to me by Karl Geiringer (1899–1989),[3] inquired about the possibility of tracing back to the eighteenth century the ancestral lineage of his wife (Ellen Louise, née Bach, born on December 4, 1911). Her great-grandfather Karl Friedrich Bach (born on October 5, 1808) was said to have come to the United States in 1848 with his wife and five children. The second son, August Reinhold Bach (born on December 10, 1835), had claimed to be born in Erfurt as a seventh-generation descendant of Johann Sebastian Bach. This was recorded in a newspaper article whose origin is no longer identifiable, which presents a detailed obituary under the heading "Reinholdt Bach Victim of Sea Disaster." It reads:

> Reinholdt Bach, a prominent farmer of this county and father of Bach Bros. of this city, lost his life in the tragic disaster of last Friday morning [May 29, 1914], when the "Empress of Ireland" sank in the St. Lawrence river. Mr. Bach was one of the Rochester party sailing on Thursday from Quebec for Germany. . . .
>
> Reinholdt Bach, who is numbered among the dead in the sad disaster on the St. Lawrence, was born in Erfurt, South Weimer, Germany, in 1836 [1835], and was 78 years of age. He was a lineal descendant of the great musician, John Sebastian Bach, being of the seventh generation. Valuable papers regarding the family lineage, which he had in his possession and took with him, are most unfortunately lost in the water tragedy.
>
> Mr. Bach came to America with his parents when ten years of age, locating at Portage, Wis., where he grew to manhood, and where he was married to Barbara Bauer in 1858. Later they moved to Marion, this county and for forty-four years he was one of the highly respected citizens of that community. . . .
>
> Mr. Bach was possessed of considerable musical ability, and for many years instructed and conducted a family orchestra of his own boys [see plate 1]. As a pastime he made a number of violins by hand of more or less value, and he also built for his own enter-

3. Cf. Karl Geiringer (in collaboration with Irene Geiringer), *The Bach Family: Seven Generations of Creative Genius* (New York: Oxford University Press, 1954).

Plate 1. The "Bach Band," c. 1889. *Standing, left to right:* Herman Bach, August Reinhold Bach (father). *Seated, left to right:* Edward Bach, Arthur Bach, Charles (Karl) Bach, Adolph Matthias Bach (grandfather of Nancy Bach Hertzog), Fred Bach, Reinhold (Reynold or R. H.) Bach. Courtesy of Nancy Bach Hertzog.

tainment a home pipe organ, making all the parts entirely by hand. He was for many years a member of the old Rochester German Sang Verein.

Mr. Bach was enjoying the best of health when he left Rochester on Saturday, May 3 [May 2], for the trip to Hamburg, Germany, to which he had looked with anticipation for some time. It was to be his first trip to his fatherland since coming to America 68 years ago, but it was ruled otherwise.

Due to the loss of important papers mentioned here, all investigations about the origins of the family at first seemed of very little promise. A further complication arose through another oral account, according to which the family was descended from Philipp Emanuel Bach (1714–88), the second son of Johann Sebastian.

Yet in 1983, there was hope that the connection might be established after all. A Carl Friedrich Bach had been mentioned in an old genealogy of the Bach family, which was prepared no later than 1782 with supplements extending to 1818.[4] He was listed, however, with a birth year of 1803, not 1808. The similarity of the numbers 3 and 8 suggests a possible writing or reading error. Assuming that such an error might have crept into the document, it might now be possible to establish a lineage—granted the absence of very few dates—that would reach back to Johann Bach (1604–73), the older brother of Johann Sebastian Bach's grandfather Christoph Bach (1613–61).

Even the account of "seven generations" handed down in family lore could be considered verified. Johann August Reinhold Bach, who died in the 1914 accident, represented the seventh generation of descendants of Johann Bach, Erfurt town musician and organist at the Predigerkirche. Thus the Cantor of St. Thomas's in Leipzig, Johann Sebastian Bach, and Johann August Reinhold Bach who perished in the shipwreck had as their common ancestor the baker and musician Johannes Bach of Wechmar who died in 1626.

The accuracy of the hypothesis put forward in 1983 was confirmed when in 1988 Mrs. Helga Brück of Erfurt was able to supplement investigations of the Erfurt Bach families—carried out over many years—through a complete genealogy of the "Andislebener Bache."[5] Even though Andisleben is only a few kilometers from Erfurt and though it had long been known through Johann Sebastian Bach's account that a descendant of the Erfurt Bach family had been a cantor there, Bach scholarship had paid no attention to this family branch. But the exploration of the "Andislebener Bache" and their largely unknown dates finally established the sought-after connection between the "musical Bach family" in Thuringia and a great number of Bach descendants in the United States. On the other hand, the results of research on Bach descendants in the United States helped to explain the fact, which initially seemed strange, that the annotations about members of the Bach family in Andisleben church records ended abruptly in 1848.

Simplified and reduced to male descendants bearing the name of Bach, the generations present the following sequence: Veit Bach (Slovakia/later Wechmar, died before 1577?)—Johannes Bach (Wechmar, died in 1626)—Johann Bach (Erfurt, 1604–73)—Johann Aegidius Bach (Erfurt, 1645–1716)—Johann Christoph Bach (Erfurt, 1685–1740)—Johann Friedrich Bach (Andisleben near Erfurt, 1706–43)—Johann Christoph Bach (Andisleben, 1736–1808)—Johann Friedrich Nikolaus Bach (Andisle-

4. Alfred Lorenz, "Ein alter Bach-Stammbaum," *Neue Zeitschrift für Musik* 82 (1915): 281–82. Cf. Charles Sanford Terry, ed., *The Origin of the Family of Bach Musicians* (London: Oxford University Press, 1929), Table III.

5. Helga Brück, "Die Andislebener Bache," BJ 77 (1991): 199–206; cf. Brück, "Die Erfurter Bach-Familien von 1635 bis 1805," BJ 82 (1996): 101–31.

ben, 1761?–1829)—Johann Karl Friedrich Bach (Andisleben, 1808–76; emigrated to the United States in 1848)—Johann August Reinhold Bach (1835–1914; came to the United States with his parents and siblings in 1848)—Charles August Bach (1862–1938)—his descendants, among them Ellen Louise Bach, already mentioned, the wife of John F. Erdle.

Its only weak spot is the absence of documentation for the birth or baptism of Johann Friedrich Nikolaus Bach, due to the fact that his father, Johann Christoph Bach (1736–1808), though born in Andisleben, did not finally settle there until around 1773. The lineage of the entire family now established, however, precludes the possibility of an error.

It should be mentioned that an older brother of the "emigrant" Johann Karl Friedrich Bach, whose name was Johann Christoph Bach (born in 1802), had left home and family soon after 1830. As can be gathered from hints in the church records of his hometown, he died before 1848, apparently as "Singemaster" in Batavia, New York. It remains uncertain whether it was he who suggested to his Thuringian relatives that they move to the New World to seek their fortune.

Johann August Reinhold Bach, who died in the tragic accident, was evidently the strongest and most influential personality among the "Andislebener Bache" who had come to the United States. With his twelve children (see plate 2), all of whom lived to maturity (of the two last born, one died in 1977 and the other in 1980 at the age of ninety-eight), as well as with their offspring, musical giftedness was, so to speak, a foregone conclusion. This alone makes it understandable that establishing a connection with the famous Cantor of St. Thomas's in Leipzig had become a family tradition.

Since the documentation for the spread of the "Andislebener Bache" in the United States available by 1990 had pointed in the main toward settlement in Wisconsin, Minnesota, Idaho, and Oregon, an April 1998 communication received in Leipzig from Springfield, Virginia, elicited a certain surprise. It reads:

> My name is Nancy Bach Hertzog, and my family is descended from the family of Johann Sebastian Bach. We live in the United States, as these Bachs came over here in 1848 (possibly because of the political turmoil in Germany). My family has had great difficulty, however, in tracing the family roots from 1848, when they arrived in America, back to Johann Sebastian. I am the 9th generation, and we have records of the fifth through ninth generations here in the U. S. We're missing the first four generations. My father is Philip Fredrick Bach (8th gen.), grandfather is Adolf Mathias Bach (7th gen.), to August "Reinhold" Bach (6th gen.), to Karl Friedrich (5th gen.) who came over with his wife and their first-born child, Leopold. The only information we have on his father, who lived in Germany, is that his name was Johann and that he was born in 1770.

Plate 2. Family of August Reinhold Bach, c. 1889. *Top row, left to right:* Louise (eldest child), Charles, Reinhold, Edith, Herman, Fred, Lizetta. *Front, left to right:* Emeline, Barbara (mother), Edward, Arthur, August Reinhold (father), Hulda, Adolph. Courtesy of Nancy Bach Hertzog.

On the basis of the information gathered, it will easily be seen that open questions concerning the supposed birth date of 1770 for "Johann Bach" and the presumed descent from the family of Johann Sebastian Bach can now be dismissed. An ensuing correspondence with Mrs. Hertzog produced pictorial material of interest[6] and numerous new dates, especially for the youngest generation of descendants—born shortly before 1990—and their musical activities.[7] There is, unfortunately, much more detail than can be presented here.

6. Family pictures, entries in the family Bible, and a photograph from around 1889, showing August Reinhold Bach and seven sons—the father with a three-stringed double bass, and the sons with two stringed, two woodwind, and two brass instruments, and a small drum (reproduced as plate 1).

7. Through these, some gaps can be closed in the 1991 article by Helga Brück. It should be noted that none of the family connections to Johann Karl Friedrich Bach have been so thoroughly explored as those to his son Johann August Reinhold Bach.

While it was possible to substantiate by hard data the information received orally about the origins of Bach family members who in 1848 emigrated to America, and thus establish with certainty the true lineage, there remains a slight uncertainty about the earliest Bach generations—Veit Bach and Johannes Bach in Wechmar. If we accept the information in Johann Sebastian Bach's 1735 document—apparently based on oral tradition—the American descendants of the "musical Bach family" can trace their genealogical roots back to the sixteenth century, that is before the era of the Pilgrim Fathers and the Mayflower.[8]

(translated by Alfred Mann)

8. Notwithstanding the fact that the riddle concerning the descendants of the "Andislebener Bache" has been solved, a number of open questions remain about Americans and Canadians bearing the name Bach and about their ancestry. We might name the capellmeister Christoph Bach (born in 1835 in Eschwege, Hesse), who was active in Milwaukee and to whom the *Milwaukee Herald* of February 14, 1906, devoted an article on his "golden jubilee"; Johann Balthasar Bach of Ottweiler (1726–96), who arrived in America in 1749 and is said to have lived in Frederick, Maryland; Johann Peter Bach (1762–1831) of Mosberg or Mannheim, and another Johann Peter Bach, who supposedly served under Napoleon; and some members of the "Hessische Bache" described in BJ 33 (1936) and 34 (1937), who are believed to have emigrated to America. A connection to Johann Sebastian Bach or the "musical Bach family" is regularly claimed—on the basis of oral tradition—but can in no case be substantiated.

Descendants of Wilhelm Friedemann Bach in the United States

Christoph Wolff

When in April 1843 Felix Mendelssohn Bartholdy dedicated the first Leipzig Bach monument, he was surprised and very pleased to encounter at the ceremony the last direct male descendant of Johann Sebastian Bach. Though very advanced in years, Wilhelm Friedrich Ernst Bach, retired capellmeister to Queen Luise of Prussia, had traveled from Berlin to Leipzig in the company of his second wife and his two daughters in order to attend the event.[1] Born in 1759 at Bückeburg as son of Johann Sebastian Bach's second youngest, Johann Christoph Friedrich, he was then the sole remaining representative of a musical family whose tradition reached back for more than 250 years. In fact, Wilhelm Bach—as he used to be called—was the only one of the Thomaskantor's grandchildren who had chosen a musical career, with the encouragement and support of his famous and influential uncles, Carl Philipp Emanuel of Hamburg and Johann Christian of London. His death in 1845 effectively marked the end of the Bach family of musicians.[2]

Historical documentation on the Bach family traditionally focused on the males, and more specifically on the vast majority of them who, during much of the seventeenth and eighteenth centuries, were professional musicians. Hence, in the family genealogy, "Origin of the Musical Bach Family," compiled around 1735 by Johann Sebastian Bach, information is provided almost exclusively on the male musicians.[3] The only two exceptions occur in the listings of Johann Nicolaus Bach of Königsberg, a surgeon (*ein Chirurgus*) who grew up as a foster child in Ambrosius Bach's Eisenach household and

1. Ulrich Leisinger, "Wilhelm Friedrich Ernst Bach: Der letzte musikalische Enkel Johann Sebastian Bachs," in *Johann Christoph Friedrich Bach (1732–1795): Ein Komponist zwischen Barock und Klassik*, ed. Ulrich Leisinger (Bückeburg: Verlag Createum, 1995), 80.

2. Christoph Wolff, "Bach," in *The New Grove Dictionary of Music and Musicians*, 2d ed., 29 vols. (London: Macmillan, 2001), 2:305.

3. NBR, 283–94.

went to school with Sebastian, and of Johann Christoph Bach of Blankenhain, a shopkeeper who supported himself with "materialists' stuff" (*Materialisten Kram*).[4] But even they were presumably devoted to music.

With the genealogy's exclusive focus on male musicians, it seems all the more surprising that Johann Sebastian Bach, in his 1730 letter to Georg Erdmann, singled out two women in his family for their musical competence: "My present wife sings a good, clear soprano, and my eldest daughter, too, joins in not badly."[5] Of course, Anna Magdalena Bach was a professional singer of distinction, who once earned the second highest salary among the Cöthen court musicians. Still, Bach's eldest daughter and apparently her younger sisters as well were musically inclined and competent, even though, for whatever reasons, they did not prepare for a musical career. Bach expressly writes in the Erdmann letter about his children that "they are all born musicians," yet only the sons chose professional musical paths.

Unfortunately, not much detailed and reliable information about the Bach family's female offspring is available. At a time when educational and professional choices for middle-class women were extremely limited, both private and public records usually reflect disinterest, if not an openly discriminatory attitude toward women, especially unmarried ones. Thus, we know virtually nothing about the fate of Bach's three unmarried daughters, Catharina, Carolina, and Regina. All we know about Elisabeth, who married her father's student, the organist Johann Christoph Altnickol, is that she survived her husband by more than twenty years.[6]

The situation in the next generation is hardly any different. Three of Johann Sebastian's four musical sons had descendants, but information on the daughters again is wanting. Wilhelm Friedemann's two sons, Wilhelm Adolf and Gotthilf Wilhelm, did not survive childhood. Carl Philipp Emanuel's first-born, Johann August, a lawyer in Hamburg, as well as his second son, Johann Sebastian, Jr., a draftsman, painter, and engraver who died in Rome at an early age, both had no children. Carl's daughter Anna Carolina never married, whereas both Friedemann's youngest child, Friederica Sophia, and Johann Christoph Friedrich's daughter, Anna Philippina Friederica, did.[7] These two women, along with the aforementioned Berlin capellmeister Wilhelm Bach, turned out to be the only ones among Johann Sebastian Bach's grandchildren who had descendants.

4. Ibid., 289–90, nos. 20 and 26.

5. NBR, no. 152.

6. NBR, 293; Hermann Kock, *Genealogisches Lexikon der Familie Bach* (Wechmar: Kunstverlag Gotha, 1995), 83.

7. Regarding the Colson family and their relationship with the Johann Christoph Friedrich Bach descendants, see Kock, *Genealogisches Lexicon der Familie Bach*, 75.

Friederica Sophia Bach, born in Halle on February 27, 1757, settled in the mid-1770s together with her father and mother in Berlin. There, after both parents had died, she married on February 10, 1793, at the age of nearly thirty-six (fairly late for a woman at that time), Johann Schmidt, a professional soldier (*musquetier*) in the Prussian army, who was four years her junior.[8] Parish records indicate that a few days before the wedding the couple had a child. Sophie Dorothea, born on February 5, 1793, was left unbaptized until after her parents were married; her christening took place on March 10. Another daughter, Sophie Friederica, was born on March 30, 1797, and baptized on April 2. Prussian army records, related to Johann Schmidt's regiment under the command of General von Arnim, show Friederica Bach Schmidt and her two daughters as Musketeer Schmidt's dependents through 1801. While the two children continue to be listed in later years,[9] the mother disappears from the records in 1802. This led to the supposition that Friedemann Bach's daughter had died in 1801–2, although her death was not registered by either the church or military authorities in Berlin. It is documented, however, that Johann Schmidt remarried in 1805; his second wife, Louise Friederica Holzhausen, was the thirty-year-old, previously unmarried daughter of another soldier.

The actual fate of Friederica Sophia, presumed dead by 1802, turns out to be substantially different from what had been deduced from the Schmidt family records in Berlin. What the archival documents do not reveal is illuminated in a remarkable way by the background and history of an American family of German extraction. Friederica did not die in her early forties. Instead, her life took a surprising turn after 1798.

In conjunction with a 1979 concert given in North Carolina by the Bach Aria Group, founded and sponsored by William H. Scheide of Princeton, New Jersey, Lydia duChateau introduced herself to him as a descendant of Wilhelm Friedemann Bach.[10] For verification of her claims, the appropriately skeptical Scheide referred her to the Bach-Archiv in Leipzig, and to me who, as he knew, had just written the entry on the Bach family for the soon-to-be-published *New Grove Dictionary of Music and Musicians*.[11]

8. The pertinent Berlin documents on the Schmidt-Bach family are presented in Heinrich Miesner, "Einige neu entdeckte Notizen über die Familie Friedemann Bachs," BJ 28 (1931): 147–48, and Miesner, "Urkundliche Nachrichten über die Familie Bach in Berlin," BJ 29 (1932): 157–63.

9. Nothing is known about the subsequent lives and whereabouts of these two grandchildren of Friedemann Bach's.

10. I must express my deep gratitude to Lydia duChateau (1905–86), with whom I had the privilege of corresponding and speaking extensively in telephone conversations in the early 1980s. She generously and proudly told me about her family background, and I regret that a planned visit to her home in North Carolina was prevented by her illness and subsequent death. I also must thank William H. Scheide for making me aware of the connection between duChateau and Wilhelm Friedemann Bach.

11. Christoph Wolff, "Bach," in *The New Grove Dictionary of Music and Musicians*, 20 vols. (London: Macmillan, 1980), 1:774–82.

As duChateau's letter to the Bach-Archiv ended up in the hands of Hans-Joachim Schulze, he and I compared notes on the matter and frequently discussed her fascinating and previously unknown story.[12] The following summary of her report, for the most part delivered verbally, has been supplemented recently by much welcome factual information provided by her son, Philippe duChateau, who has access to genealogical notes prepared by one of his mother's brothers, a scientist.

Lydia duChateau began her discussion with me on an apologetic note about why the Bach connection was for generations kept under a veil of secrecy by her devout Lutheran family. The story begins with what was considered an embarrassing incident, objectionable by traditional religious and moral standards: a child born out of wedlock. Lydia herself had learned about it only as a mature woman from her father, physician Dr. Paul Friedemann, whom she adored.[13] What was transmitted in her family is that her great-grandmother had been an illegitimate child of Friederica Sophia Bach and a man named Schwarzschulz. The fact that the story also involved a case of flagrant adultery and that Friederica had run away from her first husband was not known in Lydia's family, as information about her marriage to Johann Schmidt may have been suppressed very early on, perhaps by Friederica herself. Regrettably, therefore, we do not learn anything beyond a few meager facts about Friedemann Bach's evidently adventuresome daughter.

That she had clearly led an utterly unconventional life in Berlin is underscored further by information that surfaced in conjunction with Hans-Joachim Schulze's unsuccessful attempt in 1980 to uncover a Schwarzschulz-Bach marriage record. Instead, the Berlin parish archives yielded a previously unknown entry concerning the birth on November 5, 1780, of an illegitimate son to "Friederica Sophia Bach, daughter of a *Musikus* from Halle."[14] The identification of the mother could hardly be more unequivocal. But no reference is made to the father of the child, nor is anything known

12. See also Hans-Joachim Schulze, *Studien zur Bach-Überlieferung im 18. Jahrhundert* (Leipzig: Peters, 1984), 129 n. 521.

13. Born Lydia Emma Augusta Friedemann, she changed her middle name after her father's death to Paul, so that her married name became Lydia Paul duChateau. Lydia's father, Dr. Paul Friedemann, served as treasurer of the Salem Lutheran congregation in Stillwater, Oklahoma, and was a strong supporter of church music. As Jene Friedemann reports, "With Doctor Paul's son William at the piano, and the children pressured into their best behavior, the music from the loft at the right of the altar commanded as much attention as the pastor's inflexible sermon. Under the direction of Marie Friedemann (Oltmanns), the choir almost monotonously abounded with Friedemanns"—perhaps a distant echo of the Bach family link. Jene Friedemann, *Bread for the Third Generation: An Early History of Salem Lutheran Church* (Stillwater, Okla.: Western Publications, 1987), 94–95.

14. Information provided by the Evangelisches Zentralarchiv in Berlin, Kirchenbuchstelle. I am greatly indebted to Hans-Joachim Schulze for communicating it to me.

about the fate of the little boy. The incident took place almost four years before Wilhelm Friedemann Bach's death, and it must be assumed that he and his wife were well aware of the perhaps rash and heedless activities of their twenty-three-year-old daughter. Her behavior, in turn, may not have remained unaffected by the unsteady conduct of Friedemann Bach's own life.

According to Lydia's report, her great-grandmother, Karoline Beata, was born to Friederica Bach in 1798 (no exact date is known). Probably shortly after the birth of the child, the mother legitimized her extramarital affair and married the father of the child, a textile designer known only by the family name Schwarzschulz. Schwarzschulz lived in a place called "Zülchen" (Züllichau, or Sulechów in Polish) on the Oder River in Lower Silesia, formerly Prussian territory, about 100 miles southeast of Berlin.[15] At the time of Karoline's birth, Friederica Bach was still married to Johann Schmidt, with whom she had her second daughter, Sophie Friederica, only in 1797. However, we have no information about how Friederica Bach arranged her life in the immediate aftermath of her affair with Schwarzschulz, either within the household of her husband Schmidt or in separation from him; a divorce is not recorded. Moreover, no details are known about why, when, where, and under what circumstances Friederica linked up with Schwarzschulz, left the musketeer for the textile designer, and eventually settled with him in Züllichau.

Since Friederica had two very small daughters by 1797, it seems unlikely that she traveled away from Berlin in 1797–98. Hence, she might have met and gotten involved with Schwarzschulz in Berlin. However, the Berlin parish records show no entry for the birth in 1798 of another, if illegitimate, daughter. So Karoline Beata most likely was born in Züllichau. This is also congruent with the oral tradition in Lydia's family, according to which her great-grandmother came from Züllichau and was born as an illegitimate child. Friederica's marriage with Schwarzschulz would have occurred, then, only after Karoline's birth, in 1798 or shortly thereafter. This means, however, that by 1801–2—the time of her previously assumed death—she would have established her new life as Mrs. Schwarzschulz in Züllichau for at least a couple of years after abandoning her first family in Berlin and letting her identity as Mrs. Schmidt vanish into obscurity. We must assume that Friederica Bach and her second husband, Schwarzschulz, lived in Züllichau until they died (no death dates are available for either of them). However, if they lived long enough they might well have joined their daughter and son-in-law on their move southeastward.

15. Hans-Joachim Schulze resolved Mrs. duChateau's misleading spelling of Züllichau and also verified that before and after 1800 a number of people by the name of Schwarzschul(t)z were in that town's textile business. No records for a marriage between a Schwar(t)zschul(t)z and a Bach or a Schmidt are traceable in Züllichau (the parish registers were lost in World War II).

Friederica's daughter, Karoline Schwarzschulz, married between 1822 and 1826 one Johann Gustav Friedemann. The latter's family name must immediately have reminded the mother (who, if still living, would have been in her late sixties) and daughter of the name by which their famous father and grandfather was called.[16] Johann Gustav Friedemann, a clothmaker (*Tuchmacher*) of Lutheran faith, was born on April 16, 1799. Like Karoline's father in the textile business, he grew up in Lissa (Polish Leszno), about fifty miles southeast of Züllichau, still in Prussian territory but close to the border of Poland (after the third Polish division of 1795). His parents reportedly had arrived there in 1797.[17] Soon after Johann Gustav and Karoline Friedemann's wedding in Züllichau or Lissa (again no specifics are known), the young couple moved to Zgierz, a textile manufacturing center in the district of Łodż, Poland, where in 1827 their first son Eduard was born. Their third and youngest son also was born there on January 29, 1834. They named him Gustav Wilhelm, his middle and family names together echoing the name of Johann Sebastian Bach's eldest son, Wilhelm Friedemann. Not long after Wilhelm's birth, Johann Gustav Friedemann moved his family farther to the east and established himself in the textile industry at Supraśl near Białystok, Poland, where he set up and repaired textile machinery. Gustav Wilhelm and his older brothers grew up in the textile business at Supraśl but later relocated to villages in the Volhynia and Podolia regions of western Ukraine, then part of the Russian empire and heavily settled by Lutheran Germans.[18] Whether either of their parents joined them in their continuing southeastward journey is as unknown as are their dates of death.

In 1856, after moving to the industrial colony of Dunajewicz, Podolia, Wilhelm Friedemann married Augusta Buchholz, daughter of a German weaver, and later op-

16. Lydia duChateau reported that her great-grandmother's husband changed his name on his marriage certificate to "Friedemann"—an act that, in the absence of any documentation, cannot be verified. I assume that she erred or misremembered.

17. According to the papers of Theodore Friedemann, brother of Lydia duChateau, "there was one by the name of Friedemann (first name unknown) and his wife who came from the University City of Halle and arrived in Leszno Poland in 1797. Their first-born was a son, Johann Gustav Friedemann, b. 16 April 1799." It remains unclear, however, whether the elder Friedemann had indeed come from Halle on the Saale River, the city in Prussian territory where Wilhelm Friedemann Bach's daughter Friederica Sophia was born. Conceivably, the presumed Halle roots of the Friedemann family may have been mixed up with Friederica Bach Schwarzschulz's birthplace, where her father was organist at Our Lady's Church from 1746 to 1764 and also served as music director of the university (he lived in Halle until 1770).

A narrative account of the journeys of the extended Friedemann family after 1830 in Poland, Podolia, and Volhynia and of their emigration to the United States is given in Friedemann, *Bread for the Third Generation*, 17–19.

18. By 1871 139 German villages had been established in Volhynia.

erated the Perekore Travelers House, Ranch, and Way Station (Perkoritsky) near Kamenecz, Podolia. Six of their children were born there.[19] Two more were born at the German colony of Annette near Novograd, Volhynia, where in 1869 Wilhelm Friedemann had purchased two farms and also served as local magistrate (*Dorfschulze*). Primarily for economic reasons, he emigrated in 1892 with his extended family from Ukrainian Volhynia to the United States, where they rebuilt their lives in Oklahoma together with other settlers of German-Russian background. Their many descendants can all legitimately claim Wilhelm Friedemann Bach's daughter Friederica as their ancestress and, therefore, link up directly with the family of Johann Sebastian Bach (see table 1).

Table 1. The Bach-Friedemann Lineage

I. Wilhelm *Friedemann* Bach, 1710–84, m. *Dorothea* Elisabeth Georgi (1725–91).[a] Three children: Wilhelm Adolf, Gotthilf Wilhelm, and Friederica Sophia (only the daughter reached adulthood).

II. *Friederica* Sophia Bach, b. Halle, February 27, 1757, d. Züllichau/Sulechów (?), date unknown; m. (1) Johann Schmidt and later (2) a Schwarzschulz, whose first name is unknown. Three daughters: from her first marriage, Sophie Dorothea and Sophie Friederica; from her second, Karoline Beata. Also a son (name unknown), born out of wedlock in 1780, thirteen years before her first marriage (see note 14).

III. *Karoline* Beata Schwarzschulz, b. Züllichau/Sulechów (or Berlin), 1798, d. Supraśl (?), date unknown; m. Johann *Gustav* Friedemann, b. Lissa/Leszno, April 16, 1799, d. Supraśl (?), date unknown. Three sons: Eduard,[b] Karl,[c] and Gustav Wilhelm; possibly also one or more daughters.

IV. Gustav *Wilhelm* Friedemann, b. Zgierz, Poland, January 29, 1834, d. Stillwater, Oklahoma, January 10, 1911; m. Augusta Buchholz, b. Alexandrov, December 29, 1834, d. Stillwater, Oklahoma, January 26, 1914. Children: Emma Hulda, Julia Ida, Paul Wilhelm, Robert Julius, Adolph Gustav, Lydia Karoline, Wilhelm Andreas, and Rudolf Alexander.[d]

V. Paul Wilhelm Friedemann, b. Perecorre, Podolia, Russia, February 10, 1861, d. Stillwater, Oklahoma, March 15, 1945. Children: several sons and one daughter, Lydia Emma Augusta, b. Kiel (renamed "Loyal" in World War I), Oklahoma, January 15, 1905, d. Tryon, North Carolina, August 28, 1986 (see notes 10 and 13).

[a]For up-to-date biographical information, see Peter Wollny's article on Wilhelm Friedemann Bach, in *Die Musik in Geschichte und Gegenwart*, 2d ed. (Kassel: Bärenreiter, 1999), 1:1536–47.

[b]Eduard had a son Gustav, b. Supraśl, 1859; descendants are known to have lived in Wetzlar, Germany.

[c]No data available.

[d]Friedemann, *Bread for the Third Generation*, provides data for all of them.

19. Including their oldest son, Paul Wilhelm (William) Friedemann (1861–1945), who died in Stillwater, Oklahoma. He had been in the Russian army and received his medical training at the Russian Army Medical Institute in Kielce. After obtaining a medical degree in the United States, he practiced

Among her possessions, Friederica Schwarzschulz apparently kept and treasured a number of items that originally belonged to her father, Wilhelm Friedemann Bach. She passed the collection on to her daughter Karoline, who kept it throughout the stations of her life from Prussia to Poland and Russia. Karoline, in turn, left it to her youngest son Wilhelm Friedemann (most likely because of the name connection), who later transported it across the Atlantic to the American Midwest. Lydia Paul duChateau, his granddaughter and a sixth-generation descendant of Johann Sebastian Bach, inherited the small, old wooden trunk with the family's collection of Wilhelm Friedemann Bach memorabilia. However, as she reported with much embarrassment and deep regret, this trunk was lost around 1950, in connection with a family move to a new residence in Highland Park, Illinois, on the shore north of Chicago. It was probably accidentally discarded and destroyed, or perhaps stolen. At any rate, it never turned up again. As for the contents of the trunk, Lydia vividly recalled the items listed in table 2. The fact that none of these items ever showed up on the antiquarian market or anywhere else during the past several decades strongly suggests that they no longer exist and were indeed destroyed. The loss of this material is most unfortunate because it would have provided some welcome musical, biographical, and contextual information not otherwise available for Johann Sebastian Bach's oldest son, who remains such an enigmatic figure.

Table 2. Lost Wilhelm Friedemann Bach Memorabilia

A pastel portrait (c. 24 in. × 20 in.) of Wilhelm Friedemann Bach
A notebook with musical exercises for Wilhelm Friedemann[a] and annotations presumably by his father, including: *drei mal* ([to be repeated] "three times") and *du bist ein* (or: *mein*) *gutes Jüngelchen* ("you are a [or: my] good little boy")
A music manuscript with square notes[b]
Several medals, presumably given to Wilhelm Friedemann Bach by aristocratic patrons
Part of a diary and notes by Friederica Sophia Bach, with character sketches of her father, describing him as a sad and deeply religious man

[a]If authentic, it must have preceded the known *Clavier-Büchlein* of 1720.

[b]An eighteenth-century music manuscript is unlikely to have contained square notes, but it might well have been a copy of the set of printed performing parts for BWV 71 of 1708 (with square notes) or for the lost Mühlhausen town council cantata of 1709.

as a physician in Oklahoma. Lydia Emma Augusta Friedemann was his oldest daughter (see n. 13). I am greatly indebted to Virginia Less, who plans to publish a book on the German-Volhynian Bergstraesser family with close ties to the Friedemanns (*The Wandering Bergstraesser Clan*, in preparation), for important references.

On Miscellaneous American Bach Sources

Peter Wollny

When Gerhard Herz published his study of Bach sources in America, the unexpected wealth of material forced him to concentrate primarily on the original manuscripts and prints of Johann Sebastian Bach's works, that is, those sources and documents that were either written in Bach's own hand or prepared on his initiative and under his guidance, as well as printed editions that were issued during his lifetime.[1] There was little room for discussion of secondary sources, and items relating to Bach's family had to be excluded altogether. The latter have until now been treated only in two short articles by Karl Geiringer, which drew attention to the music collections of the Moravian congregations in Bethlehem, Pennsylvania, and Winston-Salem, North Carolina, as well as to the Stellfeld Collection at the University of Michigan at Ann Arbor.[2] Other important American collections of Bach family materials, in particular those at the Library of Congress and at Harvard University, in the meantime have been catalogued, but only a few sources have so far been studied in depth and received the scrutiny they deserve.[3]

1. Gerhard Herz, *Bach-Quellen in Amerika/Bach Sources in America* (Kassel: Bärenreiter, 1984).

2. Karl Geiringer, "Unbeachtete Kompositionen des Bückeburger Bach," in *Festschrift Wilhelm Fischer zum 70. Geburtstag*, ed. Hans Zingerle (Innsbruck: Selbstverlag des Sprachwissenschaftlichen Seminars der Universität Innsbruck, 1956), 99–107; Geiringer, "Unbekannte Werke von Nachkommen J. S. Bachs in amerikanischen Sammlungen," in *Bericht über den siebenten Internationalen Musikwissenschaftlichen Kongress, Köln, 1958*, ed. Gerald Abraham (Kassel: Bärenreiter, 1959), 110–12.

3. Manuscripts relating to J. S. Bach's second son for the most part are included in E. Eugene Helm's *Thematic Catalogue of the Works of Carl Philipp Emanuel Bach* (New Haven: Yale University Press, 1989); the holdings at Harvard are treated by Barbara Mahrenholz Wolff in *Music Manuscripts at Harvard: A Catalogue of Music Manuscripts from the 14th to the 20th Centuries in the Houghton Library and the Eda Kuhn Loeb Music Library* (Cambridge: Harvard University Library, 1992). The Rinck Collection of musical manuscripts at Yale University was catalogued by Henry Cutler Fall in "A Critical-Bibliographical Study of the Rinck Collection" (master's thesis, Yale University, 1958).

Unknown Early Compositions by J. S. Bach?

The extensive collection of central German organ music assembled by the Darmstadt organist Johann Christian Heinrich Rinck (1770–1846) was acquired in 1852 by the American music teacher and composer Lowell Mason (1792–1872), whose heirs donated it to Yale University in 1873.[4] In 1985 the Rinck Collection gained widespread public attention as a result of the discovery of some thirty previously unknown early chorale preludes by Johann Sebastian Bach (contained in a volume copied by Johann Gottfried Neumeister, catalogued as LM 4708).[5] Despite the great interest which the "Neumeister Chorales" have attracted since then, it has been overlooked that a further anthology also transmitted by Rinck (LM 4843) contains an additional series of unknown chorale preludes attributed to Johann Sebastian Bach. These were only recently published in a modern edition within the context of the surrounding repertoire.[6]

LM 4843 was copied in the late eighteenth or early nineteenth century by Rinck and a scribe working for him, presumably from various early-eighteenth-century sources. Despite the title *Chorale di Seb. Bach* on the first page of the wrapper, only six of the nineteen works assembled here are explicitly attributed to J. S. Bach (see table 1). One piece bears the name of Bach's Weimar cousin Johann Gottfried Walther, while the remaining twelve are anonymous.

Only two of the six compositions appearing under Bach's name are also known from other sources. No. 7 is a variant of the chorale partita *Christ, der du bist der helle Tag* (BWV 766). This work exists in several other sources, so its authenticity is unquestionable. The version in LM 4843 has a large number of variant readings; it contains only six of the seven variations (BWV 766/6 is omitted); and the piece bears the altered title *Christ, der du bist Tag und Licht.* This does not reflect the copyist's unauthorized interference, however, as there is a similar source in the Scheibner collection at the Musikbibliothek der Stadt Leipzig (Ms. 4, fascicle no. 16), which also contains most of the

4. On Rinck and his teacher Johann Christian Kittel, see Friedrich Wilhelm Donat, *Christian Heinrich Rinck und die Orgelmusik seiner Zeit* (Bad Oeynhausen: Theine & Peitsch, 1933), and Albert Dreetz, *Johann Christian Kittel, der letzte Bach-Schüler* (Berlin-Köpenick: P. W. Nacken, 1932).

5. See Christoph Wolff, "Bach's Organ Music: Studies and Discoveries," *The Musical Times* 126 (1985): 149–52; also the introduction to Wolff's facsimile edition, *The Neumeister Collection of Chorale Preludes from the Bach Circle: Yale University Manuscript LM 4708* (New Haven: Yale University Press, 1986), reprinted in Christoph Wolff, *Bach: Essays on His Life and Music* (Cambridge: Harvard University Press, 1991), 107–27.

6. Peter Wollny and Jean-Claude Zehnder, eds., *Aus dem Umkreis des jungen Johann Sebastian Bach: Neunzehn Orgelchoräle von Johann Sebastian Bach und dem Thüringer Umkreis aus der Handschrift Yale LM 4843* (Stuttgart: Carus, 1998). The present discussion is based on the preface to this edition.

Table 1. Inventory of LM 4843

Page	*Number*	*Item*
1–2	Blank	
3	No. 1	*Ich ruff zu dir Herr Jesu Christ* [etc.] *Aria. di Seb. Bach.*
4	No. 2	*Komm heiliger Geist erfülle die Herzen* [etc.] *di Seb: Bach:*
5	No. 3	*Chorale Von Gott will ich nicht laßen* [etc.] | *oder Auf meinen lieben Gott* [etc.] *Arioso. di* | *Seb. Bach:*
6	No. 4	*Herr Christ der einige Gottes-Sohn. di* | *Seb. Bach.*
7	No. 5	*Choral. Herr Christ der einige Gottes Sohn* [etc.] *Aria di Seb. Bach.*
8	No. 6	*Choral Durch Adams Fall ist ganz verderb. di Walter*
9	Blank	
10–14	No. 7	*Choral Christe der du bist Tag und Licht con 5 Variaz. di Joh: Seb. Bach*
15	No. 8	*Nun kommt der Heyden Heiland* [etc.]
16–19	No. 9	*Dieß sind die heiligen zehn Geboth* (pp. 18–19: *Fuga. Alio mode 2.*; p. 19: *Variat 3.*)
20–23	No. 10	*Nun freut euch lieben Christen Gemein* [etc.] | *Allabreve* (p. 21: *Variation 2.*; pp. 22–23: *Aliomode 3.*)
23–24	No. 11	*Fuga Ach Herr mich armen Sünder* [etc.] (p. 24: *Variation 2.*)
25–29	No. 12	*Erhalt uns Herr bey deinem Wort* [etc.]
30–31	No. 13	*Christus der uns seelig macht* [etc.] (p. 31: *Variatio 2*)
32–33	No. 14	*Jesu meines Lebens Leben.*
34	No. 15	*Kommt her zu mir spricht Gottes Sohn* [etc.]
35	No. 16	*Fuga Herzliebster Jesu! was hastu verbrochen*
36–37	No. 17	*Fuga Aus tiefer Noth schrey ich zu dir* [etc.]
38–39	No. 18	*Da Jesu an den Creutze stund.*
40	No. 19	*Fuga: Allein Gott in der Höh sey Ehr* [etc.]

major variants found in LM 4843.[7] Rather, the copy transmitted in LM 4843 evidently represents an early stage of the variation cycle, probably dating from Bach's years in Arnstadt (1703–7) or Mühlhausen (1707–8). No. 4 appears elsewhere under the name of "Adlung."[8] If this attribution is correct, it seems more likely that the piece was composed by Rudolf Ernst Adlung (1663–99) than by Jakob Adlung (1699–1762), since

7. See NBA IV/1, KB, 185 and 189–91; Peter Krause, *Handschriften der Werke Johann Sebastian Bachs in der Musikbibliothek der Stadt Leipzig*, Bibliographische Veröffentlichungen der Musikbibliothek der Stadt Leipzig (Leipzig: Musikbibliothek, 1964), 28.

8. Staatsbibliothek zu Berlin, Preußischer Kulturbesitz, Mus. ms. 338; this manuscript dates from around 1840. The piece is also listed in August Gottfried Ritter's "Katalog der Orgelkompositionen" as a composition by Jakob Adlung (Beuron, Erzabtei St. Martin, Mus. MS. 195, p. 13). Photocopies of the Ritter catalogue were kindly made available by Michael Belotti.

its style points to the period around 1700.[9] On the other hand, the elder Adlung worked solely as a cantor and never held the post of organist, so it may be questionable whether he ever composed any organ music.[10]

The authenticity of the remaining four pieces attributed to "Seb. Bach" cannot at present be either proved or disproved. Clearly, however, they belong to an even earlier stylistic phase than the chorale partita BWV 766. Nos. 1, 3, and 5 are described in their headings as "Aria" or "Arioso"; here the chorale melody is embedded in a free "arioso" movement that in some respects is reminiscent of Thuringian church cantatas of the late seventeenth century (see plate 1).[11] For this unusual (and probably singular) type of chorale arrangement, the authorship of the young Bach must be seriously considered. The same is true of the boldly harmonized arrangement of the hymn tune *Komm, heiliger Geist, erfüll die Herzen* (no. 2), which brings to mind the "curious *variationes*" and "strange tones" with which Bach perplexed the congregation at Arnstadt while playing chorales.[12] Moreover, this piece is strikingly similar to the chorale arrangements BWV 715, 722, and 726, which appear to date from Bach's years at Arnstadt.

There can be no doubt about the authenticity of the composition by Johann Gottfried Walther (no. 6): it is also transmitted, with slight variants, in Walther's own hand as verse 2 of a two-movement arrangement of the hymn *Durch Adams Fall ist ganz verderbt* in the so-called *Frankenbergersche Handschrift* (see n. 13).

Of the twelve anonymous works in LM 4843, only nos. 11, 13 (verse 1), 17, and 19 have been identified. No. 11 (*Ach Herr, mich armen Sünder*) is a version—with considerable differences, particularly in its second half—of a composition by Johann Pachelbel, which has come down to us in several sources. In its complete form, the piece is preserved in two copies by Walther.[13] Also, a variant of its second section is transmitted in the *Plauener Orgelbuch*.[14] In all three sources the piece is notated a whole tone

9. For an example of Jakob Adlung's musical style, see his chorale prelude *Christus, der ist mein Leben* in *Orgelmusik um Johann Sebastian Bach*, ed. Rüdiger Wilhelm (Wiesbaden: Breitkopf & Härtel, 1985), 21–23.

10. For biographical data on Rudolf Ernst Adlung, see Johann Gottfried Walther, *Briefe*, ed. Klaus Beckmann and Hans-Joachim Schulze (Leipzig: Deutscher Verlag für Musik, 1987), 66–67, 218, 222, and 275.

11. See Wilhelm Krumbach, "Sechzig unbekannte Orgelwerke von Johann Sebastian Bach? Ein vorläufiger Fundbericht," *Neue Zeitschrift für Musik* 146, no. 5 (1985): 14, especially his reference to works by Johann Michael Bach.

12. BDOK 2:20; NBR, 46.

13. The Hague, Gemeente Museum, Ms. Scheurleer, 4. G. 14 (Frankenbergersche Handschrift), pp. 137–38; Königsberg Ms. 15839, pp. 209–10 (lost; microfilm at the Stadtbibliothek Winterthur).

14. Lost; photocopy in Berlin, Staatliches Institut für Musikforschung, Preußischer Kulturbesitz, Fot. Bü 129/1, p. 167.

Plate 1. J. S. Bach (?), organ chorale *Ich ruf zu dir, Herr Jesu Christ*, BWV *deest.*
Yale University, Irving S. Gilmore Music Library, LM 4843, p. 3.
Reproduced by permission.

higher than in LM 4843. The first verse of no. 13 (*Christus, der uns selig macht*) also appeared in a now-lost copy made by August Gottfried Ritter, again under Pachelbel's name.[15] A variant version of no. 17 (*Aus tiefer Not schrei ich zu dir*), with some of the parts arranged in a different order, is known as a composition by Johann Heinrich Buttstedt (1661–1734).[16] In addition, a fughetta based on this piece (albeit reduced to nine measures) is transmitted anonymously in the Weimar *Tabulaturbuch* (Weimar, Herzogin Anna Amalia Bibliothek, Ms. Q 341b, Nr. 103). Finally, no. 19 (*Allein Gott in der Höh sei Ehr*) is the eighth variation in a chorale partita by Nikolaus Vetter (1666–1734), which mistakenly was attributed to J. S. Bach (BWV 771/8).[17] The stylistic features of nos. 10, 13 (verse 2), 15, and 16 suggest Vetter's authorship as well.

Although it is impossible to say much about the lost original from which LM 4843 was copied, the pieces now identified suggest that it originated in Erfurt, since Adlung, Buttstedt, Pachelbel, Vetter, and Walther all at some point held posts there. The only composer in this circle not directly connected with Erfurt is J. S. Bach, but he had various family ties with the town. The fact that Rinck copied LM 4843 from an earlier collection (probably assembled soon after 1700) further confirms this conclusion. Rinck spent his student years (1786–89) in Erfurt, and through his teacher, Johann Christian Kittel, may have had easy access to older source material there.

Evidence of J. S. Bach's Teaching

The Princeton University Library contains a notebook by Bach's student Heinrich Nikolaus Gerber (1702–75) that is little known and has been studied even less. The course of instruction that Gerber received from Bach during his years of study in Leipzig (1724–27) is vividly described by his son Ernst Ludwig in the famous *Lexicon der Tonkünstler*. In addition to a detailed account of the works he studied with Bach (inventions, suites, and the Well-Tempered Clavier), we learn that, "having spent two years in Bach's school, with an industry appropriate to the excellence of such a teacher," Gerber returned to his home in Thuringia and "employed two years of leisure to put into order and apply the manifold good and beautiful things he had brought with him from Leipzig."[18] It appears that those "two years of leisure" point to a period of

15. See *Orgelkompositionen von Johann Pachelbel (1653–1706) nebst beigefügten Stücken von W. H. Pachelbel (1686–1764)*, ed. Max Seiffert, Denkmäler der Tonkunst in Bayern, IV/1 (Leipzig: Breitkopf & Härtel, 1903), xviii. Ritter's "Katalog der Orgelkompositionen" (see n. 8) also lists this work on p. 307 under the name of Pachelbel and on p. 465 under "incerta."

16. See Johann Heinrich Buttstett, *Sämtliche Orgelwerke*, 2 vols., ed. Klaus Beckmann (Meßstetten: Forum Music, 1996), 2:16–17.

17. See Nikolaus Vetter, *Sämtliche Orgelwerke*, ed. Klaus Beckmann (Meßstetten: Forum Music, 1995), 13–28.

18. Ernst Ludwig Gerber, *Historisch-biographisches Lexicon der Tonkünstler*, 2 vols. (Leipzig: J. G. I. Breitkopf, 1790), 1:491–92; English translation in NBR, 322.

self-instruction during which Gerber most probably made his first independent attempts at composing in the manner and style he had learned from his teacher. Fortunately, this stage of his musical development is meticulously documented in the notebook preserved in Princeton's collection.

The provenance of the source can be traced only in part. The notebook is first mentioned early in the nineteenth century by Ernst Ludwig Gerber, who in the manuscript catalogue of his music library occasionally refers to it as the "red book."[19] Moreover, in his *Neues historisch-biographisches Lexikon der Tonkünstler* he draws bibliographical information from it for the worklists of Christian Friedrich Witt and Johann Heinrich Buttstedt.[20] After Gerber's death the book, together with other items, was acquired by the Offenbach publisher Johann Anton André (1775–1842), whose extensive collection later was divided among his five sons. The exact transmission of the notebook in the second half of the nineteenth century and the first half of the twentieth still needs to be determined. With the exception of Gerber's *Lexicon*, the manuscript is not mentioned in any musicological reference work.[21] Before being transferred to the United States, however, it was announced in Hans Schneider's antiquarian catalogue no. 72 (October 1959).

Within the confines of this article it is not possible to provide a full inventory of the notebook. For our purposes, however, a brief overview of its contents should suffice. The first layer of the manuscript (fols. 1–28) consists of six chaconnes by several Thuringian masters active around 1700:

- *Ciacona ex C di Sing. Valent. Eckelt.* [61 variations]
- *Ciacona ex C di Joh: Heinr: Buttstädt* [23 variations]
- *Ciacona in G di Sing. Witte* [15 variations]
- *Ciacona in D di Pachelbel* [13 variations]
- *Ciacona* [in C] *di Singor Körner* [20 variations]
- *Ciacona. di Christian F. Witte* [100 variations]

Johann Valentin Eckelt (1673–1732) was Gerber's first teacher in Sondershausen. It is therefore likely that Gerber received this collection of chaconnes directly from him,

19. Ernst Ludwig Gerber, *Musikalische Werke sowohl theoretische als praktische . . . berühmter Tonkünstler . . . gesammlet und angeschaft von: Ernst Ludwig Gerber Sondershausen 1791* (Vienna, Gesellschaft der Musikfreunde, 1656/36), 142–43 and 146.

20. Ernst Ludwig Gerber, *Neues historisch-biographisches Lexikon der Tonkünstler*, 4 vols. (Leipzig: A. Kühnel, 1812–14), 1:589 and 4:593.

21. The source is mentioned by Susi Jeans in her edition of Heinrich Nikolaus Gerber's *Four Inventions*, Early Organ Music 25 (Borough Green, Kent: Novello, 1973). A discussion of the notebook, mainly focusing on the organ works contained in it, is found in Hugh J. McLean, "The Organ Works of Heinrich Nicolaus Gerber," in *Aspects of Keyboard Music: Essays in Honour of Susi Jeans on the Occasion of Her Seventy-Fifth Birthday*, ed. Robert Judd (Oxford: Positif Press, 1992), 60–80.

or at least acquired them before his departure to Leipzig. This is confirmed by certain characteristics of Gerber's handwriting, which point to the time before 1725. A comparison with dated samples of his hand suggests that the first two chaconnes were copied around 1715, while the other pieces probably were entered around 1720–25.[22]

The second layer, beginning on fol. 29r, contains a more modern repertoire. Judging from the date "17 July 1727" on fol. 36r, these pieces were entered into the notebook shortly after Gerber returned from Leipzig to Sondershausen. There cannot be any doubt, however, that this layer is closely related to his academic years in Leipzig—more specifically, to his studies with Bach.

Two pieces point to fellow students of Gerber's. On fol. 29r there is a little polonaise in G major attributed to "Wild." This refers to the Leipzig student Friedrich Gottlieb Wild (1700–1762), another of Bach's pupils, who in fact introduced Gerber to his teacher.[23] On May 18, 1727, Wild received a most favorable and warm-hearted testimonial in which Bach commented on "his well-learned accomplishments on the *Flaute traversiere* and *Clavecin*" and also mentioned "the special instruction . . . in the clavier, thorough bass, and the fundamental rules of composition based thereupon" that Wild had received from him.[24] The style of Wild's piece is closely related to the polonaises that around the same time found their way into the notebook of Anna Magdalena Bach, and to some of the earliest compositions by Carl Philipp Emanuel Bach. Even J. S. Bach paid tribute to this popular dance type in his sixth French Suite (BWV 817).

The second piece illuminating the biographical constellations and musical trends current in Gerber's Leipzig years is a *Concerto per il Cembalo composto da Giovanni Adolfo Scheibe* (fols. 54v–56r). This composition belongs to a species that apparently grew out of the Leipzig reception of Bach's keyboard transcriptions of concertos by Vivaldi, Marcello, Johann Ernst of Saxe-Weimar, and others, and culminated in the famous Italian Concerto (BWV 971) from the second part of the *Clavier-Übung* (published in 1735). It is significant in this context that two of Bach's transcriptions (BWV 972 and 981) were copied by Johann Adolph Scheibe and Bach's principal copyist Johann Andreas Kuhnau during the second half of the 1720s.[25] Following Bach's example, Scheibe also arranged a violin concerto by Vivaldi for solo keyboard.[26] The piece in

22. See Alfred Dürr, "Heinrich Nicolaus Gerber als Schüler Bachs," BJ 64 (1978): 7–18, esp. 8–9.

23. See BDOK 3:476; NBR, 321.

24. BDOK 1:127; NBR, 135.

25. See Ulrich Leisinger and Peter Wollny, *Die Bach-Quellen der Bibliotheken in Brüssel: Katalog, mit einer Darstellung von Überlieferungsgeschichte und Bedeutung der Sammlungen Westphal, Fétis und Wagener*, Leipziger Beiträge zur Bach-Forschung 2 (Hildesheim: Olms, 1997), 463–64.

26. See Russell Stinson, "The 'Critischer Musikus' as Keyboard Transcriber? Scheibe, Bach, and Vivaldi," *Journal of Musicological Research* 9 (1990): 255–71. For an edition of Scheibe's Vivaldi

Gerber's notebook in addition now documents him as a composer of concertos for unaccompanied keyboard.

It is interesting to note that, when not transcribing a model, Scheibe immediately gives up the ritornello structure of the outer movements and instead adopts the bipartite form customary for keyboard suites. Still, the term *concerto* is justified by the typical gestures of the motives as well as by the virtuoso figuration and characteristic harmonic features. In employing the more flexible and varied musical language of the concerto, Scheibe created a work that itself may have functioned as a prototype in the development of the keyboard sonata, which began to take shape in the late 1720s.[27] The earliest harpsichord sonatas by Carl Philipp Emanuel Bach follow similar stylistic trends.

Although he made a copy of Scheibe's concerto, Gerber himself did not experiment with such novel genres. His more conservative approach is particularly evident in the earliest of his compositions. After a few miscellaneous studies, the notebook on fols. 31r–33v contains a series of six two-part inventions. These are deeply indebted to their famous models, albeit without reaching their elegance and complexity. Gerber's *Inventio 1* in C major appears to imitate Bach's first invention (BWV 772); his *Inventio 2*, also in C major, is related to Bach's piece in A minor (BWV 784). Both are characterized by a constant exchange of musical material between the two hands. *Inventio 3*, again in C major, continues in the same manner, while *Inventio 4*, in G major, tries to emulate the style of Bach's highly *cantabile* and rhythmically intricate settings in 9/8 meter (cf. BWV 781 and 792). *Inventio 5* in A minor is an almost strict canonic minuet, which resembles a similar composition by the young Wilhelm Friedemann (Fk 1A, Minuetto 2)[28] as well as an anonymous piece from the notebook of Anna Magdalena Bach (cf. BWV ANH. 120). *Inventio 6* in D minor, finally, pays tribute to Bach's invention in the same key (BWV 775) (see plate 2). Taking into consideration stylistic individuality and varying giftedness, an analysis of these pieces in conjunction with the earliest compositional attempts by the two eldest Bach sons might yield significant clues about J. S. Bach's teaching methods.

After several attempts at writing minuets (fol. 34r–34v), Gerber next entered into his notebook a rather strange series of six short pieces labeled *Aria* (fol. 35r–35v), each

---

transcription, see *Keyboard Transcriptions from the Bach Circle*, ed. Russell Stinson, Recent Researches in the Music of the Baroque Era 69 (Madison, Wisc.: A-R Editions, 1992), 29–38.

27. McLean ("Organ Works," 68) assumes that Gerber had access to the piece only in 1736 during Scheibe's visit to Sondershausen. However, for stylistic reasons a date of origin in the second half of the 1720s is most likely. Thus it would seem more plausible that Gerber copied it during his stay in Leipzig.

28. See Hans-Joachim Schulze, "Ein dubioses 'Menuetto con Trio di J. S. Bach,'" BJ 68 (1982): 143–50.

Plate 2. Heinrich Nikolaus Gerber, *Inventio 6. in D f*, from Commonplace book of music, 1727. Princeton University Library, Rare Books: Manuscript Collection (MSS), C0199, fol. 33r. Reproduced by permission.

comprising only eight measures (two reprises of four measures). The purpose of these seems to have been to practice the writing of harmonically logical, melodically pleasing, and altogether "natural" phrases within the strict confines of two four-measure periods. The melodic style and ornamental flourish of these little compositions are reminiscent of keyboard arias by Johann Pachelbel and his school. It therefore appears feasible to associate them with Gerber's early musical education in Thuringia under the guidance of Johann Valentin Eckelt, a student of Pachelbel's. On the other hand, one cannot exclude the possibility that Bach, too, instructed his students to write exercises of this kind in order to sharpen their sense of well-balanced and coherent phrasing, and thus to strengthen their ability to "think musically."[29]

The most significant group of works in the notebook is a series of twelve suites (fols. 36r–48v). For his suite cycle, as in his inventions, Gerber uses only simple keys with no more than one sharp or flat. The suites generally include an allemande, courante, and sarabande, plus one additional dance movement (minuet, polonaise, bourrée, gavotte, or gigue). From Suite 6 onwards, however, the sarabandes are missing; only for Suite 11 did Gerber supply one at a later point (fol. 48v). In most instances, the allemandes and courantes follow the principles of the old-fashioned variation suite: the courante is merely a *tripla* variant of the allemande. Another feature of these movements is the frequent inversion of the opening theme at the beginning of the second reprise. In keyboard suites of the seventeenth and eighteenth centuries, this technique is common in gigues but rare in allemandes and courantes. Although the rhythmic and metric design as well as certain melodic features of these movements show similarities to Bach's French Suites, it seems that Gerber stuck to (or fell back on) the earlier, Thuringian phase of his musical education when unifying the first two movements of his suites by means of variation technique. His sarabandes are stylistically more advanced; they are mostly in strict three-part texture and display the expressive melodic qualities characteristic of Bach's pieces in the same genre. Finally, the more *galant* dance types maintain a stylistic level similar to that of the above-mentioned polonaise by Wild, representing musical taste in Leipzig student circles around 1730.

The stylistic diversity of the movement types in Gerber's keyboard suites raises the question of Bach's involvement in their genesis. If E. L. Gerber's claim that his father "put into order and applied the . . . things he had brought with him from Leipzig" is correct, we have to assume that many compositions existed in drafts or sketches before they were entered into the notebook. The stylistic evidence suggests, however, that Gerber studied with Bach especially (or even exclusively) the art of composing modern, *galant* dance types. For the older suite movements (except perhaps the sara-

29. See Christoph Wolff, "Vivaldi's Compositional Art, Bach, and the Process of 'Musical Thinking,'" in *Bach: Essays on His Life and Music*, 72–83.

bande), he had to rely on his earlier training and on studying independently those works by Bach that he was allowed to copy. One might even speculate that at least some of the allemandes and courantes go back to pre-Leipzig works or drafts. This view is supported by the observation that Gerber worked most intensively on his minuets and polonaises, constantly revising melodic and structural details, while the allemandes and courantes (despite their greater complexity) generally were entered into the notebook almost as fair-copies.

Among the miscellaneous pieces that follow the suite cycle, I would like to single out a *Menuet pour l'Cimpal* in F major, which demands the crossing of hands. This keyboard technique became very popular in the Bach circle around 1730, particularly for minuets. C. P. E. Bach later characterized it rather disparagingly as "a natural and at that time very common witchcraft" ("eine natürliche und damals sehr eingerissene Hexerey").[30] It is frequently found in the early keyboard works of Wilhelm Friedemann Bach, and also in several compositions by the young Carl Philipp Emanuel (e.g., the *Menuet pour Clavessin* [W. 111; H. 1.5], published in 1731). Even J. S. Bach used it in the *Tempo di Minuetto* of his fifth Partita (BWV 829).[31] The entire musical substance of the *Menuet pour l'Cimpal*, including the passages with crossed hands, appears again in an incomplete draft of a *Concerto* in A major for solo keyboard (fol. 50v).

The remainder of the notebook consists mostly of drafts for organ pieces, among them a three-part *Inventio . . . a 2 Clav: & Ped:* in E minor and numerous chorale preludes. Although it is likely that Gerber completed these drafts and sketches at a later point, it seems that only the final form of the E-minor invention has come down to us.

The Older Bach Family

JOHANN MICHAEL BACH'S PARTIA IN A MINOR

The majority of the Lowell Mason Collection at Yale University consists of copies in the hand of Johann Christian Heinrich Rinck and a number of scribes working for him, which date from the last decade of the eighteenth century or the beginning of the nineteenth. While the collection transmits numerous compositions from the late seventeenth and early eighteenth centuries, there are few sources from that period. Undoubtedly the oldest Bach-related source is LM 4693, a little manuscript that encompasses only four folios and contains a *Partia . . . ex A Moll di I. M. Bach*. This heading

30. C. P. E. Bach's autobiography in *Carl Burney's . . . Tagebuch seiner Musikalischen Reisen*, 3 vols. (Hamburg: Bode, 1772–73), 3:203.

31. See Peter Wollny, "Studies in the Music of Wilhelm Friedemann Bach: Sources and Style" (Ph.D. diss., Harvard University, 1993), 139–41; also Ulrich Leisinger and Peter Wollny, "'Altes Zeug von mir': Carl Philipp Emanuel Bachs kompositorisches Schaffen vor 1740," BJ 79 (1993): 127–204, esp. 172.

refers to the Gehren organist Johann Michael Bach (1648–94), whose daughter Maria Barbara became J. S. Bach's first wife. The characteristics of the handwriting suggest a date of origin around or shortly before 1700; the watermark "A with trefoil" stems from the Arnstadt papermill, pointing to the immediate vicinity of J. M. Bach, perhaps even directly to the composer's family. Indeed, the title page reveals the script of Johann Michael's successor, Johann Christoph Bach (1673–1727), while the music was entered by an unidentified copyist.[32]

The instrumental designation on the title page and in the caption of the first movement reads *Spinetto. 1.*, implying that originally there was also a part for a second *Spinetto.* This is corroborated by the musical structure of the composition. The piece—a keyboard suite of modest technical demands, containing the movements *Präludium*, *Allemande*, *Courante*, *Sarabande*, and *Gigue*—represents one of the earliest examples in central Germany of a composition for two harpsichords. Works of this type later played a significant role in the Bach family: consider the early *Concerto senza Ripieno* (BWV 1061a) by Johann Sebastian Bach and similar pieces by his two eldest sons, as well as the "musicalien auff zwey Clavire" mentioned by the Jena organist Johann Nikolaus Bach in a letter of 1728.[33] Johann Michael Bach's contribution to the genre now shows that pieces for two harpsichords were en vogue in the Bach family about fifty years earlier than the date of J. N. Bach's comment.

THE MOTET *MERK AUF, MEIN HERZ, UND SIEH DORTHIN* (BWV ANH. 163)

Modern Bach research has long been interested in Johann Sebastian Bach's ownership and performance of music by other composers. Reconstruction of his music library has yielded new insights into the musical styles he favored and the influences he absorbed from other composers.[34] Learning about his musical connections has also shed light on the tight web of his personal relations, although here many questions still remain unanswered. In particular, our attention is drawn to pieces composed by mem-

32. Johann Christoph Bach is represented in the Lowell Mason Collection with two large anthologies of keyboard music (LM 4982 and 4983). See Yoshitake Kobayashi, "Der Gehrener Kantor Johann Christoph Bach (1673–1727) und seine Sammelbände mit Musik für Tasteninstrumente," in *Bachiana et alia musicologica: Festschrift Alfred Dürr zum 65. Geburtstag am 3. März 1983*, ed. Wolfgang Rehm (Kassel: Bärenreiter, 1983), 168–77. The provenance of these sources is not entirely clear; it should be noted, however, that J. C. Bach's son Johann Günter died in 1756 at Erfurt, and Rinck may have acquired the manuscripts there when studying with Kittel.

33. See Hans-Joachim Schulze, "'Die Bachen stammen aus Ungarn her': Ein unbekannter Brief Johann Nikolaus Bachs aus dem Jahre 1728," BJ 75 (1989): 213–20, esp. 216.

34. See Christoph Wolff, *Der stile antico in der Musik Johann Sebastian Bachs: Studien zu Bachs Spätwerk*, Beihefte zum Archiv für Musikwissenschaft 6 (Wiesbaden: F. Steiner, 1968), and Kirsten Beißwenger, *Johann Sebastian Bachs Notenbibliothek*, Catalogus Musicus 13 (Kassel: Bärenreiter, 1992).

bers of the Bach family (e.g., Johann Michael, Johann Christoph, or Johann Ludwig Bach), since almost all of their surviving compositions were transmitted through J. S. Bach. Without his careful collecting and preserving, most notably in the so-called *Altbachisches Archiv*, we probably would have almost no trace of the musical output of these composers. For J. S. Bach, this collection obviously was more than just a repository of family memorabilia, since the performance of quite a number of these pieces is documented during his tenure at Leipzig.[35]

To the list of compositions owned and performed by Bach, another work probably can be added now: the double-choir Christmas motet *Merk auf, mein Herz*. The piece has been known since Franz Wüllner considered it for inclusion in the motet volume of the Bach-Gesellschaft edition in 1892.[36] But since it obviously was not an authentic composition by J. S. Bach, it was at the time discarded without further study. The recent discovery of a unknown source in an American library has yielded new material to carry the question of the piece's authorship and early transmission a good step further.

When I was looking through uncatalogued manuscripts and papers at the Harvard Music Library in September 1989 I came across a complete set of parts and a full score of BWV ANH. 163, both apparently eighteenth-century sources. These had belonged to George Benson Weston, a professor of Italian literature at Harvard and a collector of Bach sources. Weston gave most of his precious manuscripts to Harvard during the 1950s. When he died in 1960, the remainder of his musical library—consisting mainly of nineteenth- and early-twentieth-century editions as well as manuscript scores and performing parts in his own hand—was donated to Harvard by his son, Charles D. Weston. At that time, it was overlooked that some eighteenth-century manuscripts were hidden among these materials. In addition to the motet *Merk auf, mein Herz*, a copy of Handel's eight harpsichord suites (HWV 426–33), a collection of arias and chorales from Telemann's passion oratorio *Das selige Erwägen* (TVWV 5:2) arranged for voice and keyboard, and a hitherto unknown symphony by the Mannheim composer Johann Anton Filtz (1733–60) all came to light.

Both the parts and the score of the motet are kept in a blue cardboard folder bearing notes and comments by G. B. Weston and the former owner, Franz Hauser. These enable us to reconstruct the provenance of the sources as follows. Hauser bought the two manuscripts in 1832 at the auction of the estate of the Thomaskantor Johann

35. See Yoshitake Kobayashi, "Zur Chronologie der Spätwerke Johann Sebastian Bachs: Kompositions- und Aufführungstätigkeit von 1736 bis 1750," BJ 74 (1988): 7–72, and Daniel R. Melamed, *J. S. Bach and the German Motet* (Cambridge: Cambridge University Press, 1995), 159–88.

36. See BG 39, xxiv–xxv. The sources available to Wüllner were a score copied by G. A. Stäps in 1759 (Brussels, Royal Library) and an early-nineteenth-century score from the collection of Franz Hauser.

Gottfried Schicht,[37] and Weston subsequently acquired them at the auction of Hauser's music library by the firm of C. G. Boerner in 1905.[38] The source descriptions in the auction catalogues may indicate (if they are not simply incomplete) that the two manuscripts were separated during the nineteenth century and brought together again by Weston. This is of only secondary importance, however, for there can be no doubt that around 1800 both score and parts belonged to Schicht.

Since the two manuscripts came from Schicht's estate, Hauser mistakenly assumed that Schicht himself had copied the score; this error was rectified by Weston in a note on the folder. The score was, in fact, prepared directly from the parts by a professional Leipzig scribe, whose name is not known but who appears regularly as a copyist for Schicht. It bears the heading *Motetto. del Sigl: Bach Cugino. del Sigl: Giov: Seb: Bach.* Since this attribution is not present in the parts, it appears probable that the scribe took it from a title wrapper that has not been preserved.

The eight parts are written on paper of the same type and size, with the watermark (*a*) heraldic lily and (*b*) monogram CV.[39] There are only the voice designations, but no title or attribution (see plate 3). The copyist is commonly known as the "scribe of the Doles scores," referring to a group of mid-eighteenth-century copies of Bach cantatas formerly believed to be in the hand of Johann Friedrich Doles but actually written by a Leipzig figure whose name is still unknown.[40] The activities of this scribe are not limited to these sources, however. In fact, his work is quite frequently found in performance materials prepared for J. S. Bach and his successor, Gottlob Harrer.[41] The scribe's handwriting changed considerably in the course of the roughly ten years during which it can be documented. The earliest samples are found in several additional parts for the cantatas *Tue Rechnung! Donnerwort* (BWV 168) and *Dem Gerechten muß das Licht* (BWV 195), as well as for Johann Ludwig Bach's cantata *Die mit Tränen säen;* these

37. See *Versteigerungs-Katalog der von dem verstorbenen Herrn J. G. Schicht, Cantor an der Thomasschule zu Leipzig hinterlassenen Musikaliensammlung [. . .], Leipzig [1832],* p. 26, no. 62 ("Bach, J. S., Merk auf mein Herz, 8 Bg. Stimmen doppelt 8 [Bg.]").

38. See *Katalog der Bibliothek Hauser Karlsruhe [. . .] Versteigerung Montag, den 1. bis Mittwoch, den 3. Mai und folgende Tage [. . .] durch C. G. Boerner, Leipzig [1905],* p. 3, no. 17 ("Bach, (Johann Nicolaus?) (1669–1753). Motette: 'Merk auf, Herz, und sieh dorthin, was liegt in den (!) Krippelein' del Sign. Bach Cugino del Sign. Giov. Seb. Bach. Für achtstimmigen Chor à capella. Part. fol. 16 Bl.").

39. The watermark is identical with no. 73 in Wisso Weiß, *Katalog der Wasserzeichen in Bachs Originalhandschriften* (NBA IX/1).

40. I am grateful to Hans-Joachim Schulze for recognizing this scribal concordance. For additional information on the "Schreiber der Doles-Partituren," see NBA I/4, KB, 46–47, and NBA I/21, KB, 124–25 and 134.

41. In Yoshitake Kobayashi's list of copyists working for Bach between 1736 and 1750, he is labeled "Anon. N 5." See Kobayashi, "Zur Chronologie der Spätwerke Johann Sebastian Bachs," 32.

Plate 3. Johann Ludwig Bach (?), motet *Merk auf, mein Herz, und sieh dorthin*, BWV ANH. 163, first page of *Alto I*. Harvard University, Eda Kuhn Loeb Music Library, Mus 627.273.579. Reproduced by permission.

were all copied in connection with Leipzig performances between 1746 and 1749. The "scribe of the Doles scores" also wrote the *Violono* part for C. P. E. Bach's Magnificat, which was performed in Leipzig in 1750 on one of the feasts of St. Mary.[42] Finally, during the cantorate of Gottlob Harrer his work can be traced in a considerable number of performing materials, including the original parts of Harrer's passion oratorio *Ich weiß nicht, wo ich bin* (1751)[43] and a copy of the *Florilegium Portense* dated 1752.[44]

The most significant feature bearing on the chronology of this copyist's handwriting is the change in appearance of the downward-stemmed half notes. In the copies dating from 1750 and thereafter, the stem invariably is positioned in the middle of the large oval note-head; in the copies prepared between 1746 and 1749, it is placed on the right side of the much smaller "white note." In the parts for *Merk auf, mein Herz*, all the half notes are stemmed on the right. In addition, the quarter rests are very similar to those in the *Violono* part of C. P. E. Bach's Magnificat and in Harrer's passion oratorio. It therefore seems reasonable to date the source around 1748–49. This is confirmed by the watermark: the paper used for the motet parts is documented in Bach's own works between about 1747 and 1749 (e.g., the autograph score of the B Minor Mass and the original parts for Cantata 195). It is fairly safe to assume, then, that the parts were commissioned for a performance under Bach's direction.

Merk auf, mein Herz is an extended chorale motet that uses seven stanzas of Martin Luther's hymn *Vom Himmel hoch, da komm ich her.*[45] The stanzas do not appear in their original order, but in the sequence 7, 3, 6, 8, 9, 13, 15. Obviously, the composer wanted to strengthen the work's rhetorical plan and create an opportunity for dialogic exchange. Such rearranging of chorale stanzas is not unique—a similar treatment of the stanzas of *Vom Himmel hoch* is found in Johann Schelle's *Actus Musicus auf Weihnachten*—but it reveals the composer's particular attention to dramatic issues. His considerable craftsmanship is evident in the final movement, for instance, in which the chorale tune is presented by the two sopranos as a *cantus firmus* in long note-values while the other voices maintain the double-choir disposition of the previous movements. This approach to the use of a *cantus firmus* is typical of concluding sections in Thuringian motets from the second half of the seventeenth century and the first half of the eighteenth. Its combination with a double-choir accompaniment is certainly unusual, however.

42. See BDOK 3:148. The possible dates are February 2 (Purification), March 25 (Annunciation), and July 2 (Visitation).

43. Gdansk, Polska Akademia Nauk, Biblioteka, Ms. Joh. 216.

44. Leipzig, Bach-Archiv, Go.S. 432. For a detailed description, see Hans-Joachim Schulze, *Katalog der Sammlung Manfred Gorke: Bachiana und andere Handschriften und Drucke des 18. und frühen 19. Jahrhunderts*, Bibliographische Veröffentlichungen der Musikbibliothek der Stadt Leipzig 8 (Leipzig: Musikbibliothek, 1977), 100.

45. See my edition, CV 30.570 in the series Stuttgarter Bach-Ausgaben (Stuttgart: Carus, 1994).

This leads to the question of authorship. The piece follows the tradition of the Thuringian motet, and there is no reason to doubt its attribution to a member of the Bach family. But the motet genre tended to adopt a deliberately antiquated style, particularly in the early eighteenth century. It is therefore difficult to decide if we have to look for a composer from the generation of J. S. Bach or one active in the second half of the seventeenth century. When I first addressed this problem, I tended to follow the attribution "Bach in Eisenach" on the title page of a copy of the motet owned by G. A. Stäps.[46] Interpreting the work's pictorial, madrigalesque style as genuinely from the seventeenth century, I concluded that it was a composition by the Eisenach organist Johann Christoph Bach (1642–1703). After further study of the motet repertoire, however, I am now inclined to regard *Merk auf, mein Herz* as a deliberately old-fashioned piece from a much later time and to attribute it to the Meiningen court cantor and capellmeister Johann Ludwig Bach (1677–1731). Many stylistic features—such as a predilection for dialogic structure, relatively simple contrapuntal texture, and equally straightforward harmonic language with a tendency towards pictorial devices—are also found, for example, in J. L. Bach's extended funeral motet *Gedenke meiner, mein Gott.*[47] Particularly striking in both works are the extended passages with sustained pedal in three voices of each chorus, combined with free figuration in the fourth. If we accept the attribution to Johann Ludwig Bach, we can add to J. S. Bach's collection of his cousin's works (eighteen cantatas and a mass setting) a double-chorus Christmas motet of considerable musical quality.

Compositions by Carl Philipp Emanuel Bach at the Library of Congress

Among many other important tasks, the newly launched edition of the collected works of Carl Philipp Emanuel Bach will have to deal with the numerous eighteenth-century copies owned by the Library of Congress. These holdings—mostly keyboard concertos and a large number of chamber and solo keyboard works—were acquired in the early 1900s from the Berlin antiquarian Leo Liepmannssohn. Ciphers on the title pages indicate that the bulk of these sources came from the estate of the director of the Berlin Singakademie, Eduard Grell (1800–1886). While their earlier provenance still needs to be examined, it appears safe to assume that many of them originated in Berlin. The

46. Cf. n. 36. The Stäps copy was announced in the 1764 Breitkopf catalogue; see *Verzeichniß Musicalischer Werke allein zur Praxis, sowohl zum Singen, als für alle Instrumente [. . .], welche in richtigen Abschriften bey Bernh. Christoph Breitkopf u. Sohn in Leipzig [. . .] zu bekommen sind, Leipzig 1764*, p. 5 ("Bach, Organistens in Eisenach, Motette: Merk auf mein Herz, à 2 Chor, 2 Soprani, 2 Alti, 2 Tenori, 2 Bassi. a 2 thl. 16 gl.").

47. The unique copy of this piece is in the Stellfeld Collection at the University of Michigan, Ann Arbor (M 2092. B 118. G 4). It once belonged to Werner Wolffheim and was auctioned in 1928 as part of his large music collection.

fact that several of the copyists involved in the preparation of these sources are also known from manuscripts coming directly from the composer's own library confirms their significance for C. P. E. Bach scholarship.[48]

Since the trio sonatas in most cases have been preserved in autograph scores and original sets of parts, the copies in Washington are not of primary significance for establishing reliable editions. However, they do offer important clues concerning the distribution and reception of these works during the second half of the eighteenth century. This becomes clear in an exemplary way from a copy of C. P. E. Bach's Trio in D Minor (W. 72; H. 596). While in the authorized sources the piece is transmitted in a version for violin and obbligato harpsichord, in the Washington manuscript (shelf number: M 422. A 2. B 13) the right hand of the keyboard part is designated *Flauto Traverso*. Although the authenticity of this arrangement cannot be proved, it is worth noting that the original performance materials for other trios provide various alternatives with separate parts for flute, violin, and continuo, as well as a combined part labeled "Traverso e Basso" for obbligato keyboard.

The Washington source bears the comments "coupirt von AKohne" and "ex partibus Monsr. Kauffman." The copyist's name refers to the Berlin court musician August Kohn(e), who was born in 1732 in Königsberg and came to Berlin in 1750 as a violinist in the chapel of Margrave Carl. Kohn studied composition with Christoph Schaffrath, entered the royal court chapel in 1760, was employed there until his retirement in 1798, and died around 1801–2 in Berlin.[49] Apart from the Washington copy of W. 72, Kohn's handwriting is also found in two other sources at the Library of Congress: a trio sonata by Carl Heinrich Graun (M 322. G 771 No. 29) and a copy of Jean Marie Leclair's trio sonata collection, Op. 4 (M 312.4 L 47 op. 4). According to the other comment on the title page of W. 72, Kohn prepared his copy from parts provided by "Monsr. Kauffman." This points to the Berlin organist Johann Friedrich Kaufmann, who was born in 1729 and from 1750 until his death in 1798 held appointments as organist at several Berlin churches.[50] Kaufmann's name also appears on the list of sub-

48. See Leisinger and Wollny, *Die Bach-Quellen der Bibliotheken in Brüssel*, 132–34; also Rachel Wade, *The Keyboard Concertos of Carl Philipp Emanuel Bach*, Studies in Musicology 48 (Ann Arbor, Mich.: UMI Research Press, 1981), 45–47.

49. Biographical data according to Robert Eitner, *Biographisch-bibliographisches Quellen-Lexikon der Musiker und Musikgelehrten*, 10 vols. (Leipzig: Breitkopf & Härtel, 1900–1904), 5:410. On Kohn's activities as a composer, see Christian Ulrich Ringmacher, *Catalogo de' Soli, Duetti, Trii . . .* (Berlin, 1773; reprint, Leipzig: Peters, 1987), 45, 63, 72, 82; also Hans Uldall, *Das Klavierkonzert der Berliner Schule*, Sammlung musikwissenschaftlicher Einzeldarstellungen 10 (Leipzig: Breitkopf & Härtel, 1928), 85.

50. See Eitner, *Biographisch-Bibliographisches Quellen-Lexikon*, 5:328; also Curt Sachs, *Musikgeschichte der Stadt Berlin bis zum Jahre 1800* (Berlin: Paetel, 1908), 183 and 212.

scribers to C. P. E. Bach's song collection *Herrn Doctor Cramers übersetzte Psalmen mit Melodien zum Singen bey dem Claviere, Leipzig 1774* (w. 196; H. 773). Since the title page of Kohn's copy of w. 72 describes the composer's position as "Màstro di Capella a Hambourg," it obviously dates from after 1767. It may, however, go back to much older exemplars circulating in Berlin. Kohn's copy offers an interesting glance at the wide range of options in eighteenth-century performance practice: a note on the flute part states explicitly that in the first movement the violin part should be played by the keyboard ("NB das Adagio aus der Viol: wird auf dem Flügel gespielt").

Another interesting group of sources contains early keyboard sonatas by C. P. E. Bach from the collections of Erich Prieger (1849–1913) and Ludwig Scheibler (1848–1921).[51] These manuscripts have been of particular interest to C. P. E. Bach scholarship, since they include some of the composer's earliest contributions to the genre. The early sonatas have survived only in rare instances, as the composer later in his life destroyed his juvenilia and replaced them with stylistically and technically more advanced versions.[52] The graphological evidence and oblong format of these sources suggest a connection with the Leipzig firm of Breitkopf, although only a few of the pieces actually show up in the thematic catalogues. Five sonatas of this group were copied by the "scribe of the Doles scores" mentioned earlier; certain characteristics of his handwriting suggest that his copies stem from between 1750 and 1755. These sources claim our special attention, since our examination of the parts for *Merk auf, mein Herz* showed that this copyist is more closely connected to J. S. Bach than had previously been suspected. Indeed, the readings in the Washington copy of the Sonata in E-flat Major (w. 65/7; H. 16) are very close to the version entered by Anna Magdalena Bach into her notebook around 1733–34, while the copy of the Sonata in F Major (w. 65/1; H. 3) corresponds with a partial autograph from around 1744.[53]

Clearly, source-critical investigations can still contribute to our understanding of the genesis and transmission of long-known compositions by members of the Bach family. And in this endeavor the American Bach sources will continue to offer useful clues.

51. See Leisinger and Wollny, "'Altes Zeug von mir,'" 130.

52. See Wolfgang Horn, *Carl Philipp Emanuel Bach: Frühe Klaviersonaten. Eine Studie zur "Form" der ersten Sätze nebst einer kritischen Untersuchung der Quellen* (Hamburg: K. D. Wagner, 1988).

53. Brussels, Conservatoire Royal de Musique, Bibliothèque, 27911 MSM.

"Father Knew (and Filled Me Up with) Bach"

Bach and Ives—Affinities in Lines and Spaces

Carol K. Baron

Separated by almost two centuries and by differences distinguishing the older German culture from that found in the New World of the late nineteenth century, Johann Sebastian Bach and Charles Ives nevertheless created musical works that exhibit strong similarities. These similarities were, moreover, set in comparable foundations. Despite the disjunctions in time and culture, they converge in circumstances governing the composers' early educations and in consequential aspects of the worlds they each inherited, involving social and religious change. Even more significantly, they converge in the ways each of these composers confronted their respective worlds and responded, through music, to their interests and concerns.

I

The musical gifts of both J. S. Bach and Charles Ives were initially nurtured by their fathers, both professional musicians. Although Bach's father, Johann Ambrosius Bach (1645–95), died when the composer was but ten years old, by then Bach's unusual gifts had been recognized and his training as an organist, violinist, and singer was well underway. Ives's first and most important teacher was George Edward Ives (1845–94). In his memos, Charles Ives wrote about his early education:

> Besides starting my music lessons when I was five years old, and keeping me at music in many ways until he died, with the best teaching that a boy could have, Father knew (and filled me up with) Bach and the best of the classical music, and the study of harmony and counterpoint etc., and musical history. Above all this, he kept my interest and encouraged open-mindedness in all matters that needed it in any way.[1]

The training the young composers received was colored by the level of stability

1. Charles E. Ives, *Memos*, ed. John Kirkpatrick (New York: W. W. Norton & Co., 1972), 115.

musicians confronted in the normative, paradigmatic musical practice of their immediate environments: Bach, the relatively stable compositional style that his father and older brother practiced and transmitted; Ives, the radical changes in musical practice that his father perceived had taken place within the recent past. Although the composers' innovations are primarily traceable to the power of their giftedness, Bach was expected to work in the contemporary styles he inherited, which he perfected and to which he, moreover, even introduced anomalous musical conceptions that seem to have been utterly personal and idiosyncratic. Among these, the Brandenburg Concertos, the Musical Offering, and the Art of Fugue are the most dramatic examples. Ives was encouraged to understand the nature of stylistic change and to seek new musical possibilities in logical musico-historical processes. As with Bach, Ives's inventiveness resulted in conceptions expressed in idiosyncratic musical designs and structures.

A striking similarity between the older generation of musicians in both families was their involvement in church music and community rituals and celebrations. The career choices made by the younger composers and the spiritual concerns that motivated much of their creative output stemmed from their families' musical values and their fathers' professional backgrounds, which are notable genealogical oddities—shared to some degree also by Mozart—in the history of modern Western composers. Bach's father, part of a large family of professional musicians, began his career as a town musician in Erfurt, from where he moved to become both a town and church musician in Eisenach (the birthplace of J. S. Bach) as a singer and instrumentalist, a performer for weddings in that city and in the general vicinity, and also part of a newly formed band for Prince Johann Georg I. Extant records chronicle his success and the community's admiration of his gifts.[2]

Charles Ives's father, George Ives, was well trained both as an instrumentalist and in theoretical matters, much of the latter acquired through his own initiative. Entries in George Ives's own student notebooks, which are preserved in the Ives Collection at Yale University, "show a thorough grounding, particularly in Bach. The copybook has pages of exercises in harmony (figured), counterpoint, and fugue—many Bach chorales (figured), two movements of *Jesu meine Freude*—parts of baroque masses, opera scenes of Gluck and Mozart, etc.—and marches and dance tunes—all in George's hand."[3] George Ives appreciated Wagner's music and, long before it was revived, Monteverdi's music also attracted his attention.[4] After serving for a short time as the

2. Karl Geiringer, *The Bach Family: Seven Generations of Creative Genius* (London: George Allen & Unwin, 1959), 69–74 passim.

3. John Kirkpatrick, appendix 13, "George Edward Ives (1845–1894) and His Family," in Ives, *Memos*, 246.

4. Jan Swafford, *Charles Ives: A Life with Music* (New York: W. W. Norton & Co., 1996), 442 n. 21, found a letter from Charles Ives noting that his father admired Monteverdi's music.

youngest bandmaster in the Union army, he freelanced in New York before returning to his hometown of Danbury, Connecticut, to be church organist and choir director at the Methodist Church. He also directed the music at revival meetings around Connecticut during the summer months, an activity that comfortably qualifies as the occupation of a church musician; led concert and marching bands in Danbury and neighboring towns; freelanced on cornet in pick-up bands in New York and Connecticut; directed musical theater productions; toured in minstrel and vaudeville shows, as well as in concerts; and taught.[5] Not too surprisingly in a small, middle-class town like Danbury, while George Ives was appreciated as a performer, few could appreciate his deeply penetrating mind in regard to past music and his prescience in recognizing a crisis in basic theoretical issues concerning late-nineteenth-century music.[6] Nevertheless, he occupies a serendipitous position in music history, wherein his ruminations about problems in contemporary theory and pedagogy could suggest ideas that would take root in his son's development as a composer.

Both Bach and Ives were child prodigies. Although not endowed with the extraordinary precocity of Mozart, they were recognized as creative and instrumental geniuses at a young age. Organ virtuosi, they both began careers as practical, professional instrumentalists when they were fifteen years old. Between the ages of ten and fifteen, Bach earned a modest salary as a choir singer while living with his older brother, Johann Christoph, in Ohrdruf.[7] When he left his brother's household, he was hired to sing in the prestigious choir at the church of St. Michael in Lüneburg, where he earned a salary for these services and "for singing in the streets, performances at weddings, funerals, etc." As part of his compensation he also received room and board, a rigorous education and, incidentally, became acquainted with the unusually fine collection of music housed at St. Michael's, the source of the choir's exceptionally large repertory. At this time Bach also began his career as an instrumentalist, as organist and violinist or violist in the small orchestra maintained by the church.[8]

Charles Ives started drum lessons when he was eight and at the age of twelve he became the drummer in his father's band, a semiprofessional organization. When he was fourteen years old, Ives's performance of Bach's Toccata, Adagio, and Fugue in C Major

5. Stuart Feder, *Charles Ives: "My Father's Song": A Psychoanalytic Biography* (New Haven: Yale University Press, 1992), 76–77; see also Swafford, *Charles Ives*, 41.

6. On George Ives's theoretical ideas and his place among other late-nineteenth-century theorists, see Carol K. Baron, "George Ives's Essay in Music Theory: An Introduction and Annotated Edition," *American Music* 10 (1992): 239–88; and Baron, "At the Cutting Edge: Three American Theorists at the End of the Nineteenth Century," *International Journal of Musicology* 2 (1993): 193–247.

7. Geiringer, *Bach Family*, 121.

8. Ibid., 124–25; also Karl Geiringer, *Johann Sebastian Bach: The Culmination of an Era* (New York: Oxford University Press, 1966), 11.

(BWV 564), technically a formidable work,[9] led to his professional career as a church musician. In early 1889, while his father was organist at Danbury's Methodist Church, Ives became a salaried professional as organist at the Second Congregational Church. Later that year, on his fifteenth birthday, he became the organist at the West Street Church, Danbury's Baptist Church, a position he retained until he left Danbury in 1893.[10] At about the same time Ives began his first regular job, he embarked on organ lessons with a more rigorous teacher, "who tutored him in the highest level of the repertoire," including Bach preludes and fugues, Mendelssohn organ sonatas, and numerous "orchestral transcriptions that were rife in those days," including "Rossini's *William Tell Overture*, a grandstanding number that would turn up on recitals for the rest of his playing career."[11] He was still fifteen when he performed a short program of virtuosic works that included Bach's Toccata and Fugue in D Minor ("Dorian," BWV 538). The remainder of the program included Dudley Buck's Variations on "Home, Sweet Home" and Mendelssohn's Organ Sonata No. 1. Seventeen days later he performed again, in a full solo recital with a totally different program "the Mendelssohn Second Sonata, a Bach Prelude and Fugue, pieces by Flotow, Batiste, and Guilmant, and finishing with Wagner's *Tannhäuser* Overture. This time the paper called his abilities 'almost phenomenal.'"[12]

Gifted and innovative, Bach and Ives also shared the hazards of being church musicians in the early eighteenth and early twentieth centuries respectively. *Plus ça change* . . . When the twenty-one-year-old Bach tried out some new, unconventional ideas in performing his duties as church organist in Arnstadt, having recently absorbed new and compelling ideas during four months of study with Buxtehude, the congregation complained about "his accompaniments of the hymns, and his improvisations between the verses [that] seemed never to come to an end." Bach was taken to task "for the 'many curious variations' he was inserting into the accompaniment" and received strict instructions regarding the use of strange and conflicting melodies or tonalities.[13] He held

9. Laurence D. Wallach, "The New England Education of Charles Ives" (Ph.D. diss., Columbia University, 1973), 135–36.

10. The *Danbury* (Conn.) *Evening News* noted that Ives had been given the job; see Feder, *Charles Ives*, 107. Swafford, *Charles Ives*, 49–50.

11. Swafford, *Charles Ives*, 51, from an unpublished memo in New Haven, Yale University Music Library Archival Collection, Ives Papers 45/D4.

12. Reported in the *Danbury Evening News* under the heading, "The Greatest Artistic Success of the Season"; Swafford, *Charles Ives*, 57 and 442 n. 34 (from Ives Papers 40, Scrapbook #2).

13. Geiringer, *Bach Family*, 134. Geiringer adds, "Strict orders were given him 'if he used a *tonus peregrinus*' (a strange key) 'to hold it out and not quickly to pass on to something else or even, as he liked to do, to use a *tonus contrarius*' (a key conflicting with the former one)." The rebuke may be found, in English translation, in NBR, 46.

the Arnstadt position for only a short time after that incident, only long enough to acquire a new one. In his next position, in Mühlhausen, Bach's plans to develop the modern cantata are said to have met with pietistic resistance to elaborately composed music and, probably, the congregation's opposition to changes in what they had come to expect. Bach soon left for Weimar, where he looked forward to "the more effective pursuit . . . in the due ordering of church music without interference from others."[14] He moved several more times, seeking a position in which his gifts would be appreciated, but he never found the ideal situation, one that would enable him to fulfill his artistic drives while also consistently providing nurturing encouragement and appreciation for doing so. Even as music director for the most prestigious Leipzig churches, the situation in which he had been so incredibly productive, Bach complained of the inadequacies of his performing forces.[15] Eventually he ran up against what he experienced as demeaning treatment from a young school superintendent, Johann August Ernesti. The town council, throughout his tenure, remained more interested in how well Bach served the St. Thomas School than how well he composed and directed the music for services and official functions. As a consequence, by the last decade of his life, having withdrawn from a number of previously held responsibilities, like teaching or supplying music for church use, Bach devoted himself to instrumental composition, revising earlier compositions, and preparing works for publication.

During this last period of his life, Bach experienced the professional isolation that Ives knew during most of his creative life, and he responded similarly. Bach composed his most personal expressions of artistic conviction and of piety, following only his creative impulses. In his new compositional activities of that period, thoughts no longer centered on pedagogically or performance-driven instrumental music, communicative religious symbolism, or communal entertainments and celebrations, but on private, intellectualized goals. The disparities between the interactions with employers and respective social milieus known by Bach and Ives are worth noting, although these lifelong differences did not ultimately determine the compositional ambitions of either one. With few exceptions, until his last years, Bach composed music on demand. For Ives, satisfying creative impulses were the only motivations driving him throughout his composing career, except when he was a young church composer on whom the most minimal demands were made.

How much more difficult it was for Ives to be professionally fulfilled as a compos-

14. Geiringer, *Johann Sebastian Bach*, 25–26, 28. The quotation is from a letter to the Mühlhausen Council in which Bach sought his dismissal. The entire letter is translated in NBR, 57.

15. His letter of August 23, 1730, to the Leipzig town council, complaining about the inadequacy of the vocal and instrumental forces available to him for preparing the church music in his charge, is well known; see translation in NBR, 145–51.

er! Ives's aspirations as a concert composer, which had emerged at an early age, could not be supported in the United States (or probably anywhere in the Western world during his lifetime). A livelihood from music would have depended on teaching, or combining church positions with teaching, or, sometime later, writing scores for sound films and then television. Although Ives's religious and spiritual inclinations were a powerful aspect of his creative drive, working as a church composer proved unsatisfactory. The church jobs he held from early 1889 until the summer of 1902, with some freelance work in churches before and after that period, comprised the only employment Ives ever held as a composer. Like Bach in Arnstadt, Ives suffered his congregations' criticism for inserting what he considered even minor deviations to the conventional hymn-setting recipes, and Ives reported a few such instances.[16] Also like Bach, Ives always faced the limited ability of church choirs to sing his music well.[17]

Ives gave leaving music as a career much thought, especially since it seemed being a church musician was the only option open. Although several college teaching positions in music had been established, they had not yet gained much respect.[18] Nonetheless, although Ives was walking away from being a church musician, there is no indication that he ever relinquished his goal to be a composer. Ives finally concluded that being the conventional composer that church congregations wanted was too limiting and that, conversely, church congregations were unsuitable audiences for the religious music he wanted to compose. However, Ives's affinity for religious expression led to compositions on religious themes conceived for concert performance: "Not until I got to work on the *Fourth Symphony*, did I feel justified in writing quite as I wanted to, when the subject matter was religious."[19] Can Ives's choice to compose the music he needed to compose be compared to Bach's compositions during the last ten years of his life? I believe they can. Like Bach, Ives continued to affirm his values through composition, even when isolated from an audience.

16. He noted on the manuscript of *Adeste Fidelis* that when it was played as an organ prelude at the 1898 Christmas service in Bloomfield, New Jersey, "Rev. J. B. Lee, others and Mrs. Uhler said it was awful"; see John Kirkpatrick, *A Temporary Mimeographed Catalogue of the Music Manuscripts and Related Materials of Charles Edward Ives, 1874–1954* (New Haven: Yale Music Library, 1960, 1973), 109, no. 3D19.

17. He noted in his memos that it was difficult to get choirs to sing the 67th Psalm *a cappella* as intended, and that his father had taken on the challenge with his choir in Danbury (Ives, *Memos*, 129, also n. 4, and 178–79).

18. Dudley Buck, for one, thought the degrees offered were "sought for or desired only by the greater or lesser frauds who would fain climb by means of it"; letter quoted in Frances Hall Johnson, *Musical Memories of Hartford* (Hartford, Conn.: Witkower's, 1931), 16, cited in Gayle D. Sherwood, "The Choral Works of Charles Ives: Chronology, Style, Reception" (Ph.D. diss., Yale University, 1995), 96. Ives's disparaging remarks about academic degrees in music (see Ives, *Memos*, 50, 87) may have been derived from Buck, who was his teacher for a short period.

19. Ives, *Memos*, 129.

The music and career decisions of Bach and Ives mirror their societies and their lives. Bach composed after absolutist rulers had been empowered by the disruptions of the Thirty Years' War (1618–48). Absolutism contributed to shaking up old social patterns based on birth and paving the way for a newly enfranchised middle class—the seminal step in its own later dissolution. Leipzig, like other larger German cities in Bach's time, was primed for trade by the absolute ruler who would forego control of the creation of wealth in exchange for added personal wealth, increased political control, and the privileges these presumably bestowed. Absolutism's tradeoff created the middle class to which Bach belonged and according to whose mores he learned to function. Bach's preoccupation with gaining a royal title and his sons' pursuit of juridical degrees can be understood as ways in which the Bach family complied with and prepared to serve the needs created by absolutism. Most of Bach's liturgical music was composed for Leipzig's mainly middle-class Lutheran congregants. Aside from a few works for the elector and his family, Bach's secular cantatas were for merchants and the déclassé nobility. As absolutism created and co-opted a vigorous middle class and disenfranchised the feudal nobility, composers and artists were again succumbing, if only for a short time, to the tastes of the aristocracy and the gallantry of court life. While proving that he could write "pretty melodies" and imitate the best of French affectations, Bach seems to have recoiled from pressures to move in this direction musically. Remaining true to himself, he composed the Art of Fugue at a time when polyphony was in a state of decline. The composer of the greatest liturgical music left this world when liturgical music for all Christian denominations was no longer serviceable.

The world in which Ives grew up was also undergoing enormous social change, stemming from industrialization. Labeled both the "Gilded Age" and the "Progressive Age," the post–Civil War period gave U.S. society both a new sense of capitalism's benefits and potential, and a newly awakened social conscience. The creation of new pockets of wealth led to social mobility and urbanization. Mark Twain enshrined the period in his novel, *The Gilded Age* (1873). The times challenged the social and political awareness of Ives and his immediate family; family history still retained a vital hold on Ives's sense of purpose and destiny. His family's commitment to democracy had been tested at the end of the eighteenth century in the New England battle for religious tolerance and, in the more recent past, in the abolitionists' crisis. The Ives family was among the liberal Protestant Congregationalists of Connecticut who joined the Massachusetts Unitarians in a religious movement that focused on social justice, and whose form of piety lay in action taken in the here and now.[20] Through Charles Ives the familial heritage took yet another step: into the realm of art. Ives attempted to realize the quality and character of an ideal American democracy in his life and to portray its symbols in

20. This history is discussed in Carol K. Baron, "The Democratic Objectives of Charles Ives and His Family: Their Religious Contexts," *Musical Quarterly* 86, no. 2 (Summer 2002), forthcoming.

his music. The musically revolutionary means he employed to fulfill his musical goals placed him at odds with all sectors of the musical world. His commitment to change and progress in music was as natural to him as contemporary assumptions that physical evolution was inevitable. Ives referred to the concerns of his age in his memos and often composed with these concerns in mind.

II

The similarities between the music of Johann Sebastian Bach and Charles Ives began to take shape during Ives's early education. Among Ives's earliest musical experiences was the tattered edition of the Well-Tempered Clavier, technically simplified by virtue of being an arrangement for piano four-hands—likely one of the first books he used with his father.[21] Bach's music was a common enough starting place for most students of keyboard instruments and composition during the almost 150 years before Ives's musical studies were initiated. However, in Ives's mature compositions, similarities developed in spatial and temporal relationships, particularly in their use of polyrhythmic textures. Ives's two early symphonies belong to the youthful period of experimentation and gaining compositional skills, when he was settling on the structural components of his mature style and solidifying what would be the convictions of his individual voice. Until Ives, I can think of no composer whose polyphonic conceptions are so directly linked to those of Bach. Therefore, although Ives was heir to the great body of Western music that included, most immediately, the symphonic music of nineteenth-century Europe and its more than competent American entries, his mature style refers back to Bach's music in a variety of ways.

Ives followed Bach's pattern of setting congregational tunes in "chorale preludes" for organ, as he referred to them. This practice was not seriously pursued even among church musicians after Bach, who preceded their hymn accompaniments in order to establish a key for the congregation. Until the Eleven Chorale Preludes by Brahms, which weren't published until 1902—a telling sign about how functional they were—such arrangements are not found among the compositions of famous composers. In the United States, Dudley Buck (1839–1909) and Harry Rowe Shelley (1858–1947), prominent church musicians and composers of original organ works, as well as Ives's teachers for short periods, eschewed original settings of church tunes but created organ arrangements and transcriptions of works by other composers, some of which were recommended for use as interludes, preludes, offertories, and postludes during church services.[22]

21. *Das Wohltemperierte Clavier: 48 Fugen und Präludien in allen Tonarten*, arranged by Henri Bertini (Mainz: B. Schott's Söhne, n.d.). Also to be found are the Two- and Three-Part Inventions, edited by F. A. Roitzsch, which contain pencil notations designating organ manuals and fingerings. The author saw this music in Ives's study in the house in West Redding, Connecticut, in October 1995.

22. One example of a collection for church use is the volumes published by G. Schirmer called *Preludes,*

Ives's hymn settings for organ comprised a significant portion of his earlier compositions, although precise numbers are unknown and we cannot ascertain anything about their structures. With one exception, *Adeste Fidelis*, all of these compositions were lost. Ives discusses several instances of incorporating arrangements of hymns in later compositions; however, the few comparisons that can be made tell us nothing about the structures of the early settings. Comparing his one extant organ setting of *Adeste Fidelis* and his uses of that tune in "Decoration Day" from the *Holidays Symphony* shows no correlation between the two. Ives discusses only church compositions whose settings were unusual, the ones that involved taking chances in regard to a congregation's tolerance for strange "sound combinations." But comparing Ives's description of his setting for "an organ *Prelude and Postlude for a Thanksgiving Service* played in Center Church, New Haven, Conn., in November 1897" (which states that the "*Postlude* started with a C minor chord with a D minor chord over it, together, and later major and minor chords together, a tone apart") yields no direct correlation in "Thanksgiving" from the *Holidays Symphony*, the associated later development, beyond the use of some of the same hymn tunes.[23]

Attempts to hypothesize about the original form of Ives's organ pieces from their transformations in movements of the violin sonatas and the Third Symphony—a few other pieces where, Ives tells us, he incorporated the organ settings in some movements—are also frustrated. Our expectation of a clear statement of the hymn tune at a point where it would have functioned as an introduction and guide for a congregation preparing to join in—as it undoubtedly originally did—is often thwarted by statements merely more or less recognizable and rarely complete. These statements are short, distorted, placed in middle voices, and overshadowed by lines more prominently set. There are exceptions, such as the last movement of the Third Symphony, where the final statement of the hymn tune shines out from the preceding murkiness like a revelation, and the last movement of the Third Violin Sonata. Ives described the latter movement in the program notes for the 1917 performance as "an experiment: The free fantasia is first. The working-out develops into the themes, rather than from them. The coda consists of the themes for the first time in their entirety and in conjunction."[24] However, *Adeste Fidelis* has no preliminary melodic fragmentation. In two parts, the left hand plays the melody in a real, nontonal inversion in the first part. In the second part, the right hand plays the melodic inversion as the countermelody to the known melody in the left. When this melody appears in "Decoration Day," the setting is com-

Offertories and Postludes, for the Organ, edited and arranged by Harry Rowe Shelley. The pieces included are a mixture of secular and religious, originally texted and untexted works. The style of these arrangements is primarily homophonic.

23. Ives, *Memos*, 38.

24. Ibid., 69 n. 1.

pletely different and the melodic intervals are distorted. Pitch distortions in the later works usually permit the recognition of only snippets of the hymn melodies. All that we can conclude about these organ settings with certainty is that Ives composed them, that this practice was not common, and that these pieces did not present opportunities in which the young composer could express himself freely, since he was restricted by the musical tastes and habits of congregations for whom simple accompaniments for congregational singing would have sufficed.

Ives's use of hymn tunes, in the works we do know, differs markedly from Bach's use of Lutheran chorales in two significant ways: He did not set each phrase of the hymns successively and completely, and he rarely maintained the integrity of the melodies. In Bach's arrangements, although interludes sometimes interrupt the continuity of the melodies, the chorales are rarely disguised, except when Bach, on occasion, sets them as a fantasia, fugue, or fughetta. Even in Bach's "paraphrase type" of setting, where the countermelody accompanying the chorale is paraphrased, the hymn is stated clearly. In his "ornamented type," the chorale is minimally embellished, while elaborate ornamentation disguises the chorale in one or more of the countermelodies.[25] Nevertheless, Bach's chorale arrangements probably exerted the single most influential force on the development of Ives's music—one that he encountered as a young organist. The textures used in Ives's "organ-derived" pieces, like those mentioned above, and in the many secular instrumental works Ives had been composing since his youth, and continued to compose, are comparable only to Bach's music in their polyphonic intensity. Bach's polyphony, even as represented in the simpler chorale settings of the *Orgelbüchlein*,[26] provided the most enduring lessons in Ives's compositional training. In these tightly constructed preludes, the variety of imitative procedures—canon, fugue, fugato, imitation in inversion, and so on—are similar to the techniques Ives uses in his early works, such as the polytonal fugues in four keys and the *Harvest Home Chorales*, as well as in the violin sonatas and in the Third Symphony, which he characterizes as "a kind of crossway between the older ways and the newer ways."[27]

If the idea of Bach's polyphonic style is limited to fugues and canons, however, then the next point is lost: Ives clearly understood that Bach's polyphony was not restricted to imitative procedures, but also existed in nonimitative, independent, distinct voices defined by discrete motives. Bach's countersubjects are not only functional in fugues.

25. Geiringer, *Johann Sebastian Bach*, 230, cites the examples of the "chorale fughetta," *Herr Christ, der ein'ge Gottes Sohn* (BWV 698), and the five-part *Fuga sopra il Magnificat* (BWV 733). Geiringer's typological analysis of Bach chorale settings (pp. 229–37) thoroughly discusses the polyphonic techniques the composer used.

26. Ives wrote "Ceal Klein" on one of his earliest manuscripts, which I believe was a "play" on the German title; there are other examples. "Ceal Klein" stands for C. E. (Charles Edward) when small.

27. Ives, *Memos*, 128.

They are also motives with either distinctive rhythms or pitch contours, often associated with expressing the meaning or character of the chorale text. In that capacity, they function like the instrumental obbligatos in the cantata and passion arias. In several organ arrangements, Bach's motives are even reduced to ostinato figures, like the recurring rhythmic figure in *Wir Christenleut* (BWV 612) or the eight-note figure in the pedal of *In dir ist Freude* (BWV 615), both from the *Orgelbüchlein.* Bach's music even offered suggestions for gaining the kind of rhythmic distinctiveness through contrasting rhythmic cells that became Ives's fingerprint. In only one measure of *In dulci jubilo* (BWV 608) are triplets on three levels: the half note, the quarter note, and the eighth note (see ex. 1). In 3/2 meter, the division of the dotted half notes implies a duple meter; two dotted half notes operate against three half notes, two quarter notes operate against an eighth-note triplet, two dotted half notes operate against three eighth-note triplets, and two quarter-note triplets operate against three half notes.

Juxtaposed distinctive motives and ostinatos are the sine qua non in Ives's polyphonic-layered structures. "Polyphonic layers" are discrete motivic, and sometimes also harmonic and contrapuntal, complexes in which polymeters play an important role. They function in polyphonic relationships, somewhat as conventionally independent, identifiable lines of single pitches do.[28] They characterize movements of the *Holidays Sym-*

2 dotted half notes: 3 half notes
2 quarter-note triplets: 3 half notes
2 dotted half notes: 3 eighth-note triplets
2 quarter-note triplets: 3 eighth-note triplets
2 quarter notes: eighth-note triplet

Ex. 1. Polymeters and Polyrhythms in J. S. Bach, "In dulci jubilo," *Orgelbüchlein*, m. 12.

28. Nachum Schoffman, "The Songs of Charles Ives" (Ph.D. diss., Hebrew University of Jerusalem, 1977), 266–67, surveys the terminology used for this Ivesian texture. The nature of the interrelationships Ives creates cannot be treated here.

phony, Three Places in New England, the Fourth Symphony, the *Set for Theater Orchestra,* the Second Orchestral Set, both piano sonatas, the *3-Page Sonata,* and the most famous of all layered polyphonies, *The Unanswered Question*—in short, most of Ives's mature conceptions.

Even Ives's one extant organ prelude, *Adeste Fidelis,* incompletely described above, which has a simple structure not necessarily representative of his other organ preludes, includes polyphonic components that point to the "layers" of Ives's mature music. In *Adeste Fidelis* (see ex. 2), throughout the first part the B-flat retained in the pedal, the B-flat-minor chord in a high register in the right-hand manual ("like distant sounds from a Sabbath horizon," Ives wrote), and the inverted melody in the left-hand manual function as independent layers. In the second part, a reasonably regular diatonic bass line in the pedal provides support for the melody in F major in the left-hand manual, while the melodic inversion is played on the right-hand manual as a countermelody. Independence is largely created by the dissonance factor between the juxtaposed melodic lines. In each of the two parts, three motivic ideas retain their autonomy—their layeredness.

Ex. 2. Charles Ives, *Adeste Fidelis,* mm. 1–6.

Early in his studies, Ives's imagination was stimulated by fugal and canonic procedures, but later they provoked his disdain, particularly as the primary pedagogical tool in counterpoint courses with Horatio Parker. When Ives wrote in the margin of an assignment for Parker, "a stupid fugue and a stupid subject,"[29] he was responding to, what was for him, the irrelevant nature of this exercise and so many others he had completed, which demonstrated imitation at intervals prescribed by Jadassohn's textbooks and adherence to Fuxian rules for alleged sixteenth-century dissonance treatment.[30]

29. Marginal note by Ives on a class assignment, from Kirkpatrick, *Temporary Mimeographed Catalogue,* 109, no. 3D15.

30. Salomon Jadassohn, *A Course of Instruction on Canon and Fugue,* trans. Gustav (Tyson-) Wolff (New York: G. Schirmer, 1887); *A Manual of Simple, Double, Triple and Quadruple Counterpoint,* 2d ed., rev. E. M. Barber, trans. Gustav (Tyson-) Wolff (New York: G. Schirmer, 1892).

Before attending Yale, Ives had broken away from the fugues composed according to Jadassohn's lesson plans with his own playful treatments of fugal entrances. Extending the standard procedure in four-voiced fugal expositions, where the *dux* and *comes* are stated in the tonic and dominant in two voices and then stated again in the tonic and dominant in the remaining two voices, Ives composed several fugues in which the voices enter in a continuous cycle of fifths. There are two short fugues with entrances on C–G–D–A and the *Song for Harvest Season* with entrances on C–F–B-flat–E-flat in his father's notebook,[31] and the *Fugue in Four Keys on "The Shining Shore"* for strings or organ and violins, also with entrances on C–G–D–A.[32] According to Ives's values, and those of his father, these kinds of innovative fugal procedures were, at the very least, attempts to strive for relevancy, if only by articulating a step in music's evolution, an evolution inherent in music's nature just as evolution was inherent in all nature.[33] Ives elaborated about his departure from standard practice as follows:

> To show how reasonable an unreasonable thing in music can be—look at a fugue. It is, to a great extent, a rule-made thing. So, if the first statement of the theme is in a certain key, and the second statement is in a key a 5th higher, why can't (musically speaking) the third entrance sometimes go another 5th higher, and the fourth statement another 5th higher? And if it must hold to the same nice key system, why can't these themes come back in the same way? "Because Bach didn't do it," Rollo says, "and that's the best reason I know."[34]

Ives then summons scientific data from Helmholtz to challenge professors who defend "tonality" and avoid tunings they call "unnatural and violating a fundamental law," which in fact exist in the overtone series, "the true, fundamental, natural laws of tone."[35]

Ives continued to use canons and fugues in his piano studies and pieces based on algorithms, where musical parameters were largely serialized but also represent a

31. Ives writes that his father's ear-training exercises in singing in two keys led to composing "in more than one, or two keys together" and "also a fugue going up in 4ths in four keys, or up in 5ths in four keys, etc." He describes his father's response to such experiments as follows: "Father used to say, 'If you know how to write a fugue the right way *well,* then I'm willing to have you try the wrong way—*well.* But you've got to know what [you're doing] and why you're doing it.'" See Ives, *Memos,* 46–47.

32. Charles Ives, *Fugue in Four Keys on "The Shining Shore,"* ed. John Kirkpatrick (Bryn Mawr, Pa.: Merion Music, 1975). Ives lists this work among the "first serious pieces quite away from the German rule book . . . [in] four keys (1896), (though this was suggested by a *Fugal Song [for Harvest Season* for] tuba, trombone, cornet, voice—in C, F, B-flat, E-flat—see Father's copy book)" (Ives, *Memos,* 38).

33. See his father's letter regarding what "Helmholtz says about natural laws—the danger of restricting music to habits and customs" (Ives, *Memos,* 47–48).

34. Ibid., 49–50.

35. Ibid., 50.

specific image, as in his *Tone Roads*.[36] However, in their diatonic and modal modern reincarnations, fugues came to represent culture's atrophic expressions. Ives relegated his best-known fugue to the "image" of a historical icon. Initially performed for a service at Center Church in New Haven in 1896, this fugue was the first movement of the First String Quartet, entitled "Chorale," before it became the third movement of his magnum opus, the Fourth Symphony. Henry Bellamann's 1927 program note for the symphony, undoubtedly prepared with Ives's guidance and approval, describes the symphony's "aesthetic program" as "the searching questions of What? and Why? which the spirit of man asks of life." The role of the fugue in this program is to represent "an expression of the reaction of life into formalism and ritualism."[37]

Symmetrical arrangements, which Bach used extensively in formal designs and tonal structures, were an important factor in Ives's tonal and formal thinking as well, particularly after he turned his back on what he saw as the rigidified molds of the classical-romantic traditions (the subject of the *3-Page Sonata*, discussed below). We are forced to wonder about astonishing similarities in the aesthetic inclinations of these two composers. In *Johann Sebastian Bach*, Karl Geiringer describes symmetrical formal design and symmetrical organization in Bach's multimovement works.[38] Eric Chafe discusses symmetry principally as an aspect of tonal design, that is, as structures expressing, through tonal allegory, the music's "musicotheological" character.[39] The coincidence of symmetrical structures in the works of the two composers considered here is curious, but perhaps it can be attributed to a symmetry in music history rather than only to influence: the organization of tonal structures in the period of the yet-

36. Ibid., 63–64. J. Philip Lambert ("Ives and Counterpoint," *American Music* 9 [1991]: 119–48) analyzes the fugal procedures in *Tone Roads No. 1* (135–38). Lambert, who makes a distinction between experimental and concert music, writes: "Ives uses canonic techniques in his experimental music more extensively than any other developmental device" (138). See also Nachum Schoffman, "Serialism in the Works of Charles Ives," *Tempo* 138 (September 1981): 26–27.

37. Quoted in John Kirkpatrick's preface to Charles Ives, *Symphony No. 4* (New York: Associated Music Publishers, 1965), viii. Bellamann assigned the fugue to the second movement, but Ives clearly assigns it to the third movement in *Memos*, 66.

38. Geiringer, *Johann Sebastian Bach*. He refers particularly to Bach's development of the concerto form and also mentions the symmetry in the Fugue in F-sharp Major from Book 2 of the Well-Tempered Clavier (BWV 882; p. 301), and in the organization of the Canonic Variations on *Vom Himmel hoch* (BWV 769; p. 254), the motet *Jesu, meine Freude* (BWV 227; pp. 181–82), and the St. John Passion (BWV 245; p. 196).

39. Eric Chafe, *Tonal Allegory in the Vocal Music of J. S. Bach* (Berkeley: University of California Press, 1991). See especially pp. 125–32, where he distinguishes between Bach's use of symmetry in tonal allegory and of symmetry involving textual antitheses, in which the "overall symmetrical planning is an image of reconciliation" (p. 127). The symmetry in numerous works is discussed throughout; see the entry "Symmetry" in the index (p. 448).

to-become drama of diatonic tonality—of the polar tonic and dominant defining sonata and symphonic structures—and their organization in the period that betrayed that drama. In both periods, symmetry was a logical structural and expressive tool; it served the needs of Bach and Ives.

In the passage quoted above regarding fugal entrances in continuous fifths (n. 34), Ives suggests a cosmic symmetrical tonal structure, wherein the entrances go up by fifths and "come back in the same way." An early work, *Gloria in excelsis*, actually modulates from F to B-flat to E-flat, "hold[ing] to the same nice key system" with "these themes com[ing] back in the same way," through B-flat back to F.[40] Geiringer makes the point that "not only the first and last sections [in Bach's symmetrically structured works] correspond, but a certain connection is established between the second part and the one next to the last,"[41] that is, Bach's symmetries are not tripartite constructions (A–B–A) but extended symmetrical structures, as are also those by Ives. Formal and tonal symmetrical structures are found in Ives's works throughout his creative years, from the youthful *Gloria*, to movements of the violin sonatas, to mature songs, to the systematic palindromes in "On the Antipodes," to orchestral conceptions like *Over the Pavements*.

Symmetrical structuring in the work of both composers implicates underlying meanings. Both Geiringer and Chafe ascribe theological interpretations to Bach's formal and tonal symmetrical structures. Ives composed symmetries in the contexts of various parametric relationships, but the meanings behind the symmetrical structuring in Ives's works cannot be ascribable to one principal source. Each piece suggests its own challenges, and much interpretive work is still needed. However, Ives attached underlying meanings to his use of such procedures, and he was negatively disposed to serializations of musical parameters as abstract organizational procedures: "Something made in this calculated, diagram, design way may have a place in music, if it is primarily to carry out an idea, or a part of a program."[42]

Nachum Schoffman describes Ives's use of palindromic symmetry in different parameters, which I mention here, since I believe they developed in conjunction with his development of those formal and structural symmetries more directly associated with Bach's music. Schoffman analyzes the symmetrical arrangements of "chord intervals" (between consecutive pitches of the chords), chord order, chord density, rhythmic patterns, ranges, and dynamics of the song "On the Antipodes."[43] In Ives's instru-

40. Kirkpatrick, *Temporary Mimeographed Catalogue*, 130, no. 5C4. See also Wallach, "New England Education of Charles Ives," 189–93; and Sherwood, "Choral Works of Charles Ives," 105–6.

41. Geiringer, *Johann Sebastian Bach*, 315–16.

42. Marginal note in *Majority or The Masses*, listed in Kirkpatrick, *Temporary Mimeographed Catalogue*, 126.

43. Schoffman, "Songs of Charles Ives," 209–34 and 48–52.

mental works, there are palindromes in *From the Steeples and the Mountains*, *All the Way Around and Back*, *In re con moto et al*, and elsewhere.

Larry Starr, in *A Union of Diversities*, directs our attention to symmetrical organization in what he labels the "stylistic arch." In the song "Ann Street," Starr analyzes nine sections, in which section 1 is an introduction outside of the arch, and sections 2 through 9 contain the arch in "distinct units of increasing complexity, rhythmic activity, chromaticism, and dissonance . . . followed by units that return to more consonant, diatonic, and rhythmically placid music." Later Starr describes the second "half" of the song, "The Things Our Fathers Loved," as "presenting a reversed and altered echo of the first 'half'"—a "'mirror' form."[44] Although Starr does not use the term *antithesis*, his discussion of this text suggests reconciliation as an aspect of symmetry in this song.[45] He also describes the "stylistic arch" in the songs "Walking" and "On the Antipodes," and in the instrumental works *Scherzo: Over the Pavements* and *Variations on "America."*[46] Starr insightfully notes that Ives's symmetry was achieved "without significant direct repetition of earlier material." I believe the implications Starr draws from this aspect of Ives's methodology offer a sound starting point for understanding Ives's cosmic, symmetrical structures and the composer's intentions in such complex instrumental works as the First Violin Sonata, which will be discussed presently: "After a succession of varied experiences, one may return toward one's point of departure, but that point can never really be reached again, since one's perception has been irrevocably altered by the intervening events."[47]

The first movement of the First Violin Sonata is an example of an Ivesian symmetrical structure. This work, Ives writes, was "a kind of mixture between the older way of writing and the newer way." Composed "in 1903 and 1908," the first movement is a complex conception, particularly rhythmically. Ives wrote: "There are things in it, rhythmically, harmonically, and structurally, which Mr. E. Robert Schmitz told me last year (1931) he didn't remember (even up to the present time) seeing in other music."[48] The opening theme is in a cross-meter of 8/4 in a notated 6/4 meter; the first section is infused with crossrhythms, whereby rhythmic units disrupt the meter. In table 1, where the thematic units are diagrammed, the analysis is limited to the symmetrical formal design of the movement. The principal theme is atonal, both the antecedent

44. Larry Starr, *A Union of Diversities: Style in the Music of Charles Ives* (New York: Schirmer Books, 1992), 26, 64.

45. My use of the term *antithesis* refers to Chafe's application of it to Bach text settings, as mentioned in n. 39.

46. Starr, *Union of Diversities*, 36–42, 86, 43–46, and 48–54, respectively.

47. Ibid., 27.

48. Ives, *Memos*, 68.

Table 1. Symmetrical Formal Design of Ives, First Violin Sonata, First Movement

ANDANTE

Section A: opens and closes with *principal theme*, characterized by fifth cycles and whole-tone cycles (and anticipation of submotive V).

Principal thematic section, first statement, mm. 1, fourth quarter–5, third quarter. Starts on F.[a]

Submotivic section II, mm. 5, third quarter–8, third quarter.

Submotivic section III, mm. 8, fourth quarter–10. Starts on C.

Submotivic section IV, mm. 11–14, fourth quarter.

Submotivic section V, from *Shining Shore* refrain, mm. 17, third quarter–29, third quarter (variation of motive in mm. 26).

Principal theme, second statement, mm. 30, fourth quarter–33, first quarter. Starts on E.

ALLEGRO VIVACE

Section B: mm. 34–62. Varies cycle of fifth and whole-tone cycle motives from *principal thematic section.*

CON MOTO

Section C: mm. 61, third quarter–65. Submotive V, from *Shining Shore* refrain.

mm. 65, sixth quarter–69. *Bringing in the Sheaves* fragment, starts on E over C pedal.

mm. 70–73, third quarter. Submotive V, *Shining Shore*, as above.

mm. 73, fourth quarter–79, third quarter, *Bringing in the Sheaves*, as above.
(Middle measure of piece = m. 75.)

mm. 79, fourth quarter–83, develops motive from *Bringing in the Sheaves*, starts on E over E pedal.

mm. 83–85. E pedal retained, fragments from Submotive V, *Shining Shore* added.

mm. 85–96. Development of motives associated with both hymn melodies.

Section D: mm. 96, fourth quarter–100. Opens with third statement of *principal theme*, distorted, in augmentation and diminution, starting on G.

Section C¹: mm. 101–4, submotive V, from *Shining Shore;* mm. 105–10, *Bringing in the Sheaves* fragment, starts on A over C pedal.

Section B¹: mm. 111, fourth quarter–130. Varies cycle of fifth, whole-tone cycle, and other motives from *principal thematic section.*

ANDANTE

Section A¹: opens and closes with statements of *principal theme.*

Principal thematic section, fourth statement, mm. 134–38, third quarter. Starts on D.

Submotivic section II, mm. 138, fourth quarter–141, third quarter. Starts on F.

Submotivic section III, mm. 141, fourth quarter–142. Starts on B.

Principal thematic section, fifth statement, mm. 143, starting on E. Extended to end, m. 151.

[a]The indicated starting notes do not imply keys.

and consequent phrases being equally divided by tonal and whole-tone elements. Motive V, familiar as the second phrase of *Shining Shore* and other gapped hexachordal melodies, functions as a countermelody in sections B, B¹, C, and C¹.[49] Although the opening phrases of two hymn tunes are noted in table 1, they are covered by the nature of the concurrently sounding materials, which do not set these tunes but incorporate and even conceal them.

Musical hermeneutics is required in understanding the music of Bach and Ives. Research in the role of rhetoric and the doctrine of affections in baroque music, and the more recent hermeneutic analyses of Bach's music, particularly by Eric Chafe, Susan McClary, and Michael Marissen, convincingly demonstrate the role of extramusical dimensions.[50] Hermeneutic forms of analysis have not generally been applied in interpreting Ives's music.[51] Yet Ives's discussion of questions regarding the nature of meaning in music and of musical representation is the subject of his "Prologue" to *Essays Before a Sonata*, which originally appeared in 1920 to accompany the publication of the *Second Piano Sonata, Concord, Mass., 1845*. For want of a systematic way to address the extramusical problem, he uses the term *program music* in a very broad sense: "Is not all music program music? Is not pure music, so called, representative in its essence? . . . As we are trying to consider music made and heard by human beings (and not by birds or angels), it seems difficult to suppose that even subconscious images can be separated from some human experience."[52] However, Ives rejects "the theory that music is the language of the emotions and *only* that," and that emotion is only an "expression of" itself. He associates emotion with "meaning in a deeper sense" in which "the intellect has some part."[53] Ives put into practice his vision of the extramusical dimension: in meaning derived from perception or "actual experience"—visual, spa-

49. Identified by Clayton W. Henderson, *The Charles Ives Tunebook*, Bibliographies in American Music 14 (Warren, Mich.: Harmonie Park Press, 1990), 51.

50. Chafe, *Tonal Allegory;* Susan McClary, "The Blasphemy of Talking Politics During Bach Year," in *Music and Society: The Politics of Composition, Performance and Reception*, ed. Richard Leppert and Susan McClary (Cambridge: Cambridge University Press, 1987), 13–62; Michael Marissen, *The Social and Religious Designs of J. S. Bach's Brandenburg Concertos* (Princeton: Princeton University Press, 1995).

51. This approach underlies the discussion of Ives's music in Carol K. Baron, "Meaning in the Music of Charles Ives," in *Metaphor: A Musical Dimension*, ed. Jamie C. Kassler, Australian Studies in the History, Philosophy and Social Studies of Music (Sydney: Currency Press, 1991), 37–50; and Baron, "Ives on His Own Terms: An Explication, a Theory of Pitch Organization, and a New Critical Edition for the *3-Page Sonata*" (Ph.D. diss., City University of New York, 1987).

52. Charles Ives, *Essays Before a Sonata: The Majority and Other Writings*, ed. Howard Boatwright (New York: W. W. Norton & Co., 1970), 3–8. Ives admits to the need for literary "programs," which he frequently provides in the form of memos, titles, actual program notes, and so forth, to clarify his intentions and the music's content (see Ives, *Memos*, 97–98).

53. Ives, *Essays*, 4.

tial, emotional, and intellectual. Furthermore, rejecting the idea that music is the language of emotion, Ives rejects, as his own mode of expression, musical styles in which the extramusical dimension is primarily emotional, and in which tonal language becomes the vehicle for emotional content, as in the classical and romantic periods. Having dismissed the philosophical improbability of abstract music and the aesthetic value of music as the language of emotion, Ives needed other models. Indeed, Ives's music in classical-romantic styles is found only among his early works, which include his first two symphonies.

For Ives, intellectual perception is the ultimate source of meaning, since it alone "reduces" all experience to "a tangible basis; namely, the translation of an artistic intuition into musical sounds"—this process being intellectual.[54] The extramusical dimension represents music's content or, in his terminology, its "substance." Noteworthy in Ives's substance-manner dichotomy is the ultimate lack of dialecticism, which generally accompanies its discussion. "Manner" constitutes the musical-linguistic or systematic dimensions, into which Ives also includes formulaic and conventional aspects of composition: Manner is the vehicle or medium through which "substance" is conveyed and, itself, contributes to a work's substance and conveys meaning.[55]

Ives's aesthetic values are closely related to Bach's compositional aesthetic: Ives's depictions of spatial, pictorial, and intellectual perceptions through allegory, satire, word-painting, and metaphor, which are effected by tonal, timbral, registral, stylistic, and figurative techniques, are comparable to those of Bach. On the simplest level, imaging through pitch configurations also describes Bach's imaginative rhetorical figurations. One example of coincident imaging is found in their depictions of fire. Bach's musical image is found, for instance, in the instrumental obbligato of the bass aria from the cantata, *Nimm von uns, Herr, du treuer Gott* (BWV 101), where "deines Eifers Flammen" ("your flames of wrath"), the *locus topicus*, is depicted by a sharply angular, sequential opening figure that dips and leaps in opposite directions and rising and falling scale passages; canonic imitation takes over beginning in measure 5, with lines that rise and fall back but drive on to the flames' high point, from which they fall precipitously, as may be noted in example 3. Ives's configuration in "Hallowe'en," depicting "the sense and sound of a bonfire, . . . growing bigger and brighter," consists of rising and descending scale passages, broken into short accented phrases of unequal lengths, as shown in example 4, which represent the rising and falling of licking flames.[56] The visually kinetic complexity of flames—the texture of fire—is further captured in the

54. Ibid., 7.

55. A discussion of the question Ives posed, "What part of substance is manner?" (in the "Epilogue" to Ives, *Essays*, 99), may be found in Baron, "Ives on His Own Terms," chapter 3, 63–75. The chapter title is Ives's question.

56. Ives, *Memos*, 91.

Ex. 3. J. S. Bach, Cantata 101, fourth mvt., mm. 1–8.

Ex. 4. Charles Ives, "Hallowe'en," from *Three Outdoor Scenes*, mm. 1–4 of string quartet parts.

musical texture of the two paired canons. Did Ives learn this musical depiction from Bach, or is the coincidence evidence of minds working along similar tracks? I think both were at work.

Without doubt, Ives studied various aspects of the Art of Fugue with his father. One detail that could not have been missed, since George Ives was highly critical of the inadequacies of staff notation, was the unlike pitches that are made visually identical on the lines and spaces of the staff by means of the dispositions of clefs and points of imitation.[57] We can imagine some hilarity accompanying Charles Ives's youthful discovery, in Contrapunctus IX and Contrapunctus XI, of this peculiarity. In both fugues, Bach links the soprano-tenor and the alto-bass entrances. In "Hallowe'en," Ives creates a notational pun. In a double canon, in which Violin 1 and Viola are linked, and Violin 2 and Cello are linked, Ives achieves Bach's notational effect with, however, *atonal* points of imitation. By pairing the C-major passages using the G clef and the D-flat major passages using the alto C clef, the pitch-class notation for these two keys is visually identical, displaced by the octave. The same result is achieved by linking the B-major passages using the G clef, and the D-major passages the F clef.[58] In a memo primarily about this piece, Ives puns, a bit sarcastically, about the nature of its key relationships: "The four strings play in four different and closely related keys [B, C, D flat, and D], each line strictly diatonic. Then it is canonic, not only in tones, but in phrases, accents, and durations or spaces."[59]

Bach's idiosyncratic treatment of single musical parameters has been shown to signify extramusical meaning of the most profound nature. For instance, the meaning of Bach's polymetric conception in *In dulci jubilo,* described above, undoubtedly lies in the infusion of the Trinity on all levels. The canonic procedure represents "divine law" in the first chorus of *Ein feste Burg ist unser Gott* and elsewhere.[60] The studies by McClary and Marissen reveal the extramusical dimension in Bach's instrumentation, while Chafe reveals it hidden in tonal structures.[61] Similarly, in Ives's song "Remembrance," the canon carries the weight of a rhetorical image. It is the *locus topicus,* the echo from the distant past: "O'er shadowed lake . . . my father's song." Ives's mature songs, un-

57. George Ives's concerns with staff notation are described in Baron, "George Ives's Essay," and "At the Cutting Edge."

58. This work is discussed in another context in Baron, "Meaning in the Music of Charles Ives," 39–40.

59. See Ives, *Memos,* 90–91, for the composer's extensive commentary on this work (quotation on p. 91).

60. In *Ein feste Burg ist unser Gott* (BWV 80), a canon in the highest and lowest voices of the first chorus symbolizes "the rule of the divine law throughout the Universe" (Geiringer, *Bach Family,* 219–20).

61. These three studies are cited in n. 50.

like those imitating romantic lieder, often have the constructive tautness and precision of Bach arias and, sometimes, their elegance. Like the single musical images in the instrumental obbligatos of Bach's arias, they also often have a single musical image that articulates the primary meaning, or an analogue, of the text.

In the *3-Page Sonata,* Ives creates meaning through formal dislocations in what he perceived as the conventionalized formulas of classical sonatas.[62] He creates a hilarious satire of the sonata by manipulating the formal designs of each movement with incongruous content and procedures. He underscores the conflicts between the unconventional and unstylistic procedures practiced in this work and those commonly known and practiced for over one hundred years by means of the piece's verbal correlative in "Memo 5" and in marginal notes on the manuscript that spoof conventional sonata procedures.[63] The *3-Page Sonata* was directly inspired by a book of music criticism, *What Is Good Music?,* written by one of the leading music critics in New York, William James Henderson.[64] This book was so popular that it went through six editions and was reprinted in fifteen different years. John Kirkpatrick identified Ives's copy as a third edition, published in 1905.[65] The *3-Page Sonata,* composed in the same year as the publication of his copy of the book, is a musical diatribe against the values of the contemporary musical establishment in general, and the community of music critics in particular, who resist the evolutionary impulse in musical creativity, armed with ignorance and power.[66] Henderson's officiousness caught Ives's attention, particularly this passage:

> No one presumed to pronounce an opinion on the merit of a picture or a statue who had not at least learned the difference between a pen-and-ink drawing and a watercolor, and few persons would have ventured to write down Shakespeare an ass before

62. The two published editions are Charles Ives, *Three Page Sonata,* ed. Henry Cowell (New York: Mercury Music Corp., 1949); and *3-Page Sonata,* ed. John Kirkpatrick (Bryn Mawr, Pa.: Mercury Music Corp., 1975). A third edition is in Baron, "Ives on His Own Terms," appendix 4, 148–80, © Mercury Music Corp., 1986.

63. Ives, *Memos,* 30–32.

64. William James Henderson, *What Is Good Music?* (New York: C. Scribner's Sons, 1898). Henderson was music critic for the *New York Times* from 1887 to 1902 and for the *New York Sun* from 1902 to 1937.

65. Ives, *Memos,* 31 n. 3.

66. A note beneath the last measure of the composing score says: "End of '3 page Sonata' Fini at Saranac Lake with Dave Aug '05." This note and marginal comments found on the score are in the same handwriting as the music; the comments are an aspect of the compositional process. J. Peter Burkholder, *All Made of Tunes: Charles Ives and the Uses of Musical Borrowing* (New Haven: Yale University Press, 1995), 240, 466 n. 45, dates the piece between 1907 and 1914 but gives no evidence to support his revision.

> having acquired a sufficient knowledge of poetry to tell a sonnet from a five-act tragedy. But it was deemed altogether fitting and, indeed, intellectually satisfying that Beethoven should be smugly patted on the back, Brahms viewed with lifted brows, and Wagner convicted of lunacy by persons who could not, while in the concert-room, detect a fantasia masquerading as an overture, nor a suite disguised as a symphony—nay, more, who could not tell when the composer dropped the elementary rhythm of the valse to take up that of the polonaise.[67]

In the *3-Page Sonata*, Ives parodies Henderson's cleverly worded, sarcastic statement, lampooning it in a verbal paraphrase: "He has been able for many years to detect a fantasia masquerading as an overture, or a suite disguised as a symphony—nay more, he can now tell when the composer drops the elementary rhythm of the valse to take up that of the polonaise. He does not lift his brow at Brahms, and he does not convict Wagner of lunacy (see Rollo's own book, pages 3 and 4)."[68]

Ives's attack on Henderson is integrated into the design and procedures used in the *3-Page Sonata;* their meaning is reinforced by the sarcastically worded instructions in the margins of the composing score. The composer's note in the first measure of the third movement, "March time (but not a March, Rollo)," recalls Henderson's statement about those unable to tell "when the composer dropped the elementary rhythm of the valse to take up that of the polonaise," unambiguously linking the piece to "Memo 5." In the music of the third movement, Ives "drops" the "elementary rhythm" of the march to take up that of the waltz by cleverly combining both. It is clear that the deviations that dramatically violate expected sonata conventions are the subject or content of the music, its "program" and its "substance": the music is the program and the program is the music.

In the present context, I shall draw attention to Ives's references to Bach and to Bachian procedures, which were the referential center from which his own mature thinking and characteristics were emerging. Indeed, Bachian procedures are often the vehicles, on different formal and technical levels, through which Ives deconstructs the classical sonata and communicates the meaning of the *3-Page Sonata.* Because of space limitations, the following hermeneutic approach is restricted to an overview of germane musical signifiers in each movement.

The first movement parodies Henderson's statement about "persons who could not, while in the concert-room, detect a fantasia masquerading as an overture, nor a suite disguised as a symphony" by employing fugal procedures while referring to "1st theme" and "nice Sonatas" in the marginalia ("nice" being a pejorative for Ives). Here, a fugal subject is made to "masquerade" as a first theme, and the second theme is "disguised"

67. Henderson, *What Is Good Music?*, 3–4.

68. Ives, *Memos*, 32.

as a fugal episode. Recognizable themes, homophony, and rhythmic regularity—procedures generally associated with the first movements of sonatas—are replaced by abstract motives, polyphony, and nonmetrical rhythms.

The formal design of the first movement is idiosyncratic. Using both fugal and sonata-allegro procedures in contradictory postures, the movement raises such questions as: Is the opening theme the first theme of a sonata or the subject of a fugue? What is the second theme doing between two statements of a fugue? The following outline of the formal design shows the amalgam of fugal and sonata-allegro procedures underlying Ives's comical statement of formal contradictions and facetious imbalances:

- First statement of the fugal complex ("1st Theme")
- Bridge
- Second statement of the fugal complex, in diminution
- Bridge
- "2nd Theme"/Episode
- Third statement of the fugal complex, in inversion
- Repeat sign!
- Bridge
- New "Octave Theme"
- Bridge
- "2nd Theme"/Episode
- Variation of new "Octave Theme"
- Ending phrase

In yet another reference to the Art of Fugue, the B-A-C-H motive from Contrapunctus XIXc is the "1st Theme"/fugue subject (see ex. 5); conventional techniques of diminution and inversion are used in the second and third fugal statements. A touch of invertible counterpoint appears in the second bridge with rhythmic groups of five against six! The references could not be more obvious. At the same time, however, the linear integrity of the polyphony is, in effect, obliterated by chordal writing. The contrapuntal fugal procedure is made to contrast with a wickedly contradictory chordal

Ex. 5. Charles Ives, *3-Page Sonata*, first mvt., first fugal complex.

texture: Ives obfuscates the expected contrapuntal procedures of the fugue with chordal textures created by "parallel fourths" for the subject and by a note-for-note accompaniment of the countersubject.

In the second movement, conceived in two parts, an Andante followed by an Adagio, the *appearance* of a homophonic melody and accompaniment in the opening section—the characteristic texture of a "textbook" sonata slow movement—is another Ivesian deception in which Bach's influence lurks. Ives composed a polyphony of independent structures or layers—perhaps the ultimate contradistinction to homophony, as shown in example 6. The derivation of this Ivesian technique from Bach's motivic polyphony, as exemplified in many arias and, especially, in the organ chorale settings of the *Orgelbüchlein*, has already been discussed. Two other factors preclude the interpretation of the slow movement as authentically homophonic: the metrical distinctiveness between the layers and, more powerfully, their independent pitch-rhythmic configurations. The result is a succession of figurative motives in the upper layer of the right-hand part and broken chords in the left-hand part that share the same time frame. However, the implied metric units in each line deny the authority of the given meters within the individual layers, reducing them to practical frames of reference rather than received musical perceptions (i.e., metric independence, not syncopations against given meters).

A third layer, introduced in the last two measures of the Andante, opens the texture into three coexisting, independent layers that are retained through to the end of the Adagio section (mm. 13–31). Each layer unfolds within its own spatial dimension: through different and contrasting motivic figuration in the upper layer and, primarily, through rhythmic and metrical differences in each of the three layers. The given meters serve as a frame of reference; the perceived, implied meters are articulated by melodic phrases, mainly simple, repetitive pitch patterns that straddle the measures.

The third movement targets Henderson's statement about ignorant critics who are unable to tell "when the composer dropped the elementary rhythm of the valse to take up that of the polonaise." Ives added the note, "March time (but not a March, Rol-

Ex. 6. Charles Ives, *3-Page Sonata*, second mvt., mm. 1–2.

lo)," to the first measure of the score, thereby immediately alerting one to its character. He proceeds with the ingenious strategy of using a series of three different, characteristic dance rhythms (march, waltz, and ragtime) as motives placed in changing relationships to each other. Ives's highly charged intention to make tricky distinctions between "dance" rhythms is accompanied by purposefully misleading references to "1st Theme," "2nd Theme," and "1st development"—all implying sonata-allegro procedures. Vernacular rhythmic forms are used to satirize the conventionalized inclusion of dance movements in the sonata and symphony, while suggesting, with the help of marginal notes, a unique integration of sonata-allegro procedures and dance forms in which neither can be recognized.

Ives would have rested assured that the challenges this piece hypothetically presented to the critic, on the levels of formal design and texture alone, were formidable. Analytical attempts to use classical concepts and terminology to describe this work have been as defeating as trying to fit the work into classical formal molds.[69]

* * *

In reaching maturity, Ives returned to his pursuit of nondiatonic systems, polyphonic imaging, and original and relevant formal structures. He was forthright in citing the centrality of Bach's music in his training and confident about his responsibility to move into new territories. That acknowledgment of the past and the certainty with which he persisted in moving into uncharted musical territories were derived from religious beliefs in which progress, as one moved into the future, was mandated—indeed, was an act of piety. Progress necessitated looking for whatever possibilities existed in nature and revealing them; operating out of habit was, in effect, sinful. Thus, Ives's musical activities, like his intense political meditations, lay in the realm of a personal, religious commitment. The challenges Ives set himself therefore involved him in the kinds of struggles that Bach never had to face, having inherited a musical universe that offered whatever was needed. Ives could accept nothing for himself, just as it was. Musical parameters needed to be viewed in new ways, juxtaposed in new ways, and reinvented. The intellectual and schematic nature of Bach's music, with its less emotionally oriented, and more intellectually and visually oriented programmatic content, suited Ives's gift for musical imaging in ways that the sonata and symphony failed to do.

69. Other interpretations of this work are discussed in Baron, "Ives on His Own Terms," 52–62. See also Burkholder, *All Made of Tunes*, 240; David Nicholls, *American Experimental Music, 1890–1940* (Cambridge: Cambridge University Press, 1990), 34–40; and Lora L. Gingerich, "Processes of Motivic Transformation in the Keyboard and Chamber Music of Charles E. Ives" (Ph.D. diss., Yale University, 1983), 126–55.

The Role and Meaning of the Bach Chorale in the Music of Dave Brubeck

Stephen A. Crist

In an essay on Felix Mendelssohn's reception of Bach's music, Wolfgang Dinglinger states, "The conviction that Mendelssohn's preoccupation with the music of Bach is of fundamental importance for his life and works is one of the indisputable and self-evident premises of any examination of this composer."[1] The same cannot be said about the relationship between Johann Sebastian Bach and Dave Brubeck. Since many people are not yet aware of the fundamental importance of Bach for Brubeck's life and music, let us begin by examining some general evidence concerning this subject before turning to the specific topic of this study.

Throughout his career, Dave Brubeck has consistently named Bach as one of his greatest musical influences. As early as 1957, he listed Bach (along with Stravinsky, Bartók, and Milhaud) as one of his "favorite composers."[2] Likewise, an entry in the previous year's *Current Biography Yearbook* noted that "Brubeck injects [into his jazz improvisations] classical counterpoint, atonal harmonies and modern dissonances which hint at composers like Debussy, Stravinsky, Bartók, and Bach."[3] In recent years, however, the rhetoric has

A version of this essay was presented at the biennial meeting of the American Bach Society, at the Library of Congress, Washington, D.C., on April 8, 2000. I am most grateful to Dave Brubeck, Iola Brubeck, Constance Emmerich, Russell Gloyd, Richard Jeweler, and George Moore for their invaluable cooperation and assistance.

1. "Die Überzeugung, daß die Beschäftigung mit der Musik Bachs von grundsätzlicher Bedeutung für Leben und Werk Mendelssohn's ist, gehört zu den unbestrittenen und selbstverständlichen Voraussetzungen jeder Auseinandersetzung mit dem Komponisten." Wolfgang Dinglinger, "Aspekte der Bach-Rezeption Mendelssohns," in *Bach und die Nachwelt, Band 1: 1750–1850*, ed. Michael Heinemann and Hans-Joachim Hinrichsen (Laaber: Laaber-Verlag, 1997), 379.

2. Sharon A. Pease, "'The Duke' Good Example of Brubeck's Solo Style," *Down Beat* 24, no. 3 (Feb. 6, 1957): 45.

3. "Brubeck, Dave," in *Current Biography Yearbook 1956*, ed. Marjorie Dent Candee (New York: H. W. Wilson Company, 1956), 80.

intensified. For instance, in the early 1990s Brubeck published the *"Chromatic Fantasy" Sonata,* a full-length work for piano solo, which will be discussed in some detail later. The unsigned preface notes that this piece "was inspired by the great German composer, Johann Sebastian Bach, who is Dave Brubeck's favorite composer."[4] Similarly, in the remarks accompanying a brief composition in four-part chorale style titled "Suspense and Resolution" (1970), Brubeck himself states, "I've always loved suspensions, and the master of all writers of suspensions is my favorite composer, J. S. Bach."[5]

Another factor that testifies to his connections with Bach is the size of Brubeck's family and their choice of vocation. Of Dave and Iola Brubeck's six children, four have pursued careers as professional musicians (Darius, Chris, Dan, and Matthew). In addition, Dave's mother, Elizabeth Ivey Brubeck, and his two older brothers, Henry and Howard, all earned their living from music. The parallels between the two families were not lost on Brubeck's biographer, Fred Hall, who noted:

> Given their maternal grandmother's and uncles' notable careers in music, and their father's eclectic interest in *all* things musical, along with his constant reaching toward new horizons, the Brubeck clan is one of the more productive and altogether interesting since the heyday of another notable musical family—that of J. S. Bach.[6]

The similarities also captured the imagination of Christopher Hogwood, who made the following statement in an interview during the Bach tercentenary: "Bach is alive now and playing on a grand piano, . . . but he's called Dave Brubeck. Brubeck's running the same kind of musical family, he's a phenomenal improviser with a very mathematical mind, and he's a great educator. That's a fair analogy, I think."[7] After becoming artistic director of Boston's Handel and Haydn Society in 1986, Hogwood on several occasions engaged Dave Brubeck and his sons as guest artists. The program of one such concert, titled "Bach & Sons, Brubeck & Sons," is reproduced in plate 1.[8] It featured music by Johann Sebastian Bach and his two eldest sons, Wilhelm Friedemann and Carl Philipp Emanuel, alternating with music by Dave Brubeck and his brother Howard, performed by Dave Brubeck, two of his sons (Chris and Dan), and others. In connection with the main topic of this essay, it is worth calling attention to the title of the second item of the final set: a "Chorale" by Dave Brubeck.

4. Dave Brubeck, *"Chromatic Fantasy" Sonata* (Miami, Fla.: Warner Bros. Publications, 1994), 1.

5. *Dave's Diary: A Collection of Dave Brubeck Piano Solos* (Miami, Fla.: Warner Bros. Publications, 1995), 36.

6. Fred M. Hall, *It's About Time: The Dave Brubeck Story* (Fayetteville: University of Arkansas Press, 1996), 97–98.

7. Quoted in Stuart Isacoff, "The 'Now' Sound of the 16th Century," *Keyboard Classics* 5, no. 2 (1985): 8.

8. I am grateful to Dave and Iola Brubeck for providing a copy of this program.

Handel & Haydn Society
Christopher Hogwood, Artistic Director
John Finney, Associate Conductor
1997–1998 Season

Friday, January 30, 1998 at 8:00 p.m.
Sunday, February 1 at 3:00 p.m.
Symphony Hall, Boston

Christopher Hogwood, Conductor

Dave Brubeck, Piano
Chris Brubeck, Electric Bass/Bass Trombone
Dan Brubeck, Drums
Bobby Militello, Alto Saxophone/Flute
Russell Gloyd, Guest Conductor

Brandenburg Concerto No. 3, BWV 1048 — Johann Sebastian Bach
(Allegro)—Adagio—Allegro

Marian McPartland — Dave Brubeck
Theme for June — Howard Brubeck
The Things You Never Remember — Dave Brubeck
Brandenburg Gate

Sinfonia in E Minor, H. 652 — Carl Philipp Emanuel Bach
Allegro assai—Andante moderato—Allegro

—INTERMISSION—

The Basie Band is Back in Town — Dave Brubeck
Lord, Lord
Waltzing

Sinfonia in D Minor, F. 65 — Wilhelm Friedemann Bach
Adagio—Allegro e forte

Thank You — Dave Brubeck

Three To Get Ready (Dave Brubeck)
Chorale (Dave Brubeck)
Take Five (Paul Desmond)
Blue Rondo a la Turk (Dave Brubeck)
The Brubeck ensemble with the H&H Orchestra
Russell Gloyd, conductor

Plate 1. Program for "Bach & Sons, Brubeck & Sons" concert. Used by permission of the Handel and Haydn Society.

To conclude this brief preamble, let us consider a compact disc by Dave Brubeck's son Chris, titled *Bach to Brubeck*.[9] Along with Chris Brubeck's Concerto for Bass Trombone and Orchestra, this recording features his arrangements of compositions by his father (including "Blue Rondo à la Turk") and by Bach (BWV 924a, 846a, 926, and 997), performed by Bill Crofut on banjo and Joel Brown on guitar, with the London Symphony Orchestra conducted by Joel Revzen. The cover art by Erika Crofut—with a bust of Bach on the left pedestal and a bust of Dave Brubeck on the right—speaks volumes about the relationship between the great composer of European "classical" music and the famous American jazz pianist (see plate 2). Along with the examples

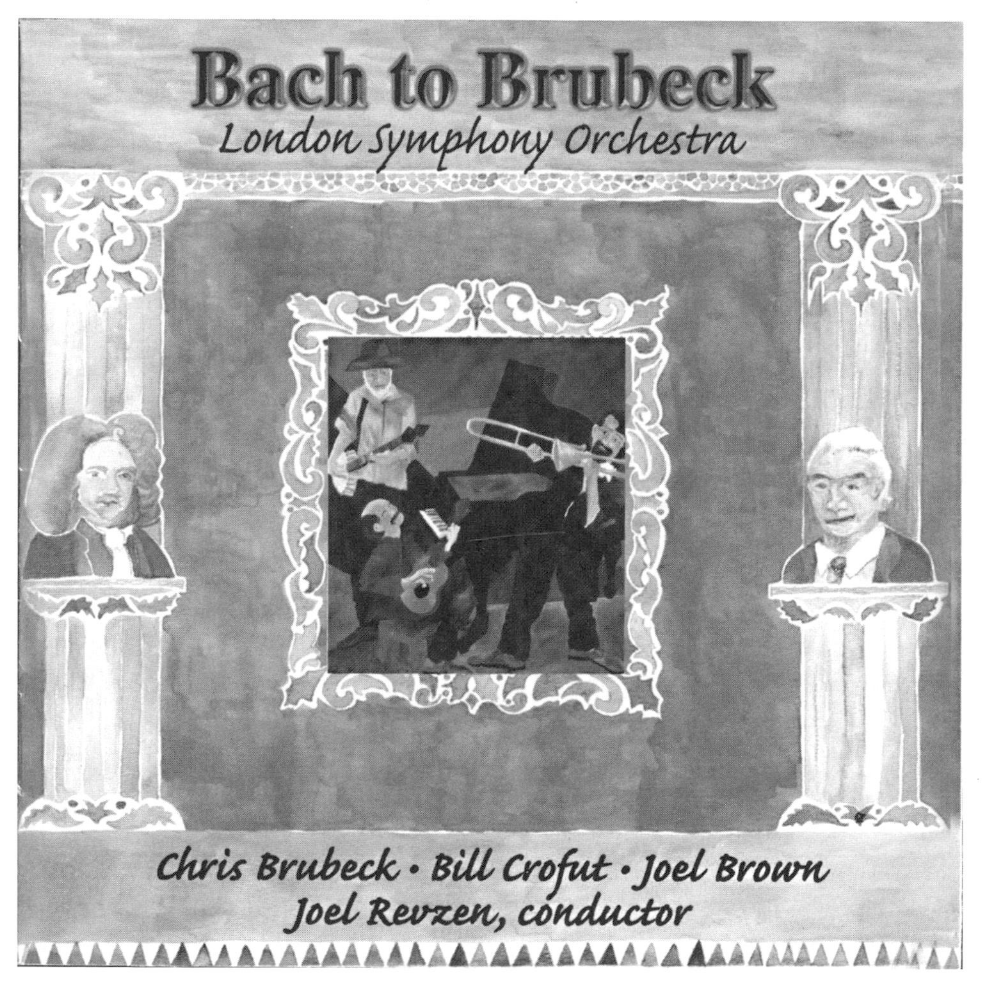

Plate 2. Cover art by Erika Crofut for *Bach to Brubeck* recording. Used by permission of Koch International.

9. Chris Brubeck et al., *Bach to Brubeck*, Koch International Classics, 3–7485–2 H1 (2000).

discussed above, the *Bach to Brubeck* project testifies to the very real and meaningful connection between these two indisputably odd bedfellows.

* * *

Anyone who explores Dave Brubeck's extensive jazz discography, as well as the oratorios, cantatas, and other "serious" works he has composed over the past several decades, will discover that Bach's music has been an important creative stimulus throughout Brubeck's career. Indeed, the influence of Bach on Brubeck has more dimensions than can be addressed here. I have chosen, therefore, to focus on just one facet of the complex relationship between these two figures: namely, the presence of actual Bach chorales, as well as original compositions in the chorale style, in Brubeck's music.

Let us start with Brubeck's jazz recordings. On occasion, specific tunes by Bach are quoted in Brubeck's improvisations. For instance, in "Fare Thee Well, Annabelle" (recorded live at the Basin Street nightclub in New York on October 12, 1954) the ritornello of "Jesu, Joy of Man's Desiring" makes a brief appearance.[10] The opening of Brubeck's arrangement of this song by Mort Dixon and Allie Wrubel, from the 1935 film *Sweet Music*, is striking on account of the three-part counterpoint and canonic imitation between the piano, alto saxophone, and bass. (In the original liner notes, George Avakian noted that "Brubeck enjoys making these arrangements exercises in fugal . . . writing.") After a lengthy saxophone solo by his long-time sideman, Paul Desmond, Brubeck takes his turn. Early in the piano chorus, Brubeck hits upon a triplet passage that is vaguely reminiscent of "Jesu, Joy of Man's Desiring" (ex. 1a). A bit later, he reintroduces the triplet motion and includes a more recognizable quotation of the same tune (ex. 1b).

This recording is cited in Ilse Storb's book—one of the few scholarly studies of Brubeck's music—as an example of Bach's influence.[11] But, as interesting as it may be, it ultimately is not very illuminating. For Brubeck's momentary quotation of this familiar melody by Bach is not qualitatively different from the quotation of any number of "common-coin" tunes that intelligent jazz musicians frequently weave into their improvisations. Moreover, only Bach's ritornello is heard in this performance. The chorale cantus firmus that he set in Cantata 147—*Werde munter, mein Gemüte* by Johann Schop—is not present.

A more substantial example of Brubeck's use of a Bach chorale is the song "Because All Men Are Brothers," in which his jazz trio (piano, bass, and drums) is joined by the

10. The Dave Brubeck Quartet, *Jazz: Red Hot and Cool*, Columbia, CL 699 (1955); rereleased on Columbia/Legacy, CK 61468 (2001).

11. Ilse Storb and Klaus-Gotthard Fischer, *Dave Brubeck, Improvisations and Compositions: The Idea of Cultural Exchange, with Discography*, trans. Bert Thompson (New York: Peter Lang, 1994), 81.

a.

b.

Ex. 1a–b. Two excerpts from Brubeck's improvisation in "Fare Thee Well, Annabelle."

folk trio Peter, Paul & Mary. In this 1970 recording,[12] the chorale "O Sacred Head, Now Wounded" is fitted with a new, secular text by Tom Glazer, which reflects the aspirations of the civil rights movement:

Because all men are brothers, wherever men may be,
One union shall unite us, forever proud and free.
No tyrant shall defeat us, no nation strike us down,
All men who toil shall greet us, the whole wide world around.

My brothers are all others, forever hand in hand,
Where chimes the bell of freedom, there is my native land.
My brothers' fears are my fears, yellow, white or brown.
My brothers' tears are my tears, the whole wide world around.

Let every voice be thunder, let every heart be strong.
Until all tyrants perish, our work shall not be done.
Let not our memories fail us, the lost years shall be found.
Let slavery's chains be broken, the whole wide world around.[13]

12. Dave Brubeck, *Summit Sessions*, Columbia, C 30522 (1971). This song and several others from the original album were rereleased on Dave Brubeck, *Vocal Encounters*, Columbia/Legacy, CK 61551 (2001); according to the liner notes, it was recorded on March 17, 1970.

13. The lyrics sung by Peter, Paul & Mary (given here, Copyright 1948, Songs Music, Inc., Scarborough, N.Y., and used by permission) differ slightly from those in Tom Glazer, ed., *Songs of Peace, Freedom, and Protest* (New York: David McKay Co., 1970), 21–22. This song dates from the late 1940s. Tom Glazer is best known for his children's songs, especially the comic parody "On Top of Spaghetti" (to the tune of "On Top of Old Smoky"). See Irwin Stambler and Grelun Landon, *Encyclopedia of Folk, Country and Western Music* (New York: St. Martin's Press, 1969), 107–8.

After all three singers present the first stanza and a second chorus on the syllable "oo," the chorale tune then is used as the basis for a jazz improvisation, after which stanzas 2 (Mary Travers alone) and 3 (trio) are sung.

The original liner notes to *Summit Sessions* by Alexander Coleman make explicit the connection with Bach, identifying the melody as "a chorale sung just after the moment when Christ is crowned with thorns" in the St. Matthew Passion. The notes also mention that the tune originated "around 1600 as a weepy tavern lament entitled 'My happiness has left me, my girl has gone away,' composed by one Hans Leo Hassler."[14] The fact that the so-called Passion Chorale was originally a secular love song is extremely important to Brubeck, and has encouraged him in his efforts to unite sacred music and jazz. In a personal interview, Brubeck told me about a performance of this song that he had once heard, with the original words translated into English. He said:

> It was the bawdiest song you'd ever want to hear in your life. . . . And the fact . . . that Bach used drinking songs in his most sacred pieces, . . . this thrilled me to death. You know, stupid people were saying, "How could a jazz musician write sacred music?" . . . But you see how important this was to me: to know, from that day forward I wasn't going to listen to anybody [who said that] sacred music shouldn't be composed by jazz musicians. Because, if Bach were aware enough to know that the congregation would know this melody and respond to it, . . . it just is so enlightening to know from the greatest composer of sacred music, and he was right down to the people. This is important.[15]

14. The date and attribution are secure: a five-voice setting first appeared in Hassler's *Lustgarten neuer teutscher Gesäng* (Nuremberg, 1601). But whether one wishes to characterize this polyphonic lied as "a weepy tavern lament" or translate "Mein Gmüth ist mir verwirret, das macht ein Jungfrau zart" in this way is another matter

15. Dave Brubeck, interview by author, tape recording, Wilton, Conn., April 28, 1998 (hereafter Brubeck interview). One wonders what kind of translation or paraphrase Brubeck may have heard, since the original text hardly seems "bawdy":

> Mein Gmüth ist mir verwirret, das macht ein Jungkfrau zart,
> Bin gantz vnd gar verirret, mein Hertz das kränckt sich hart.
> Hab tag vnd nacht kein ruh, führ allzeit grosse klag,
> Thu stets seufftzen vnd weinen, in trauren schier verzag.
>
> Ach dass sie mich thät fragen, was doch dir vrsach sey
> Warumb ich führ solch klagen, ich wolt jrs sagen frei,
> Dass sie allein die ist, die mich so sehr verwundt,
> Köndt ich jr Hertz erweichen, würd ich bald wider gsund.
>
> Reichlich ist sie gezieret mit schönn thugend ohn ziel,
> Höflich wie sie gebüret, ihrs gleichen ist nicht viel,
> Für andern Jungkfraun zart führt sie allzeit den preis,
> Wann ichs anschau, vermeine ich sey im Paradeiss.

Quotations of actual Bach chorales are rare in Brubeck's jazz performances. More frequently, he borrows stylistic features of the Bach chorale for newly composed pieces. For instance, the texture and voice-leading at the beginning of "Danse Duet" resemble in some ways those of Bach's four-part chorale settings (see ex. 2).[16]

> Aber ich muss auffgeben vnd allzeit traurig sein,
> Solts mir gleich kosten sLeben das ist mein grösste pein,
> Dann ich bin jhr zu schlecht, darumb sie mein nicht acht,
> Gott wölls für leid bewaren durch sein Göttliche macht.
>
> I'm all mixed up; this a tender maid has done to me!
> I'm totally lost; my heart is sick and sore.
> I get no rest by day or night, my pain is always so great.
> I'm sighing and crying all the time; I'm almost in despair.
>
> If only she would ask me: What's the matter with you?
> I would tell her straight why I carry around such pain,
> That she alone is the one who hurts me so.
> If I could soften her heart, I'd soon be well again.
>
> Her lovely virtues adorn her, rich and without end.
> Gracious is her bearing; few can compare with her.
> Before other tender maidens, she always takes the prize.
> When I look at her, I think I am in Paradise.
>
> But I must give up and be miserable forever,
> Even if it should cost me my life; this is my greatest pain.
> I am not good enough for her; she doesn't care about me.
> May God keep her safe from suffering, through His divine power.

German text (including a fifth stanza with similar content) in Hans Leo Hassler, *Lustgarten*, ed. Friedrich Zelle, Publikation aelterer praktischer und theoretischer Musikwerke 15 (Leipzig: Breitkopf & Härtel, 1887; reprint, New York: Broude Brothers, 1966), 24. Translation courtesy of the San Francisco Bach Choir; used by permission.

16. *The Genius of Dave Brubeck*, Book 2 (Miami, Fla.: CPP/Belwin, 1984), 32–38. "Danse Duet" was recorded on June 28, 1961, and was included on the album The Dave Brubeck Quartet, *Countdown—Time in Outer Space*, Columbia, CL 1775 (1962). It is one of four tracks that originated as part of Brubeck's 1956 ballet, *Maiden in the Tower* (the others are "Fast Life," "Waltz Limp," and "Three's a Crowd"). According to the composer, "the titles are descriptive of the ballet situation. . . . *Danse Duet* opens with a rubato statement of the theme by the piano [see ex. 2], followed by a stately 4/4 *pas de deux*. A transitional phrase moves into waltz time, which is designed as a solo dance for the Heroine ["1st Improvisation"]. She is then answered by the Hero who dances a solo in 4 ["2nd Improvisation"]. The piece closes with a restatement of the solo piano theme." Dave Brubeck, *Deluxe Piano Album, Number Two: Countdown—Time in Outer Space and The Real Ambassadors* (New York: Charles Hansen Music and Books, 1973), 6.

Ex. 2. Brubeck, "Danse Duet," mm. 1–11. Copyright © 1962 and 1963 by Derry Music Company. Used by permission.

Another composition with strong ties to Bach is "Brandenburg Gate."[17] When I asked Brubeck what he likes about Bach's music, and which compositions he finds most meaningful, he immediately said, "The Brandenburg Concertos, from which I got my piece 'Brandenburg Gate.'" He told me about hearing them at the Carmel Bach Festival in 1946, shortly after returning from military service during World War II. He was especially impressed with the last movement of the Second Brandenburg Concerto (BWV 1047), noting in particular "its rhythmic drive and melodic inventiveness."[18]

"Brandenburg Gate" is one of six pieces that were composed during an extensive tour in 1958, sponsored by the State Department, which began in England, Germany, and Poland, continued on through the Middle East, and ended over three months later in India, Pakistan, Afghanistan, and Ceylon. In the liner notes for *Jazz Impressions of Eurasia,* Brubeck said, "I did not approach the writing of this album with the exactness of a musicologist. Instead, as the title indicates, I tried to create an *impression* of a particular locale by using some of the elements of their folk music within the jazz idiom." The generative idea that unites the album and provides the thematic material for each of the six pieces is the inflection of the words "thank you" in different languages. The German phrase "danke schön" suggested the descending motive constituted by the first three notes of "Brandenburg Gate" (see ex. 3).

Beyond the obvious play on words in the title, between the Brandenburg Gate as a symbol of Germany and the Brandenburg Concertos as a kind of symbol of Bach, this composition contains at least three stylistic features associated with baroque music, and with Bach in particular: (1) a predominantly polyphonic, contrapuntal texture; (2) imitation between the saxophone and piano, indicated in ex. 3 by an "echo" effect (the drop from *mezzo forte* to *mezzo piano* in the repetitions of the four-note ascending-scale motive); and (3) its distinctive harmonic language. Although the style of Bach's four-part chorales is not at the forefront of "Brandenburg Gate" in the same way as it is in "Danse Duet," Brubeck has noted that "the root progressions of this piece are similar to those of a Bach chorale, with some modern alterations of the chord structure."[19] The "modern alterations" appear in mm. 3–4, with the dissonances on the first part of each beat. But what is extraordinary about its harmonic structure is that, throughout the entire piece, the root motion proceeds almost exclusively by descending fifths.

17. The Dave Brubeck Quartet, *Jazz Impressions of Eurasia,* Columbia, CL 10251 (1958); rereleased on Columbia/Legacy, CK 48531 (1992). "Brandenburg Gate" is included in *Dave Brubeck's Two-Part Adventures: Original Two-Part Arrangements* (Miami, Fla.: Warner Bros. Publications, 1999), 30–31.

18. Brubeck interview.

19. Dave Brubeck, *Themes from Eurasia,* ed. Howard Brubeck (Delaware Water Gap, Pa.: Shawnee Press, 1960), 7.

Ex. 3. Brubeck, "Brandenburg Gate," mm. 1–13. Copyright © 1959 by Derry Music Company. Used by permission.

* * *

In 1967 Dave Brubeck disbanded his quartet, one of the most successful jazz ensembles of the 1950s and 1960s, in order to devote more time to his family and to composing. On the face of it, this may have seemed a bold and unexpected move. But it actually represented a return to earlier aspirations. As early as 1952, the second year of the quartet's existence, *Down Beat* magazine reported: "Dave Brubeck is in a unique position for a jazzman. His time and interests are about equally divided between formal classical composition and his increasingly emergent position as the leader of one of the country's most stimulating modern jazz units."[20] The next year, Brubeck was quoted as saying, "I want to compose and play jazz to the extent of my ability."[21] The cover story in *Time* magazine, which catapulted Brubeck to international fame in 1954, included the following prediction: "One of these days, restless Dave Brubeck thinks he may go back to his original ambition of being a composer."[22] And a full decade before he restructured his schedule, Brubeck said, "Composition has always been one of my great loves, maybe the strongest. . . . I would like to develop as a composer. I think I would like to write for larger groups, too. I don't know what I'm capable of here because I haven't pushed myself in this direction because I haven't had time to. I've been so involved in the quartet and traveling."[23]

Among the fruits of Brubeck's labors as a "serious" composer over the past several decades is a series of vocal works, many of which contain chorales.[24] These movements bear various degrees of similarity to the four-part chorales of Bach (see table 1).[25] In some cases, the distinctive style (especially the texture and voice-leading) of Bach's chorales is present in only part of the movement, while in others it permeates the entire movement. Although we shall examine only a few representative examples in detail, the very fact that Brubeck has composed a significant number of vocal works containing chorales over a period of thirty years is a testament to his admiration of Bach. In

20. "Brubeck Has Double Life as Jazzman, Classic Composer," *Down Beat* 19, no. 24 (Dec. 3, 1952): 6.

21. Bob Fulford, "Horns Swing Alone in Brubeck's Crystal Ball," *Down Beat* 20, no. 9 (May 6, 1953): 8.

22. "The Man on Cloud No. 7," *Time* 64, no. 19 (Nov. 8, 1954): 76.

23. Ralph J. Gleason, "Brubeck: 'I Did Do Some Things First,'" *Down Beat* 24, no. 17 (Sept. 5, 1957): 15.

24. The best survey of this portion of Brubeck's *oeuvre* is Harmon G. Young III, "The Sacred Choral Music of Dave Brubeck: A Historical, Analytical, and Critical Examination" (Ph.D. diss., University of Florida, 1995), which also includes an extensive analysis of *The Light in the Wilderness* (194–238). See also Storb and Fischer, *Dave Brubeck*, 118–47.

25. I am very grateful to Nancy Wade, a choral director and close friend of Dave and Iola Brubeck, for making available to me numerous scores and recordings of unpublished materials.

Table 1. Selective List of Chorales in Vocal Works by Dave Brubeck

Year	Work
1968	*The Light in the Wilderness* (oratorio)
	IIa. Forty Days
1969	*The Gates of Justice* (cantata)
	IIIb. Open the Gates Chorale
1971	*Truth is Fallen* (cantata)
	VI. Yea, Truth Faileth
1975	*La Fiesta de la Posada* (Christmas pageant)
	6. We Have Come to See the Son of God
	14. God's Love Made Visible
1978	*Beloved Son* (oratorio)
	Abba, Father
	Weep Ye Waters
1983	*Pange Lingua Variations*
	Movement II (mm. 13–54)
1985	*Voice of the Holy Spirit* (oratorio)
	11. Though I Speak with the Tongues of Men and of Angels
	15. Benediction
1987	*Upon This Rock* (chorale and fugue, with fanfares)
1991	*Joy in the Morning*
	IV. Psalm 121: I Will Lift Up Mine Eyes
1992	*As the Moon Is to the Sun*
1998	*Hold Fast to Dreams* (cantata)
	I Dream a World: Chorale
2001	*The Power Chorale and Fugue*

the words of John Salmon, a pianist with long-standing ties to Brubeck and his music, "Brubeck writes serious oratorios and cantatas in order to express deeply held religious convictions, and because he simply loves Bach."[26]

The vocal work with the most overt connection to Bach is *Beloved Son*, a forty-minute oratorio on the passion and resurrection of Jesus Christ that was commissioned by the American Lutheran Church Women and premiered at their national convention in Minneapolis on August 9, 1978. Brubeck told me that Bach's influence is felt "all the way through it," that the "He is Risen" section at the end "has a canon that I wouldn't have written had I not loved Bach," and that "the chorales are so

26. John Salmon, "What Brubeck Got from Milhaud," *American Music Teacher* 41, no. 4 (February 1992): 28.

much indebted to Bach."[27] Moreover, he mentioned that "my favorite chorale that I've ever written is 'Weep Ye Waters.'"[28]

It is not difficult to understand why Brubeck should be especially fond of "Weep Ye Waters," for it is a hauntingly beautiful chorale that is sung at a pivotal moment just after Christ's death on the cross. In his remarks on the occasion of the awarding of an honorary doctorate to Brubeck from the University of Duisburg, John Salmon said, "Mr. Brubeck's chorales give expression to mankind's deepest agony and the Christian gospel of atonement and redemption."[29] This most certainly is true in the present case. Much of the movement's expressive power derives from its chromaticism (especially intense in mm. 1–2, 8, and 15) and its rich harmonic palette (see ex. 4). The C-minor tonality, appropriate to the mournful text, is enriched by pungent augmented sixth chords at the beginning of all but one of the four phrases (downbeats of mm. 1, 5, 13). The plentiful nonchord tones (suspensions, passing tones, appoggiaturas, and the like) include some harsh dissonances, such as the second b' in m. 7 of the soprano part, which clashes with the tonic triad. In addition, the diatonic harmonies encompass not only sevenths but also ninth and eleventh chords, and even an occasional quartal sonority (m. 11, fourth beat). An especially tender passage occurs in the third phrase (mm. 10–11), where the submediant A-flat major is tonicized briefly through the introduction of a fourth flat (D flat).

Not long after he composed *Beloved Son*, Brubeck fulfilled a commission from the Roman Catholic publisher, Our Sunday Visitor, to create a contemporary Mass. *To Hope! A Celebration* received its first performances in April 1980 in Philadelphia and at the convention of the National Association of Pastoral Musicians in Providence, Rhode Island. Though it contains no chorales, Brubeck's work on *To Hope!* was personally quite significant. By the time he had finished it, he had embraced the Roman Catholic faith. As he put it in the preface to the published score,

> The heart of the Mass is found in the words themselves, living language full of deep meaning, born from the very human need to know God. . . . I approached the composition as prayer, concentrating upon the phrases, trying to probe beneath the surface, hoping to translate into music the powerful words which have grown through the centuries. Emotions that are life, from sorrow to exaltation, were part of my experience in writing TO HOPE! When the work was completed, I felt a strong sense

27. These portions were published (Delaware Water Gap, Pa.: Shawnee Press, 1979) as choral octavos A-1499 ("He Is Risen") and A-1500 ("Two Chorales: I. Abba, Father; II. Weep Ye Waters").

28. Brubeck interview.

29. "Mr. Brubecks Choräle verleihen der tiefsten Pein des Menschen und der christlichen Botschaft von Sühne und Erlösung Ausdruck." Ilse Storb and John Salmon, "Dave Brubeck," *Jazz Podium* 43 (June 1994): 14.

5

II. WEEP YE WATERS

Text by
HERBERT BROKERING

Music by
DAVE BRUBECK

Ex. 4. Brubeck, *Beloved Son*, "Weep Ye Waters." Copyright © 1979 by St. Francis Music Company and Malcolm Music, Ltd. Used by permission.

6
a tempo
ten.
accel.
gar - den_weep-ing,_ Je - sus' bod - y wrapped in_ lin - en,_ Wo - men mix - ing_
they have pierc - ed,_ Son of wo - man, Son _ of_Jah - weh,_Pierc - ed_side_for_
top to_bot - tom,_ Rocks are tum-bling, graves_re - o - pen._Sure - ly_He _ is_
gar - den weep- ing. Je - sus'_bod - y_ wrapped in lin - en, Wo - men mix - ing_
they have pierc - ed. Son of_wo - man, Son of Jah - weh, Pierc - ed_side_for_
top_to bot - tom, Rocks are tum- bling,_ graves re - o - pen. Sure - ly_He _ is_
(opt.div.)
oil_ and_spic - es._ All ye wa - ters_ of the Jor - dan_
blood and_ wa - ter,_ Not a bone in_ bod - y bro - ken._
Son_ of_ Jah - weh._ All ye wa - ters_ of the Jor - dan_
oil_ and_spic - es._ All ye wa - ters of the Jor - dan_
blood_ and_ wa - ter,_ Not a bone in bod - y bro - ken._
Son_ of_ Jah - weh._ All ye wa - ters of the Jor - dan_

(A-1500)

7
rit.
a tempo
Pour up-on, pour up-on, pour up-on the cross of Je-sus. Weep ye wa-ters of the Jor-dan.
Mar-vel now, mar-vel now, mar-vel now at blood and wa-ter. Weep ye wa-ters of the Jor-dan.
Pour up-on, pour up-on, pour up-on the cross of Je-sus. Weep ye wa-ters of the Jor-dan.
Pour on, pour on, pour up-on the cross of Je-sus. Weep ye wa-ters of the Jor-dan.
Mar-vel, mar-vel, mar-vel now at blood and wa-ter. Weep ye wa-ters of the Jor-dan.
Pour on, pour on, pour up-on the cross of Je-sus. Weep ye wa-ters of the Jor-dan.
Pour on, pour on, pour up-on the cross of Je-sus. Weep ye wa-ters of the Jor-dan.
Mar-vel, mar-vel, mar-vel now at blood and wa-ter. Weep ye wa-ters of the Jor-dan.
Pour on, pour on, pour up-on the cross of Je-sus. Weep ye wa-ters of the Jor-dan.
rit.
a tempo
1., 2.
3.
Mar-y, weep.
Mar-y, weep.
Mar-y, weep. Mar-y, weep.
Mar-y, weep.
Mar-y, weep.
Mar-y, weep. Mar-y, weep.
1., 2.
3.
(A-1500)

of wholeness and affirmation. I pray that those who experience the work will share my feelings.[30]

The composition of *To Hope!* led to several more commissions from Roman Catholic organizations in the 1980s, three of which have implicit or explicit ties to Bach and his chorales. The *Pange Lingua Variations* were commissioned by the Cathedral of the Blessed Sacrament in Sacramento, California, in connection with the restoration of that historic edifice, and were premiered there on May 21, 1983. The work consists of six movements, each of which embellishes a stanza of the medieval hymn *Pange lingua* (in an English rendering by Brubeck's wife, Iola).[31] The first five variations each are preceded by a stanza of the hymn, sung in Latin to the traditional tune in the style of Gregorian chant. In the first half of the second movement (mm. 13–54), Brubeck introduces the four-part chorale style. This produces a historically improbable amalgam of the *Pange lingua* (whose text, by St. Thomas Aquinas, concerns the Roman Catholic doctrine of transubstantiation) clothed in the garb of the quintessentially Lutheran Bach chorale (see ex. 5).[32]

Brubeck's next sacred vocal work, *Voice of the Holy Spirit*, was commissioned by the National Association of Pastoral Musicians (whose 1980 convention had hosted a performance of *To Hope!*). Since its composition and premiere coincided with the tercentenary of Bach's birth in 1985, it is not surprising that this seventy-five-minute oratorio includes musical styles associated with Bach.[33] The most prominent such section occurs toward the beginning, in a movement titled "Full Authority," which features an extended choral fugue on the words, "In the name of the Father, and of the Son, and of the Holy Spirit; Amen."[34] But the work also contains a setting of St. Paul's famous discourse on love (1 Corinthians 13), "Though I Speak with the Tongues of Men and of Angels," in the style of Bach's four-part chorales.[35]

30. Dave Brubeck, *To Hope! A Celebration* (Miami, Fla.: Warner Bros. Publications, 1979), 3. This work was recorded at the Washington National Cathedral by the Cathedral Choral Society Chorus and Orchestra, with the Dave Brubeck Quartet, on Telarc, CD-80430 (1996).

31. Dave Brubeck, *Pange Lingua Variations* (Miami, Fla.: CPP/Belwin, 1989).

32. When I discussed this with Brubeck, he speculated that Bach "might have" set the *Pange lingua*, "if he liked the tune." However, the orthodox Lutheran theological climate in eighteenth-century Leipzig surely would not have permitted such a broadly ecumenical outlook. This portion of the *Pange Lingua Variations* was recorded under the title "To Us is Given" on Dave Brubeck, *A Dave Brubeck Christmas*, Telarc, CD-83410 (1996), and published in *Selections from A Dave Brubeck Christmas* (Miami, Fla.: Warner Bros. Publications, 1997), 23–26.

33. *Voice of the Holy Spirit* was first performed on July 27, 1985 in Cincinnati.

34. Published separately as the choral octavo *In the Name of the Father* (Chapel Hill, N.C.: Hinshaw Music, 1985), HMC-956.

35. Dave Brubeck, *Though I Speak with the Tongues of Men and of Angels* (Miami, Fla.: Warner Bros. Publications, 1996), OCT02607.

Ex. 5. Brubeck, *Pange Lingua Variations*, mvt. 2, mm. 7–57. Copyright © 1989 by Derry Music Company. Used by permission.

9

an in - vi - o - late Vir - - gin,
C
He who did pass through this world,
Sow - ing the seed of the Word,

10
clos - ing His so - journ a - mong us,
Per - fect in or - der and har - mo - ny.
D
p unis.
Of an in - vi - o - late Vir - gin,
pp*
Pan - ge
p
pp
*This phrase may be sung an octave lower.

A composition in which Bach's influence is especially palpable, and the last vocal work to be discussed here, is *Upon This Rock*. This short choral piece was commissioned by the Roman Catholic Diocese of San Francisco and Oblates of Mary Immaculate, and was first performed on September 18, 1987, as Pope John Paul II entered Candlestick Park to celebrate Mass before a crowd of 79,000.[36] Brubeck himself is quite fond of it. In response to an interviewer's question, "If you could hear only three of your works, which three would you choose?," Brubeck replied, "My favorite is *Upon This Rock*. . . . [It] is my best writing; there's nothing in it I would change."[37] The influence of Bach is evident, first of all, in the design of the work, which consists of a chorale and fugue, framed by brass fanfares (an excerpt from the chorale is given in ex. 6).[38]

But Bach's role extends far beyond Brubeck's choice of the Bachian genres of chorale and fugue. Indeed, Brubeck told me that he "could never have written that piece for the Pope, *Upon This Rock*, if it hadn't been for being aware of Bach." When the Diocese of San Francisco first approached him, he turned down the commission because he "couldn't do it; didn't know how to do it." But he went to bed and during the night "dreamt the fugue." When he got up, he "called them and told them [he] could do it, [he] was going to do it."[39] In short, the catalyst for the composition of *Upon This Rock* was Brubeck's dream, as well as his own conscious attempt to imagine how Bach might have approached this task. This intellectual exercise enabled Brubeck to overcome his initial reluctance about fulfilling the commission and provided the creative spark without which the piece would never have come to fruition. In his words, "I just woke up with the subject and kind of the countersubject, or the answer, going through my mind, and I knew . . . this is the way Bach would have done it. Then I thought, he would have done a chorale. . . . This is the answer how I can do this."[40]

* * *

A parallel compositional track, which began much earlier than the vocal works, involves Brubeck's use of the Bach-chorale style in instrumental pieces. One of his earliest compositions, a "Lullaby" written for his future wife, Iola, in 1942 (when they both were students at College of the Pacific in Stockton, California), has the four-part polyphonic texture and predominantly stepwise voice-leading of Bach chorales (see ex. 7).[41]

36. A detailed description of this festive occasion is provided in Young, "Sacred Choral Music," 148–50.

37. Elyse Mach, "With Dave Brubeck the Music Never Stops," *Clavier* 40, no. 5 (May 2001): 9.

38. The chorale was published in Brubeck, *Dave's Diary*, 44–47.

39. Brubeck interview.

40. Ibid.

41. Brubeck, *Dave's Diary*, 3–5. This piece also was published in Dave Brubeck, *Nocturnes* (Miami, Fla.: Warner Bros. Publications, 1997), 10–11.

Ex. 6. Brubeck, *Upon This Rock* (chorale), mm. 1–20. Copyright © 1994 by Derry Music Company. Used by permission.

Lullaby

Lullaby - 2 - 1
P1085P9X

Ex. 7. Brubeck, "Lullaby," mm. 1–18. Copyright © 1994 by Derry Music Company. Used by permission.

Twenty years later, Brubeck included a "Chorale" as the sixth movement of his ballet *Points on Jazz.* The origins of this work date back to the same 1958 tour during which he wrote "Brandenburg Gate." On the train from Łodż to Poznán in Poland, Brubeck composed a Chopinesque piece called "Dziekuje" (Polish for "thank you"), which the Quartet played as an encore and subsequently recorded on the album *Jazz Impressions of Eurasia.* An American choreographer of Polish descent, Dania Krupska, heard the recording and approached Brubeck about composing a ballet based on this tune. After several delays and setbacks, the work finally received its premiere by the American Ballet Theatre in 1961.[42]

The musical content of the theme and variations, whose titles allude to standard styles and genres of classical and popular music, corresponds to the story provided by Krupska in the following manner:

I. Prelude. "The Boy is the Theme. He is all alone on the stage—detached. Gradually movement begins. The Girls make their entrances. He tries to reach out and make contact with them, but cannot."
II. Scherzo. "Now The Girl enters. She is fresh and bubbling with life."
III. Blues. "Here comes the Temptress. She entices The Boy, then leaves him to summon other men to gather around her. They fight for her in a primitive dance and she is tossed wildly from one man to another. Then The Temptress snaps her fingers and walks out on the men."
IV. Fugue. This movement was designed as a choreographed "chase," with entrances of the dancers corresponding to the musical entrances.
V. Rag. "Now The Girls and The Boys are happily together again. They are wacky, happy couples."
VI. Chorale. "Their happiness makes The Boy feel even more alone."
VII. Waltz. "The Girl reaches out for The Boy. She wants to comfort him. He recognizes her as The Girl of the Scherzo. they dance a romantic *pas de deux.*"
VIII. A La Turk. "The Girl is overjoyed. She must call everyone to share her happiness. In the confusion of their celebration, The Boy and The Girl are separated. After a climactic search they find each other, embrace, and walk away arm in arm."[43]

Of greatest interest in the present context are the "Prelude," "Fugue," and "Chorale," three movement types with close associations to the music of Bach. The "Chorale" (ex. 8) is an emblem of loneliness and isolation, represented by the simultaneous use of two tonalities: E-flat major in the right hand, and C major in the left.

42. The compositional history of *Points on Jazz* is described in greater detail in Storb and Fischer, *Dave Brubeck,* 105–6.

43. Dave Brubeck, *Points on Jazz,* transcribed for piano solo by Howard Brubeck (Miami, Fla.: CPP/Belwin, 1993), 3. John Salmon has recorded this version on *John Salmon Plays Brubeck,* Phoenix, PHCD 130 (1995).

Ex. 8. Brubeck, *Points on Jazz,* mvt. 6 ("Chorale"). Copyright © 1962 and 1963 by Derry Music Company. This arrangement copyright © 1994 by Derry Music Company. Used by permission.

About thirty years after *Points on Jazz*, Brubeck composed another "Chorale" as part of his *"Chromatic Fantasy" Sonata*, a work that—as I mentioned earlier—was inspired by Bach (this also is the "Chorale" on the 1998 concert program, reproduced in plate 1 above). The *"Chromatic Fantasy" Sonata* originated as a piece for oboe, violin, viola, cello, and piano, which was commissioned in the late 1980s by the New York chamber ensemble An die Musik and recorded by them in 1993.[44] In the liner notes for a subsequent recording of the work—Brubeck's version for string quartet, recorded in 1997 by the Brodsky Quartet—Brubeck mentions that "the original commission stipulated that I should write variations on a theme by a composer who had been of special significance to me. I chose J. S. Bach and used the opening bars of his *Chromatic Fantasy* as a point of departure."[45] The second movement of the versions for string quartet and for piano solo is titled "Chorale." It begins with a quiet passage in four-part harmony, in which the bass traces a chromatic scale descending from c' to the octave below (see ex. 9).

About halfway through the movement—beginning in m. 48—a lyrical melody is introduced, with an arpeggiated accompaniment in the left hand (see ex. 10). Although the four-part chorale texture is no longer present, this passage is notable on account of its thoroughgoing chromaticism. One can readily trace several simultaneous ascending chromatic step progressions.

While the composed versions of the "Chorale" are certainly quite competent, the most successful incarnation, in my opinion, is the jazz version recorded in 1997, which takes the lyrical tune as its point of departure.[46] However, the fact that Brubeck and his flutist, Bobby Militello, do not play the music from the beginning of the movement creates the curious situation of a piece called "Chorale" that really has none of the stylistic features of a true chorale. Indeed, it sounds much more like a gentle ballad.[47]

It is worth lingering on the *"Chromatic Fantasy" Sonata* a bit longer because its complex compositional history demonstrates so clearly the rich interconnections between the worlds of jazz and "classical" music, and more specifically between improvisation and composition, in Brubeck's music. Brubeck has noted that for him the process of composition begins with improvisation: "I guess because I am fundamentally an improviser, I call upon all the musical resources of my past experience, and in the process of selecting, honing, and developing, that which is basically an improvisation becomes a composition."[48] Indeed, his pursuit of a dual career as a preeminent

44. *Jazz Sonatas*, Angel, CDC 5-55061-2-2 (1994).

45. Brodsky Quartet, Silva Classics, SILKD 6014 (1997).

46. The Dave Brubeck Quartet, *So What's New?*, Telarc, CD-83434 (1998).

47. The same is true of the version published in Brubeck, *Nocturnes*, 40–41.

48. David Ewen, *American Composers: A Biographical Dictionary* (New York: G. P. Putnam's Sons, 1982), 100.

11

II. Chorale

Ex. 9. Brubeck, *"Chromatic Fantasy" Sonata*, mvt. 2 ("Chorale"), mm. 1–11.
Copyright © 1993 and 1994 by Derry Music Company. Used by permission.

EL 03971

Ex. 10. Brubeck, *"Chromatic Fantasy" Sonata*, mvt. 2 ("Chorale"), mm. 48–55.
Copyright © 1993 and 1994 by Derry Music Company. Used by permission.

improviser of jazz and as a "classical" composer has led Brubeck to deemphasize the distinctions between these two musical realms: "Sometimes I hear a jazz composition that is more classically written than a classical piece. So for that reason, I put music into two categories: improvised and written, rather than 'jazz' and 'classical.'"[49]

As was mentioned earlier, the impetus for the composition of the *"Chromatic Fantasy" Sonata* came from a classical musician. On July 23, 1988, pianist Constance Emmerich first approached Brubeck about the possibility of composing a piece for her chamber ensemble An die Musik. In her initial proposal, Emmerich played on the perceived dichotomy between "classical" and "popular" music:

> The reason for this letter is to prevail on your compositional muse. An die Musik would very much like to have you write a piece for us for our new project, THE COMPOSER'S COMPOSER. ANDRE PREVIN has agreed to write one for us for the first concert in this project: each concert will feature two composers and as you are our absolute favorite "popular" musician/composer/performer, we were dreaming of having you be the one to share the premiere event with Mr. Previn. Is there a chance? . . . AS I mentioned, each concert of THE COMPOSER'S COMPOSER would have TWO contemporary composers and we came to the idea that one "popular" and one, so-called "classical" composer would be a fascinating story about our times in music.[50]

Emmerich's query left much room for creative license, specifying only that the piece should be "VARIATIONS on a THEME of [a] past composer. ANY THEME from ANY work. (ANY kind of variations or referral to the THEME)."[51]

In his response, Brubeck stated that Bach "would be the classical composer most related to me I think, or vice-versa." He mentioned the possibility of "taking two or three choral fugues I have written for some of my sacred music; transcribing them for An die Musik and adding a third or fourth movement, which I have been thinking about as a string quartet, but I can hear that the oboe could substitute for violin and I could add a piano part." He also expressed his hope that she "would understand if I later decided to write it as part of a longer string quartet, string orchestra or any other combination." Brubeck then sketched another alternative, noting that he had just asked a friend if he had a copy of Bach's Chromatic Fantasia and Fugue in D Minor (BWV 903): "He did not have it, but I cannot remember anything about this music, having only heard it one time in my life. I've been inspired by Bach and maybe this chromatic fan-

49. Ilse Storb, "An Interview with Dave Brubeck," *Jazzforschung* 16 (1984): 150. This interview took place on April 25, 1980.

50. Constance Emmerich, letter to Dave Brubeck, July 23, 1988. I am grateful to Emmerich for providing copies of her correspondence with Dave Brubeck concerning the *"Chromatic Fantasy" Sonata*, and to her and Brubeck for their permission to quote from these materials.

51. Ibid.

tasy and fugue could be incorporated somehow into the final movement that I will write if I proceed with this project. . . . My greatest musical influence is Bach."[52]

In a subsequent letter, Emmerich expressed her excitement that Brubeck was interested in the project and rearticulated the parameters of the commission: "You are free to choose ANY theme from ANY Bach piece and have it as a reference for your piece. And it needn't be a complete theme, but any sort of reference to it that you choose to use. We thought of a piece that would be from 10 to 15 minutes in duration. . . . Please feel free to use our instrumentation (oboe, violin, viola, cello and piano) in ANY way you wish. . . . There doesn't have to be any specific number of movements—it can be ALL ONE MOVEMENT or ANY number of longer or shorter movements—just as you feel it as it develops. Absolute freedom to do as you feel is the only rule!"[53]

Several months after this initial exchange of correspondence, in February 1989, Brubeck underwent triple-bypass surgery at the Yale–New Haven Hospital. Remarkably, he began performing and composing again just a few months later. A story in the *New York Times* about his recovery included Brubeck's thoughts about the overall structure of the "*Chromatic Fantasy*" *Sonata:*

> Mr. Brubeck's current projects include . . . a theme and variations for an ensemble of violin, oboe, viola, cello and piano. . . . "It's variations on a piece by my favorite composer, Bach," said Mr. Brubeck. . . . "It has the first two bars of the Chromatic Fantasy. There are five variations: the first is the Chromatic Fantasy; the second is a chorale on a 12-tone theme; the third is a jazz variation; the fourth is maybe a passacaglia using a different 12-tone theme; and the fifth is a fugue where the subject is the first 12-tone theme, and the answer is the second 12-tone theme."[54]

By early in the summer of 1990, Brubeck had settled on a four-movement plan for the project, and he had nearly completed the third movement (the "Chaconne" of the published version for piano solo). He wrote to Emmerich:

> This [movement] seems to me to be more reflective of a jazz musician writing for An die Musik than the other three movements. I have the feeling this will be the piece you will program the most, but how does it relate to the Bach chromatic fantasy? This, in the true definition, is a chaconne, and the ostinato bass figure appears throughout in various voices. It is also an extension of the chromaticism of the first Bach theme, but it is contemporary to the point of almost being minimalistic. I think you could make a case for the ostinato bass being a precursor of minimal music. I had fun chang-

52. Brubeck, letter to Emmerich, Aug. 9, 1988.

53. Emmerich, letter to Brubeck, Aug. 24, 1988.

54. Valerie Cruice, "A Healthy Brubeck Keeps the Jazz Flowing," *New York Times*, May 21, 1989, sec. 23 (CN), p. 20.

ing the rhythmic pattern far more quickly than the minimalists, but I hope you can see there is a relationship to Bach.[55]

Like the "Chorale," this movement has a dual identity. Though conceived as part of the *"Chromatic Fantasy" Sonata,* it also has served as a vehicle for improvisation, under the title "Jazzanians." In 1992 Brubeck recorded the piece with his sons, Chris (electric bass) and Dan (drums).[56] In the preface to the published version, Brubeck explains the origin of its unusual name, but does not mention its connection with the *"Chromatic Fantasy" Sonata:*

> A few years ago a student band called The Jazzanians came to the U. S. from the University of Natal, Durban, South Africa to perform, under my son Darius' direction, at the International Jazz Educator's conference in Detroit. The members of the band reflected the multiple cultures of South Africa—Zulu, Xhosa, English, Indian, Dutch—and they played a passionate music that stemmed from African roots with an overlay of Western jazz and popular township music. After their visit I wrote this tribute to them.[57]

In a postscript to his letter of June 14, 1990, Brubeck asked for a deadline for the entire work, noting that "the third movement has turned out to be twice as long as anticipated. If I run out of time we could end here, and not go on to the fugue, movement IV." As it turns out, the fugue did not make it into the published piano solo version of the *"Chromatic Fantasy" Sonata* (1993/1994). This is ironic, because the fugue apparently contained the generative idea for the entire composition. When I asked Brubeck why the fugue was not included, he said:

> I hadn't written it yet. . . . The first time I started writing this I was in a place outside of Vienna that does jazz festivals in the strawberry field [Wiessen]. The dressing rooms are on the siding of the railroad track where they put old sleepers, and the various musicians use those. And I asked my son [Chris Brubeck] and Bill Smith, the great clarinetist, just to play these two themes together. That's how it started. But I never did ever finish that fugue until later. But it actually was the first thing.[58]

In a letter concerning the details of the recording by An die Musik, Brubeck noted, "It's a good thing I didn't finish the fugue, as that would have put it way over in time. However, I do intend to finish it some day." He also mentioned that "someday there

55. Brubeck, letter to Emmerich, June 14, 1990. A shortened version of these comments subsequently appeared in Brubeck's liner notes for the recording of this movement on *Jazz Sonatas* (see n. 44).

56. *Trio Brubeck,* MusicMasters, 65102–2 (1993).

57. *At the Piano with Dave Brubeck: Intermediate Solos* (Miami, Fla.: CPP/Belwin, 1993), 5.

58. Brubeck interview.

is going to be an orchestral version, as well as solo piano and string quartet versions."[59] On March 16, 1994, An die Musik premiered the "Chorale" and "Chaconne" at the Kennedy Center in Washington, D.C., under the title *Quintet Sonata*.[60] Finally, in 1997, Brubeck's plans to finish the fugue and write a version for string quartet simultaneously came to fruition in the recording by the Brodsky Quartet of the four-movement *Chromatic Fantasy for String Quartet*.[61]

* * *

By now it should be clear that chorales have been an important strand in Brubeck's music over the past five or six decades. Before discussing one final example, let us consider the meaning of the Bach chorale for Dave Brubeck.

Brubeck's engagement with the chorale has both personal and aesthetic dimensions. Bach's chorales were intimately associated with two individuals of signal importance in his musical development. The first was his mother. Elizabeth Ivey Brubeck was a classical pianist and teacher who studied in England with Tobias Matthay and Dame Myra Hess for several months in 1926, when Dave was just beginning grade school.[62] She gave her son his first lessons in both piano and harmony, and made use of Bach chorales in this early instruction.[63] Moreover, she was a choir director and took Dave with her to rehearsals when he was a young boy.[64] The association of Bach chorales with the memory of his mother is made explicit in *They All Sang Yankee Doodle* (1976). This orchestral work, dedicated to Charles Ives, was commissioned by the New Haven Symphony Orchestra to celebrate the American bicentennial, and subsequently was transcribed for two pianos as well as for piano solo.[65] Brubeck has described this composition as "an autobiography, made up of memories and snatches of tunes imprinted from my early childhood: hymns and Bach chorales from the church next door where my mother was choir director and the cowboy songs and turn-of-the-century ballads that I have always identified with my father."[66]

59. Brubeck, letter to Emmerich, Aug. 27, 1993.

60. Mark Adamo, review in *Washington Post*, March 18, 1994.

61. See n. 45. The "Chorale" also is included on a compilation by the Brodsky Quartet, titled *Elegie*, Silva Classics, SILKD 6701 (2000).

62. For Brubeck's first-person account of this period, see Gene Lees, *Cats of Any Color: Jazz Black and White* (New York: Oxford University Press, 1994), 44–45.

63. Storb and Fischer, *Dave Brubeck*, 1–3.

64. Brubeck later recalled, "My first job was in a church to play the organ for $1 per Sunday." Cruice, "Healthy Brubeck Keeps the Jazz Flowing," 21.

65. The solo piano version was published in *American Contemporary Masters: A Collection of Works for Piano* (New York: G. Schirmer, 1995), 11–32, and recorded on *John Salmon Plays Brubeck* (see n. 43).

66. Hall, *It's About Time*, 132. "Yankee Doodle" appears in four-part chorale style at mm. 149–80.

The other person who was extremely influential in Brubeck's early musical training was the French composer Darius Milhaud. Brubeck studied composition with him privately upon graduating from college in 1942, and as a graduate student at Mills College (Oakland, California) from 1946 to 1948, after his stint in the army. Again, the Bach chorales—in Albert Riemenschneider's 1941 edition—formed the foundation of these studies.[67] Brubeck's recollection of this phase of his compositional training was that "the Riemenschneider chorales Bach book was the Bible in the class. He was very strict on that."[68] Or, as he told me, Milhaud "just saturated you with Bach chorales, to get that voice-leading."[69] Moreover, Brubeck considers the study of Bach's chorales to be an important heuristic device not only for learning composition, but also for learning to improvise. When asked what advice he could offer to classically trained musicians who want to improve their improvisational skills, Brubeck said,

> I would advise a developing musician to study Bach first; a thorough understanding of Bach is the greatest training a pianist can have. Begin by playing in the Bach *Riemenschneider* edition, the *371 Harmonized Chorales*, then improvise new melodies over the chord progression of a selected chorale. Next write Bach-like chorales and improvise new melodies over the chord progressions.[70]

A fascinating artifact of this period of study with Milhaud is the "Chorale" recorded by the Dave Brubeck Quintet (Dave Brubeck, piano; Paul Desmond, alto saxophone; Dave van Kriedt, tenor saxophone; Norm Bates, bass; Joe Morello, drums) in 1957, in which Bach's harmonization of *So gehst du nun, mein Jesu, hin* (BWV 500) is played at the beginning and end by the jazz ensemble, and is used in between as the basis for improvisation by each member of the group.[71] The version of this chorale in the Riemenschneider edition originally appeared in the Schemelli *Gesangbuch* in 1736 (see ex. 11).

Comparison of the arrangement by Dave van Kriedt (see plate 3) with Bach's harmonization reveals the extent to which the jazz version is indebted to the original.[72] The most significant differences are (1) the introductory drum solo, (2) doubling of the note values (predominantly half-note motion, instead of quarter notes), and (3) the

67. *371 Harmonized Chorales and 69 Chorale Melodies with Figured Bass by Johann Sebastian Bach*, ed. Albert Riemenschneider (New York: G. Schirmer, 1941).

68. Storb, "Interview with Dave Brubeck," 153.

69. Brubeck interview.

70. Mach, "With Dave Brubeck," 9–10.

71. The Dave Brubeck Quintet, *Brubeck/Desmond/Van Kriedt: Re-Union*, Fantasy, 3268 (1957); reissued on Fantasy, OJCCD-150–2 (1990).

72. Dave van Kriedt was a classmate of Brubeck's in Milhaud's composition studio. He also was a member of the Dave Brubeck Octet, which recorded his "Fugue on Bop Themes" and other original compositions and arrangements in the late 1940s.

Ex. 11. *So gehst du nun, mein Jesu, hin* (BWV 500) from Albert Riemenschneider, ed., *371 Harmonized Chorales and 69 Chorale Melodies with Figured Bass by Johann Sebastian Bach.* Copyright © 1941 by G. Schirmer, Inc. Used by permission.

introduction of syncopation at the end of each phrase (accented eighth notes). In the recording, the alto saxophone, tenor saxophone, and bass each take a twenty-four-bar chorus (as indicated in the chart), while Brubeck stretches his solo to forty bars and infuses it with Bachian harmonies and figuration.

Since this recording dates from 1957, it is surprising to hear this chorale again nearly forty years later on *A Dave Brubeck Christmas*, as the introduction to his arrangement of "O Tannenbaum."[73] One might reasonably assume that Brubeck had become reacquainted with the chorale when the 1957 recording was rereleased in 1990. But Brubeck's producer and personal manager, Russell Gloyd, told me emphatically that this was not the case, and that it was instead an excellent example of Brubeck's prodigious imagination and musical memory.[74]

When I asked Brubeck what he finds so attractive about chorales, he invoked their affective and aesthetic qualities:

> It must be a combination of the emotional sound of the chorale and the emotional sound of voices. . . . The thing that move[s] me the most [are] the chorales, *a cappella.* That's what I love the most. . . . Just that sound, and no instruments, and the human voice, and just what it's conveying from the choir.[75]

73. Brubeck, *A Dave Brubeck Christmas;* this arrangement was published in *Selections from A Dave Brubeck Christmas*, 27–29 (see n. 32).

74. Russell Gloyd, telephone conversation with author, March 22, 2000.

75. Brubeck interview.

Plate 3. "Bach Chorale," arranged by Dave van Kriedt. Copyright © 1958 by Derry Music Company. Used by permission.

"BACH CHORALE" by David van Kriedt

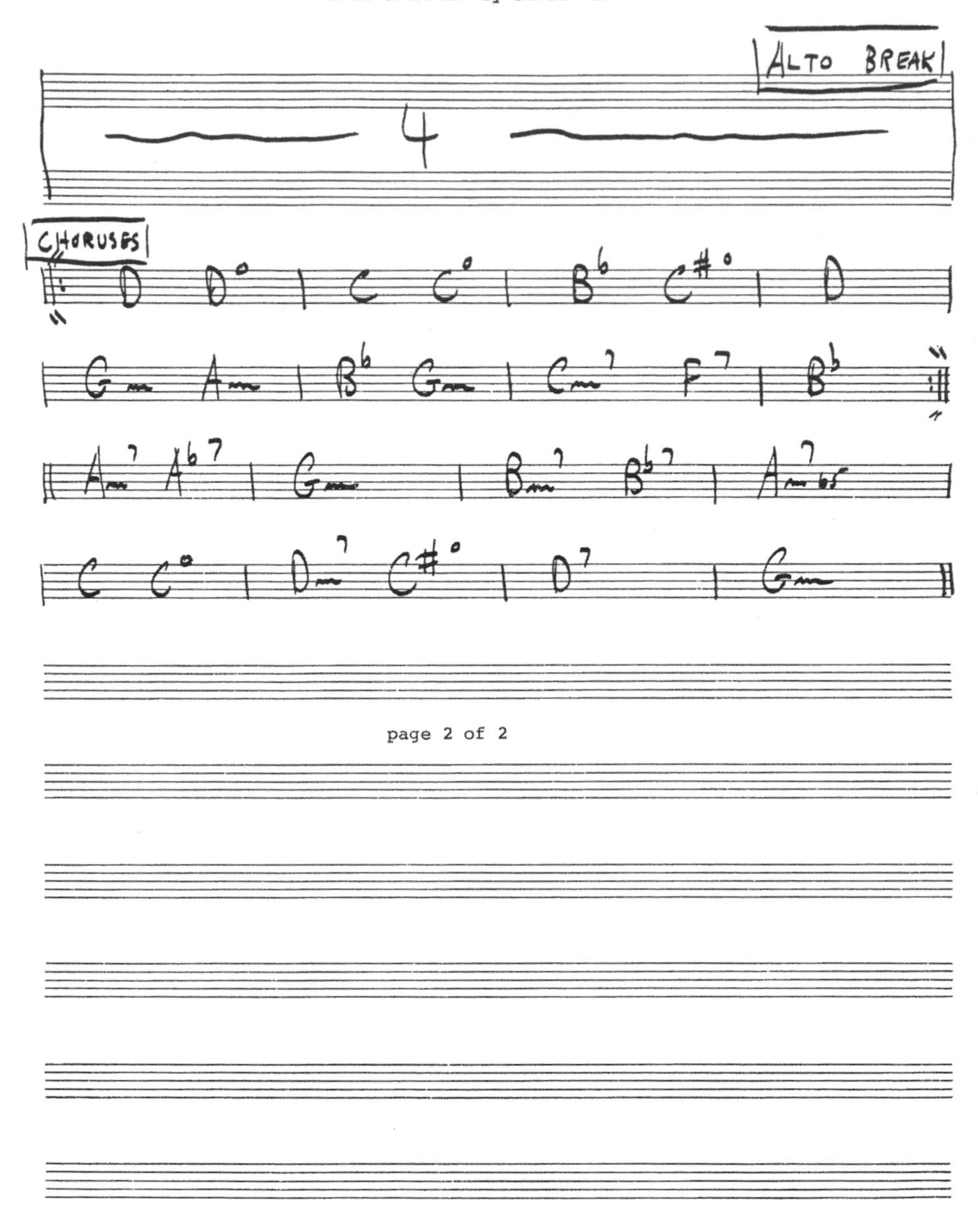

Brubeck's lifelong preoccupation with the chorale, then, stems from its powerful, formative associations with his mother and his esteemed composition teacher, as well as from his love for the sound of diverse human voices making music together, and, finally, from his profound admiration for the legacy of Johann Sebastian Bach.

CONTRIBUTORS

CAROL K. BARON is a fellow in the Department of Music at Stony Brook University, where she was executive director of the Bach Aria Group Association, Inc., and of the Bach Aria Festival and Institute at Stony Brook (1980–1997). She taught at Hunter College, York College, and Adelphi University. Author of numerous articles on twentieth-century music, she was awarded an ACLS grant, was twice recipient of the ASCAP-Deems Taylor Award, and twice recipient of NEH Public Humanities Program grants. She was associate editor of *Perspectives of New Music* from 1991 to 2001.

MICHAEL BROYLES is a professor of music and professor of American history at Pennsylvania State University. His most recent books are *"Music of the Highest Class": Elitism and Populism in Antebellum Boston* (Yale University Press), and *Mavericks and Other Traditions in American Music* (in press). With Denise Von Glahn of Florida State University, he is currently writing a biography of Leo Ornstein.

STEPHEN A. CRIST is an associate professor of music at Emory University. His publications on J. S. Bach have appeared in *The Cambridge Companion to Bach, Oxford Composer Companions: J. S. Bach, The World of the Bach Cantatas, Journal of the American Musicological Society*, and many other books and journals. He is coeditor of the forthcoming volume of essays, *Interpreting Sources in Music Scholarship* (University of Rochester Press). He has served as officer and chaired numerous committees in both the American Bach Society and the American Musicological Society.

MATTHEW DIRST is an associate professor of music and director of the Collegium Musicum at the Moores School of Music, University of Houston. His publications on the music of Johann Sebastian Bach and its reception include a forthcoming book entitled *Bach and the Public Sphere: Early Advocacy of the Keyboard Works* (Cambridge University Press). A noted performer, he has won major international prizes in both organ and harpsichord, including first prize at the American Guild of Organists National Young Artist Competition and second prize at the inaugural Warsaw International Harpsichord Competition.

MARY J. GREER is a conductor and a musicologist based in New York City. In 2001 she founded "Cantatas in Context," a Bach cantata series, in collaboration with the Orchestra of St. Luke's. She holds B.A. and M.A. degrees from Yale, and received her Ph.D. from Harvard. She has held faculty positions at Yale University and Montclair

State University, and has presented papers at meetings of the American Musicological Society and the American Bach Society, as well as at various international Bach conferences. Her book reviews have appeared in *Notes* and *Journal of the American Musicological Society*. She served as editor of the Newsletter of the American Bach Society from 1996 to 2000, and is currently secretary-treasurer of the organization.

BARBARA OWEN holds degrees in music from Westminster Choir College and Boston University, and has also studied in Germany, Italy, and England. The author of four books and numerous periodical articles, she is the recipient of the Alumni Merit Citation of Westminster Choir College, the Curt Sachs Award of the American Musical Instrument Society, and the Distinguished Service Award of the Organ Historical Society. Currently she is music director of the First Religious Society of Newburyport, Mass., curator of the AGO Organ Library at Boston University, and editor of the *Westfield Journal*.

HANS-JOACHIM SCHULZE is former director of the Bach-Archiv in Leipzig. The author of *Studien zur Bach-Überlieferung im 18. Jahrhundert* and coeditor of *Bach-Dokumente*, *Bach-Compendium*, and *Bach-Jahrbuch*, he is widely recognized in Bach scholarship for his archival work. He was appointed honorary lecturer at the Martin Luther University in Halle-Wittenberg in 1990 and honorary professor at the Hochschule für Musik und Theater in Leipzig in 1993.

CHRISTOPH WOLFF is William Powell Mason Professor of Music and former dean of the Graduate School of Arts and Sciences at Harvard University. He currently serves as chair of the Zentralinstitut für Mozart-Forschung in Salzburg and director of the Bach-Archiv in Leipzig. He has published extensively on the history of music from the fifteenth to the twentieth centuries, especially on Bach and Mozart. *Mozart's Requiem* (University of California Press), *The New Bach Reader* (Norton), and *Johann Sebastian Bach: The Learned Musician* (Norton) are his most recent books.

PETER WOLLNY is a research fellow and the curator of the Manuscript and Rare Books Collection at the Bach-Archiv in Leipzig, teaches at the universities of Leipzig and Dresden, and codirects a research project on seventeenth-century German ensemble music at Würzburg University. He is contributing editor for the Neue Bach-Ausgabe, executive editor of *Carl Philipp Emanuel Bach: The Collected Works*, coeditor of *Leipziger Beiträge zur Bach-Forschung*, and is associated with the Bach Repertorium. He serves on the board of directors of the Neue Bachgesellschaft and on the editorial board of the *Journal of Seventeenth-Century Music*.

GENERAL INDEX

INDEX OF BACH'S COMPOSITIONS

The University of Illinois Press
is a founding member of the
Association of American University Presses.

Composed in 10/14 Janson Text
by Jim Proefrock
at the University of Illinois Press
Designed by Dika Eckersley
Manufactured by Thomson-Shore, Inc.

University of Illinois Press
1325 South Oak Street
Champaign, IL 61820-6903
www.press.uillinois.edu

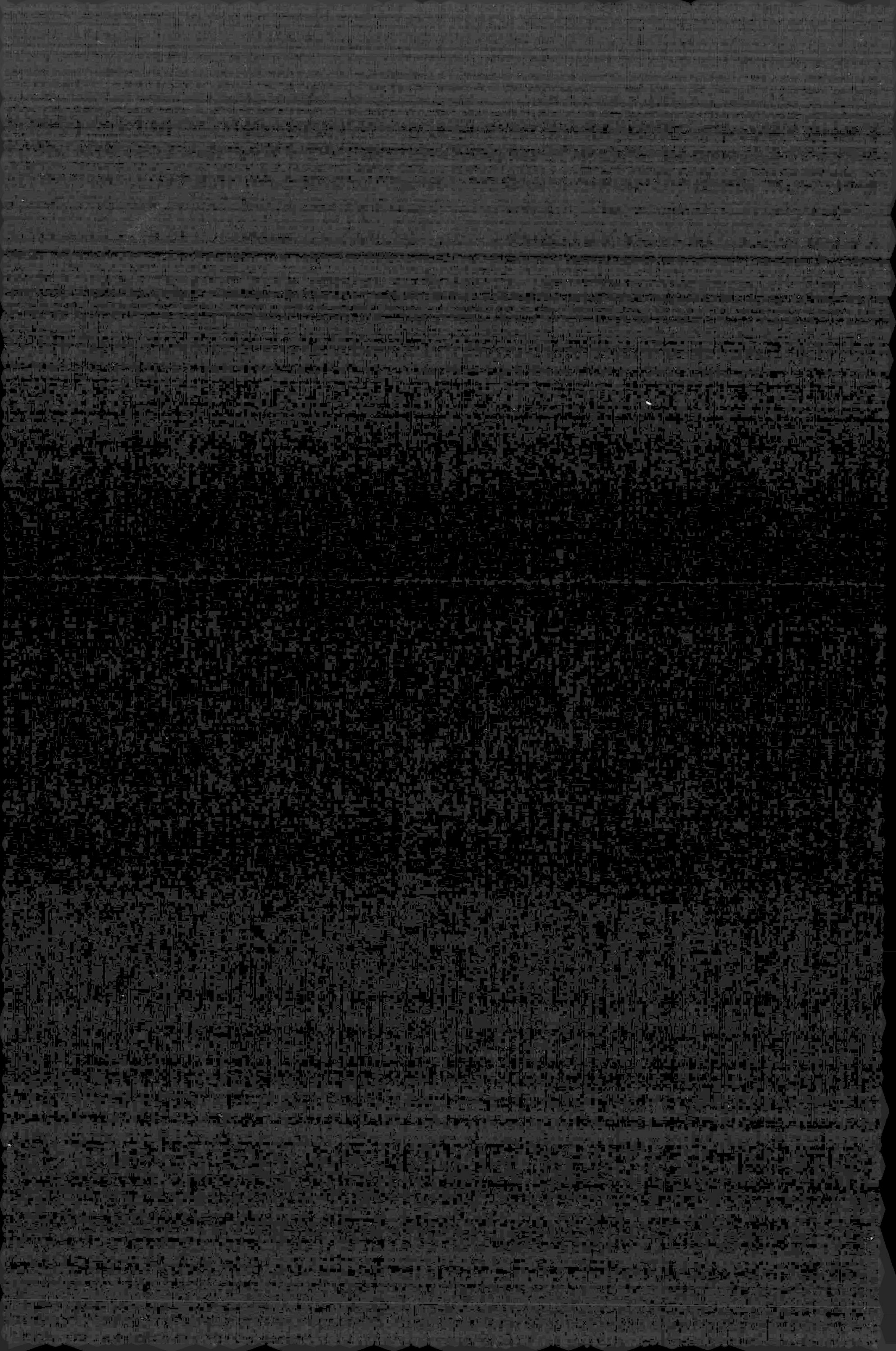